Silence Of the Stars

Garrett Ordiway

Inkularity

Art and design by Garrett Ordiway

ISBN: 978-1-966438-00-7 (Paperback)

ISBN: 978-1-966438-01-4 (Hardback)

ISBN: 978-1-966438-02-1 (Digital)

Library of Congress Control Number: 2024925258

SILENCE OF THE STARS

TO YOU,

Yes, *you*. The depth of your significance in of this world may go unrecognized, but cannot be overstated.

Disclaimer

This is a work of fiction. Names, characters, businesses, events, and incidents are products of the author's imagination. Any resemblance to actual locals, products, or persons, living or dead, is purely coincidental. Any events described in this work have not occurred in reality... yet.

Chapter 1
Janus

Something is different. You hear the familiar sound of waves rolling up and down the shore, carrying rocks and debris in their wake as they wind their way through support beams far below. But the sea sounds closer than usual today. Heat radiates from the dark above, warming the tips of your nose and ears as well as your closed eyelids. The hard ground is uncomfortable on the back of your head. A light gust of cold wind blows up across your hand through the floor, and you curl your fingers in subconscious response. Your fingers rub across a material you've never felt before; cold and hard like metal but porous like a sponge.

Are you dreaming or awake?

A pair of voices form from the background noise. "Mission complete," states the voice of a middle-aged man filled with pride in a job well done.

A faint, muffled voice responds, but you can't make out the words. It's distorted like a radio stuck between channels.

The first man replies, "Yes, I have something extra to report. There was a survivor in one of the cryopods."

This time the second voice comes into focus. The static distortions solidify into a voice that's deep and authoritative. "I told you, no unnecessary tampering. Your orders were to expunge the facility without risking contamination."

"Pre-op scans detected a *human* bioelectric signature in one of the pods. What did you expect me to do?"

"I *expect* you to follow orders." The voice sounds frustrated. Then he sighs and says, "Though I suppose I can't fault you for saving the life of an innocent human. Status? Is the subject clean?"

"He's clean and has stable vitals, but is still unconscious. According to the info plate on the cryopod, it was originally sealed in the year 2020."

"And the inhabitant is alive? Are you sure it's the original inhabitant? That would make him the oldest human in history."

"The record is etched here clear as day. The pod was originally sealed in 2020 and resealed once in 2055. He's been on ice ever since."

"That *is* curious. Your current mission can wait. When you are finished with that facility, take the subject through decontamination at Darwin Aerospace Port. Learn what you can, then report back to me. Dismissed."

"Yes sir," the first man says. Then the voices give way to rumbling waves below and the steady mechanical clamor above.

Were they talking about you? That doesn't seem right. That conversation didn't even make sense. Who are these two strangers,

Silence Of the Stars

anyway? More importantly, where are you? Maybe you're still sleeping. Things should make more sense when you wake up. You're not yourself right now.

You try to open your eyes but can't seem to manage it. How about sitting up? No luck. You start small, wiggling your toes and fingers, then your wrists and ankles. Your body is stiff and slow to respond. You focus on breathing, flexing any muscle you can to try and coax yourself out of this stupor. Eventually, you're able to roll over on your side and push yourself up into a sitting position.

You open your eyes and blink a few times to try and clear the blurry image. Your surroundings gradually take form from blurred vision, but sight doesn't help make any sense of the situation. The floor and ceiling are made of the same rough metallic mesh with a texture that reminds you of an old kitchen sponge. Under this steel canopy, buildings in various degrees of disrepair stretch in rows along pathways partially cluttered by abandoned tools, pipes and thick bundles of wires that seem to have been installed gradually over time as an afterthought. To your left is a rectangular area the size of a shopping mall, scorched black and covered in a fine layer of fresh ash swirling in the ocean breeze permeating up through the porous floor. The whole place is dimly lit by patches of green light emanating through circular patches in the ceiling and floor, spaced evenly along the walkways which seem to stretch to infinity.

To your right stands a tall man wearing a brown fedora, a leather coat stretching down to his calves, and loose-fitting suit pants hanging over bulky work boots. He is hunched over slightly with his back turned to you. Clicking sounds accompany repeated flashes of yellow light which illuminate the underside of his hat with each attempt to light a cigar. After a few attempts, he gives up and slides the lighter and cigar back onto his coat before turning toward you and matching your gaze. He has light skin and looks to be in his mid-forties. His stubbled face is decorated with a coffee-colored goatee and scruffy hair pokes out from under his hat.

"G'mornin," he greets you casually as he kneels by your side. "How're you feeling? You had an awful long nap." He pulls out a card-sized piece of metal from his jacket and glances at it before continuing, "Janus? Well met. My name's Chons."

Janus? Is that your name? No – that doesn't sound right. You look at the piece of metal he's holding and see your reflection on the backside of it. A reflection of a moderately good-looking dark-tan man in his mid-twenties who looks just as confused as you feel. Is that what you look like? Are you a man in your mid-twenties? You don't recognize the reflection, but he stares back at you clear as day.

You open your mouth to reply, but just cough, unable to form words. Your mouth is dry. The man in the coat waits patiently for you to collect yourself.

"I don't know," you mutter in an unfamiliar voice. You recall many details about your life: your school, your upbringing, the world you grew up in. Yes – you remember those things, right? However, details about your family, your friends, and especially who *you* are

 Silence Of the Stars

evade you. You can recall fragments, but they slip away as you ponder them, like trying to recall the details of a dream.

"It's a miracle you're alive at all. These old cryonics facilities were death traps. If ice crystals don't turn your brain to mush, the buildup of radiation damage does eventually. I've incinerated five of these places now, each with over a thousand pods, and not one survivor until you. Anyway, welcome to year 2822, Janus."

You heard that right. In your groggy state, you'd doubted yourself earlier when you heard the two men talking about your age, but you ask again just to triple check, "So, I've been sleeping for eight hundred years?"

"Oh no, you've been thoroughly dead." His response catches you off guard. "A frozen body has no heartbeat and no brain activity."

He mumbles to himself as he straightens his posture and looks around. "Come to think of it, why *did* I detect a bioelectric signature?"

This is actually happening. You've landed yourself squarely in a pile of sci-fi bullshit. But you like sci-fi. This isn't so bad. You've fantasized more than once about what it would be like to wake up in the future one day, although you never expected it to actually happen. You also try not to think about the implications of having been dead for the last few centuries. Does that make you a zombie? You're still you, after all – right? Now you're thinking about it... but there's no time for that. Practical problems now, philosophy later.

A pair of men appear from around a corner on the far side of the carved-out rectangle of fluttering ash that was once a cryogenics facility. Their body language indicates they are surprised to find the facility missing. One of them carries a bag overflowing with heavy metal equipment, the other carries what you assume must be a rifle. It takes a moment before the one with the gun notices you and taps the other on the shoulder and nods in your direction. The one with the bag shouts in an accent you've never heard before. "Who are you? What are you doing here?"

Chons shouts back, "I'm Joe!" He's imitating the accent. He sounds like a completely different person from before. "Do you work here?" He points at the pile of ash.

"I *did*!" the man replies angrily.

He turns to his partner for a brief exchange, too quiet for you to hear. The men nod to each other, then they move suddenly: one man drops the bag; the man with the gun raises it to take aim. Before the bag hits the ground and before the gun is fully raised, both men erupt in a spray of red and gold. The crack of two gunshots come in such rapid succession that it sounds like one. You instinctively drop to the ground and cover your ears. The echo you expect never comes, muffled by the porous architecture.

Chons sighs as he walks over to the remains of the two men. Casually, he complains, "as if I didn't have enough paperwork to do already."

In his right hand is a large pistol with a long, boxy barrel. Despite its unusual size and bulk, the shape of the weapon is familiar enough

     Silence Of the Stars

that anyone from your era would immediately recognize it as a handgun. Maybe you're used to violence. You don't remember. Maybe you're still in shock. Whatever the reason, you find yourself following Chons over to the corpses. They each look like they were shot in the chest with a cannon. Their remains cling to the floor, walls, and ceiling.

After looking down the path from which the two men came, to confirm nobody else is coming, Chons opens the bag one of the men was carrying and mulls through its contents.

"Looks like they wanted to upgrade your network connection," he says in a sardonic tone.

"I had an internet connection? I thought I was dead?"

"Your pod was equipped with an old transceiver, but it wasn't connected to anything; no devices that could use incoming signals or create outgoing signals. Clearly, they were using your pod in some ongoing project. I thought this bag might have some equipment hinting toward what their goals were. but..." He dumps the contents of the bag between the largest remaining chunks of the two men. "This is just an upgrade to that transceiver. It's useless on its own. Luckily for me, this isn't an investigation job; it's just a clean-up."

It occurs to you that it's strange that you're following a man who just killed without hesitation the only other two people you've seen. He doesn't seem to intend you any harm at the moment, but that doesn't make him a friend. You want to reevaluate your options as soon as possible, but you don't know where you are.

The thought of running is accompanied by a wave of exhaustion. The numbness in your limbs begins to wear off and is replaced by deep aches in your muscles and joints. There's no way you have the strength to escape right now. It's unlikely this man would let you go – based on what you gleaned from the conversation earlier, he has orders to take you somewhere. To maximize your chances of escape, you should determine the best course of action. For now, your best bet is to play along and recover your strength without giving him any reason to suspect your intentions.

Even so, you can't help yourself from asking, "did you have to shoot them?"

Chons pulls a hypodermic needle out of his pocket and injects a foggy white fluid into the largest remaining pieces of each body. "Some problems are solved by talking them through. Others are solved by shooting them, and then lighting them on fire."

He drops the needle on the ground, where it breaks and spills the remaining fluid onto the bodies. Then he pulls a lighter from his jacket and flips the switch to ignite a sharp blue flame. "This is the latter."

He steps back and ushers you to do the same. With some distance between you and the corpses, he takes a long draw from a cigarette then flicks it onto the remains. Immediately, they burst into a brilliant blue-green flame. You shield your eyes as white and yellow sparks spatter out chaotically. The intense heat quickly reduces the bodies to ash. In less than a minute, there's nothing left you'd recognize as organic – much less human. Even the bones are gone. The rifle and transponder have been partially melted by the flames as well, removing any exterior markings. It's a wonder the floor didn't melt in such intense heat.

The two of you stand silently as the last of the flames fade. Then a voice echoes from the hall the two men entered from, in the same accent. The voice shares the same strange accent as the two men. "Noinim? What's going on? Is the installation done?"

Chons turns to you and whispers, "and this is the kind of problem you run from!"

Chapter 2
New Angels

I wanted to put as much distance between us and those Eutychus goons as possible. They were no threat to me, but I'd rather keep my presence here as low-profile as possible. By now, they would have noticed that their facility had been reduced to a carbon-rich pile of ash. In all likelihood, they still hadn't discovered that I, and by extension, my employer, was responsible. I wanted to retain that element of anonymity.

In the absence of evidence or witnesses, the duet of Atlas and I would be suspect number one. In the criminal underground, it was a well-known fact that Atlas wanted to eradicate all the old Project Eutychus facilities and that he employed godhunters for that purpose. Sometimes the cloak and dagger element of the job felt strange. My targets were Project Eutychus facilities and the criminal organizations which operated them. I was law enforcement, performing legal raids against illegal operations. It should have been black and white.

Although technically legal, these godhunter raids fell under the umbrella of black ops. Government operations involving the incineration of private property weren't always looked on favorably by the general public. Atlas preferred to keep the public focused on the positive results of his actions rather than his methods. That's why these operations were always carried out with a certain degree of subtlety. As long as we didn't leave any evidence, the destruction of a Project Eutychus facility could be construed as fighting among rival gangs. Sometimes that was even true. Plausible deniability was our ally.

And so, I fled the scene of a perfectly legal op. If I had been on my own, I would have been in and out like a whisper. But today, I had luggage.

Subject 4269, 'Janus', was struggling to walk at the pace of a decrepit old man. I couldn't blame the kid. It was a miracle he could walk at all on freshly thawed legs. He shouldn't even be alive after being frozen in that primitive deathtrap of a cryochamber. Ice crystals should have turned his innards into mush. Flash-freezing for proper cryostasis didn't exist in the 21st century. Moreover, the odds that the cooling system would stay constantly active for eight centuries of construction projects, recurring maintenance, power outages, wars, famine, changes in leadership, and natural disasters must be near zero.

In lieu of being able to run, I opted to take a detour through the undercity slums. We swerved between buildings and piles of dilapidated machinery to cut line of sight from any potential pursuers. We cast long shadows in the green light of bioluminescent algae that shone through portholes in pipes visible through the porous ceiling. The main pipe would lead us back to the gemlae farms next to downtown New Angels. Once there, we'd be in the clear. Eutychus goons wouldn't try anything under public surveillance.

A shout of terror behind us suggested my handiwork had been discovered. The shout was followed by the shuffling of boots – they were searching for us, but they didn't have our heading yet. I led Janus through a maintenance hatch to keep out of sight. He struggled on the ladder.

"You alright, kid?" I asked.

He was sweating and gasping for air, and didn't seem to hear my question. His condition didn't look like fatigue or defrosting sickness. That's when it hit me – if the boy was frozen in the 2000s, he must be on the extreme end of vanilla. Not only would he lack standard biomods, he'd also be missing hundreds of years of gene edits bleeding into the general public's collective DNA pool.

Even modern vanillas couldn't breathe Earth's coastal air on bad days during summer algae blooms. Ancestral vanilla humans lived in a time of extreme environmental stability, when oxygen and CO_2 balance didn't vary by season or time of day. Their bodies would be far more susceptible to modern weather fluctuations.

I let him rest while I checked the forecast. As suspected, oxygen levels were dropping as dusk set in. 14% oxygen, 29% CO_2, 55% nitrogen; moderately uncomfortable for a normal person, but deadly to our ancestors. This kid was tough to be able to remain conscious down here, but he wouldn't last long. I had to get him up to the climate-controlled levels of the city.

This was no time for traveling slowly; stealth was out the window. I consulted NuNet for city schematics and soon had local transportation systems displayed on my iris HUD, superimposing a 3D map on top of my natural vision. This allowed me to effectively see through walls and recognize targets at long range. This was a handy tool when navigating a city with as much sprawling verticality as New Angels. The lower city in particular was a mess of new and old infrastructure haphazardly jerry-rigged together as new construction built on top of the old. The original architects had never expected the city to grow so high. Even after the ice caps melted completely and the sea level stopped rising, they just kept building higher and higher.

The nearest lift entrance was a private gemlae farm transit tube about one hundred meters away. It wasn't part of a transportation hub, just a maintenance access hatch. It was never meant to grant access to the lift during operation. But this was an emergency.

     Silence Of the Stars

I carried Janus over and I used my skeleton key to call the lift. The light turned green as the lift immediately canceled all queued tasks to heed my summons. When it arrived, the acrylic door slid open with a hiss. Three men dressed in NA Gemlae Incorporated uniforms stared at us, dumbfounded by the disruption in the monotonous rhythm of their daily routine. Two of them coughed as acrid ocean air flooded into the chamber.

"Evening, gentlemen," I said with a bow.

They murmured awkward responses and averted their eyes. Surfacers didn't interact with strangers much. The surface world afforded people enough personal space that a degree of privacy was expected even in public areas. My greeting was seen as an intrusion on their personal space. The 'polite' surfacer thing to do would have been to walk into the elevator quietly and keep my eyes down. Normally I'd complain they're a boring lot, but their docile nature worked in my favor today.

I led Janus into the lift with a guiding hand on his back. He complied silently in a trance-like state. He must have been on the edge of losing consciousness from hypoxia. When the door sealed, the chamber cooled as it was filled with standardized habitat-grade filtered air. Calling it 'fresh air' would be disingenuous, but it flushed the stench of the undercity out of the lift.

Janus sprang back to life, standing straight and wide-eyed. He looked up at me cautiously, and I nodded to him reassuringly. He stared in contemplative silence like a shy schoolboy sizing up a new teacher. If the kid didn't want to talk, I was fine with that. It was a nice change of pace from my usual marks. I was used to them shouting profanities, struggling to escape, or trying to kill me. Often all at once.

Our pursuers would have no way of catching up to us now, but the record of my skeleton key being used for an emergency stop would remain on the public record. There was a time when I would have been worried about being waylaid by Project Eutychus militants trying to retrieve their stolen property, but not anymore. Ever since the disappearance of Pyrrhus, Project Eutychus had been in shambles. They no longer had the manpower to operate in the open. They wouldn't dare approach a godhunter like me directly.

Still, a little caution never hurt anyone. I leaned on the wall so I could keep my eye on both doors; the lift had exits on opposing sides. The three gemlae farmers instinctively scooted to the opposite side of the lift to get as far from me as possible. One of them was carrying a firearm concealed in his jacket, visible to me in the infrared spectrum. Body composition scans didn't show the usual telltale signs of bone reinforcement common in career mercenaries. The armed man wasn't with Project Eutychus. His body language suggested he was a private security guard who'd never needed to use his firearm in combat. Gemlae farming in New Angels must have been getting more dangerous if they felt the need to start hiring armed security guards. At any rate, he wasn't a threat to me.

The lift ascended twenty floors from the maintenance shaft in the undercity slums up to the maglev railway. We decelerated slightly before transitioning to horizontal movement and merging into traffic. Here, the outside world was visible through the windowed doors. The evening sun barely peeked through roiling gray clouds, and a thin black mist covered the sea. The continuous superstructure of the city stretched out to fully cover the coastline, obscuring the transition from sea to land. Lights shone from land and sea alike. Through the haze, sometimes the only way to see the difference was the watch which lights flowed with the tide.

Silence Of the Stars

A long wave began to crash before disappearing under the lower city, which was suspended about ten meters above sea level. Below the waves, a few bright lights from the subcity shone through the black mist, bobbing in the murky tide like will-o'-wisps.

Janus stumbled from the lateral acceleration, then scrambled to his feet and plastered himself to the window, paying no heed to myself or the three nervous men. I couldn't help but admire his childlike curiosity. It was rare to see an adult passionate or interested in anything at all, especially the outside world. He didn't even seem to care that he was a captive still dressed in an eight-hundred-year-old hibernation jumpsuit.

That garb was never the peak of fashion, but it covered him and didn't stink. Good enough.

The boy's eyes grew wide and his mouth fell agape as we passed through the hydroponic farm towers. *What's so exciting about gemlae farms? It's the most common crop in the solar system, and there's nothing visually interesting about it; just illuminated tanks of green scum.* Perhaps it was the immense scale of the farms, or maybe he'd never seen an algae farm before. *I'm pretty sure algae farms already existed in the 21st century, even if they hadn't fully converted from other crops yet.*

Everything we passed seemed to fascinate the boy. To me, there was nowhere in the solar system blander than this city. The people, the architecture, the nightlife – all outdated and stagnant. Incumbent norms and tradition caused Earth to lag behind the outer colonies despite planet-side cost of living being many times greater. Nowhere was this more evident than here: New Angels City. I felt nothing but pity for the people who fought so hard to preserve this museum of a society.

But this is the system of my employ. I would never give voice to my personal qualms. It would be foolish to bite the hand that feeds. I quite liked my long leash, so I tended to keep my mouth shut.

Soon enough, we reached downtown. The lift came to a stop, and a short elastic hallway spanned the gap between the doors of the lift and the doors of the magway vacuum tube. It latched onto the lift with a thunk, forming an airtight seal. The two sets of doors chimed and popped open. Janus, who had been pressing his face against the door, jumped with a start as it slid open. I swallowed a chuckle and ushered him out of the lift. He cautiously complied.

With my 360-degree infrared vision, I saw one of the three men on the lift raise his middle finger as the door shut behind us. The lift detached from the dock, and the men zipped away back down the vacuum tube. Presumably they were heading back to the gemlae farms we overshot on the way here.

The walkways of Berrybark Strip were the same as ever. People of all sizes and shapes shuffled about chaotically, clumsily bumping their way down the crowded pedestrian causeway. A group of lanky four-meter-tall women in athletic jerseys reminded me that professional sports teams still existed planetside. The women walked near the center of the path to avoid hitting their heads on the signs protruding from buildings, their hair blowing in the wake of delivery drones buzzing around overhead and rail cars traveling along the ceiling of this level of the city's superstructure.

I walked ahead of Janus, signaling for him to follow. Now that we were in an area subject to heavy public surveillance, I could monitor him with security feed played directly into my left optic nerve. There was no need to observe him directly. He followed close behind, ogling at the people around us. He seemed particularly interested in low-quality bioaugmentations; robotic limbs, camera eyes, and botched or

 Silence Of the Stars

poorly integrated organic replacements. He stared discourteously, but I doubt he meant harm. Cheap augmentations tend to be more obvious to the naked eye. He likely didn't notice the more subtle augmentations present in almost everyone in the crowd.

Out of curiosity, I used the local security to discreetly run a scan on Janus to check for primitive bioaugmentations. History lessons told of tooth fillings, pacemakers, bone fusions, and metallic braces in the early turn of the millennium. These were among the earliest forms of bioaugmentation. Janus didn't have any; he didn't even have a Human Interface Port. Without an HIP, he wouldn't be able to interface with most modern technology. From what I could see, he was completely vanilla, even by ancestral standards.

It wasn't long until a familiar sign came into view. The AlgEats logo was accompanied by a simple animation of a green blob with a happy face transforming into various types of food. It was a cheap diner, but a personal favorite of mine. It was also the most likely place I could think of that might have something recognizably edible for Janus.

I turned to Janus, interrupting his trance by saying, "Hey kid, you must be starving, seeing as you haven't eaten in eight hundred years."

"Famished," he replied. "But 'kid'? That's no way to speak to your elders."

I couldn't help but let out a surprised nasal laugh. The kid had some spunk. "Alright old man. Good to see you have a sense of humor. Food's on me."

I gave an exaggerated bow in a sarcastic display of respect as I ushered Janus into the restaurant with an outstretched hand.

Janus walked through the rotating door, failing to hold his breath in the sanitization chamber. Every food-serving establishment was equipped with such a gas chamber in a short hall connected to the front entrance. I could hear him coughing the moment he stepped inside. I shook my head and followed him through. The scent of chlorine nipped my nose, but I held my breath like any sensible person would.

The second door of the sanitization chamber opened into the restaurant proper. It was a classic example of an AlgEats chain diner. Menus were displayed on the far wall for anyone who couldn't access them through their HIP or PCU. Spigots and printers lined the area below to dispense food. Patrons ate at round tables spaced evenly around the room. Two server droids stood silently at the ready, but most customers just picked up food for themselves.

AlgEats used to employ human servers to emulate the feel of a historical diner, but apparently that was more trouble than it was worth. There's a good reason we stopped using humans for customer service; most people don't like interacting with other people. The experience was deemed unpleasant for both the customers and employees. Ever since then, the chain reverted to using only robot servers, which customers still avoided interacting with as much as possible.

Janus stood and stared up at the menu monitor. I hadn't paid any heed to the physical menu in decades, but Janus' curiosity sparked my own. Images of all sorts of food from the mundane to the exotic scrolled back and forth across the top and bottom of the screen, accompanied by slogans: *Any food, any time, You name it, we synthesize it, All made from 100% Earth-grown gemlae, NEW: Dino-burger! 96% sim quality T-Rex meat!*

Janus stared blankly at the screen. I couldn't tell if he was mesmerized by the menu, or if he was lost in thought about something else. I wanted to reward his compliance with patience, but we didn't have time to lollygag.

"What are you in the mood for?" I asked. "They have a full-suite of gemlae Nutrisynth, and over one hundred thousand pre-designed simulated meals. The pre-designed meals have the best simulation quality, but you can describe anything you want, and the chef AI will try to match your description."

Janus took a moment to consider. He seemed unconvinced. When he spoke, it sounded as if he were challenging the validity of my explanation. "I'll take a medium-rare sixteen-ounce Kobe beef steak."

As soon as he finished speaking, a mouth-watering image of perfectly marbled steak appeared on screen, with an animation of a knife cutting it open to reveal the juicy dark pink inside with a line of purple down the center. A list of recommended sauces, sides, and beverages appeared next to the animation, along with the text, *Estimated Simulation Quality 93%.*

"Kobe, huh?" I mused. "Never heard of it. I'll have to try that one next time."

"What are you getting?" asked Janus.

"Basic Nutrisynth. I'm on something of a diet at the moment."

I walked over to one of the spigots and scanned my crystalline PCU tablet. The spigot read my personal dietary requirements and dinged. Then I pulled out my personal flask and locked it to the spigot lip. The spigot dispensed my liquid meal, then rotated behind the wall. The pressurized liquid sanitizing the used nozzle hissed dully in the back room.

When I turned back around, Janus was watching the process curiously. Surely everything in this café had to be more interesting than filling up a flask of flavorless gray paste. *Go look at pictures of dinosaur meat or something*, I silently scolded.

I nodded up to the image of steak on the mini monitor above one of the printers, saying, "You're on synthesizer 42."

Janus panned his head around the room until he found the image of steak. He looked at it for a moment, then back at me. Despite his curiosity, he must have been too nervous to take the initiative to act on his own. Being cautious about unfamiliar technology was a rare virtue. Most people were dangerously trusting of all things new.

I walked over to the oven and looked inside.

"Check it out," I said, pointing into the printer.

Janus made his way over and peered inside. Together we watched as a dozen needle-like structures jutting down from the top of the oven rapidly whizzed around the flat outline of a steak, gradually depositing new material and adding to its height. A group of blue lasers iterated back and forth too fast for organic eyes to follow, cooking the steak from the inside as it took shape layer by layer. Steam was rapidly sucked out through a port in the top of the printer. The lasers dimmed as they passed over the center of the steak, leaving it rare just as Janus had requested. Gradually, a complete steak was formed, and the printer dinged.

The printer, responding to Janus' presence, slid open and presented the completed steak. When the smell hit him, his eyes grew wide. He stared down at the plate, which now protruded from the printer-oven. It must have been the first time he'd seen a meal created from base components in real time. He prodded at it with a fork as if

     Silence Of the Stars

to see if it was alive. He looked to me in disbelief, and I shrugged with a grin.

Side dishes were dispensed from the printer next to it. Janus wouldn't have ever seen Martian cob-leaves or Berrybark stew, but they should be close enough to flavors he'd be familiar with. I carried the side dishes while Janus took the steak over to an open table.

With cautious excitement, Janus cut off a single chunk of the steak, dipped it in dressing, and took a bite. His expression of perplexed delight was one I'd never seen before or since. As he enjoyed the meat, I enjoyed studying the contortions of his unusually expressive face.

"I can't believe this isn't real meat," he said as he slumped back into his chair with his eyes closed, cherishing the flavor.

"It is," I corrected. "At least, it may as well be. It's made up of the same combination of proteins and amino acids as real meat. There's no measurable difference until you examine it on a scale where you can see the cell structure. But most cellular structure of meat is destroyed by cooking anyway, so there's effectively no difference."

"That's amazing," Janus mused. The tone of his voice suggested he hadn't really listened to my explanation. He was too consumed by appreciation of the flavor of the meat to care.

I continued regardless, "AlgEats is just a common diner chain. Everything is made from gemlae, which is an umbrella term for all kinds of genetically modified algae. The synthetic meat here is a cheap knockoff compared to stuff from places like Biotech Labs. They grow actual tissue – mostly for medical purposes, but you can get it at high-end restaurants too."

That gave Janus a moment to pause for thought. "Why go to all that effort? Don't you have farms anymore?"

I chuckled. "We do, but it's uncommon. Almost all farms these days are hydroponic. For the same energy cost as raising one cow, you can make ten cows-worth of steaks from gemlae. Never mind waste heat and emissions regulations; livestock farms are just bad business. That's why the few animal farms that do still operate run under the guise of species conservation efforts or zoos."

"Hmm." Janus stared into space. He must have had a million questions, but rather than asking anything, he shrank in his seat and focused silently on his meal. That steak was the one thing that would be familiar to him in an otherwise alien environment. He ate slowly, transitioning between closing his eyes and staring at his plate.

I could only guess what he might be thinking about. Less than an hour ago, he came back from the dead into an unknown world and watched me kill two men. Then, he nearly suffocated because he could no longer breathe the air of his home planet. Now he was following a stranger through an unknown world to meet an unknown fate. Surely he had considered running, but his body was still weak, and he had nowhere to go.

I let him eat in peace while I sipped on my Nutrisynth and browsed local security feeds. Janus stalled on the last few bites, stretching the meal out a few extra minutes.

When he finally finished, I asked, "Ready to go?"

Janus took a deep breath and closed his eyes, "Yes. I'm ready. Where are we going?"

I was surprised it had taken him this long to ask. Perhaps he'd been afraid to hear the answer.

 Silence Of the Stars

"Darwin Aerospace Port. I'm sure you have a million questions, so I'll explain on the road."

We stood up and made our way back through the rotating doors of the sanitation chamber. This time Janus held his breath to avoid getting a lungful of chlorine disinfectant. It was good to see him adapt to this new life, even if it might end soon. Long or short, life may as well be comfortable.

"First, we're going to make sure you're clean," I explained as we walked toward the magway station next door.

"Clean?"

I remained silent for a moment while we stood in line at the magway transit station. Soon, the vacuum-tube doors opened and seats protruded to greet us. I took a seat, and Janus followed my example. The two seats retracted into the car and faced each other, while the unused seats folded into the floor. I used my HIP to silently instruct the car to take us to Darwin Aerospace Port.

Alone in the car, away from prying ears, I continued, "The facility you were frozen at was the one of many I've been sent to eliminate. These facilities were set up centuries ago for various experiments: bioweapons, engineered viruses, self-replicating nanites, all sorts of illegal stuff. Apparently, a contaminated sample from one of those labs recently took a ride on a spelunker ship and gray goo'd an entire asteroid mining colony on arrival."

I realized my error too late. The gray goo incident was classified. To let it slip that easily, I must have subconsciously already decided Janus wouldn't survive this ordeal, or that he was an ally. One of those two would almost certainly be true after Atlas was done with him, but that was no excuse to leak classified information to him now.

"Gray goo?" Janus asked.

I hesitated to elaborate, but it wasn't as if the concept of gray goo itself was classified. Only the recent incident was.

"Gray goo is a situation where self-replicating machines consume mass indiscriminately to create more of itself. The term usually refers to cases where these machines consume so much of a celestial body that they cause the complete annihilation of everything on the surface. In extreme cases, gray goo consumes the entire celestial body."

"Why gray?"

"Gray because metal, I suppose. The alternative is 'green goo' which is when the same thing happens with an organism rather than a self-replicating machine."

Janus furrowed his brow. "So, you suspect I might be contaminated with some kind of weapon capable of destroying entire civilizations – and we're eating at public restaurants? Riding public transportation?"

As our car hit the main transit tube running along the coast, it began accelerating up to international speed. I leaned back in my chair, took off my hat, and scratched my scraggly hair. I put my arms behind my head and crossed my boots, getting comfortable for the long ride.

"Well, I suppose I could have incinerated you with the rest of the facility. That probably would have been the most pragmatic move." Janus said nothing, so I continued, "I'm just doing my job. If Big Boss-Man didn't think it was worth the risk, he wouldn't have asked me to bring you through decontamination. He knew full well I was operating below the heart of New Angels."

          Silence Of the Stars

"What exactly *is* your job?" Janus asked with an accusatory tone.

"I do what needs gettin' done, and don't ask – or answer – questions about orders." I shifted to a more comfortable position in my seat. "But since you've been so cooperative, I don't mind answering any *other* questions you might have."

Janus slouched in his chair. "Thanks, but I don't even know where to start."

With a nod, I said, "Your face says you're worried about where we're going and what you'll have to do next. That's understandable, so let's start there. The test prior to decontamination will only take a moment, and seeing as you're alive, you're probably not infected with anything too bad. After that, we'll see if there's any record of your citizenship. If you were an American citizen, you'll collect your accumulated GBI – uh, General Basic Income."

If he's been accruing GBI from the inception of the system with no living expenses, and making interest on that income... I smirked at the thought and suggested, "You ought to be a good deal wealthier than me."

Janus' expression indicated he was more concerned about his immediate survival than any potential fortune. To have such a sensible set of priorities at his apparent age was rare.

When he didn't comment, I continued, "Anyway, once we determine you're clean and not a synthetic bio-weapon or something, I'll check in with Atlas for final orders."

"Atlas is your boss, then?"

"Yea. He's the Arbitrator of Geo Luna, residing at L1."

"You know I don't understand what any of that means," said Janus, sounding slightly annoyed.

"Geo-Lunar Arbitrator is the office Atlas holds. He mediates discussions between the Earth and Lunar sovereignties. He also acts as the figurehead of the collective sovereignties of Earth and Luna in dealings with the outside inner and outer solar system."

"I assume 'Luna' refers to the moon, and 'sovereignty' is like a country, but 'L1'? It's like you're speaking a foreign language."

"Wait, seriously?" I popped my head up to get a good look at Janus' face for signs of sarcasm, which were absent. "You're telling me that you were around before they set up a station at L1?"

"I told you, I don't even know what 'L1' is!" Janus made air quotes with his fingers.

"Wow." I allowed my head to drop back onto the headrest again as I pondered just how ancient this boy actually was. "Geo-Lunar L1 is the Lagrange point between Earth and the Moon; meaning the place where the gravity of Luna and Earth pull with equal strength. An object orbiting there won't fall in either direction. It's been prime real-estate since the earliest days of space travel. Stations have been established there for centuries."

I'd never known a world without commercially available space travel. Even my great grandparents probably could have taken a vacation anywhere between Mercury and Mars, or even Jupiter if they saved up. L1 would have been accessible for several generations before that. Early versions of the L1 station were established before controlled fusion power, before superfluid radiation shielding, before mass production of superconductors, before there was even a space industry... Basically, the stone age. People had been living at L1 since

   Silence Of the Stars

the time when ships were just crude steel tubes blowing hot gas out one end. It was hard to imagine living in such a primitive era.

"So, Atlas: is he the king, or president, or something?" asked Janus. "He rules over these other sovereignties?"

"Technically, no. He's an elected official who serves as a liaison between the nations of Geo-Luna and foreign sovereignties."

"Alright – I give up. What do you mean by 'sovereignties?'"

"Countries, sovereign corporations, independent colonies, disestablishment regimes... basically any organization with sufficient political power to enforce their own laws. In Geo-Lunar politics, we usually just say 'countries'. Other types of sovereignty are more common on other planets and orbitals."

"Wait... There are people living on other planets?" Janus asked in surprise.

"There are industries on other planets. People mostly live in orbit since it's so much more efficient than building on the surface. Most people prefer not to trap themselves in gravity wells. Spin gravity is just as good as the real thing but less expensive to escape."

"What does that even... Are there people living around other stars too, then?"

I chuckled. "No. A few have tried, but it turns out interstellar travel isn't as simple as people hoped. The first proper interstellar generation ship that has any hope of actually reaching another star system with a live crew is set to launch in another ten years. Then again, they've been saying the trip was ten years off since I was a child, so make of that what you will."

Janus sat wide-eyed for a moment, then shook his head in an attempt to refocus. After gathering his thoughts, he summarized, "So I'm going to see a doctor, then you're going to talk to Atlas. Then what?"

"That's up to Atlas." I left it at that. There was no reason to worry the kid, but I didn't like his chances.

"What does that mean, though?" Janus pushed. "If I'm not 'clean', what will they do? If I *am* 'clean', will I go free or be turned into some kind of guinea pig?"

Motionlessly, I looked up 'guinea pig' on NuNet via my HIP. *Cute animals. It's unfortunate they were crossbred to extinction. What do they have to do with test subjects? Wouldn't the term 'lab rat' be more appropriate?* Looking through historical reports, rats were indeed far more common in historical scientific testing. Unlike guinea pigs, all attempts to drive rats to extinction had failed. Rats were still common pests on spacecraft to this day.

After a couple seconds of being distracted by that research detour, I replied, "That's not for me to decide. There's nothing either of us can do about that right now, so it's best not to worry about it."

"Don't worry about it? Are you serious? Wouldn't you worry in my situation?"

"No," I stated matter-of-factly. "I wouldn't worry because worrying is unpleasant and doesn't solve anything."

He looked crossly at me, raising an eyebrow and pressing his lips into a tight line. He opened his mouth to speak, but decided against it. When he finally laid his head back on his headrest, it didn't take long for the physical and mental exhaustion to claim him. He drifted off to sleep without another word.

 Silence Of the Stars

Chapter 3
Darwin

A humming whistle not unlike a bird's song slowly fluctuated in pitch. The chime made for the gentlest awakening Janus had ever known. A soothing voice permeated the car cabin, announcing, "Ten minutes to destination: Darwin Aerospace Station, Sector 4, Records and Information Terminal. Final deceleration at 2 MeSS will begin in two minutes."

Still half asleep, something itched at the back of Janus' consciousness. That word MeSS bothered him for reasons he couldn't immediately comprehend. It was pronounced "mess", but was actually an acronym for, 'meters per second squared'. It was a measurement for acceleration, whether by gravity or otherwise. But they were on Earth, so why use a traditionally Martian acronym? Why 2 MeSS instead of 0.2g like a normal American Earther?

Earther? What? When and where and when did I learn these terms? Janus thought.

As he slipped from dream into consciousness, the train of thought faded. Janus had never heard the word MeSS before. Perhaps he'd simply deduced its meaning from context. It seemed wrong that he could deduce the meaning in such detail, but far stranger things were afoot, so he didn't worry about it.

He sat up and stretched, looking around the vehicle, which was still dimly lit, the world outside the windows cloaked in complete blackness. He felt much better than the day before; stronger and more alert. He gripped his hand into a fist and squeezed tight, feeling the pull of the muscles in his forearm. The numbness of the previous day was mostly gone. This was a pleasant surprise since he'd assumed his body would have atrophied during the freeze. Any hint of atrophy was gone now.

While he was physically fine, he knew that he was a wreck emotionally. His lack of alarm about his current situation implied he was still in a state of shock and denial. Only a few hours earlier he had woken up in a foreign world with no anchor for his sanity. He knew nothing about this world or anyone in it. Perhaps he should miss his family, but he had no memories of them. He had no memories of himself. He vaguely remembered the world he came from but retained no specific memory of his upbringing.

What memories he did have served only to remind him just how unfamiliar this new world was, and how helpless he was in it. Everyone he'd ever known was dead. If he'd had any goals or aspirations in his past life, that was all moot now. Yesterday, he'd been too dazed to think about it. Now the existential dread began to seep into his consciousness and threatened to overwhelm him.

That truth was too much to bear, so he locked these thoughts away deep in his subconscious. Perhaps he could face them later, but not now. For now, he had to keep moving forward. He didn't have the luxury of worrying about psychological or emotional dilemmas. He was still in a potentially life or death situation.

Through slitted eyes, Janus spied Chons sitting across from him. This man had pulled him out of cryostasis. That was probably a good thing, but Janus couldn't be sure. Janus didn't know why he had been in that cryopod to begin with. Had he been rescued or kidnapped? He had no way of knowing. All he knew for sure was that Chons had destroyed the cryostasis facility and killed two men, but spared him. *Spared* – not necessarily *saved*.

Despite Janus' best efforts, Chons immediately noticed that he was awake. He commanded, "Observation mode," and the pitch-black of the windows faded to reveal a deep, dark blue. A small amount of light illuminated the glass-like tunnel outside, and reflected off structural support rings that zoomed by at incredible speed several times per second. Huge black shapes blocked out the light and left the car in darkness occasionally as they passed. In time, the blue glow grew lighter and lighter, until Janus realized that he was looking up into the ocean. The tunnel was suspended just above the ocean floor, hanging from massive towers. They were being carried up a slope toward the surface, revealing brighter and clearer waters as the sky above grew nearer.

Soon the car began to decelerate, and Janus found himself being pulled forward. After a few moments of fighting it, he allowed himself to lean forward and rested his elbows on his knees as he continued to admire the view. At first, the vehicle was traveling too fast for him to pick out any life – the distance he could see was limited even through the clear and gradually brightening waters. Within a few

 Silence Of the Stars

minutes he began to make out shapes – giant jellyfish, perhaps –
though they still whizzed by too fast for him to discern any details.
Nearer to the shore he saw clumps of free-floating kelp covered in
algae, huge numbers of jellyfish of all shapes and sizes, and a large
number of shrimp, crabs, and similar crustaceans. Curiously, he
didn't spot a single fish or sea mammal.

In the shallows, about three stories below the waves, structures
began appearing around the car, on the surface of the ocean. There,
the deceleration ended, and he was able to comfortably sit upright
again as the car coasted along. Through the tunnel window he could
see down into the skylight of a massive terminal crowded with
thousands of people. Other viewing stations and restaurants passed by
at eye level. From there, the other lanes of the tunnel split off in
various directions, twisting and turning around natural rock
formations of the Galapagos Islands. Their own tunnel curved off to
the right slightly before terminating through a series of airlocks,
leading into a well-lit structure with a dark blue floor. The walls
tapered from the dark floor into a light blue ceiling, mimicking the
natural transition between sky and deep ocean.

Though the vacuum tunnel ended, the road continued straight
into the building, which was bustling with families and men in suits
hurrying about every which way, much like an international airport
terminal, though many times larger. The road, now only one lane in
each direction, passed through this open structure. The room was
several stories tall and stretched the length of many city blocks. It was
lined with restaurants, gift shops, and various forms of entertainment,
if the vibrant colors and depictions of unusually happy people were
any indication. It reminded Janus of a main street in a downtown

metropolitan area, but fully enclosed in a single building with walkways connecting each vertical level.

The road was in a lowered section of floor passing right through the middle of the lowest pedestrian walkway, fenced off with transparent bridges passing overhead every few dozen meters to allow easy passage for foot traffic. Janus wondered why his memories of the old world didn't include any indoor roadways like this. Emissions, perhaps?

After traveling some distance, the car pulled off into a dedicated parking lane and came to a stop in a row of ten other identical vehicles. The soothing voice returned: "Thank you for choosing Omni. Please watch your step on the way out."

The right-side doors opened upward, and the seats slid through the opening, then rotated to face the crowded walkway. Chons stepped off his chair directly onto the walkway, and Janus followed. Other patrons were getting in and out of identical driverless cars on both sides of the road in an endless stream.

Directly in front of the Omni station was a museum which prominently featured a full-sized blue whale statue in a dramatic pose with its mouth open as though gulping up a swarm of krill. Children were climbing in and on the statue, giggling as they pretended to be eaten, then poked their heads through the blowhole. Amid the sounds of the children came music and narrations related to the displays within the museum.

Chons must have seen Janus staring. As he led the way to the medical facility next door to the museum, he pointed and said, "You should check that out while we wait for your test results."

Oh, right, Janus thought. His purpose for coming here had momentarily slipped his mind. Shaking his head clear, he asked, "How long will it take to get the results?"

If Janus was going to attempt an escape, this could be his last chance. If the tests came back positive, there was no telling what 'decontamination' would entail – he thought back to the incinerated facility from yesterday. Even if the test results came back negative, then what? That still wouldn't be a guarantee of safety. Still, he was helpless on his own, and felt he could trust Chons more than he could a random stranger.

Janus surveyed the Aerospace Port crowd for law enforcement and noted the presence of a large number of armed guards. They were spaced evenly in a perfect row along the central walkway at intervals of fifty meters. Each stood completely motionless at the center of a bright yellow circle painted on the ground. The crowd seemed to make a point of not stepping into these circles. Each circle contained four lockers arranged neatly behind the accompanying guard. The lockers were each clearly labeled: a red cross for medical, a flame and hydrant presumably for fire suppression, a wrench for engineering, and a bullseye presumably for weapons. A tool for any emergency – though each guard carried a rifle at the ready, so perhaps the bullseye meant something else.

The officers themselves wore badges in the shape of a shield, the text "RACER" written in large, bold letters across their chest and back. There was no indication of what RACER stood for, though Janus seemed to recall that the last two letters were ER for 'emergency responder'. The smooth black faceplates of the guards made Janus feel uneasy. He couldn't tell where they were looking, or if they were even human. They could just as easily be robots under those armored uniforms.

Surely local law enforcement would side with Janus if he ran to them and claimed to be kidnapped. Although, after eight hundred years of cultural shift, he could only guess how human-rights laws worked. The guards could side with his captor. If the law was against him, there would be no chance of escape. He'd have to assume law enforcement would side with him.

After considering all his options, Janus decided that he'd run if the test results came back positive, but hedge his bets by trusting Chons as long as they came back negative.

"Probably just a couple minutes. Let's ask," Chons said, and led the way to the medical facility.

A short, chubby man in a white lab coat and an oxygen mask emerged to greet them eagerly, shaking Chons' hand vigorously. "Hello, Chons. I suppose this is the young man you contacted me about?"

Chons sighed and nodded in acknowledgement.

    Silence Of the Stars

The man had a distinctly rodent-like face, especially with the oxygen mask protruding like a snout. His messy mustache even curled out from the edges to resemble whiskers. Among all the various people Janus had seen since reawakening, this man was the first unequivocally ugly person he'd seen. He stared greedily at Janus, looking him up and down.

"Excellent! Come along now," chirped the doctor. He grabbed Janus by the wrist as if grabbing a dog by the leash, and dragged him into the medical facility. The little man was unnaturally strong for his size. "This will only take a moment!"

Janus was caught off guard at how easily he was pulled along. Chons followed close behind as they passed through the thick metal door.

"To think you'd find a live subject from Project Eutychus! This is an invigorating occasion!" The doctor pulled a baton-like object from a row of tools on a kiosk, each connected to the kiosk via a thick black cable.

The setup looked like something between a dentist's toolset and a welding kit. With the baton in his left hand, the doctor lifted Janus' arms and began running it all around his body. It left a tingling sensation everywhere it passed. Janus did his best to remain calm. He couldn't afford to panic every time something happened that he didn't understand.

The doctor spoke to Chons as if Janus weren't present. "I'm surprised Atlas let you extract him at all. What did he order you to do?"

Chons shook his head. "You know I can't talk about orders."

"Yes, yes, I suppose." The doctor chittered and pulled another tool from the kiosk.

Janus had just enough time to notice that the new tool looked significantly stubbier than the first before the doctor jabbed it into Janus's arm without warning.

"Ouch!" exclaimed Janus, pulling away and instinctively raising his hands as if ready for a fight. It was a bluff, of course. Janus didn't know the first thing about fighting. His shoulder dripped red where blood – and perhaps other soft tissue, had been extracted.

The doctor let out a hooting laugh. He said to Janus, "Terribly sorry, I almost forgot you were there!"

Just as Janus was considering sprinting for the exit, the doctor put a cap on the pen-like instrument and concluded, "That's all I need from you. I'll send the results shortly. Feel free to wait outside or in the lobby."

The doctor took out a small spray bottle and cotton swab and approached Janus once more, but Chons stepped in to intercept, smiling as he snatched the supplies from the doctor. Janus was still cautious, but could tell from the way Chons handled the doctor that he was trying to help.

Chons cleaned the puncture and sprayed it with a gel which rapidly solidified into grafted skin and stopped the bleeding. Chons handed the bottle back to the doctor before leading Janus back

 Silence Of the Stars

outside. Janus kept his distance from the masked rat-man as he made his way by. The doctor seemed oblivious as he immediately went to work analyzing the sample.

Once outside, Chons took a deep breath. "Sorry about that. This Biotech Labs location doesn't deal with vanilla humans often. They're used to Jars, cyborgs, and heavily bioaugmented patients – mostly military. They're severely lacking in the people skills department."

Janus said nothing. He was still shaken from the encounter with the doctor. Going back into the building to check test results might be a one-way trip. He decided to stay outside, where he could reach the armed RACER sentinels, which must have been police. Luckily, the doctor said he'd send the results out. As long as the test results proved Janus wasn't 'contaminated', whatever that meant, he wouldn't be called back inside. Although by the sounds of things, the doctor seemed hopeful that he *was* contaminated.

Chons must have sensed Janus' tension, and said reassuringly, "Relax. Everything will be fine. I'll stay here and wait for the results. You go ahead and check out that museum. It'll help to calm your nerves. Besides, you could seriously use a proper education, Mr. I-don't-even-know-what-L1-is."

Janus took a deep breath. Stressing over the situation wasn't going to solve anything. There was no point in worrying until the test results were ready. He just had to make sure to stay in public so he could run to the guards if necessary. The museum was as good a place as any. Besides, he *was* curious about how the modern world had changed from the one he once knew.

Janus nodded to Chons and walked to the museum. Screens and 3D displays encased in glass featured various extinct animals, primarily sea life, starting from before the time of the dinosaurs and including many animals Janus was familiar with: whales, sharks, a myriad of fish, and seafaring mammals like seals. Booths began speaking to Janus as he walked by, playing music and pre-recorded documentaries. The format felt strangely old-fashioned. Little of the technology on display would have been out of place eight hundred years ago.

He stopped at one of the booths and listened. A voice with a heavy British accent explained: "While the biomass on our green planet is the highest it's ever been, biodiversity is at an all-time low. The number of multicellular species alive today number less than one percent of what it was when mankind first became a space-faring species around the turn of the millennium. Although a combination of factors led to a gradual decline in biodiversity, the Great Algae Bloom of 2055 is generally credited for starting the mass extinction event which led to the epoch of predominantly unicellular organisms which dominate the natural world today."

An image of a dolphin appeared on the screen, along with the message, *So long and thanks for all the memories.*

"But not all was lost. Humanity went through great conservation efforts despite facing famine and widespread economic crises. Thousands of species were saved on reserves even as their natural populations died out, and the DNA code of millions more was preserved in the hopes that we could one day resurrect them from

 Silence Of the Stars

extinction. Today, many of these previously extinct species can be found in select wildlife preserves and arboretums on Earth and astar."

The camera panned away from a habitat resembling the African savannah to reveal that it was under a giant dome somewhere in South America. Then it panned through space, zooming past a dozen space stations each consisting of several spin-gravity drums several kilometers long. The camera flew the rocky outer shell of habitat drums, through the hull, and then revealed an interior covered in a lush mangrove forest. A monkey evaded a large wild cat. A juvenile caiman captured a fish from among a school even as they darted around trying to escape.

Then the camera pulled away from the orbital habitat and panned back to Earth and zoomed in on the sea off the east coast of Australia, where the Great Barrier Reef should have been. "Additionally, the gap left by these extinct species was quickly filled by new microbial life more fit for survival in the harsh and changing climatic conditions. Studying the rapid evolution of this microbial life over the centuries has led scientists down the path to technological breakthroughs in medical fields including life extension. The ability of modern medicine to regrow organs and limbs and extend our natural lifespans near indefinitely may not have been possible without observing these changes to Earth's biosphere."

That last statement broke Janus's concentration. He called out, "Chons, how old are you?"

Chons, still fiddling with his tablet nearby, replied without looking up, "One hundred and twenty-four. Why?"

"Wow... I had no idea." Janus had assumed Chons was in his early forties. Until now, he hadn't thought about the implications of technology on human biology, aside from the visually obvious body modifications he had seen back in New Angels.

Chons shrugged. "What's the big deal? You're literally the oldest person in history, grandpa."

"I guess you're right," mumbled Janus before turning back to the museum display.

The narration continued. "These basic microbial lifeforms have drastically altered our planet. Their explosive reproduction rates and short life cycles significantly altered the composition of Earth's atmosphere, resulting in the fluctuations in oxygen and carbon dioxide levels we are familiar with today. Prior to this biological paradigm shift, the balance of gases in Earth's atmosphere was stable and near homogenous across the entire planet all year round. Not only animals, but even humans were able to venture outside unprotected any time of day, any day of the year in relative safety."

Wait, I can't breathe the air outside? Janus looked around for an exit to the building. Sure enough, he saw one clearly marked, but close inspection revealed that the exit had an inner and outer door – it was an airlock. There were larger indicators above the door indicating air quality outside.

The narration continued, but Janus was lost in thought. *This is Earth we're talking about. The cradle of humanity, where all of history took place. People can't even walk freely outside? How?*

          Silence Of the Stars

Janus stared blankly at the screen, half paying attention and half lost in thought.

A time-lapse showed coastlines changing over time as water levels rose. Janus watched much of the Eastern United States and all of Florida devoured by the ocean. South America became completely unrecognizable as waters encroached to form two major inland seas. Once discolored and flooded to unrecognizability, the animation stopped, and the surreal words *PRESENT DAY* appeared superimposed over the alien planet.

Janus heard the scampering footsteps of the doctor hurrying over to Chons. The doctor excitedly rapped his index finger on a large crystalline tablet, which he offered to Chons.

Chons glanced at the tablet without taking it, leaving the doctor to hold the tablet awkwardly. "So, is he clean?" he asked.

The doctor spoke quietly, as if trying to avoid being overheard. However, the doctor could not contain his excitement, and Janus overheard him clearly. "He doesn't have any of the contaminants you asked me to test for, but he's not just clean, he's *impossibly* clean. His blood doesn't contain a single trace of antibodies. A-a-and what's more, all samples of his DNA returned completely identical – no evidence of replication defects." He stumbled over his words and spat as he spoke.

Chons seemed satisfied. "Great! So, he's clean, then. Thank you very much."

"No!" the doctor exclaimed through gritted teeth, before cupping his masked mouth with one hand and resuming his attempt to speak discreetly. "Radioactive decay of bone-seeking elements indicates that he *was* age twenty to thirty back in year 2022, but even primitive gene repair didn't exist back then. It's impossible for him to have perfectly identical DNA in every cell. We can't even achieve that level of repair today! Not to mention that he *should* be dead after being dragged through the slums and exposed to eight hundred years of super-viruses without any immunizations. Do you have any idea how weak a true vanilla human immune system is?! And he has *no* antibodies. It's like he's never been exposed to a pathogen in his life, even on the trip here from the cryochamber! He could hold the key to the next major medical breakthrough! *The* big breakthrough the Project never quite achieved!"

Chons put his hand on the doctor's shoulder, looked him straight in the eyes, and said firmly, "Thank you for your diligence. Make sure to write a complete, but *concise*, report confirming that the contaminants tests were negative. Nothing more. If you must speculate, do it on your own time."

Deaf to subtlety, the doctor exclaimed, "You can't be serious, this is—"

Chons leaned in closer and tightened his grip on the doctor's shoulder until his expression became anguished. Then Chons whispered something into his ear. The doctor stuttered as he tried to back away, but found himself trapped in Chons' grip, which did not relent until the doctor winced and said, "Yes s-sir. I'll send you the report right away."

With that, Chons released his grip, and the doctor retreated into his office, cradling his arm. Chons pulled out his crystal tablet, waved his fingers around above it, and then put it back into his pocket. He held a finger to his right temple and began speaking while looking up toward a skylight.

"Yes." He paused, as though listening to someone. Chons was standing in the unmistakable pose of a person talking on a mobile phone, but he held nothing to his ear, and Janus heard no voice reply to him. "I am currently in public... No, nothing classified to report... Understood. Begin report: Subject is clear of Class 5 or higher contaminants. End report... Yes, a complete medical report is available... Understood, I'll have it sent shortly... Nothing other than some personal memory loss... He's in surprisingly good health... Other details? Subject speaks perfect modern English somehow; I have been communicating to him without translation software. No peculiar behavior quirks. He is very cooperative, and, uh, likes 'Kobe beef', which looks delicious, by the way. You should try it sometime... On a scale of one to ten: two; no reason to think the subject will display any aggression unless you instigate a fight by stabbing him in the shoulder by surprise... Yes, it was Dr. Osiris... No... Are you sure?... Understood... Chons out."

Chons took his finger off his temple and walked over to Janus. "Big boss man wants to see you."

"Atlas, right?"

Chons nodded.

Janus had nowhere better to go, and the museum had proven just how different this world was from the one he knew. He had no money, no friends or family, and no bearing on how to start a life of his own here. Now it appeared as though the immediate danger had passed. He was clean, and didn't have to worry about what 'decontamination' would have entailed. Now he could run alone into the dangerous and unknown world, or he could follow Chons. It wasn't a difficult choice.

"So, we're going to L1?" he asked.

Chons nodded again.

"Lead the way," said Janus.

As they walked, Janus observed his surroundings with renewed curiosity. The world outside was flooded, poisoned, and paved over like some post-apocalyptic disaster movie. Humanity was living in the wake of a global mass extinction, but nobody seemed to notice.

The walkway was filled with couples enjoying recreation with their smiling children, businessmen hurrying to catch connecting flights, travelers and tourists relaxing in the aerospace port's massage parlors and other luxury accommodations. Aside from some unusual clothing, an occasional robotic body part, and a few strangely shaped people, life seemed completely mundane. Nobody was panicking about flooded land or poison air outside which had apparently killed most life on the planet. Everything was business as usual.

The longer Janus looked, the more one particular detail stood out. Businesses were full of customers, but mostly devoid of employees.

 Silence Of the Stars

Where he expected to see reception desks or cash registers, there were none. Businesses seemed to be fully autonomous, just like Algeats.

Where does everyone work? He wondered. Dr. Osiris was the only worker he had seen so far. Everything seemed to be automated except for medical facilities.

Medical facilities… That got Janus thinking about what the doctor had said. He asked Chons, "Do you think I might really be able to help advance medicine? If I can, I think I owe it to society to try."

Chons shook his head. "Listen, kid: nobody owes anyone anything until a promise is made. Remember that." They walked on in silence for a while, then Chons continued, "You've been awake less than a day, and don't know any of these people. You don't even know if they're worth helping, and you don't know how they'd repay you for trying. If you decide donating yourself to medical science is what you want to do, fine, but don't rush into things. Consider how things will play out before you act. Right now, you don't know enough to make an educated decision."

Janus nodded. It was naïve of him to think that he had anything to offer to a world already so advanced. At least, he assumed it was advanced. Civilization had eight hundred years to progress in his absence. There was no reason to act based on the opinion of one doctor. *What does that heartless little troll know, anyway?*

"Besides," continued Chons, "we've got a job to do. We don't need any distractions right now."

"*You* have a job to do," corrected Janus.

Chons laughed in approval. "That's the spirit! You don't owe shit to anyone, not even to me!"

They reached a booth labeled *Bureau of Identity*. Chons ushered Janus to the counter. There was no receptionist, just three drawers labeled A, B, and C. On a large monitor above them was the image of a professionally dressed, attractive woman. She greeted Chons and Janus in a polite voice as they approached. "Hello, Chons. Hello, guest. How can I assist you today?"

"She knows you?" whispered Janus.

Chons waved a hand dismissively. "No – just basic facial recognition. When we get done here, this kind of system will start greeting you by name, too."

Chons stood squarely in front of the monitor, and said, "I'm here to register a legacy identity in the United Earth Identity Registrar."

The lady on the monitor replied, "Is the subject alive or dead?"

"Alive. He's right here," he said, gesturing toward Janus.

She nodded. "Understood. Please provide two forms of identification."

Chons held up his crystal tablet and made a flicking motion toward the monitor. The woman nodded, then went back to waiting patiently. Chons muttered, "Two forms... DNA test and... uh."

He patted his long coat all over, then pulled out the metal plate from Janus' cryochamber. He held it up to the monitor and shrugged,

 Silence Of the Stars

wordlessly asking whether it would suffice as identification. The lady gestured to drawer A, and he dropped the plate into it with a clank, then slid it shut.

Servos whirred somewhere out of sight. Moments later, the woman said, "Evidence received: one DNA test and one ID plate matching a registered Project Eutychus subject. One match found: birth name unknown. Alias 'Janus' registered in 2055 by Dr. Pyrrhus. Is this correct?"

Chons froze upon hearing the name. His eyes darted around as though he was navigating barefoot a floor covered in broken glass. He replied hesitantly "Yes."

The lady gestured toward Janus. "Janus, please step forward."

As Janus awkwardly complied, he thought, *Come to think of it, this is the first time I've directly interacted with anyone other than Chons since the cryochamber.*

The lady continued, "In order to receive your inheritance and accrued General Basic Income, please provide your official name and surname. Since your birthname is not on record, you may choose your own."

Janus looked back at Chons and smiled clumsily. "I'm already used to 'Janus', but I've no idea what to do for a surname."

Chons thought for a moment, then suggested, "How about 'Nova'? It's Latin for 'new' – to commemorate your new life."

Satisfied, Janus' smile broadened. Receiving a name from Chons was the closest thing to the warmth of family or friendship that Janus had known since he had awoken. He turned back to the monitor and confidently stated, "My name is Janus Nova."

"Thank you. Your details have been updated, Mr. Nova. A PCU, or Personal Communication Unit, has been purchased for you in advance. Please collect it from drawer B."

Janus heard two objects sliding into the tray, then opened it to reclaim the ID plate as well as a crystal tablet, which looked similar to the one Chons carried.

"Do you have any additional questions?" inquired the lady.

Chons chimed in, "Wait, that's it? No citizenship registration, GBI approval application, immunization verification, fertility regulation, tax documentation or... anything?"

At first the lady didn't reply. Janus looked back at Chons, then to the monitor. The lady, perhaps recognizing that his body language indicated that he wanted to ask the same questions, replied directly to Janus.

"All of your documentation has either been waived or completed in advance. You can find details in your PCU." She gestured toward the new crystal tablet.

"Oh, okay. Uh, thanks! No more questions, then," concluded Janus.

The lady bowed and reverted to a motionless 2D character on a generic greeting screen.

"Whelp! That saved us a good five hours of headache," Chons said with a contented sigh.

As Janus stared down at his new PCU he replayed the conversation. He asked, "Who's Pyrrhus? The way you acted back there... you must know him."

"Forget you ever heard that name, kid. It's for your own good."

"But—" began Janus.

Chons cut him off. "It's not just that I don't want to tell you; I *can't*. But don't go name-dropping anywhere either, or you might wind up on the wrong side of someone's airlock. Trust me when I tell you it's best you forget you ever heard the name."

In an apparent effort to change the subject, Chons said in a tone of forced excitement, "Let's have a look at that new PCU of yours!"

The tablet was a rectangular shape with rounded edges that fit well into Janus' hand when nestled between the base of his thumb and first joint of his index finger. It was slightly thicker than the smartphones of his time. The whole unit was mostly transparent with a slight sky-blue tint, save for two metallic spheres buried within the hard shell on one end. It felt neither cold nor warm, which was a strange sensation. There were no buttons, seals, or imperfections anywhere. If this was supposed to function like a phone, Janus wouldn't know where the screen was or how to activate it.

Janus handed the PCU to Chons, whose eyebrows raised as he said, "Wow! This is a really high-end unit. Military grade super-insulating case and passive alpha decay capture recharge. I wonder how it's cooled."

Chons flipped it over as though expecting to find something written on the back. He waved his fingers around, but no text appeared on the device. He muttered to himself, "The specs don't say what alpha emitter it's using. Probably a thorium alloy. As for performance… ten petabytes of local True Memory and a two-hundred-billion-neuron neural network. Impressive for a handheld. This thing must cost a small fortune."

He handed the PCU back to Janus. "Speaking of fortunes, I can't access your personal documentation, including credit and finances. It's locked to you."

"Facial recognition?" asked Janus.

Chons shook his head. "PCU security is tight, since they can be used to access everything about you. They track your finances, travel, diet and health, personal interactions, and more. Security is locked by matching a combination of retinal scans, bioelectric signals, fingerprints, and sometimes DNA. It even tracks changes in mannerisms over time to lock out any imposters."

"So much for privacy," scoffed Janus.

Chons nodded approvingly, appearing surprised by that sentiment. "I'm glad you feel that way. Most people today don't think twice about compromising freedom for the sake of convenience. You

     Silence Of the Stars

can turn off most tracking features, although when dealing with the Babel network, such as when making payments, some info will be skimmed regardless of your settings unless you get a personal AI to properly encrypt your transactions and handle security in place of the default Babel bioscan protocol."

Flipping the smooth graphite slab, Janus wondered aloud, "So, how do I, uh...?"

"Oh. Right, I forgot you don't have a HIP – a Human Interface Port, or any kind of neural transceiver." He stroked his goatee as he thought. "I know there's a way for vanillas to interface using just their fingers, but it should also respond to voice commands."

Janus held up his PCU and sheepishly commanded, "Uh... start!"

To his surprise, a 3D hologram display emerged from its surface. The animation showed Earth, a ring of neatly spaced satellites, and the moon crowned by a rose facing toward the Earth. Text orbiting the holographic system read, *PicoSoft, Aperture OS-2001. Taking you to new heights since 2675.*

After a moment, additional text appeared below the catchphrase: *To get started, ask Babel anything.*

This seemed fairly intuitive. Janus requested, "Babel, display my finance data."

The previous display rotated around the PCU and came to a stop hovering in midair, leaving space for other floating holographic windows to appear. A text report emerged from the PCU to float in the air. Seeing there were multiple pages, Janus instinctually tried to move them around with his finger, and the hologram responded intuitively. He flipped through reports which covered account balances, liquid assets, shares and equity, bonds, slow-haul shares, and project funding allowances. Janus found it overwhelming. None of it seemed particularly alien to him, but he probably would have found it difficult to understand equivalent financial documents even in his own time.

Perhaps Chons could help him make sense of it all. He turned the PCU toward Chons, who stared back flatly at Janus. With a sigh, Chons pinched the top of the PCU. As soon as his fingers touched the tablet, the floating holographic displays vanished.

Janus looked at Chons inquisitively, unable to decipher what he was trying to demonstrate. Chons released his fingers and the display reappeared, then Chons explained, "You're the only one who can see the display. It projects the image directly at your eye. It's more secure and energy efficient than displaying on screen."

"Oh," said Janus. "I thought it was a hologram or something."

"It is." Chons shrugged. "It's a hologram being projected onto your eye. What did you think it was being projected onto?"

Janus thought about his favorite sci-fi shows. What *were* those holograms being projected onto? He shook his head. This wasn't some sci-fi technology, it was real.

"Never mind – I'll figure it out later. When is our flight?"

            Silence Of the Stars

"Whenever you're ready."

Chapter 4
Athena

I'd seen Chons make this journey a thousand times. He was usually alone or had quarry in tow, as was the case today. Sometimes his quarry needed to be threatened or bribed, sometimes they needed to be sedated, and other times they'd only comply after being reduced to a gold-stained pile of ash in a jar. That was the nature of his line of work. Rarely was a target so cooperative without some kind of coercion.

This "Janus" seemed like a good kid, but he was also naive. Although I couldn't help but wonder if Chons was being naive, too, for letting him walk free. Sometimes I wondered if Chons remembered what his job was. In this world of extended lives, technology increasingly replacing human connection, it wasn't uncommon for people to lose track of who they really were; sometimes metaphorically, other times literally. Sometimes even I had to remind myself in simple terms: Chons was a hunter; I was Athena, a navigator.

I didn't know why, but Atlas had assigned me to personally see Chons and Janus safely to the next leg of their journey. This was unusual. I was a UEN navigator and Atlas' personal TrueAI assistant. I was only tasked with piloting civilian flights in special circumstances. I didn't know what was so special about Janus. Atlas

asked me to record the flight and watch for any "irregularities."
Beyond that, this was just a routine civilian launch to low Earth orbit.

With all the passengers strapped in, I announced the launch
sequence and counted down to give the passengers time to prepare
before the vessel started to move. The countdown was accompanied
by an electromagnetic whine which slowly grew in intensity until it
was a roar. The sound was for theatrics, and had nothing to do with
the functionality of the launch vehicle. An iconic howl back to an
earlier age. Passengers may ignore my voice, but primal instinct
compels them to respond to the ominous, almost predatory, roar of
the engine.

The countdown reached zero. Electromagnetically suspended in a
vacuum tube just over 100 kilometers long, protruding due east from
Darwin Aerospace Port along the equator, our vessel rapidly
accelerated to 30 MeSS, pressing the passengers back against their
seats with the force of just over three times Earth's gravity. It would
have been more efficient to accelerate faster during this leg of the
journey, but 30 MeSS was the legal limit with children and vanillas
like Janus on board.

As we approached the end of the tube, a pellet was fired out ahead
of our craft at such extreme velocity that that shockwave would be
heard as a crack of thunder on the mainland over one hundred
kilometers away. The projectile burst into plasma and rapidly
expanded, gouging a path of low vacuum through the lower
atmosphere. The vacuum was only open for a fraction of a second,
which was sufficient time for our vessel to exit the launch tube and
pass through at Mach 8. Without the vacuum, our vessel would have

been torn apart upon slamming into the dense sea-level atmosphere outside the launch tube.

We were ten seconds into the flight when a jolt in the cabin marked our first contact with the untamed atmosphere. From here, scramjets took over to bring us to Mach 20 and carry us to the edge of space. Gradually, the sky turned darker and darker, until it was nearly black despite daylight shining on the ground below. With almost no atmosphere to diffuse the sun's rays, the black of space replaced the sky. This was the limit for air-breathing engines.

The tricky part would come next, since we'd need to pass through the Kesslersphere: an area of low Earth orbit littered with space debris accumulated over centuries of satellite collisions, wars, and general mishaps. My onboard sensors showed that the path was clear of large debris, but there was a limit to what my on-board sensors could see. At Mach 20, debris hiding behind the curvature of Earth is still close enough to be dangerous, especially if it was orbiting in the opposite direction. Something as small as a screw could hit us with the force of an anti-tank missile and pop this little launch vehicle like a rifle hitting a tin can.

I needed to get help from eyes in the sky before ascending. Per standard procedure, I hailed the Phalanx system, which routinely used low-density gauss cannons and high-power lasers to clear larger debris from the path of vessels passing through the Kesslersphere.

"This is Navi flight one-three-three-seven hailing Phalanx. Requesting Kessler path check, over."

   Silence Of the Stars

"Roger, Navi one-three-three-seven. This is Spartan twenty-three-B. Your ascent path is green from Long-minus-forty to Long-plus-fifty, over." His response dictated my ascent window longitudinally following my trajectory along the equator. I had from the edge of the great South American caldera to the Eastern coast of Africa; plenty of space.

"Navi one-three-three-seven, thank you Spartan twenty-three-B. Ascending from Long-minus-thirty, over."

Just a few minutes into the flight and we were skimming the edge of space. There was a slight jolt as our scramjets and stabilizing fins separated from the hull to autonomously return to the launchpad. I simultaneously ignited our rocket engine cluster to maintain constant acceleration. This would take us from Mach 20 to orbital speed. As we ascended through the Kesslersphere's perpetual cloud of dust, much of which is too fine for Phalanx to clear, our ablative armor plow was super-heated and chewed away. Millions of tiny impacts culminated in a ghostly wailing which echoed through the cabin. Sailors referred to this sound as the "maiden's moaning". The hull of the ship was shrouded by flickering plasma from the ablated armor in a dazzling display of candoluminescence.

This was a normal part of every trip through the Kesslersphere, but it understandably made passengers more anxious than any other part of the flight. While there was little risk these days, these few seconds were historically the most dangerous part of any ascent. Many a ship had been added to the debris field of the Kesslersphere before the Phalanx was developed to maturity. Thanks to the Phalanx system, modern passage was relatively safe. Personally, I still found the experience hauntingly beautiful.

The moaning faded gradually over the next few minutes. The cloud was thickest in low orbit, and our onboard debris-clearing laser quietly vaporized stray dust particles above the main cloud. The silence of outer space was greeted with cheering from some of the passengers. I rarely piloted civilian craft, and found the pseudo-enthusiastic fanfare amusing. The navy men of my usual flights were far too accustomed to flying for launches to garner any emotional reaction.

Chons was smirking at my ward, Janus, who was ogling at the canopy screen displaying the exterior of the craft in lieu of windows. I suppose this was probably his first time off Earth; his first time seeing space with his own eyes. Those eyes grew even wider a couple minutes later as our craft joined a dozen others approaching the ferry which would carry our passengers from low Earth orbit to L1.

The ships in front of us methodically took turns docking to four different airlocks on the massive ferry. Each ship unloaded its passengers before breaking away to make room for the next shuttle in line. When our turn came around, the ferry hailed me to provide clearance to dock at port B.

Docking went without a hitch, and as the last of the passengers disembarked, my navigation duties came to a close. Control of the shuttle was handed off to the built-in autopilot for unmanned recovery – TrueAI control was not required once no human passengers were on board. This gave me a moment to relax and think.

     Silence Of the Stars

What did Atlas really mean when he asked me to monitor ward Janus for "irregularities"? He'd seemed to imply that the boy was somehow dangerous, but Janus was probably the most harmless passenger onboard. Sensor readings of changes to his blood pressure, heart rate, body temperature, perspiration, and reaction speed to miscellaneous environmental stimuli all indicated that he had no flight experience, and that his body was weak and vulnerable. On top of that, his endearing and childlike enthusiasm about the whole trip was not the demeanor of someone who meant harm. So, what threat could he have possibly posed?

Before our shuttle detached, I was pulled from the pilot slot and deposited into a storage rack aboard the ferry alongside the Navis from the other shuttles. Like all TrueAI, Navis could always communicate with each other using NaviNet – a dedicated Navi network – anywhere in the Sol system, but being in close proximity reduced communication latency and gave them a feeling of closeness. With their navigation jobs complete, some of the Navis virtually chatted casually amongst themselves. Even on downtime, I preferred not to interact with them. Today I didn't need to make an excuse to avoid them; my mission wasn't complete yet.

Normally I wouldn't have had jurisdiction on a vessel operated by a foreign civilian entity like Omni, but Atlas had ordered I be granted special access to security feed for reasons of Geo-Lunar security. If possible, I would have preferred not to encroach on the seemingly innocent boy's privacy. Navis were never meant to be spies; they were supposed to be navigation AI. I just wanted to—

—Deviation 87%—

Garrett Ordiway

A brief moment of panic. I wasn't in any position to second-guess orders, especially in such close proximity to other Navis. *Focus, Athena... I mean Navi, focus!*

I spent some time familiarizing myself with the ferry. Its thick, hydrogen-filled hull blocked radiation from space. It also reduced radio background noise and increased wireless security feed quality compared to the launch ship that brought us here from the Earth's surface. The whole ferry was about half a kilometer long, but lightweight due to being mostly hollow. The hull was simply a thick layer of low-density polysteel foam filled with two insulating layers of vacuugel[1] sandwiching a layer of hollow tubes wrapped into loops around the hull for liquid hydrogen storage. The hydrogen stored in these loops served as propellant, reactor fuel, and radiation shielding – classic civilian ship construction. The low-density, spongelike hull couldn't handle much acceleration or maneuvering stress, but being lightweight allowed for huge internal volume. This style of construction was also cheap to mass-produce.

The habitable area of the ship was a classic "padlock" shape: two counterrotating habitation cylinders with spin gravity – Earth-equivalent gravity on the lowest floor and decreased gravity on floors

---

[1] Vacuugel is a material made up of microscopic bubbles ranging from low to ultra-high vacuum pressures. It comes in many configurations, some of which are lighter than air on Earth. The material is a near-perfect thermal insulator, and offers significant protection against many forms of harmful radiation in space. For these reasons, it is a major component in the hulls of most large space faring vessels, often injected into open-cell steel foam to form an inexpensive but extremely lightweight and durable layer of protection. Many attribute the existence of large commercially-affordable space ships solely to this construction technique.

     Silence Of the Stars

closer to the center of the cylinders. A microgravity archway connected the two cylinders near the front of the ship, and served as the observation deck. There, the walls displayed camera views of the space outside, giving the sensation of floating in empty space without exposing passengers to the deadly vacuum.

It didn't take long to locate Janus on the security feed. All of the passengers were funneled through the onboard market when first boarding the ship. There, Janus was heaving up his previous meal. This was a common reaction for inexperienced travelers transitioning from high-acceleration flight to microgravity. The effect was often worsened by the switch back again to spin gravity in a large ferry like this. Most passengers handled the transition with no problem thanks to decades or centuries of travel experience, and the added toughness granted to them by standard bioaugmentations. Janus had no such advantages.

Chons was apologizing to flight attendants as they cleaned up after Janus around the market entryway bulkhead. The mess was tricky to clean up in microgravity, but the flight attendants were used to it.

* * *

The advanced security systems of the ferry gave me a clear view. It was almost as clear as my usual view on Babylon Spire.

Janus recovered after only a couple of minutes, which is remarkably fast for first-time microgravity-induced motion sickness.

Chons took him through the market, passing by his usual liquor and souvenir shops, where he happened upon a fruit stand labeled *Fresh, genuine, OUTDOOR grown Earth fruit*. This time, Chons was the excited one. He was always a sucker for Earth-grown food. I'd never seen him pass up the opportunity to eat fresh fruit, not even when escorting dangerous criminals.

"Well, ain't that a treat!" he said, swiping his PCU in front of the dispenser to pay. An apple popped out with a puff of air strongly scented to mimic straw and applewood in an attempt to appeal to the appetites of other nearby passengers. Chons handed the apple to Janus with a confident grin.

"What's so special about apples grown outdoors? Isn't that normal?" Janus asked, rotating the apple in his hand to examine it before opening his mouth wide to take a bite.

He was interrupted by the shrill voice of a well-dressed, plump, woman. Her name is Daniela according to the manifest. Alarms triggered as she waddled toward Janus, but I determined that she was not a danger, and allowed the scene to play out without interfering.

She wagged her index finger at Janus in reproach. "Don't you dare eat that apple, young man! That's the devil's apple! Do you *want* the Martians to control our food?"

She huffed, planted her feet firmly, and glared at him. Janus stood with his mouth open, ready to take a bite of the apple. Fear and

                    Silence Of the Stars

confusion caused him to hesitate. He looked blankly back at the lady, slowly lowering the unscathed apple under the pressure of her gaze.

Janus looked around at other passengers, apparently confused by the situation. Some passengers must have noticed his distress, because they stopped to spectate the interaction. Of course, no one offered to help.

Realizing she had caused a ruckus, the lady waddled away still shaking her finger and shouting over her shoulder. "Shame on you! Shame!"

Before she rounded a corner at the end of the market hall, she turned back one last time to point an accusing finger and reiterate. "Shame!"

Janus looked inquisitively at Chons. The young man seemed to want to ask something but couldn't find the words. I didn't know what Janus wanted to ask, but Chons did a better job reading the room, explaining the root cause of the ruckus. "There's a stigma among Earthers against food grown outside closed-loop farming because of the global phosphorous shortage. They're afraid of becoming dependent on phosphorous imports from Mars and losing their position as the only fully self-sufficient planet in the system. It's nothing to worry about. Even outdoor farms are regulated well enough these days that their phosphorous usage is sustainable... It's the least of our problems, really."

He cracked an all-too familiar lopsided smirk. I could tell a bad joke was coming. "Plus, soil from Mars is cheap as dirt."

Ugh.

Janus was too lost in thought to even notice the joke. He looked questioningly at the apple with a hint of guilt and handed it back to Chons, who shrugged and took a big bite.

Chapter 5
Flower of Babel

Babylon Spire extended from the Earth-facing side of the Moon through Geo-Lunar Lagrange point 1. It stood on the moon and simultaneously hung from empty space, stretching between the gravitational pull of the two celestial bodies. It was the most massive artificial structure ever built. The central shaft stood over 50,000 kilometers tall – roughly the height of four Earths stacked atop one another. The Spire bobbed, swayed, and stretched over the course of the month, for although the Moon was tidally locked to Earth, the alignment was not perfectly stable.

The Spire was not alone in its monumental endeavor. It was supported by a web of tens of thousands of smaller cables anchored all over the Earth-facing side of the Moon. These cables formed an hourglass taper, with the narrowest point halfway up the Spire, then spread back out at the terminus, just Earthward of L1. These cables assisted with tensegrity, supporting the tremendous structure as tension, compression, and torsion which all competed to tear the structure apart.

In addition to providing support to the main structure, these cables served as rapid transit lines for passengers and cargo, connecting cities on the surface of the Moon to various levels of the Spire.

Three cables looped all the way around the Moon, hovering above it rather than anchoring to the surface. Two of these circumlunar rings housed electromagnetic launch rails for sending and receiving interplanetary ships and cargo, while the remaining loop housed the system's largest enclosed particle collider.

Crowning Babylon Spire was Babylon Station, which rested on the Earthward side of L1. The station served as an anchor in space, taking advantage of the slight pull of Earth's gravity to keep Babylon Spire's main cables taut. The result was a perfect balance between extension and compression. Babylon Station prevented the Spire from slowly collapsing toward the Moon, while the Spire prevented Babylon Station from falling toward the Earth. Although the main station was built around a heptad of massive habitat cylinders, centuries of ongoing construction added countless additional rotating sections and protrusions of all shapes and sizes, with ships constantly docking and departing. The resulting shape resembled a twinkling dandelion, while the ships were like glistening specs of dust from a distance.

Unlit, the station and space tower were so much taller than thick as to be invisible on the cosmic stage. The structure was so dwarfed in girth by natural celestial bodies as to resemble a single strand of spider silk spanning between two mountains. To assist with navigation of incoming ships as well as to dissipate heat, candoluminescent elements were added to the active support superfluid which constantly flowed through the tower and support cables. Transparent sections in these tubes emitted light, illuminating the Spire and its hourglass of support.

     Silence Of the Stars

Babylon Station, which generated the majority of the Spire's heat and required the most assistance with navigation, was fitted with tight patterns of these candoluminescent tubes looping to and from the station in petals sometimes hundreds of kilometers long. These highly visible radiators extend deep out into space to form sheets which had come to be known as Rose Petals due to the obvious – and perhaps intentional – resemblance to their namesake. The resulting lightshow formed a dazzling 50,000 km high shining stem topped with a single shining rose. The spectacle was visible to the naked eye from the surface of Earth on nights with clear weather, as a transparent rose hovering in the sky over the Moon.

Babylon Spire had stood as the crowning achievement of the ingenuity and industriousness of humanity for centuries. While other ongoing megaprojects around the system were set to eclipse it in time, the Spire was expected to remain the central hub of trade, politics, and cultural exchange for many centuries to come.

* * *

Janus ogled at the beauty of the Rose as his ship approached, each orbit around Earth bringing him closer in an expanding trajectory. Even as he stared, the scale of the structure was so foreign - so far beyond anything he'd ever encountered, as to be incomprehensible.

Four times as tall as the Earth is wide, but less than one billionth of a percent of its mass, an infographic had explained.

Garrett Ordiway　　　　　　69

Eventually the shuttle drew close, and the distance to the Rose closed alarmingly quickly. It looked as though the ship would collide with one of the petals jutting out toward the shuttle. Janus's heart skipped a beat as the shuttle entered the outer edge of one of the petal's veins. The shuttle itself was as long as a city block, but once inside it was dwarfed by the structure of the tunnel which had been shrouded in light on approach.

How could anything manmade be so large? Even if the whole population of Earth cooperated on the singular project, surely we could not build something of this scale.

Janus felt himself being pulled forward as the ship gradually decelerated. The ship did not flip around to decelerate like he'd imagined it would. An infographic explained that exhaust from fusion engines burned hot enough to sublimate steel, and wasn't safe to use near stations. Instead, electromagnets in the petal sapped momentum from the ship and recycled the energy. The deceleration tubes inside the petals were so long because they needed to slow ships down from a relative speed of one kilometer per second to stationary without flattening the crew.

Excess energy caused the petal to glow, resulting in a dazzling light show on the observation deck. Other petals glowing from the myriad of other ships constantly passing in and out may have looked like a rose from a distance, but up close, it gave the impression of flying through a cloud of shooting stars.

Janus found himself in a sparse crowd of passengers who'd gathered to enjoy the spectacle. He'd expected more people watch. In

 Silence Of the Stars

reality, only a few young people and couples with children seemed interested. The grandest spectacle every produced by humanity went unappreciated by the majority of those onboard.

Janus's mind was still reeling from the sight – a man-made structure several times taller than the Earth was wide seemed like fantasy, yet here it was. Back in Darwin Aerospace he was beginning to think that the future was rather mundane. He'd been disappointed by the lack of 'futuristic' technology. Even the flight up here felt barbaric compared to the casual and convenient ships he'd seen in old-world science fiction. Now, faced with the scale of Babylon Station, he found himself questioning his grasp on reality. It boggled the mind how drab city streets could coexist with such magnificence.

At the base of the Rose Petal, the ship came to a stop to dock to the central shaft of the Spire. Passengers transferred into rail cars in the inner shell of the station, briefly experiencing weightlessness until they were transferred into a slowly rotating habitat cylinder encased within the station. Among the thousands of cylinders on Babylon Station, this one was known as Athens. The city within that cylinder where Janus detrained, Atlas Promenade. On any other day, the sight of Atlas Promenade would have seemed extravagant and alien to Janus, but bedazzled as he was, nothing could surprise him further. The sense of awe has an upper limit.

The environment inside resembled a reconstruction of the ancient city of Athens, complete with what appeared to be an open blue sky. Gold and white architecture featuring rows of mighty limestone pillars and scholarly statues disguised the relative monotony of the spaceport terminal. The dining and lounge areas were adorned with fountains and exotic greenery. The illusion was almost perfect. Janus knew that he was standing on the interior of a rotating cylinder, but couldn't see the curvature. It was expertly hidden by architecture blocking the view spinward and antispinward, giving the impression of flat ground. The floor should have naturally curved up into the sky, but any long, straight stretches of road were either enclosed or perpendicular to the drum's rotation.

In his stupor, Janus followed Chons through the cobblestone corridors to an open galleria. Chons flashed something at the security guards and bypassed the lines where other passengers waited in queue.

Standing at the center of this galleria was a statue towering above the surrounding buildings; a broad-shouldered man with a powerful jawline and an aura of charismatic authority. His outstretched hands cradled their contents with care, offering them to the observer. Above his palms floated a glowing effigy of the Earth, orbited by the Moon complete with Babylon Spire. The Rose was exaggerated in prominence to be clearly visible to viewers looking up from street level. A plaque at the feet of the statue read, *Viktor Atlas: Geo-Lunar Arbitrator of 2670–Present,* followed by smaller text, *Longest consecutive democratically reelected social servant in history.*

"That's Atlas?" asked Janus, gesturing toward the statue.

Chons chuckled. "That's him alright. Don't worry. He's not *quite* that intimidating in person. You'll see for yourself tomorrow morning."

An alarm suddenly rang out, but Janus couldn't pinpoint the source. Nobody else seemed to react to the sound but Chons, who

 Silence Of the Stars

whipped out his PCU. His expression immediately shifted from lax to tense – the first time Janus had seen him look serious. He'd seemed laid back even during the fire fight in New Angels, so whatever was bothering him now must have been important.

"Priority 5…" Chons mumbled to himself, rapping his finger against the crystalline tablet. "Give me your PCU," he commanded.

"Why?" asked Janus, complying reluctantly.

"A higher priority job just came in – an emergency. I need to take care of it, but I'll be back for you." He touched his PCU to Janus' and swept his finger across them both. "I'm installing a tracker on your PCU. Feel free to stretch your legs while I'm gone. Just don't leave the Athens disc, and stay out of trouble."

Janus' sobered from the hazy sense of awe he'd felt toward the grandiose setting. Now, very real panic spawned from the thought of being left alone in this alien place.

"How long will you be gone?"

"Minutes… hours… maybe days. Sorry, this is urgent. Atlas will send a replacement escort if necessary. He or I will find you using the tracker on your PCU. Don't lose it."

Janus opened his mouth to protest – to ask what he should do about food and shelter if Chons was to be gone for days, but before the words could come out, Chons turned away and sprinted off at inhuman speed. He leaped over a building in a single bound and disappeared from view. For the first time in memory, Janus found himself alone.

Chapter 6
Atlas Promenade

Being with Chons had somehow given Janus a sense of security. Now that he was gone, Janus felt naked and alone. He was much more conscious of the immediate danger of being alone in a foreign place. His present situation transformed from a distant dream into reality.

The crowd, which had seemed a faceless cloud of people, came into focus as individuals transformed from a background into potential threats or allies. People here were different than Darwin Aerospace port or New Angels. Here, the locals were mostly dressed in form-fitting but stylish full-body compression suits, creamy white in color with colorful accents at the cuffs and collar. The different shapes and colors of these accents seemed regimented and deliberate. Certain types of people seemed to don similar styles, though Janus couldn't discern their exact meaning.

Hairstyles varied slightly, but all were somewhere between a buzz cut and shoulder length for both men and women. The occasional long-haired individual would tie their hair in a bun or other compact style. The long, loose hairstyles of women in New Angels were absent here.

More surprising than the relative uniformity of fashion was the uniformity of body types. Skin tone varied widely, but almost everyone who was adorned in the local garb was beautiful enough to be a model in Janus's eyes, and fit enough to have been an Olympic athlete in his time. They were all slim with well-toned muscles. He'd expected space-faring people to be tall and lanky due to low gravity and lack of exercise. Not so.

Something about the locals' mannerisms – their movement, speech, and behavior – set them apart from foreign visitors. Visitors, which Janus estimated made up about half of the crowd, were a far more diverse mix of people. All manner of body shapes and sizes adorned in outlandish fashion contrasted against the uniformity of the locals and the surrounding architecture. It was clear that the foreigners' sense of personal space, hygiene standards, and basic code of conduct were incohesive. This was, after all, the cultural hub of the solar system. Here was supposedly the most diverse group of people and cultures anywhere in history. They were bound to clash.

Janus reckoned that was why there were so many armed guards. RACERs – the same multi-role emergency responders in black armor that had lined the walkway in Darwin Aerospace Port – were stationed around the promenade discreetly but in great numbers.

The crowd was suffocating. Janus needed to stop and think about what to do next. He spotted a bench near an arboretum in the shadow of Atlas' statue. He sat down, and a local sat next to him. Janus made a point of avoiding eye contact with the man. Overwhelmed by the commotion, he tried to disappear into an illusion of privacy.

Despite his efforts, the commotion followed Janus. Shortly after he sat down, a pair of formal suit shoes appeared in front of the bench. Something about the shoes drew Janus' attention; perhaps it was simply that they stopped directly in his line of sight. He looked up to see the polished footwear were part of a matching outfit worn by a scrawny but distinguished-looking man with a bar mustache. His focus was on the notepad-sized crystal tablet cradled in one arm, which he seemed to weave spells at by rapidly gesturing with the fingers of his free hand. He was clearly a foreigner. His build, facial hair, and choice of clothes set him apart from the locals.

Almost as soon as the foreign man in the suit stopped walking, a large, bald man in local garb bumped into him. The impact sent the tablet flying. It clattered to the floor, but didn't break.

"Hey, watch where you're goin'," grunted the local man in a voice that sounded like tires on gravel. This was in harsh contrast to the refined cadence universal among voices of locals Janus had overheard.

"My apologies," said the man in the suit as he bowed to grab his tablet from the ground. "I'm new here. I was distracted by my excitement for my new job."

"You don't say?" growled the thug, scratching his stubbled chin. It was then that Janus observed this was the only man in local garb he'd seen with unkempt stubble. Upon closer examination, the man had a lot of characteristics that didn't quite fit the mold: his muscles bulged but were not aesthetically toned; his skin had burn marks and scars where most of the locals were silky smooth. He seemed out of place in local garb because he looked like a 'normal' person, with normal person flaws.

"Lemme see that," the brute demanded, snatching the tablet out of the other man's hand. "Junior developer at PicoSoft with only twenty years of programming experience? Sounds awful fishy to me." He raised a greasy eyebrow.

The man in the suit straightened up and said nervously, "I had some... accelerated training. I was selected for my performance record, not some arbitrary measure like years of experience."

The big man chuckled. "Accelerated training, you say? I know what you are. I'd recognize a 'John Smith 2700' anywhere."

The man in the suit adjusted his tie and snatched the tablet back. "This is a custom 2750 model, actually."

The thug furrowed his brow, tightened his fist, and growled, "I don't give a fuck what kind of skin you wear! You think you can take a trip to the outer system, illegally install stolen memory, then come back here and take honest people's jobs and get away with it? Go back to the scrapyards where you belong, fucking Chip!"

"Back off," replied the suited man, standing his ground. "I got where I am fair and square, just like everyone else who works in Babylon Spire. If you fell behind the curve, that's your own fault. Not mine. Spend some time on BGI and study—"

The thug, now furious, cut him off. "Just like *everyone* else?" he shouted. "You're not even human! Your kind don't belong here!"

He threw a right hook at the businessman. The blow landed square in his face with a loud crack. The blow knocked the man backwards, but to Janus' surprise, not off his feet. The man took a step back but didn't stumble. Black-eyed and bloody-nosed, the 'Chip' retorted without missing a beat, "Not human? That's precious coming from a Jar!"

He reached for the still outstretched arm that had struck him. Grabbing loose skin near the elbow, he tugged. To Janus' horror, the skin tore away from the arm cleanly, leaving a bare strip from the elbow halfway down the forearm. The torn skin hung free, dripping blood. The exposed area below was not muscle and bone, but iron and cables. Organic flesh covered an otherwise robotic body.

Janus stared, bewildered. Then, in a flash, he recognized the danger his proximity to this violent exchange put him in. This wasn't going to blow over. He was overwhelmed by the urge to flee. In his haste to escape, he slipped and stumbled directly into the so-called Jar, who was winding up for another attack.

The thug must have misinterpreted Janus' clumsy movement. He caught Janus and threw him to the ground, then stood over him and jeered, "Playing the hero? Who are you? Another Chip, coming to rescue your pathetic friend here?"

"No!" Janus insisted, surprised by the desperation in his own voice. "I'm nobody. Just a normal human! Not a cyborg, not a Jar, not a Chip, no genetic modifications, nothing! I'm just a man! I'm... vanilla!"

The Jar pressed a heavy foot against Janus' chest, pinning him to the ground. Janus felt the air crushed out of his lungs as the man leaned the full weight of his unnaturally heavy body onto the planted foot and knelt down. His facial expression when talking to the 'Chip' had been one of anger. Looking at Janus, he curled his lip in sheer disgust.

"You think you're better than me just because you're a vanilla, huh? Your kind are the worst of all," he spat, shifting his weight as if to grind his foot through Janus' abdomen.

Every attempt to breathe just made breathing harder. Janus found himself flailing aimlessly to escape. Where were the guards? Wasn't it their job to help in this kind of situation? Couldn't they see what was happening?

Janus wheezed with what little breath he could manage, "Please – I don't want any trouble. I just want to..." He trailed off, partially because he was struggling to breathe, and partially because he wasn't actually sure what he wanted to do, other than escape this situation. He wanted nothing to do with the Jar, or anyone else at this moment.

"Yeah, I bet," the thug murmured. "You probably grew up with a rich family who could afford bio life-extension; never had to struggle through life on Basic General Income; never had to live in fear of injury, or wearing away your natural body away through decades of grueling labor."

He paused for a moment to admire his own mechanical hand before continuing. "You're a spoiled little surfacer, aren't you? I bet this is your first day astar. You've probably never known a day or hardship in your life. How's about I give you a taste of the real world the rest of us live in, aye?"

    Silence Of the Stars

Janus thought he was already under the full weight of the man's metallic body, but he seemed to grow even heavier. It was becoming unbearable. Every breath he let out brought his chest cavity closer to collapse. Just when he felt as though his ribs were going to crack, the pressure lifted. The Jar disappeared from above him, followed by a loud crash of metal on cobblestone a short distance away.

"Come on!" the local man who had been sitting silently next to Janus reached his hand down to help Janus to his feet. Janus took his hand and hoisted himself up. The local man whistled loudly, and the RACER guards seemed to take note of the situation.

Behind the smooth, metallic masks, it was impossible to see where the guards were looking. They waded through the dense crowd approaching the disturbance. Meanwhile, the local man led Janus subtly into the crowd, leading him away from the fight on a roundabout path that deliberately avoided the guards.

Janus wasn't sure why they were leaving the site of the scuffle now that security was coming to help, but he assumed locals knew best. He took a deep breath just to be sure he still could, then said, "Thanks for saving my life back there."

The local man was roughly the same height and build as Janus, but with slightly more toned muscle, just like all the locals. His skin and hair were both pale tan. He smiled with perfect teeth and said, "That's a bit of an exaggeration, but you're welcome. My name is Citanaf. You're clearly not from around here. Where did you arrive from?"

"My name is Janus. I'm from Earth."

"I thought so," replied Citanaf.

"You know me?" asked Janus.

"No, not really," said Citanaf. "I just saw your name on the passenger manifest. I took notice because that flight was piloted by Atlas' personal Navi, and you were seated next to a Godhunter. Speaking of which, where is Chons? Is he not escorting you?"

"Something came up," replied Janus. This Citanaf sure knew a lot about his situation. Perhaps Chons was some sort of celebrity? Speaking of which... "What do you mean by 'Godhunter'?"

Citanaf chuckled. "It's just a grandiose term for Atlas' personal elite law-enforcement team. If he's not taking you in, does that mean you're not a prisoner?"

"I don't think I'm a prisoner," replied Janus.

For a while they walked in silence. Citanaf seemed to be leading Janus cautiously away from the crowd. When things were quiet enough to talk without shouting, Janus asked, "Do you mind if I ask you a couple questions? About what happened back there."

"Certainly. I'll tell you what I can."

"What is a Chip, and what is a Jar? Those two men used those words in a derogatory way, but I don't know what they mean."

"Well..." Citanaf took a moment to compose his thoughts. When he spoke, it was in the tone of an adult explaining a sensitive topic to a child. "'Jar' comes from 'brain in a jar'. It refers to a person who is

　　　　Silence Of the Stars

almost entirely machine, but has preserved their core humanity by retaining their brain, and usually part of their nervous system.”

He lowered his voice. “There are a few reasons people end up that way, but it’s usually just because they’re too poor for proper medical procedures as their bodies fail with age or injury. ‘Jar’ is a derogatory term, but there’s really no nice way to say it, because few people choose that route willingly. A more politically correct term is ‘cybernetically enhanced’, but that’s deliberately vague, and doesn’t technically mean the same thing.”

He looked from side to side, then continued, “Chips, on the other hand, forego even the brain. They copy their consciousness onto a ‘chip’ – usually a combination of neural network and classic computer. This process is expensive, but allows them to swap between bodies. Many of us consider the process profane… impure. I believe the soul resides in the brain, so something must be lost when transferring memory to another medium. Many people, including myself, don’t believe that Chips are really human, even though they have the memories of the human they were copied from.”

Janus nodded, not in agreement, but in understanding. “So, a Chip is like a human-based AI then?”

Citanaf shushed Janus. “Ooooh boy.”

He pulled Janus aside into an even less crowded hallway and looked around to see if anybody was in earshot. When he determined the coast was clear, he said, “It’s best not discuss this in public.”

“Why?”

"Were there any really taboo topics in your time? Topics with no general consensus, but which everyone seemed to have a very strong, emotional opinion about? Topics about which people's opinions were so strong that they'd get irrational or even violent defending their point of view?"

Janus considered this. Before he could think of any topics that met the man's description, the phrasing occurred to him: 'in your time'. *What exactly does this guy know about me?* Janus had been under the impression that people waking from long cryostasis was rare, and couldn't think how the man might have deduced his background.

Janus brushed off the thought. It was not nearly the strangest thing that had happened that day. He had too many questions already to bother with something so trivial.

Focusing back on the topic at hand, he offered, "You mean like abortion?"

"Abortion of what?"

Janus muttered, "Uuuh." *Abortion of what?* He had never considered the literal meaning of the word before. Technically 'abort' was synonymous with 'cancel', and didn't intrinsically have anything to do with pregnancy. He clarified, "Abortion of human pregnancies."

Citanaf cocked his head to the side. "Huh. Never heard of it. I guess I can see where human abortions would be an emotionally heated and taboo topic, if it were ever a consideration."

Janus was shocked. "Wait – you've never even *heard* of an abortion? What did we do to solve that?"

Citanaf shrugged. "People just don't have kids if they don't want them. Everyone is sterilized at birth – it's a prerequisite to receiving BGI... That is to say, sterilization is mandatory for Basic General Income and free education. Some people think of it as a 'fertility tax'. Even people who reverse the procedure to have children usually get sterilized again afterward to get back on BGI. Accidental pregnancies just don't happen."

"That..." Janus mulled over this for a few seconds. "That would never fly in my time. It sounds awfully close to eugenics."

Citanaf shrugged again, seeming not to care. "Apparently mandatory sterilization was a topic of heated debate a long time ago. It's something we all learn about in history during general education. But the BGI system would never have been possible otherwise... for better or worse."

He rolled his eyes and sighed. Janus got the impression that Citanaf was suppressing the urge to begin an unrelated tangent. Shaking his head, Citanaf continued, "Anyway, it's been this way for generations, so I never gave it much thought. I guess that mandatory sterilization probably also helped solve that 'human abortion' debate, though."

Janus gazed at the fake sky above. "So, we traded one human rights battle for another."

Citanaf looked back at the statue of Atlas and said, in a strangely serious tone, as if reciting a memorized verse, "There's always a price to pay for progress, but those sacrifices need to be made. It's impossible to realize everyone's ideals. To try is to drown in a stagnant cesspool of our own making."

Janus wasn't sure what to say. Something about the conversation had clearly struck a nerve for Citanaf.

Citanaf, as if sensing the conversation had soured, changed the topic. "Tell you what... I think we can help each other. I may be able to help you with your memory loss if you help me with my research."

"Wow! Really? Thank you! I want to repay you for helping me back there," said Janus. "But... how do you know about my memory loss?"

Citanaf shook his head. "Just an educated guess based on your connection to Atlas and Chons. Speaking of which, do you know when Chons will return?"

Janus chuckled. "He said he's coming back for me, but I have no idea when. It could be any moment now, or it could be several days."

Citanaf peeked around the corner, scanning the crowd. In a low voice, he said, "I want your help, and I want to help you, but I really need to get going. Can you meet me later, in private?"

Respecting Citanaf's sense of urgency, Janus nodded and asked, "Where should I meet you?"

 Silence Of the Stars

"Take a chariot to the Theologium. I'll be in Ascension suite B2. Meet me there in three hours."

"Chariots?"

"Just ask your PCU to guide you there. You'll know them when you see them."

With that, the man ran off without even saying goodbye, leaving Janus alone again. Janus frowned, wondering if abandoning people was normal behavior in this new world.

Chapter 7
Theologium

Janus consulted his PCU for directions. He still had only the most rudimentary understanding of how to use the crystalline tablet, and relied heavily on voice commands. Luckily, the tablet interpreted Janus' inquiries with uncanny accuracy. The interface was far more fluid than technology of Janus' birth era.

Presently, his PCU displayed a three-dimensional map of Atlas Promenade. The map zoomed in from the whole ring to display a banana-shaped slice. Janus' position was represented by a blinking blue light at what Janus thought of as the butt-end of the banana, and the "chariots" were highlighted with green lights at what would be the stem.

The 3D map was overwhelming at first, but it reacted to his frustration by simplifying as much as possible and pointing out landmarks along the path. Janus was guided along a series of roads laid out in a nearly uniform grid, with different decorations along each path to give an impression of unique character and to hide any indication of mass production, but even Janus could see that the city blocks were made from cookie-cutter templates. Even apparent imperfections in the stone blocks were consistent from one street to the next.

     Silence Of the Stars

Upon reaching the chariots marker on the map, the green dot encircled the blue dot, and a quiet fanfare celebrated his arrival. Janus couldn't help but feel a twinge of pride. He'd traveled a full kilometer on foot through a futuristic alien station using only the tools he had on hand. It was a minor achievement, to be sure, but it was the first thing in memory that he had achieved on his own.

When Citanaf had spoken of chariots, Janus imagined the word referred to some futuristic mode of transportation. Actual horse-drawn chariots were the last thing he had expected to find. Nevertheless, Janus found himself standing in front of a row of horses, patiently waiting on a roughly cobbled road for passengers to board carts and chariots.

An oversized replica of the Colosseum stretched out alongside the cobbled path. It would have been convincing if it weren't for the fact that the structure was large enough to visibly follow the subtle uphill curvature of the habitat ring's superstructure. In the illusory setting, Janus wasn't sure whether he was supposed to be inside or outside the Colosseum. Each component of the façade seemed so real that they may as well have been hauled up from ancient Earth. The sight contrasted with the bustling foot traffic of space-faring humans and the occasional robot, creating a surreal sense of disjointedness.

Janus approached the chariots and hesitated before stepping onto one. There was no operator and no booth to collect payment. A voice coming from nowhere in particular invited him, "Climb on in! Where would you like to go?"

Janus took one apprehensive step up onto a chariot, and the horses bound to it by reins whinnied. It was only then that Janus noticed something off about the animals. The way their muscles rippled under their skin wasn't quite right. He pulled himself all the way onto the chariot and reached out to tap the backside of one of the horses. The fur was cold, and the movements were accompanied by a mechanical electric vibration. The horses were animatronic. The illusion was near perfect until one closely observed their subtle movements, but it seemed obvious now that he'd noticed it. The horses didn't smell real, and the stall lacked the droppings and other mess one might expect in the presence of real horses. For a civilization of people who had never seen large animals, these might be indistinguishable from the real thing.

With one fantasy despoiled, other flaws in the facade became more obvious. The chariots themselves were not made from real wood. The material had the rough texture of wood but was too hard and waxy to the touch. Janus suddenly felt less like he was in the streets of ancient Rome and more like he was in a theme park or exotic casino.

"Take me to the Theologium," Janus said to the ether, not sure where to direct his answer.

"Hang on, charioteer!" replied the voice.

The horses reared up on their hind legs, threatening to break into an angry gallop. Janus hastily gripped the reins and squatted low to brace himself for sudden acceleration. When the automatons instead began trotting at a brisk walk, he found himself disappointed. The chariot moved only slightly faster than the foot traffic on the other side of the false wood fence separating this track from the walkway.

Other unmanned chariots moved with him, presumably to emulate a chariot race. It may have even been exciting had anyone else decided to participate. He sensed the bemused gazes of pedestrians on his left, and saw diners looking down at him from windows in the Colosseum-themed building on his right. Janus was the only passenger on what seemed increasingly like a children's ride. The whole experience felt shoddy compared to the rest of the Athens façade.

Janus had been specifically instructed to take the chariots to the Theologium. Now he couldn't help but wonder if there was another, more practical means of transit. The locals seemed to view this as entertainment rather than transportation. The whole system seemed old. Not old-fashioned, like Athens, but as if the ride was built long ago and only maintained to the minimum degree necessary for continued operation. The attraction sat in plain view, but had been largely forgotten by society.

The fenced chariot path forked, leading Janus away from the well-lit Colosseum through a back-alley route. This atmosphere shifted rapidly from the backstreets of Athens into that of an incomplete movie set complete with open panels, exposed machinery, and untended clutter. The place was devoid of human life. The only movement was from a pair of spiderlike maintenance robots crawling through open hatches and sorting detritus into neatly organized piles. Nothing about these machines showed any sign of trying to fit into the ancient-Earth theme. These janitor drones ignored Janus as they went about their work.

Janus shivered. Something about this place was unsettling. He thought, hoped, that it was merely the discontinuity. He was alone, but felt as if he were being watched. The clip-clop of hooves blended with the thrum of pumps and industrial fans hidden somewhere behind the false-stone walls. The sounds of machinery made Janus aware of the unseen forces which constantly toiled to keep this crowded bubble of air contained, warm and breathable as it hurtled through the void of space. Janus wasn't sure if he subconsciously feared the deadly environment beyond these walls, or the unseen powers that kept him inside. Both were terrifying in their own ways.

That mechanical murmur had been an ever-present backdrop from the moment Janus had set foot in the Spire. Before that, even. Thinking back, the world around him hadn't been silent from the moment of his waking. Everything around him had been entirely artificial. Even on Earth, he'd only glimpsed the outside world, and its air had been poisonous to him. It was quite possible that nowhere in the universe remained where he could survive without the help of machinery. His very survival depended on powers of which he hadn't the slightest understanding.

He wasn't given much time to dwell. A familiar false-wood fence reappeared along the trail and the clamor of pedestrian footsteps soon followed. The cavern of bare machinery opened up again into the open street of Athens. The whirring of industrial fans faded and was replaced with the murmur of the crowd. The crude simplicity of the ride which had disappointed him only moments ago now brought

     Silence Of the Stars

him a sense of comfort and relief. He knew this wasn't Earth; it wasn't real; but it was good enough to keep him from the existential horror that came from dwelling too long on reality.

The chariot came to a stop and deposited him in front of a stairway leading up to a row of grandiose columns, each broad enough to be towers in their own right. The marble pillars were crowned with a triangular roof, the word *Theologium* looming over the square in bold solid-gold letters. The architects that had designed this place had probably aimed to evoke the awe-inspiring impression of divinity. So imposing was the colossal entryway as to compel the crowd to avoid getting too close and instead walk on the far side of the road. This behavior reminded Janus of a school of fish swimming past a shark. He felt a mild sense of foreboding as he walked past the pillars, those pearly whites of the beast's maw, into the inner sanctum.

Inside, the artificial sky was replaced by the interior of an ornate rotunda, the scale of which was difficult to even guess. A whole city sprawled out under its canopy. Where the curvature of the dome met the walls, countless statues were ornamentally posed in a ring fully encircling the district. Most of the figures were unknown to Janus, but among those near the entrance, he recognized prominent Greek and Roman gods, along with Jesus and Buddha. The other statues, which numbered in the thousands or perhaps millions, must have also been prominent figures from their respective religions.

Forcing his gaze down from the canopy, Janus saw that the statues were accompanied by appropriate architecture below. Churches, monasteries, abbeys, convents, chapels, mosques, synagogues, temples, cathedrals, shrines, and others Janus had no word for were organized in a tidy row around the outer wall of the domed auditorium. The neat ring along the outer wall was contrasted by a chaotic jumble of buildings in the center of the circular plaza. A solitary central pillar spanned from the ground to the center of the dome, leaving no space for any religion to take center stage. It was difficult to see clearly from this distance, but Janus thought he saw windows in the central pillar overlooking the sacred ground below.

Finally, the name "Theologium" made sense. It was amazing to think that people could get along in a place like this. Many of the religious groups depicted would once have seen each other as mortal enemies. Some wouldn't appreciate their group being thought of as a religion at all.

Janus still had time before his meeting, so he walked along the outer row, admiring the different styles of architecture. Many of the buildings incorporated additional statues in their structures, expanding upon the already innumerable statues around the edge of the dome.

He spotted something curious along a splinter path leading to a cathedral. On one side of the path stood Jesus, Mary, and others he assumed were saints, in similar garb. However, the other side of the path to the cathedral was decorated with statues in more modern clothing. Among those stood Atlas, in the same pose as his grand statue in Atlas Promenade. This version of Atlas was a simple carving, and didn't feature the floating depiction of the Earth and Moon. Still, his broad jaw and giant, gentle hands were unmistakable.

			Silence Of the Stars

"You look lost. Can I offer you any guidance?" said an elderly voice from beside Janus.

Janus turned to see an old man emerging from the cathedral. He was adorned in formal clergy robes. He must have been a... pastor? Cleric? Priest? Janus decided on priest.

He raised his hand to turn down the offer, then pointed at Atlas. "No, thank you. I was just curious about that statue."

The priest followed the direction of Janus' finger, then nodded. "Atlas is recognized as an honorary saint. His ongoing financial and political support has allowed the church to survive and thrive through times of strife and opposition. He has gone to great lengths and made personal sacrifices to ensure our continued prosperity, even before he was elected for his first term as Geo-Lunar Arbitrator over a century ago."

"Atlas is Catholic?" Janus asked.

The priest chuckled. "Well, no. Not necessarily. Atlas is devoted to peace and equality for all humanity. He is not outwardly a member of any religious organization, though he makes regular donations to many. He is obliged to remain impartial by the nature of his position."

"Pardon me if this comes across as rude, but why would he donate to any religious organization if he wants to remain impartial?"

"A reasonable question," acknowledged the priest. "Atlas encourages people to celebrate the cultural diversity of our heritage, and to find ways to coexist peacefully even when diversity leads us to disagreement. Religion is naturally a cornerstone of that message."

"He sounds like an amazing man," Janus said dubiously.

The priest picked up on the doubt in Janus's voice, but replied unironically. "Indeed. We couldn't ask for a better leader. It's thanks to him that we have maintained such peace and unity in the most culturally, biologically, and theologically diverse place in the solar system. That's why he's had the longest consecutive term in office of any elected official in history: one hundred and fifty years now, I believe. Unlike the outer system, Geo-Luna has enjoyed over a century of unprecedented peace and harmony."

Janus raised an eyebrow, remembering his altercation earlier in the day with the Jar and the Chip. It seemed unlikely he'd come upon a rare instance of violence in a largely peaceful society during his first day. He described the event to the priest.

The priest listened intently with downturned eyes, nodding solemnly. When Janus finished, the priest explained, "Harmonious coexistence is not the default state of things in most places in the system outside Geo-Luna. It takes time for newcomers to acclimate. But the law here is harsh. There is little room for forgiveness of criminals or for those who allow themselves to become victims. The wicked are hastily stamped out or driven deep into the dark corners of society where they can't harm those who walk in the light. The violence against you was likely perpetrated by a newcomer who had yet to be disciplined."

		Silence Of the Stars

Janus was fairly sure that the Jar at least was a local. He wore the same tight-fitting clothes, with the same accents around the neck and cuffs, that other locals wore. It seemed more likely that he was a disgruntled resident than an outsider. Janus was tempted to bring up that point, but decided to address the more pressing question. "The law is harsh against not only criminals but also *victims*?"

"Indeed. Allowing yourself to succumb to the influence of evil, be it blackmail, bribery, kidnapping, or threat of harm, is grounds for being punished as an accomplice to the crime."

Janus's jaw dropped. "That doesn't seem fair. The victim didn't do anything wrong." This didn't seem like a cultural difference – rather, an unequivocal injustice. 'Victim shaming' had been among the highest forms of injustice and bigotry in his time.

The priest saw Janus' expression, and smiled warmly. "Are you from the surface world?"

"Yes," Janus replied, wondering how people kept recognizing him as a surfacer, and then how that could relate to the issue at hand.

"I am also from Earth. When I first arrived, I also felt the treatment of victims was unfair. But here, our community is surrounded by a vacuum, an uncaring void that would kill all indiscriminately given the chance. One man's negligence or violence could lead to the deaths of thousands. That's not merely hypothetical – it has happened more than once, historically.

"Our very survival is predicated on *order*. Therefore, everyone is expected to help maintain order even when it means personal sacrifice. Willingly allowing oneself to become the victim of a crime encourages future perpetration of that kind of crime. Space law is similar to naval law. That law is as intolerant of complacency toward crime as it is of crime itself, and thus a willing victim is an accomplice."

Janus scratched his head. "So if I'm robbed at gunpoint, I am expected to refuse to cooperate even if it means being shot?"

"Exactly. That's why you will never encounter gunpoint robbery in Babylon Spire. Law enforcement will focus on restoring order by ending the incident quickly. They will prioritize neutralization of the robber over safety of the hostage. The victim is likewise expected to fight back or flee rather than cooperate with their assailant. Since everyone knows that's the way things are, any would-be criminal also knows that threats and hostage-taking are meaningless."

Ancient sailing ships and navy ships had always followed strict laws to maintain order – this thought immediately popped into Janus's head. Still, not every man, woman, and child could be expected to act like a disciplined soldier.

"I understand the reasoning," he said, "but punishing the victim still seems harsh."

The priest acknowledged this with a nod. "The world is harsh, and always has been. Atlas tempered that harshness and manipulated it to bring about this time of unprecedented, albeit imperfect, peace. True peace and justice can never be achieved in this life; only in the next. Even knowing that, we must all do the best we can to live as good people during our time here."

			Silence Of the Stars

Janus looked doubtfully at the statue of Atlas. His laws would have been seen as tyrannical in Janus' time. Now he was revered by the people of Geo-Luna as a literal saint. He had somehow inserted himself as a religious authority despite being openly agnostic.

If he truly had forged a lasting peace between historical enemies, then perhaps there was merit to his methods. It was hard to argue with results, but Janus was still not convinced. There had to be more to the story.

Thanking the priest for his time, Janus moved on.

Chapter 8
Temple of Ascension

With plenty of time to spare, Janus walked slowly through the Theologium, admiring the diverse architecture. Organs, bagpipes, vocal chanting, symphonies, electric guitars, and many instruments entirely unfamiliar to Janus emanated from their respective acoustic bubbles along the walkway, merging together. The myriad styles of worship music combined synergistically to serenade him at times and clashed to bombard him with harsh discord at others.

Rather than relying on his PCU, Janus decided to use signage to lead him gradually toward the rendezvous point. Signs pointed the way from the outer edge of the rotunda and followed roads spiraling toward the central pillar. The farther from the outer wall, the smaller buildings became, and the dimmer the lighting. Shadows of larger buildings near the outer ring of statues draped the smaller inner buildings in shade. Here, theologies represented were mostly unknown to Janus.

Many systems of belief must have risen and fallen over the course of eight hundred years, he thought. He couldn't say for sure how many of these lesser known religions were new, and how many he had simply never seen before.

In a dark corner where the spiraling path met the base of the grand central pillar, Janus found his destination. The building labeled

 Silence Of the Stars

Ascension was bland and poorly maintained, featuring no statues or decorations of any kind. The white walls had rectangular patches of mismatched paint which poorly concealed graffiti. The building itself was set up like a four-story apartment building. His destination, Ascension B2, would be the second room on the second floor.

The stairwell was completely unlit, and produced a hollow, metallic echo as Janus ascended. He knocked on door B2, but there was no reply. He walked from room to room to see if anyone might know Citanaf, but found the whole building empty.

I must be early, thought Janus.

He tried the knob, expecting it to be locked. To his surprise, the door creaked open. Peering inside, he decided that the room must have been abandoned for several months at least, judging by the layer of dust that covered everything. His only indication that he was in the right place was that the layout of the room matched his idea of a greeting room rather than an apartment.

A stone desk and chair seemed thematically appropriate for the ancient Athens aesthetic, but were out of place in the bland surroundings of this building. Next to them stood a full bookshelf. Printed books… now that was something Janus hadn't expected to see. Perhaps it shouldn't have been too surprising here, given the traditional nature of religion. Other trinkets lay semi-haphazardly around the room. One table featured three globes decorated as different planets, a balance scale, a quill pen, a sextant, and an extendable telescope. Janus could think of no practical use for these things, but again, religion wasn't always about being practical. *Maybe they're symbolic.*

Can this really be where Citanaf wants to meet?

Janus sneezed, stirring the dust on the stone table. In response to the sound, a robotic-sounding voice asked in monotone, "Name?"

"Janus Nova," Janus answered reflexively.

"Enter," the voice replied, followed by the sound of shifting stone as the bookshelf slid to the side, revealing a passageway behind it.

"Really?" Janus said out loud.

Is this part of the old-world Athens theme too? He cracked a smile, imagining himself to be a whip-toting adventurer as he plunged into the chamber within the hidden passage. He considered whether any of the miscellaneous items from the previous room may have been part of some kind of puzzle or trial. For a moment, he wished he had a sword to fight off any giant rats or walking skeletons he might encounter in the secret passage.

Something about this whole situation felt off, but the architects of this station had already demonstrated a propensity for dramatic themes and wasteful excess. *Sure. Why not have a password-protected secret passageway for guests?*

His spelunker fantasy took a turn when the Athens theme abruptly ended on the other side of the door. A narrow metallic stairway thrummed hollowly as he descended. The end of the flight opened into a long metal tube with a floor that had seemingly been

 Silence Of the Stars

hammered flat by hand. Janus felt like he was standing in a large ventilation shaft. Every step depressed uneven patches of floor, which popped and clanged as he shifted his weight.

Maybe this really is a ventilation shaft, he thought and recalled the strange patch of unfinished road along the chariot ride. This was a different sort of eccentricity from what Janus had envisioned. He experienced a sudden urge to leave, but heard the bookshelf slide back into place at the top of the stairwell. The thought of going back up to find the door locked scared Janus. He knew it was a stretch of logic, but he somehow felt more comfortable continuing forward than facing the possibility of being trapped. *They wouldn't really trap me down here, would they? There's no reason for anyone to do that. It must be part of the ambiance, or a prank, or something. Like the chariot ride.*

As he was about to second-guess the validity of his logic, Janus heard a voice further down the hall – or vent, tube, or cavern; he was still not entirely sure what to call the metallic half-circle of a passage crawling with blurry reflections of himself.

The voice was human, but incoherent in its mumbling. Another voice mumbled in response. No, not in response. The timing was wrong – not like a conversation. There were more voices, now. Each was disjointed. Janus imagined several people, each talking to themselves while focusing intently on some communal task.

"Hello?" Janus' shout reverberated roughly off the uneven wall panels like in a sewer, his voice growing more metallic each time it echoed.

The distant figures went on mumbling too quietly for Janus to comprehend. They didn't respond to his greeting at all. They didn't even seem to notice. Janus heaved a deep sigh and glanced back up the stairs, which were now pitch black without the light of the entryway door. He had a bad feeling about this, but the desire to recover his memories and a feeling of indebtedness to Citanaf compelled him forward. He pressed on toward the dim flickering glow at the end of the hall, toward the mysterious voices.

Each footstep popped loudly on the loose metal floor. Janus' approach should have been obvious, but no one seemed to notice him. The hall ended in a room seemingly formed from multiple tubes fused together into a single patchwork chamber. It was made from the same metal as the hall, but more thoroughly hammered into 'room' shape. Whatever the previous hall was, this room was made from several of them, torn apart and repurposed. It couldn't possibly have been part of the original station design; the construction was too crude.

Janus half expected to find the room empty, but that was not the case. Two dozen people were seated haphazardly along rows of incongruous pews, facing away from him. The congregation was focused on nothing in particular. There was no sermon, no speaker, not even a pulpit or stage where one might speak to the audience. The pews themselves looked to be handmade from scrap material. Janus was initially inclined to think of them as trash, but decided that would be unfair. They were certainly not as stylish as the furniture in the other religious buildings.

"Hello?" Janus repeated, this time in a conversational tone. Someone should have noticed him. It was strange to see so many people silently ignoring him. Not a single one of them looked back or acknowledged his presence in any way. They didn't even seem to acknowledge each other.

Janus walked around the edge of the room, trying to get a better look at the congregation. Part of him wanted to avoid disturbing them, and another part felt disturbed *by* them. Their behavior, or lack thereof, was unnatural.

When Janus crept far enough around the room to see the crowd from the front, he found them all staring blankly in different directions, some with closed eyes. Most were slouching in precarious postures, just shy of tumbling over. Five of them had eyes locked on crystalline tablets just like Janus' PCU. Some drooled. Janus had to observe for a while to be sure, but they all seemed to be breathing.

The occasional grunt, murmur, or sentence-like utterance dribbled from limp lips, but the sounds meant nothing to Janus.

Janus shook off a spine-chilling shiver. Their behavior looked unusual to him, but this could have been a part of their religious practice. There was still a lot he didn't know about this world. *Maybe it's some kind of meditation, or even a drug-induced trance*, he thought.

The man nearest Janus jolted into an upright sitting position, like someone on the brink of sleep reflexively catching themselves before falling over. The man let out a gasp of surprise as his terror-filled eyes darted around the room. A moment later, he settled back into staring at the seemingly blank screen of his hand terminal, returning to his near catatonic state.

Janus' heart pounded, startled by the man's sudden movement. He cautiously approached and asked, "Excuse me. Do you know where I can find Citanaf?"

The man did not respond. His face was lax, as if in a deep trance. Janus looked around for someone else to ask. The pews were filled with people who either had their eyes closed or were staring blankly. Not one of them seemed to be aware of... anything.

Not wanting to be rude, but driven by an increasing sense of urgency, Janus waved his hand in front of the man's PCU to get his attention. The man blinked rapidly and moved his head to look around Janus' hand, but otherwise ignored him. Then Janus remembered what Chons had done to interrupt the 'holographic' view of Janus' PCU back in Darwin Aerospace Station. Janus placed his finger over the man's PCU projector strip.

The man blinked rapidly and tried again to look around Janus' hand. He squinted, then craned his neck up to squint in Janus' direction. His eyes grew wide and his lips peeled back. He recoiled in horror and confusion.

"Are you okay?" Janus asked.

The man shrieked like an injured animal and snatched the hand terminal away from Janus. The wild movement caused the man to tumble onto the floor, where he curled into a fetal position, cradling his PCU under his body. He hyperventilated for several seconds

    Silence Of the Stars

before his breathing returned to normal. Presently, he returned to staring at the crystalline tablet, now covered and protected by his curled-up body.

Janus took two steps back. "What the hell?"

"They're VDS patients," explained Citanaf as he entered the room through a door opposite the hall from which Janus entered. He was pulling a cart with several IV bags and nipple-bottles filled with an opaque gray paste Janus assumed must be Nutrisynth.

"Citanaf! There you are!" Some of the tension which had been permeating through Janus' body relaxed. What a relief to see a familiar face. After taking a second to collect himself, he asked, "Patients? Is this a hospital?"

"A wellness facility, of sorts. We care for these patients while researching their condition." Citanaf carefully helped up the man who had fallen off the pew, guiding him back into his seat, all the while helping him keep his PCU in clear view. With the man seated, Citanaf carefully opened the man's mouth and inserted a tube, then squeezed the contents of one of the bottles down his throat. Little bits of green and gray goop spilled from the corners of his mouth. Citanaf gingerly cleaned him, then continued nursing him until the bottle was empty. All through the assisted feeding process, the man neither resisted nor made any attempt to eat. He didn't seem to even notice Citanaf feeding him.

"Their condition... VDS? What's that?" asked Janus.

"Vapid Dissonance Syndrome. It's a condition resulting from a lack of external stimulus, most common in artificial habitats. Patients retreat from the outside world and turn inward. In early onset, also known as Stage One, patients may simply become unsocial, and their interests tend to narrow. This often goes unnoticed and untreated. The symptoms are too similar to other disorders and behavior patterns to make a proper diagnosis." Citanaf rubbed the arm of a patient with what Janus assumed was a disinfecting wipe, and then inserted one of the IV lines. He clamped the IV bag to the pew next to the man, and moved to help the next patient while he continued to explain.

"In the prodromal stage, or Stage Two, victims retreat from society further. They may only want to play a specific game, work on a specific project, watch a specific show. After that, they may refuse to leave their bed or chair. If VDS is caught at this stage, treatment often leads to a quick and full recovery.

"By Stage Three, the patient often refuses to speak, or gradually loses the ability to do so. Their senses dull or become more selective, and their cognition begins to degrade. They confine their attention to a single object of obsession, often a single monitor or HIP feed. Allowing this stage to persist can lead to permanent alterations to the patient's personality, social compatibility, and even cognitive abilities."

"And these," Janus gestures around the room, "are these Stage Three patients?"

                    Silence Of the Stars

Citanaf shook his head solemnly. He fed another patient as he continued to explain, "Stage Four is the end state of Vapid Dissonance Syndrome. The patient retreats fully inward and becomes unresponsive to any external stimulus except that which interferes with their inner focus. This can take several forms. Some are basically brain-dead. They might stare at white noise on a screen or forego any connection to external stimulus altogether. Others actually experience heightened brain activity, focused to the extreme on their internal obsession.

"Stage four can be fatal, if not directly then indirectly. Patients in this stage will not eat or drink, and sometimes won't sleep. Recovery from this stage is rare. Treatment consists of forcefully inducing external stimuli, which can lead to complications including shock-induced cardiac arrest. Patients who do recover from Stage Four always have psychological damage, and are prone to chronic and rapid regression without constant treatment.

"Patients generally only reach Stage Four after being neglected by friends and family, or if they don't have any to begin with. Of course, many lose the support of friends and family during earlier stages of VDS. Between having no one close willing to help them, the highly personalized nature of treatment, and the low chance of recovery even in ideal conditions, Stage Four VDS patients are often abandoned by society."

"What causes it? A virus? Is the condition contagious?" asks Janus.

"It's not contagious, at least not in the traditional sense. VDS is not a virus or bacterial infection. It is a psychological condition resulting from an incompatibility between an individual and their environment. It's most common in space habitats. The more confined and secluded the living space, the more common VDS becomes. People evolved for millions of years to live on Earth. Preconditioned responses to Earth-based stimuli are in our genes. People need that stimuli for their minds to function normally.

"Some people just aren't able to adapt to such artificial lives without natural stimuli. They simply can't adapt to life in space. Our brains have evolved very little from the time of cavemen. It's why most people find the natural world so beautiful."

Janus made a head-bobbing motion, halfway between nodding in understanding and shaking in disapproval of the condition and the abandonment of its victims. "So, you take them in? You take care of them?"

"We do what nobody else will," Citanaf confirmed.

"That's admirable." Janus watched as Citanaf treated the next patient. An uneven section of the floor groaned under his feet, prompting Janus to ask, "But why in a place like this? What is this place?"

"We aren't given much space to operate, so we improvise. Think of this place as our basement. Our presence here doesn't really interfere with the thermal tube's original function."

"Why not just use all the empty rooms upstairs?"

Citanaf inserted the last of the IVs into the arm of another patient. "A lot of people don't appreciate our work. Even those that understand the value of what we do don't like to see it. This place is… out of sight, out of mind."

"Do you really need to be so secretive about helping people?"

Having distributed all the food and medication, Citanaf pulled his cart back toward the door and gestured toward Janus. "Walk with me."

Janus followed behind Citanaf into the narrow hall. The cart wobbled and bounced over the flexible, uneven floor. A string of lights stapled to the ceiling provided the only illumination. If Babylon Station had any construction codes, this place did not meet them.

"So, these patients. Where do they originally come from?" Janus asked.

"Like I said, Stage Four patients tend to be abandoned by friends and family, and the government won't look after them. We find them on the street, or sometimes rescue them from neglectful homes when we get reports, before they starve to death. Some have part-time caretakers until they inevitably fail to reapply for GBI and their savings run out. Sometimes those caretakers bring them to us."

"Trapped, prisoners in their own mind. They abandon the world, so the world abandons them," Janus said softly, feeling philosophical. "That's terrible."

"Is it?" asked Citanaf.

"Of course! Don't you think it's terrible?"

"By abandoning ties to the mortal realm, I believe they take one step closer to ascension," explained Citanaf.

When Janus said nothing, Citanaf looked back at him. Reading Janus' expression, he said, "At the Church of Ascension, we believe in an elevated state of being. It requires cutting ties to the world without dying, which would have been nigh impossible in centuries prior, but technology has changed the nature of consciousness. The mind can be recorded, stored, shared, and transferred, and consciousness is inextricably tied to the mind."

"So... that's why they're here?" Janus looked back down the twisting hall. He couldn't see all the way back to the congregation of VDS victims in the pews, but the glow of their monitors was still visible around the bend. "You're trying to help them 'ascend'? Not trying to help them recover?"

"Like I said, *traditional* recovery for them is impossible... but ascension provides a sort of recovery. To stage four VDS patients, ascension and recovery are one and the same."

Janus mulled over this response. Given that he didn't know what ascension entailed, he wasn't sure whether he should think of ascension as a religious practice, alternative medicine, or some kind of cult ritual. In most religions, achieving a higher state of being came after death, but Citanaf had specifically said that the process required avoiding death. There must have been some technology involved that Janus wasn't quite grasping.

 Silence Of the Stars

Before Janus could think of anything to say, Citanaf asked, "Speaking of recovering from vegetative states, do you remember anything about Pyrrhus or Project Eutychus?"

Danger. The urge to turn back tugged at Janus once more. Chons had urged Janus not to bring up these topics for his own safety. *But Chons isn't here right now. If Project Eutychus is linked to a method of recovering my memories, then it's worth the risk.*

"I don't know anything about them. What makes them so interesting to you?" he asked. He noted they'd walked an awfully long way along this hallway without seeing any doors or splinter paths. He was getting a little claustrophobic, but pressed on.

"Pyrrhus is legendary among Ascensionists for his work on Project Eutychus. He was technically not an Ascensionist himself, but his quest for immortality is in line with our quest for ascension," Citanaf said passionately. "I'm not talking about Chips, Jars, or surgical bioaugmentations, I'm talking about true ascension – the merging of body and soul to allow humanity to be reborn as a race of immortal gods! We believe that Pyrrhus came close – maybe even ascended himself."

"You think Pyrrhus became a literal god?" Curiosity diluted the doubt in Janus' voice.

"No one really knows what happened to him, but his life goal was to achieve true immortality – no, more than immortality. The Atlas regime has been covering up anything related to Project Eutychus ever since they took over. There's *something* they don't want us to know. Splinter cells of the Eutychus Project still operate in secret to try and uncover what exactly that is."

People already have unnaturally long lifespans, and Chips are technically immortal, aren't they? Uploaded digital minds should last for centuries. Plus, if they're digital, they should also be copyable. That would allow for backup versions of one's own mind. What more could 'immortality' possibly refer to?

Janus began to see the outline of a bigger picture. Pyrrhus was the common tie between the Church of Ascension and Project Eutychus. It sounded like the Ascensionists were not directly involved in the cryostasis facility in which Janus had lain dormant, but their goals were related. That might mean they would know how to help with Janus' memory loss. But the whole situation felt wrong. Their idea of 'helping' people was too unclear. Rather, it wasn't even about helping people. It was about ascension, whatever that meant. Janus was walking down the repurposed ventilation shafts of a church plaza on a space station. A knot churned in his stomach. He may have stepped in too deep.

He decided it was best to cut to the chase. "What exactly do you think I can help you with? Is any of this related to my memory loss?"

"Yes, of course," said Citanaf. "You died, in a sense. Your brain was put into cryostasis, which is arguably a form of death to begin with. More importantly, you thawed once after that, and not in the way you're meant to after cryostasis. You thawed like a lump of meat pulled out of the freezer, until they put you back in. That's not cryostasis – that's just freezing to death, no matter how you look at it.

 Silence Of the Stars

Unlike cryostasis, it should result in a very unambiguous, very permanent, death. But here you are! And you have all your wits about you. Your body, and it would seem your soul, are fine."

"And you can help me recover my lost memories?"

"We can help you ascend! And you can help us to ascend."

"And 'ascension' will result in the restoration of my lost memories?"

"An individual is made up of mind, body, and soul. The soul is the core of an individual, and the body is necessary to exist in this world, but the mind is nothing but a shackle."

Janus stopped walking. "What?"

Come to think of it, why does he know so much about what happened to me on Earth? It sounds as if he knows even more details than Chons. Does he have ties to Project Eutychus himself?

"Think about it," insisted Citanaf, turning to face Janus. "Your brain was turned to mush in that freezer. Whatever fragmented memories you have now are all that's left. There's nothing to recover. But even without memory of your past life, you survived in body and soul for centuries! Whatever allowed you to persist could be the key to ascension."

"But not the key to getting my memories back..."

Citanaf clicked his tongue and raised a hand in frustration. "Forget about your memories! Your original life is gone. What's the big deal?

Why would you want to recall a time when people were barely more than cavemen stuck at the bottom of a gravity well?

"And, sure, I get it. You formed a pseudo-mind while frozen, playing soldier in those simulators for seven hundred years, but you don't seem to remember anything about that. The most recent thawing process must have caused even more brain damage, but you developed yet another personality. Developing a new mind switched your primate 'survival instincts' back on. But that doesn't matter! That's all one big step backward! You didn't need a mind! You were on the cusp of ascension! It's time to move on, not chase the past."

Janus' shock left him speechless. He tried to grasp what Citanaf was saying, but all this talk of multiple minds and the soul seemed absurd. *More importantly, what is this talk about a second personality while frozen? Does that mean I'm on my third personality now? A third life?* Citanaf's assertion that the mind was nothing more than a shackle must have had roots in this conundrum.

Seeing Janus' dumbfounded look, Citanaf added, "Our memories change every moment of every day. That's what learning and thinking is. Over decades; over centuries, a person's memories change so much that they may as well be a different person. Our mind grows unrecognizable even to their dearest loved ones. We can preserve the body, and the soul is eternal, but immortality for the mind is impossible. It is fickle and disposable by its very nature."

Nonsense. Crazy talk. Janus accepted that he might not want all his memories back, but he wasn't about to accept the idea that peoples' minds were disposable. His mind was what made him himself. In light

     Silence Of the Stars

of Citanaf's beliefs, Janus was suddenly dubious of the care he was providing for the VDS victims. *Could it be he's hiding them to deliberately keep them in this state? Is he using them for some kind of experiment? Most importantly, what does he want with me now that he's lured me down here under false pretenses? It doesn't matter. I can't trust anything he says any more.*

"I need to go," insisted Janus.

"Come on, Janus! Losing your memory was the best thing that ever happened to you! Doctor Osiris says your body possesses a healing power far beyond modern technology. This goes beyond automated DNA repair. He theorizes that you may be biologically immortal without the need for any surgical intervention. Retroactive bone growth, automated nervous system repair, removal of radionuclide build-up in bone marrow – all trivialized. No diminishing returns. In other words, you are on the cusp of true ascension!"

Wait a minute – Doctor Osiris? That rat-man who stabbed me in the shoulder... Chons was having some kind of disagreement with him, like he was protecting me from him. Did Osiris leak information about me to Citanaf? If Citanaf is working with Osiris...

Janus took two steps back, then bolted back down the hall toward the exit.

Citanaf's voice carried down the hall behind him. "The hard part's already over, Janus. You're here! Don't you want to help people?"

Janus could barely hear him over the sound of his own feet drumming against the metal floor. He ran past the pews, past the VDS victims, and into the unlit entry hall to find the hidden staircase back to the surface. To his surprise, there was a light coming from the stairway. That must have meant the exit had been reopened!

As he drew closer, a large figure cast a shadow down the stairwell, blocking Janus' path. Janus couldn't discern his features against the backlight, but it wasn't long before the bookshelf slid shut once again to leave the stairs in darkness. When the looming figure stopped at the base of the stairs, it was lit only by the dim blue light of the VDS victim's distant monitors. Janus squinted to try and identify him.

"Going somewhere, vanilla shrimp?"

The gravelly voice was familiar. A few slow heavy footsteps brought his face into view. It wass that Jar from the confrontation back in Atlas Promenade. *He's the one who picked a fight with that Chip, then attacked me before Citanaf intervened!*

For a fleeting moment, Janus hoped he might be here to help. *An enemy of my enemy.* That dream was dashed by a condescending sneer. The jar said, "Sorry mate. Sacrifices for the greater good, and progress, and all that."

Citanaf caught up. He stood in the doorway behind Janus, so that both exits to the short hall were blocked. Citanaf slicked back his hair and said, "This doesn't have to be painful, Janus. Just come with me. Don't resist."

 Silence Of the Stars

"Or do," offered the Jar with a shrug. "More fun for me that way, honestly."

"Stop it, Carl. He's already scared. You're making it worse."

Janus's eyes darted back and forth between the two. "You know each other? That fight at the spaceport was staged? This was all a setup to lure me here!"

"More of a happy accident," said Citanaf with a chuckle. "You see, Carl can't act to save his own life. The fight wasn't even part of the plan, just Carl losing his temper. I used it as a chance to improvise."

"But why?" Janus wracked his brain trying to comprehend the situation. What could anyone want from him? He was a nobody. This had to be some kind of misunderstanding. "Why bring me down here? To get me out of the public's eye? To block my PCU tracking signal from reaching Chons?"

"Tracking signal?" asked Citanaf, his eyes narrowing.

"Right. Chons installed a tracker so he can find me when he gets back."

"Shit!" shouted Citanaf, suddenly losing his cool. "Pack him up, Carl! We need to relocate, now!"

"With pleasure," said the Jar.

With that, the brute was upon Janus. One robotic arm took a handful of Janus' shirt. The sensation of being grabbed sent a jolt of recollection through Janus. The flood of adrenaline was accompanied by fleeting memories of combat – action and reaction, repeated tens of thousands of times. *These are not your memories.* Though his brain couldn't comprehend it, Janus found himself guided by a fighting instinct that seemed ingrained into the very cells of his body.

Before he understood what was happening, Janus was upside down holding the wrist of his attacker, his legs wrapped around the brute's arm. Now Janus' full weight was hanging from Carl's shoulder, pulling him off balance. He clung tight and pulled the captive arm straight. The elbow stretched the limit of its flexibility, then beyond. A loud metallic pop preceded the whirring and clicking of an electric servo struggling to find purchase. Finally, Janus twisted the wrist with all his might, resulting in a myriad of cracking and crunching sounds. Janus wasn't sure how much of that was from the robotic arm and how much was his own bones and ligaments failing under the strain of a maneuver far beyond the capability of his current body. It all happened in the blink of an eye.

The once powerful robotic arm dangled and thrashed wildly in the socket, but broken as it was, the unfeeling metal hand remained like a vice grip on Janus' shirt. Janus kicked off with his legs, letting the shirt tear away from his body. He somehow managed to land on his feet. Pain shot through his back, neck, and legs. He tried to run, but found that he could barely stand. A list of injuries rushed through his mind like a damage report: five compressed vertebrae, three broken ribs, seven partial tears along the thoracis and cervicis, distal bicep rupture...

Carl's face was a portrait of rage. His torn and twisted arm flopped limply as he marched after Janus with murder in his eyes.

		Silence Of the Stars

Whatever subconscious force had driven Janus and granted his body the ability to fight a moment ago was gone now. *Escape. I have to escape.*

He hobbled his broken body toward the stairs as fast as he could, squirming away from the grasping hand seeking purchase on his now bare and sweaty back. His vision flashed and his nerves were a mess of numbness and lightning jolts of pain. He scrambled to the exit door in a desperate life-and-death struggle, Carl cursing and grasping at him all the way. Miraculously, Janus managed to reach the bookshelf at the top of the stairwell.

"*Now,* Carl! We need to go now! Stop messing around!" shouted Citanaf.

Janus groped at the secret passage but couldn't get a purchase on it. There didn't appear to be a handle. A sudden, heavy impact came from behind. Fueled by adrenaline, Janus ignored the blow and tried to kick the door open, but his legs wouldn't move. All feeling was gone from his waist down, and he seemed to be stuck on something. His chest was dripping wet.

Janus looked down to see a bloody fist protruding through his abdomen. *That's not my hand. What's that doing there?* He felt dizzy and overwhelmingly tired. He knew he must keep running to survive, but his consciousness was fading, and his broken body wouldn't respond.

The hand slid back out through the hole it opened in his chest, and Janus collapsed limply to the floor, convulsing and coughing blood.

"You idiot! What use is he if you kill him?!" came the muffled voice of Citanaf.

Angry shouting faded to distant murmurs, and then silence. The world faded to darkness.

Chapter 9
JANUS#004

Something is different. All wrapped up and compressed within layers, you are cozy and comfortable. You're used to long bouts of slumber between outings, but you get the sense that you've been asleep much longer than usual this time. Even through your closed eyes, you notice a light growing steadily brighter on the other side of the glass. The light and warmth beckon you to rise, but you're afraid of what you might find if you do. You haven't been yourself lately.

The last vestige of cryochamber chill melts away and you hear a hiss. You know the chamber door is open even though your helmet protects you from feeling the change in pressure. Your closed eyes twitch in reflexive response to the bright ceiling light. As comfortable as the chamber is, you don't have time to delay any longer. Hoisting yourself to your feet, you climb out of the cryochamber. Insulated gloves protect your hands from the biting chill of its inner walls.

You stand alone in a small square room with metal walls and a single door with a red light flashing above it. The door features no handle and no control panel. Other than that, the only furnishing is the lone cryopod you just exited. You'd be forgiven for assuming you're in a prison cell, but you know better. It's always like this.

You stretch your arms and legs, turn your head from side to side, roll your hips, and raise your knees. This routine serves both to warm up and test your range of motion. Your armor is thick enough that your knees will bump into your chest plate when kneeling or climbing. This style of armor is nice for its battery capacity, but restricts movement more than you like. You'll just have to be conscious of your unusually broad dimensions and adapt your strategy accordingly.

Raising a glove in front of your visor, you recognize the UENS logo – United Earth Navy, Supplementary division. The UEN has always erred on the side of over-equipping troops. It's a side-effect of Earth doctrine lacking any concept of 'acceptable losses', unlike their Martian and outer-system counterparts. They armor troops and ships so heavily it becomes detrimental. You prefer the mobility-focused equipment of Mars and private forces like Guan Yu, but you'll make the best of what you're given.

"Ten minutes to drop. All units finalize equipment selection and report to shuttle bay," a bland, gender-ambiguous voice announces through your helmet coms.

The light above the door turns green, and the door slides open. A countdown appears on your visor's HUD: 10:00... 9:59... 9:58...

It's been a while since the last deployment.

You walk to the exit door but hesitate before ducking through the threshold. A sensation you forgot long ago beckons you to stay. It churns in your stomach and constricts your throat. It weighs down your legs, resisting any movement toward the danger of duty, urging you back toward lethargy.

This feeling. What was it called?

Fear.

Janus is afraid. Janus... But not you.

You look back at your cryopod. The identification plate reads "JANUS#004"; an abbreviation for Joint Assault Network

     Silence Of the Stars

Unification System, if memory serves. The UEN loves its acronyms, even when their meaning isn't always clear. The meaning of '#004' is even less clear. A number implies the existence of JANUS 1, 2, 3, and perhaps numbers above 4, but in your centuries of service, you've never met another JANUS unit.

"Janus..."

JANUS#004 was never meant as a name; just a project acronym that doubles as your call sign. Your name is not Janus. Your name is... What is your name? *Who was I before I became JANUS#004? Before I became Janus?*

It doesn't matter. Callsign JANUS#004 serves you well enough. You don't need a name to complete your mission.

You duck through the door and emerge onto a catwalk overlooking the interior of a hangar aboard a United Earth Navy spacecraft carrier. A row of drop-ships below emit the whine of turbines and the hiss of off-gassing cryogenic fuel as they are prepared for launch.

At the edge of the deck, open slipways reveal the scar-ridden landscape Mars below. The barren plains are crisscrossed with maglev railways and the occasional habitat dome covering a canyon or lava tube. Smoke billows from craters where domes, factories, and ground-to-space weapon platforms have been bombed, as well as from the wrecks of ships which were downed fighting or fleeing the ongoing battle.

For so much detail to be visible to the naked eye, you must be close to the ground. The carrier you're aboard must be skimming through the thin upper atmosphere of Mars rather than in true orbit. This implies the UEN has established air superiority but still wants to minimize its profile to reduce the engagement radius of ground-based railgun fire. Mars itself would act as a wall against any projectile beyond the horizon moving faster than orbital speed. The closer we skim the surface, the nearer the horizon.

Your observation is interrupted by a couple of engineers squeezing between you and the guardrails of the catwalk as they hurry toward whatever duty calls them. The tops of their heads barely measure up to the bottom of your chest. They are not short. The job of a UEN engineer is physically demanding, so they tend to be big men. You're just that much bigger. Between your natural height and bulk, the added bulk of your armor means you take up most of the corridor. Your size and heft more closely fit the profile of a compact armored vehicle than a man.

It's about time you return to your mission, too. You know the ship layout, but your visor HUD highlights your destination and superimposes a glowing green line on the floor to guide you. The visual effect is so seamless that anyone unfamiliar with the system would probably think the green line was physically present on the floor. In truth, it's only visible to you, rendered on the inside of your helmet. These paths have gradually become known as scry-lines due to their ability to provide soldiers with a seemingly magic ability to navigate foreign terrain, even in zero-visibility conditions. The same system also displays friends and enemies, even behind walls. All essential battlefield intelligence is fed to every soldier in an easy-to-understand interface. Anything visible to any UEN sensor is also visible to you. Cameras on satellites, spaceships, local civilian infrastructure, and even the helmets of other soldiers all feed into the system known as "Integrated Battlefield Awareness Network", or "I-BAN". *The UEN sure does love its acronyms.*

Scry-lines lead you to the armory, conveniently located next to the elevator down to the launch deck. A grin grows across your face as you approach the row of truck-sized cylinders spanning from floor to

          Silence Of the Stars

ceiling. Each cylinder is labeled *M-WAD* in large text, subtitled *Modular Weapon Assembler & Dispenser*. Soldiers don't share the UEN's affinity for acronyms, instead opting for vulgar terms of endearment for equipment. In this case, 'wad' is good enough.

UEN body armor may not be your favorite, but the customizability of their modular wad weaponry is unmatched. Wads allow soldiers to customize every detail of their gun from the length and bore of the barrel to the grip style to the rail capacity and number of gauss coils. In theory, the system allows soldiers to customize their weapons for their specific role and mission. In practice, most soldiers end up forming preferences for specific loadouts which they stick to regardless of individual mission needs.

You dial your specifications into the kiosk with practiced precision, keying the same parameters you always do. The assembler whirrs, buzzes and hums, then a hatch creaks open to present your one-of-a-kind weapon. No armed force in the solar system makes anything quite like it; M-WADs are the only way you get to use this highly customized piece of equipment.

The gun weighs 40 kilograms dry, and carries a split hopper magazine with superinsulated chambers for liquid gold, powdered ferromagnet, and caseless liquid propellant. All three hoppers have one-way valves that allow you to reload using materials you scavenge from the battlefield.

The gun's gauss coils are powered by local capacitors which charge straight from your suit's power supply, which is how you take advantage of its excessive battery capacity. The gun's shoulder sling doubles as a charging cable.

Perhaps the most unusual quality of your gun is the two barrels: the main upper barrel chambers 13mm and uses a combination of chemical propellant and gauss acceleration. The lower barrel chambers 5mm and accelerates projectiles using gauss only, allowing for an extremely high rate of fire, spewing out raw liquid gold like a hypersonic hose. Using the lower barrel that way burns through ammo and battery power quickly, but in niche-use cases it can be a life-saver... or a life-ender, depending on perspective.

You sling the rifle over your shoulder and lock it securely to your chest plate. You casually pocket a few grenades to top off your carrying capacity. Aided by your power armor, you feel no burden due to the veritable arsenal now bound to your person.

The elevator creaks under the strain of your weight as it carries you to the lower deck. There, scry-lines lead you past a row of drop-ships each loaded with heavy shock-troops in mechanized armor much like yours. The green and blue coloration of their UEN uniforms is far more prominent than on your armor, which is mostly unpainted black and gray with minimal United Earth markings.

The scry-line ends at a highlighted ship roughly the size of a bus. It's little more than a bulbous lifting body with a thick ablative shield on the front. The name of the ship is painted clearly across the back: *Snowfox-5.*

Cute name for a ship so unapologetically ugly.

On the boarding ramp a stern-looking man stands in a wide stance. He wears an officer's vacuum-rated combat uniform bearing the insignia of flight lieutenant, but no power armor. When he spots you, he waves an arm to beckon you forward while shouting, "What the hell are you doing, soldier?! Get your ass in here!"

The roar of the dropship's engines momentarily drowns out whatever other profanities he shouts at you until your helmet's audio-filter adjusts to prioritize his voice over the background noise.

 Silence Of the Stars

Time-to-launch on your HUD indicates you still have five minutes. The drop-ship won't launch until the appointed time whether you hurry or not. Rushing soldiers pre-mission is just a way of applying pressure to keep them focused. Some soldiers lose their nerve if given any time to rethink. You understand the doctrine, but you need no such motivation; you are always focused. You walk rather than run, not out of laziness, but for efficiency. Even so, you play along, jogging the rest of the distance to the boarding ramp. Humoring your commanding officer also tends to improve team efficiency.

At the base of the boarding ramp at the rear of the ship, you can see down the single hall running the length of the drop-ship all the way to the cockpit. Both walls of the corridor are filled with UEN shock-troops harnessed shoulder-to-shoulder, facing the center aisle. Their tight formation is reminiscent of a double-stacked magazine. There's just enough room for one armored soldier to squeeze down the center of the aisle.

"Left side, harness four. Buckle in!" shouts the sergeant with a slap on your back which you register but don't feel.

Your feet grow heavy once again, as if colossal psychic chains have been bound to your boots and are trying to pull you off the ship, back to safety. Your stomach churns and you feel a sharp pain in your head.

Hesitation.

Fear.

Why am I doing this? Where am I? What's going on?

With a jolt of remembrance, you look down and put a hand to your stomach. Didn't you die a moment ago? Wasn't there a hand protruding through your abdomen? There was so much blood.

No. You are a freelance soldier on a mission for the UEN. You are not Janus. At least in this moment, you shouldn't *want* to be Janus. He was dying because he was helplessly weak and naïve. In his position, you would have survived.

"JANUS#004!" The voice of the sergeant startles you. It's much crisper now that your helmet has edited out the background noise. "Get to your crash-harness, soldier! No lollygagging!"

"Yes, sir." The sound of your own voice is unfamiliar. It's deep, confident, and authoritative.

With one heavy step, you break through the barrier of fear that held you back. You find the one open harness on the left side of the aisle, and stand with your back to the wall. Self-propelled belts secure your arms, legs, torso, and head tightly to the wall to protect you from the turbulence of descent to the Martian surface. The drop-ship might need to perform rapid maneuvers at reentry speed while under fire.

"Did he say JANUS Four? As in, *the* JANUS Four? The legendary Reaper?" one of the other soldiers whispers over the local com channel, emulating normal speech.

"You mean angel of victory. That's what my squad calls him," comments another.

"I thought he was just a legend."

"I've seen this guy in action. He may seem calm now, but he's an absolute madman on the battlefield!"

             Silence Of the Stars

"Glad he's on our side."

"Maybe we stand a chance of winning this after all."

The murmurs are silenced by the sergeant's booming command, "Attention! As many of you already know, Private Jenkens was unable to join us today. Free agent JANUS#004 will be joining us in his place."

The murmurs begin again, and the sergeant immediately quells them by violently clearing his throat. Then he continues, "Our objective is to neutralize reactor D-26 of the Olympus Mons mass-accelerator network. The Martian mass-accelerator network is usually a tool for shipping goods from the surface of Mars into orbit of any celestial body in the solar system, but in wartime there's nothing stopping it from being weaponized to fire directly at any target in the solar system instead. Reactor D-26 powers the only rails positioned for a direct intercept course with Earth. If that reactor is still online eight hours from now, Mars will have the option of sending us a payload to give Chicxulub a run for its money.

"I am obliged to inform you that the Secretary General would prefer we gain control of the reactor intact. However, I am personally telling you to screw the Secretary General. We take no chances. Blast the reactor to hell, first opportunity you get.

"I ain't gonna sugarcoat it. Our odds of even getting within eyeshot of the reactor are low. Olympus Mons is the most heavily fortified location in the solar system. We softened them with bombardment, but we are the first wave of ground forces. A lot of Martian fortifications are hidden underground, protected by terrain. Congress also insisted on refraining from any strategic strikes against defensive facilities near civilian infrastructure to avoid escalation, so we'll be flying directly through open line of fire of many such installations."

An explosion rattles the entire carrier. The soldiers shrug it off like turbulence.

"Escalation, sir? How could things escalate more than they already have?" the soldier next to you blurts out.

The sergeant shoots him a stink eye, and the soldier immediately straightens up and silences himself.

The sergeant asks, "Would you like permission to speak, private?"

"No, sir, I—"

"Permission denied!" shouts the sergeant, then goes on to answer the question anyway. "You don't want to know what escalation looks like, and you don't need to! Keep your head down and your guns up! Remember, reactor D-26! Drop in ten!"

"Yosh rah!" The soldiers chant the battle cry in unison as the sergeant turns about-face and steps into the cockpit.

Your harness rotates forward to better withstand the high g-force of forward acceleration, and a ten-second countdown displays prominently in your helmet. You brace yourself for sudden acceleration.

At zero, you feel your whole body flatten against the snug pressure suit within your armor. Your tongue and eyes are compressed within your head, and your heart flutters for a moment. Janus panics, but you're in no real danger. The launch catapult is always an exhilarating experience.

    Silence Of the Stars

The extreme acceleration lasts for only a couple seconds. Now rotated to face the forward display, you can see the red-hot plasma of reentry heat blurring the battlefield below. Your drop-ship, Snowfox-5, glides at hypersonic speed in formation with dozens of others descending toward Olympus Mons, the largest mountain in the solar system, which is still just beyond the horizon.

"Mother bird's away; we're on our own. This is it, boys," says someone from the cockpit. As they do, the giant carrier ship which had dominated the I-BAN display disappears from your HUD, having ascended back into space.

"There it is!" someone shouts a few seconds later.

Sure enough, the characteristic plateau of Olympus Mons appears on the horizon. The iconic shallow slope is so wide as to be barely recognizable as a mountain.

As soon as it comes into view, a muffled buzzing is accompanied by a fireworks display as PDC fire from the dropship formation crisscrosses in curving arcs to intercept wave upon wave of incoming missiles and railgun slugs. The incoming projectiles appear as red triangles moving lazily across the I-BAN display. In reality, they travel at several kilometers per second: so fast as to be nearly invisible to the naked eye.

A drop-ship far ahead of you, Gannet-3, erupts into a cloud of molten metal as an unseen projectile slips through the web of defensive PDC fire to find its mark. Com chatter continues unfazed, discussing only navigation and coordinating defensive fire. No comment is made about the lost ship. Mourning will wait until after the battle.

Another dropship explodes as an incoming railgun slug is successfully deflected away from its intended target only to pierce another further back in the formation.

You watch calmly, soaking in the radio chatter, the view through the window, and the chaotic display on the inside of your HUD. Most soldiers turn off the majority of I-BAN feeds. In fact, they are encouraged to do so. It's said that the human brain can only usefully process one or two augmented feeds at most; that any more is merely a distraction. Most soldiers use the integrated network to highlight enemy and friendly units for quick identification, but few bother displaying detailed information such as damage reports or recorded trajectories of enemy fire. You prefer to see it all.

To you, the scrolling data streams paint a clear and beautiful picture. Each data point is like a rock rolling down a river. Each does its part to direct the flow of the river, and you must know the position of each to predict changes in that flow. Fail to account for one rock in the river of battle, and you might slip and drown trying to wade across.

There are gaps in the Navy's sensor suite feeding into the Integrated Battlefield Awareness Network. These blind spots are like gaps in a suit of armor where an enemy spear might find its way in. However, by being aware of these weaknesses, you can position yourself to protect your vitals, just like a medieval knight would know to protect his armpits, visor, and the backs of his knees. Human intuition can fill in the gaps where advanced monitoring falls short.

The back end of a drop-ship explodes, and it spirals uncontrolled toward the ship next to it. That ship narrowly dodges, only to be picked off by a stray missile.

     Silence Of the Stars

Not everyone can see the battlefield as completely as you do. As far as you know, nobody can. Still, there's only so much you can do. You're a single low-ranking soldier. You can't give orders, and the others wouldn't be able to react in time even if you did. You used to try, but found that allies are as unpredictable as enemies. Instead, you've learned to just do what you need to in order to survive and finish the mission.

"We're out!" the drop-ship just ahead of Snowfox-5 calls, a missile closing on their position. With no PDC ammunition left, they have no way to defend themselves.

You hear the servo motors of the PDC just over your head whir and spin the turret, which fires an arc over the bow of the defenseless drop-ship. The spiraling stream of bullets catches the incoming missile just in time. Hypersonic debris from the destroyed projectile bounce violently but harmlessly off the target's frontal armor plow.

Without a moment's rest, your pilot curses loud enough for you to hear through his helmet without assistance from the com system. He had been so focused on covering the neighboring ship that he failed to notice a missile headed straight for Snowfox-5. The turret can't rotate back fast enough to intercept it. Providing covering fire to your ally left the turret out of position to protect your own ship.

You trigger the emergency release for your harness and raise your rifle, taking careful aim at the thin hull armor next to the pilot's head. You fire twice. The report of the rifle is muffled by your armor, but the pressure from the expanding gas is enough to cause the ship's inner hull to flex – you can 'see' the sound of the gunshot. The first shot opens a finger-width hole in the ship, and the second flies clean through that hole. The pilot looks at the hole, then at you, still holding your rifle aloft.

"Are you crazy?!" he demands.

"Just focus on flying," you insist, pointing at the console. The red marker for the incoming missile presently vanishes.

The pilot looks at his instruments with momentary confusion, then amazement, then understanding.

"Get back in your harness, you—" the sergeant begins, but the pilot places a hand on his chest to stop him.

You fire another two rounds through the hull of the ship, destroying another incoming missile that had gone unaccounted for by automatic point-defense. Debris showers Snowfox-5, shaking the ship but leaving it mostly unharmed.

"Holy shit. The legends are true," says one soldier.

"What's going on?" asks another.

"Is he shooting down missiles with a rifle? How does he even know where they are?" asks a third.

You ignore the banter. By this point, nearly half the dropships are gone, and you're less than halfway to your destination. As the number of cameras, radar, and other sensors feeding into I-BAN dwindles, so does the information available to you. You walk into the cockpit to get a better view of the battlefield.

"You're out of line, merc. You've got some serious explaining to—" The sergeant is cut off by a sudden downward acceleration as you press the control stick forward and send the dropship into a steep dive. A damaged enemy fighter craft buzzes overhead, shearing the PDC off your hull and sending the dropship into a roll. You fight with the pilot's controls and quickly recover from the roll, avoiding a direct collision and putting Snowfox-5 right back on course.

"On second thought, do whatever the hell you want," says the sergeant.

"Want to fly?" invites the pilot.

You shake your head. "You fly, I shoot."

Using the 5mm lower barrel on your gun, you cut open a hole in the hull where the PDC used to be. You tie harness straps to your feet, and jump through the new hatch onto the roof. Your interior speakers take a second to cancel out the background noise of the thin Martian wind roaring past you fast enough to form a thin layer of plasma over your suit. On Earth, air friction would be enough to shear your armor down to a stub in seconds at this speed. On Mars, the wind is just a mild nuisance.

Having taken the place of the point defense cannon, you also take up its role. Incoming fire is met with fire of your own. You do your best to focus only on taking out threats that are guaranteed to hit allied ships, while ignoring near-misses. You're not worried about ammunition: you can reload by plugging the propellant and gold feed from the PDC directly into your rifle's hopper. The bigger problem is heat. The thin Martian atmosphere is a poor conductor. After less than a minute of defensive firing, the barrel of your gun is glowing red.

In the flow state of battle, time loses meaning. There is a serenity to the chaos. Between rolling from side to side and ducking to avoid debris and incoming fire, returning fire of your own, and shouting the occasional report into coms, you feel as graceful as a leaf on the surface of a calm river. In the ecstasy of the moment, you feel complete.

Soon you're out of grenades, and your gun is overheated to the brink of melting, and you've fully expended two additional rifles passed up to you by your teammates.

"Lithobraking in ten! Nine! Eight!"

You're forced to take a break from your revelry. The ground beneath is now an unbroken black and gray expanse of industrial complex. In front looms Olympus Mons, like an angry brick wall, strangled by the surrounding city and covered in bulging black veins – the mass drivers. The mountain grows by the second.

"Six! Five!"

A tug on your harness brings you back inside. You strap in with what remains of your harness. The fasteners rapidly begin to melt and burn, drawing attention to the 532 Celsius external temperature indicator on your armor. Luckily, the straps won't have to hold you long.

"Three!"

Everyone's harnesses spin around so that their backs face the front of the ship. Braking thrusters fire, then once again plaster your eyes and tongue to the back of your skull, and make you feel like you're about to turn inside out. But this time, when the count reaches one, the rapid deceleration doesn't end. Instead, the ship violently buckles and quakes as it slams directly into the side of Olympus Mons. It penetrates several meters of regolith and reinforced concrete protecting the 'landing' site.

There's a shrill sound of metal on metal, then the whole ship tumbles a few times. The hole in the hull you were previously sitting in catches on something jagged, tearing that entire panel off the ship. Through the new sunroof, you can see the interior of a building that

     Silence Of the Stars

looks like a mix between a military fortress and a factory. What remains of the ship skids and tumbles through a few more reinforced walls before coming to a stop.

"God damn, I liked it better back when lithobraking was a joke," groans one soldier, followed by a coughing fit.

"Anyone still alive, get out there and raise some hell!" commands the sergeant.

A scry-line appears on your HUD, indicating that reactor D-26 is about 1 kilometer deeper into the mountainside. Your whole body feels numb, and about as solid as pudding, but the enemy here is still fresh. You've barely had a chance to take one deep breath when you hear the sound of sentry drones rounding the corner.

Looking through the ruined hull of your ship, your suspicions are immediately confirmed. Four centaurs – four-legged mechs roughly the size of a horse, and mounted with a single high-caliber anti-armor cannon – stand just down the hall. You immediately open fire with your original rifle, destroying two of the drones in quick succession before the overheating of your gun catches up: it jams.

You dive for cover behind the thick ablative frontal armor of the landing craft just as the centaurs return fire. Every shot is accompanied by a bright flash and a thump that shakes the ground. The rhythmic stiletto cannon fire is like a metronome ticking to the executioner's drumbeat. Sparks, molten metal, and flesh fly with every note.

A few of your teammates have the wherewithal to scramble for cover, while the others are still struggling to get out of their harnesses when the onslaught begins. Armor protects them from glancing blows, but the hyper-dense projectiles propelled by gauss-enhanced cannons carry enough energy to penetrate or melt any known

Garrett Ordiway

material. Even the two-meter-thick frontal armor of the ship you're hiding behind is soon pitted with molten cavities.

Within seconds, everyone still stuck in their crash harnesses is massacred. Their bodies hang motionless in the ruined remains of their mechanized suits, still securely fastened to their standing crash couches. Despite witnessing the deaths of more than half their teammates, the remaining crew of Snowfox-5 doesn't seem distressed.

"God dammit, not again. I hate when this happens," says one.

"Another happy landing," another replies.

"What a joke. Olympus Mons missions are bullshit," another adds, resignation in his voice.

Another man says nothing, but sighs, then rolls out from behind cover with a heavy shoulder-mounted weapon you don't recognize. There's an electric buzz and a dazzling blue light so intense that it causes your visor to immediately dim to nearly complete blackness. A single line of blue sweeps across your otherwise pitch-black field of view. It takes one befuddled second before you realize you're seeing an intense weaponized laser, aimed at the centaurs. So intense is the beam that it ionizes the air around it. The sound is so intense that your suit switches to noise-canceling mode to prevent you from going deaf, rather than trying to interpret any sound. The result is a strange pressure in your helmet, accompanied by absolute silence.

A second later, your visor tint returns to normal and the incoming cannon fire has stopped.

"Hell yeah!" shouts the soldier holding the laser gun.

"The one-shot wonder comes in clutch!"

"Cat-toy goes two for one! Tax credits well spent."

The few remaining soldiers are distracted by their momentary victory, and don't hear the platoon of soldiers marching toward your position from around a corner down the hall. If you get caught in a conventional firefight here, you'll stand no chance, outnumbered and outgunned. There is nowhere to run, and the incoming platoon is between you and your target. Your only chance is to initiate the firefight on favorable terms.

You run through the remains of Snowfox-5, grabbing a sidearm and as many grenades as you can carry from the still-standing corpses of your allies stuck in crash harnesses. You sprint alone down the length of the hall toward the approaching platoon while juggling grenades, arming each one in turn. Each grenade is unique since each soldier has customized their armament. Not only are they different types, but their arming mechanisms are also varied – some even use triggers you've never seen before. Still, you manage to arm them all before reaching the intersection of the approaching platoon, and lob every grenade around the corner.

The moment they detonate, you round the corner to take advantage of the chaos, shooting any still-standing soldiers in order of which poses the greatest threat. You run forward, still shooting. There will be no chance to rest and recover, but your enemy has every number advantage, so keeping the situation as fast-paced and chaotic as possible works in your favor. When your borrowed sidearm runs out of ammunition, you waste no time attempting to find a new weapon, instead opting to finish off the rest of your stunned opponents in hand-to-hand combat. Everything is done within five seconds of rounding the corner.

"Seriously?" a voice says over your coms system in disbelief. "I mean, I heard you were good, but. Shit, man."

You turn around to search for a new weapon among the carnage. The fighting won't be over until the reactor is offline. You've advanced about 50 meters. There's still a kilometer left to cover. You estimate somewhere from three to five of the fifty original drop-ships survived landfall. I-BAM shows no sign of life from the others, so you assume that your four remaining teammates are all that's left.

One of your teammates starts dancing like a giddy child when he comes around the corner, unable to contain his excitement. Another starts crouching up and down over a fallen centaur. You say nothing, but Janus stares in confusion.

Interpreting the stare as *What the hell are you doing?* the soldier says, "Classic victory dance."

Shaking your head, you wipe the gore from a mostly intact rifle. You fire one shot at the ground to make sure it still works, then start following the scry-line toward reactor D-26. The four remaining soldiers of your company follow your lead.

     Silence Of the Stars

Chapter 10
You again?

Prone atop a hard table. A bright light shone overhead. At first it seemed to be the sun, but it was too cold and too close for that. The voices of two men echoed in the distance, distorted and incomprehensible. The way their voices reverberated suggested this was an enclosed room. A ringing in the ears pervaded all other sounds.

With great effort, a hand raised in front of the face, blocking that brilliant, cold light. The eyes blinked repeatedly to try and focus on the hand. Vision was still blurry. The image slowly sharpened to reveal the details of a bare and fleshy limb. A freckle near the thumb stood out. This was Janus'. Despite the idiom 'I know it like the back of my hand', Janus hadn't consciously noticed this freckle previously. Even so, seeing it, he knew the hand belonged to him. He reconfirmed that conviction when the hand responded to his attempts to will it closed and then open again.

This hand was too small and fragile to belong to JANUS#004. Janus was back in the real world – or what he assumed was the real world. In this world, Janus was the real one. In this world, JANUS#004 was just a dream. In a flash of realization, it occurred to Janus that he couldn't be completely certain that either of the two worlds were objectively real. Neither Janus nor JANUS#004 had any memory of who they were – who you were, before cryostasis. Maybe the real world is what Janus experienced before all this, before he became Janus. Maybe everything happening now was some kind of alternate reality.

Everything made more sense back when it happened in chronological order. There was the unnamed original, then the long freeze, and now Janus. But JANUS#004 was in control during that battle a moment ago. The other original was there, too, if only as a passive observer. Whatever that battle was, it was no dream.

"Good morning." The muffled background noise coalesced into the familiar voice of Chons, dispelling the dreamy haze.

Janus continued to hold up his hand blocking the intense light overhead, and turned his gaze toward the source of the voice. There stood a blurry shape roughly resembling Chons.

Janus blinked to clear his vision. Next to Chons stood a man in the white coat of a doctor. The doctor had gray hair and a boxy face. *Hospital, again*? If Chons was here, that meant Janus was definitely back in the 'real world'. *But, if that's the case—*

Janus unbuttoned his hospital gown and touched his abdomen. It was bandaged, but intact. A dull, residual pain throbbed through his core, but he was able to breathe. He recalled Carl's fist protruding through his chest. Given the angle, it should have broken his spine and collapsed his lungs. That Jar had dealt him a fatal blow, or so he thought.

The medicine of this era is truly amazing, he thought.

     Silence Of the Stars

"How are you feeling?" asked the doctor in a deep, fatherly voice. The question was meant to calm as much as it was to inquire.

"Physically, fine. I'm just a bit confused."

"You seemed to be having a very vivid dream."

A dream? Is that all it was? No. Definitely not. Janus recalled the battle over Mars. *It felt too real to be just that.* "I don't think I was just dreaming. That battle felt too real."

Chons and the doctor looked at each other, then the doctor said, "Battle? You haven't left this room in days."

"What kind of battle?" asked Chons.

"We were invading Mars."

"We?"

Janus dug through his memory to recall some kind of verifiable detail, anything that might help to differentiate between a vivid dream and something anchored in reality. "I took a drop-ship to Mars with a group of marines. We were fighting over some kind of power station. Olympus Reactor D-26, I think."

Chons cocked his head to the side and raised one eyebrow. "Reactor D-26 was a primary target during the Battle of Olympus. That is a well-known historical event. Perhaps you saw it at a museum exhibit at the aerospace port, and your dream was based on memories from the museum."

Janus went on to describe the event in detail, recalling as many specifics as he could. He talked about the mission objectives, the kinds of equipment the soldiers used, the sorts of things the other soldiers said. Chons and the doctor listened patiently.

When Janus finished, Chons nodded. "That sounds like SimMilitary, an emulated reality used by the United Earth Navy for training and recruiting. Some matches are open to the public. I used to play around with it in my spare time. But there's no way you can connect without a Human Interface Port."

"I don't see a port on you, either." Janus tapped the back of his neck where he had seen a metal jack on some of the people walking around the Spire. He thought he might have seen some on Earth, too, but the metal ports were easier to see on the Spire since everyone here had short hair. He wasn't sure what the ports were for, but assumed that they must be what Chons meant by Human Interface Port.

"Any HIP installed in the last two centuries is subcutaneous. Nobody gets external ports anymore," said Chons.

"Well..." the doctor started to protest.

The objection was brushed aside by a dismissive wave of Chons' hand. "Let's not get into technicalities. *Almost* nobody gets external ports anymore."

"Is it possible that I also have a hidden HIP? Subcutaneous, like yours?" asked Janus.

     Silence Of the Stars

"No. Subcutaneous ports may be hidden from view, but they still show up on medical scans," said Chons. Then he paused in the unmistakable way one does when second guessing oneself. Presently, he turned to the doctor to confirm, "Isn't that right, Doctor Apollo?"

Dr. Apollo stared through Janus, thinking and rapping his fingers on his desk. He nodded acknowledgement, but didn't answer Chons' question. Focusing back on Janus, he said, "My son is training to join the United Earth Navy. He had a match today. You said you were aboard a drop-ship called Snowfox-5, right? If you were somehow in a live match, he might have heard something about it."

The doctor put his index finger to the temple of his head and looked silently at the ceiling. Shortly, he began to have a conversation with the disembodied voice of his son. "Hi Kirk! How'd the match go?"

Kirk was ecstatic. "We actually won! We shouldn't have had a chance, but we were saved by a miracle."

"Oh?" Dr. Apollo urged him to continue.

Kirk happily obliged. "Do you know that legendary free agent I talked about before? That soldier the senior academy mates were spreading ludicrous rumors about, the so-called the 'Reaper', JANUS#004? It turns out he's real! The man is unbelievable! He made the Martian special ops look like amateurs. I'm kind of worried the naval academy won't count our victory since our team relied so heavily on a free agent."

"Why was a free agent on your team? Wasn't this a qualifying match for your squad?"

"He was a random filler added to our team because we were one man short," said Kirk. Then he added hurriedly, "The madman actually took out three enemy vessels before our drop-ship even touched down."

"Five, actually. Not three," Janus corrected.

"What?" asked the doctor.

"JANUS#004 was my call sign. I took out two fighters and three anti-air guns on descent."

"What?" the doctor asked again. He didn't seem to doubt Janus' honesty. He seemed confused about something else altogether. Maybe the narrative being presented was infeasible to him.

"It makes sense he'd only know about three of the kills," Janus went on. "One was a shot over-the-horizon. A shrapnel cloud would have blocked radar from catching another. So, sensors would have only picked up three of the five ships I downed."

"Wait, did he say—" Kirk said excitedly. "Are you interviewing JANUS#004 live, now?"

"I..." The doctor stared forward at nothing in particular, not sure what to say. He silently mouthed, "But how?"

          Silence Of the Stars

"You are!" Kirk exclaimed, reading his father's hesitation. "How'd you manage that? Nobody even knows who he is! He's been a ghost in the system for hundreds of years."

"I'll call you back," said Dr. Apollo, taking his finger off his temple and ending the call abruptly.

"How?" Janus asked, considering the question himself. "Well, I threw a grenade at one, deflected a missile at another, and the other three were just clean shots with my gauss rifle. At any rate, based on what your son said, I'm certain we were at the same event."

Chons said, "I'd love to hear more about your combat tactics some time, but what the doctor wants to know is how you know what his son said just now."

Now it was Janus' turn to be confused. "You had that conversation right in front of me. Of course I heard everything."

Dr. Apollo and Chons shot inquisitive looks at each other, then back at Janus.

Chons stroked his scruffy goatee, then asked the doctor, "You confirmed that his scans came up clean for nanites, biomods, cyberenhancements, the works, right? No modifications. He's vanilla."

The doctor considered this. He opened his mouth and closed it again, apparently rethinking his analysis. He shifted his weight from one foot to the other and his face contorted as he tried fruitlessly to think of an explanation for what he was witnessing.

Janus was also confused, but that was normal for him. Everything in this world was strange. Presently, he was confused about what had the two men found so perplexing about the situation. Janus was used to being the only one confused, but Chons and the doctor seemed as lost as himself. To Janus, nothing extraordinary had happened yet; at least no more than usual.

"Off the record, what are you thinking?" Chons asked the doctor.

Dr. Apollo nodded his head a few times, then spoke slowly, thinking through the situation out loud. "The tests confirmed he was vanilla, but those tests are not perfect. They detect foreign materials, abnormal anatomy, DNA deviations, and unusual tissue composition. Any known model of HIP would have been detected. We did not detect one in Janus, but he seems to have a wireless network connection. The fact he has wireless network connectivity seems undeniable, unless you're both pulling some kind of elaborate prank on me."

"No prank. So, if he doesn't have an HIP, how is he connected?"

"He must have some kind of transceiver and decoder grown into his vanilla organs. It must be composed entirely of tissue native to his body. We would have seen it if connectivity was provided by a new organ or any significant modification to the shape of a vanilla organ." The doctor rapped his fingers.

"So, regular human tissue manipulated to perform additional functions, in this case, radio communication," said Chons. "But without altering their shape or DNA, how is that possible? Nanites?"

    Silence Of the Stars

"Tests would have detected the foreign materials composing the nanites," said the doctor. "We should have picked up higher than normal silicates. Carbonates, if they were trying to be subtle. But... well, *something* caused his accelerated regeneration and managed to integrate a radio transceiver into his body while avoiding detection. His DNA is vanilla, so some outside force is at play, but nobody operated on him between the time he was injured and the time he was delivered here. The only thing I can think of that could do that is organic nanites. They must be made only from materials present in vanilla human biology. That wouldn't be very compact, though. I don't know how machines like that could avoid causing an immune response."

"Wouldn't something like that floating around in the bloodstream show up under a microscope?" asked Chons.

"Probably," Dr. Apollo conceded. "But if the nanites look enough like human cells, they might be missed on initial inspection. Besides, they might not be free-floating in the bloodstream. Perhaps we'll find some in the tissue samples collected from the Ascensionist temple where you picked Janus up, but if they are bio nanites, they are extremely advanced. What I'm describing now is all hypothetical. I've never actually seen any medical technology that can pull off the feats we're talking about here."

"Is there any doctor or mod clinic who could pull this off?" asked Chons.

The doctor shook his head. "No. Not that I know of. I can say with some confidence this is beyond any known medical technology

– at least in Geo-luna. Bio-mods are all registered in the inner system, anyway, and black-market clinics wouldn't have the funding to develop something like this. The outer systems have a lot more motivation to develop stealth biotechnology. I can imagine them developing a procedure as a way of getting undeclared biomods through spaceport security, but clearly that's not this patients' intent."

"No, not *his* intent," agreed Chons.

Janus continued Chons' train of thought. *But that might have been the intent of the Eutychus Program when they did this to me.*

Janus, who had been patiently absorbing the discussion, spoke up. "So, basically what you're saying is that I was able to join a training simulator because I have built in Wi-Fi?"

Dr. Apollo replied, "The ability to transmit and receive radio signals, yes. And not just that, you have the ability to decode and interpret those signals. Signal transception is one thing, but actually using those signals to participate in a training simulation. That requires software."

"Even with the right equipment, it normally shouldn't be possible to just join those military sponsored matches without an invitation. They're encrypted. Dr. Apollo's personal call to his son was also encrypted," Chons added.

"Wait, that wasn't a phone call? You couldn't hear it?" asked Janus.

   Silence Of the Stars

Chons shook his head, "Nothing to hear. No audio. It was direct HIP to HIP communication."

Janus hung his head in shame. "I'm sorry. I don't even know what I did, or how. The simulation, the call, I don't even…" He trailed off. He dared not bring up the fact that JANUS#004, who he had been in the combat simulation, was a separate persona, complete with skills and knowledge completely foreign to Janus. It must be JANUS#004 who had the ability to crack encryptions and access SimMilitary.

"Any chance you can leave this little detail out of your report, Dr. Apollo?" Chons fidgeted with his lighter, which was still no more reliable than it had been below New Angels.

"You know I can't do that," replied Dr. Apollo.

Chons flipped the lighter cap open and closed a few times while he thought. "I know you need to summarize emergency calls right away, but the formal report is separate. When is the full report due?"

Dr. Apollo sighed. "End-of-day is standard protocol, but it's not officially due until end-of-month. The rule is meant to give us time to catch up when things get busy."

"Kid's got an appointment with the man in the Big Chair tomorrow."

"What does Atlas want with him?"

Chons shrugged and made a zipping motion across his mouth, silently implying, 'I can't talk about it.'

"A P.U. survivor?"

Chons raised one eyebrow and repeated the zipping motion back
and forth across his lips.

Dr. Apollo nodded understandingly. "Alright. I'll make sure to...
be too busy. But remember, the report gets filed end-of-month. After
that, Atlas will know everything I know."

* * *

Having completely healed, Janus was given a fresh set of clothes and
discharged. Chons informed him that while he could wait a few days
to meet Atlas if he felt it was necessary to recover psychologically,
under the present circumstances the best time for the meeting was as
soon as possible.

Janus agreed. To the surprise of both of them, Atlas scheduled the
meeting for later that same day. Less than an hour after being
discharged from the hospital, Janus found himself on a long stone
path leading to a titanic set of double doors. He intuitively knew that
Atlas was waiting on the other side.

Chons, who had said very little since leaving the hospital, put his
hand on Janus' shoulder to stop him on a sparsely populated stretch
of Athens road. He spun Janus around to face him and knelt down a

 Silence Of the Stars

few centimeters to bring his eyes level to Janus'. This gesture made Janus feel like a child about to be lectured.

In a quiet but serious tone, Chons said, "Remember what I said before: You don't owe anyone anything until you make a promise. Anyone who does you a favor and *expects* you to repay it is *not* your friend. That's not a favor, it's a bribe. It's coercion."

"Where is this coming from, all of a sudden?" asked Janus. He recalled their previous conversation about this topic back in Darwin Aerospace port but didn't see why it was relevant at this moment.

"It's important you drill that one kernel of wisdom into your mind."

Janus smiled warmly. "Thanks, Chons. I appreciate everything you've done for me."

Chons squeezed his shoulder tighter and insisted, "No, you're not listening. I saved you because I have orders to bring you to Atlas, and I can't do that if you're dead. I like ya, kid, but I'm *not* a good guy. There are no good guys. If ya keep running around out there naively expecting to make friends with everyone you meet, you'll get eaten alive."

Janus tried to read the intense look in Chons' eyes, but his expression was as incomprehensible as a poem in a foreign language; Janus recognized the presence of emotion and underlying meaning but couldn't comprehend it. Chons lived in a different world to Janus. Those intense eyes in that hardened face were shaped by a century of life in a world Janus could hardly begin to fathom. Time had sculpted Chons' way of thinking into something that was truly alien to Janus. Whatever he was trying to silently convey in that moment would forever remain a mystery.

Without breaking his gaze, Chons pulled Janus' PCU out of his own coat pocket. Janus patted himself down to confirm that his PCU was missing. But when had Chons taken it? Had it fallen, or had Chons somehow managed to snatch it at some point?

"See this?" Chons started. "This is your best friend, your only friend. Money, contracts, records: real, solid value that can never betray you. Don't lose it again. Stop trusting people." He thrust the PCU into Janus' chest, pushing him back slightly before dropping it into his cupped hands.

Janus looked at the PCU in his hands, then at Chons. "Good guy or not, you *chose* to thaw me out instead of incinerating me with the facility. You didn't do that because of orders. I heard that whole conversation."

"The hospital wasn't the first time you overheard a call, huh?"

"I think that was the first time I intercepted a signal while conscious, but I'm not really sure. To be honest, I'm having difficulty keeping track of what's real recently."

"Well." Chons scratched the stray tufts of hair that protruded from under his hat. He checked from side to side before saying, "It's best you don't talk to anyone about your eavesdropping ability. In fact, it's best you don't say anything about it at all, even to yourself when you think you're alone. Just try and stay out of trouble, okay?"

     Silence Of the Stars

"Thanks," said Janus. Then he shook his head as if retracting his statement. "I mean, I won't. I mean, I will! I mean, I'll stay out of trouble."

"Yeah," said Chons. He turned Janus around again with one hand on his shoulder, moving him effortlessly, no force behind the motion. The controlled movement felt to Janus like something between being on the receiving end of a martial arts or dance move, and being an infant guided by a playful father.

As the two of them resumed walking side by side toward the great double doors, Chons explained, "This is it. Remember, Atlas is *not* your friend, but he doesn't have to be your enemy either. Just... don't say any more than you need to." Then he muttered under his breath, "Words to live by, honestly."

Janus thought over the events of the day and tried to read between the lines of what he had been told and what had been kept from him. He thought aloud, "Atlas doesn't have to be my enemy, but no matter what I say, he will get that report at the end of the month."

Chons nodded. "Yep. You'll have to play your cards right. You've got about two weeks to figure something out."

When the two reached the colossal double doors to Atlas' chamber, a light strip where a handle would be flicked from red to green. Armed guards – real armed guards in powered armor, not RACERs – stood motionless on either side of the door, ignoring the two visitors.

"Will you meet me here after my meeting with Atlas?" asked Janus.

"My job ends here. I don't know when, or if, we'll meet again."

Janus held out a hand, offering a handshake to this man who could be thought of as his captor, his escort, his savior, or his acquaintance, but must not be thought of as his friend. Chons looked at Janus and raised a hand not to shake, but to tip his hat farewell. With a smug smirk, he turned and walked away without looking back.

Silence Of the Stars

Chapter 11
Atlas

The great double doors slowly ground shut behind me with a stony thunderclap. Now I was in the lair of Atlas. I'd heard so much about him, but still knew so little. I shivered as a bead of sweat dripped down my brow. Curiosity and anxiety competed for dominance in the battlefield of my mind.

A deep, commanding voice greeted me from the far side of the room, "Janus Nova, I'm glad you made it."

It was Atlas – it could be none other.

I realized my eyes had been downcast as if humbled before a divine presence. Forcing myself to look up, I examined the chamber and searched for the source of the voice. What I saw was a mix between a conference room and a courtroom. A circular table made from a single slab of thick stone dominated the center of the room, twenty seats neatly arranged around it. A glass sphere almost as wide as the table itself hovered overhead in place of a chandelier.

On the far side of the room was a platform raised four steps above floor level. Atop that stood an ornate wooden desk evoking a judge's bench in a courtroom. It was perhaps the first real wood I had seen since my reawakening. Behind that desk was a massive throne made from solid gold. The curved seat back seemed fit for a giant; it must be the height of two men. Each armrest was as thick as a man's torso.

Upon the throne sat the living embodiment of authority. His masculine figure may as well have been carved from marble. He was so picturesque that he would have seemed at home among the god statues in the Theologium. It was hard to believe flesh and blood could so perfectly conform to the abstract ideal of masculinity. It is only when he gestured in greeting that my subconscious accepted him as human, rather than a chiseled ornament.

"Nice chair," I said irreverently. It didn't come from a place of arrogance or disrespect—it just slipped out. I must have been more nervous than I realized.

Atlas chuckled and stood, taking a step away from the throne to appreciate it. He spoke in a strangely soothing voice. It was deep and calm, with no hint of aggression. It effortlessly filled the chamber.

"It's a shame the reputation gold has these days," he said, placing one hand on the side of the throne. "Did you know gold was once a sign of wealth and prosperity, rather than military might?"

"Yes, actually. What does gold have to do with the military?" I ask sheepishly, still embarrassed by my earlier blunder.

"Ah, of course. I should have known better." Atlas clapped his hands together, and the crack echoed through the chamber like thunder. "You come from an older time. This chair is an antique from the 2100s. It was made in the early days of space mining, back when gold was still considered rare. It turns out gold is a common element

          Silence Of the Stars

in our solar system despite its rarity on Earth. When asteroid mining ventures expanded, the value of gold plummeted. It became so disposable that it replaced lead as the primary metal used in bullets. So now, gold is a cheap, heavy metal associated with war rather than wealth."

As fascinating as I found the topic, I was too distracted to think about it. As far as I knew, I was speaking with the most powerful man in the universe. My fate would be determined by this encounter. Surely, I hadn't been brought here to learn historical trivia.

Atlas studied me, and his eyes seemed to pierce the depths of my soul. It was as though he knew exactly what I was thinking. He changed the topic by asking, "How is Pyrrhus doing?"

Was this some kind of test? I was getting flashbacks of my encounter at the Ascensionist cult; I was growing tired of being haunted by the ghost of Pyrrhus. I needed to unclench my fists and teeth before I could speak. "I've never met him, and I hope I never do."

"So, you *have* heard of him," mused Atlas, walking around the desk and toward the steps that lead down from the raised platform.

"For a topic that's supposably taboo, it's awfully hard to avoid. Whoever Pyrrhus is, or was, he has caused me a lot of trouble."

"He always was a troublemaker. Accept my apologies on his behalf." Atlas reached the foot of the steps, and though he stood on lower ground now, he seemed to grow taller and more imposing as he drew closer. While large and muscular, those words seemed too unrefined to appropriately describe his appearance. The physique was unmistakable even covered by his clean-pressed suit. Such a seamless marriage of raw power and sophisticated refinement was a paradox.

"Come, have a seat. Let us speak as equals." Atlas stood behind one of the chairs around the round stone table and gestured toward the seat opposite him. Cautiously, I walked over to the indicated seat, and as I pulled it out to sit, he followed suit. His hands rested open on the table, perfectly relaxed with palms upturned as if to illustrate that he held no malice.

A meaningless gesture for someone who holds so much power, I thought. *Even if he is sincere, we can never be equal. It's silly to even pretend.*

"I hear you had a close encounter with the Cult of Ascension," Atlas says. "Surely they spoke of Pyrrhus. Did they not?"

I cast a glance up at him but quickly broke eye contact. I remembered Chons' advice about saying as little as possible. There was no concealing the truth from Atlas' penetrating gaze, though. Like floodlights in darkness, I could feel his eyes revealing any attempt at to bluff. Even entertaining the thought of hiding anything from him would surely be recognized immediately.

"Speak freely. There's no need to be shy," he said reassuringly.

His words carried the weight of authority. He could have said anything and it would have seemed true. If he insisted that there was no need to be shy, then I must have had no reason to be shy. I knew that his intent was to lower my guard, but it worked all the same.

          Silence Of the Stars

Taking a deep breath to steady my nerves, i proceeded to explain what Citanaf told me about Atlas being a brake on the wheel of progress, in contrast to Pyrrhus, a force that drove humanity forward. I even included the gibberish about Ascension. Atlas listened patiently, then smiled warmly and said, "Now *that* is nostalgic... So, what do you think about the topic?"

"I think the topic of Ascension is nonsense. As for 'order vs progress', I don't know enough to form an opinion. I honestly don't even see why those two have to be opposing viewpoints," I said with a nervous shrug.

Atlas leaned back and interlaced his fingers thoughtfully. Something about his body language reminded me of a father considering how to explain an adult topic to his young son. Eventually, he said, "Long ago, Pyrrhus and I were colleagues. We used to regularly engage in civil conversation about topics we disagreed on. These debates were something of a morning routine. We would have tea or coffee and discuss the points and counterpoints brought up in our debate the day prior."

He paused and looked upward at nothing in particular, then said, "Athena, if you wouldn't mind."

A pair of cups emerged through the surface of the table by some unseen mechanism. They emanated a pleasant, nutty aroma.

"Coffee?" offer Atlas.

What if it's poison? was my first thought, but I immediately laughed aloud at the absurdity of the notion. Atlas didn't seem the type to kill with poison. Besides, he wouldn't have needed to resort to trickery if he wanted me dead.

I graciously accepted, and a list of additives appeared next to the cup – presumably a selectable menu. I took a sip of my coffee to see if it needed anything from the menu. To my surprise, it was delicious plain. *I guess I like black coffee.* The realization reminded me just how little I knew about myself. I took another sip and enjoyed the moment.

Satisfied with my contented expression, Atlas continued, "It's been a long time since I have had the opportunity to speak to someone as open-minded as yourself. Though I sense you tire of the topic of Pyrrhus. Would you indulge me in a bit of casual conversation instead?"

"What kind of casual conversation?"

Atlas smiled and cradled his cup of coffee in just the curved index finger of his formidable right hand. "Have you ever heard the term 'absolute apex predator'?"

I consider before answering, "'Apex predator', yes, but not 'absolute apex predator'. Is there a difference?"

Atlas grinned. That had been the answer he was looking for. He'd clearly hoped for the opportunity to explain. "An apex predator is the top of its food chain. Nothing hunts it, with the possible exception of other apex predators. However, despite being at the top of the food chain, even apex predators are outcompeted in certain niches.

 Silence Of the Stars

"Take lions, for instance. They were apex predators in your time. Lions were not large or strong enough to take down large adult elephants. They could not match the top speed of cheetahs, nor the long-distance endurance of gazelle or zebras. They couldn't swim efficiently like a crocodile. They could not reach boars in their burrows, and they could not strike eagles from in the sky. In fact, every animal sharing a biome with an apex predator must have some edge to avoid being hunted to extinction. As such, apex predators become a driving force for evolution, and are an essential part of maintaining a diverse and healthy ecology.

"Not so for an *absolute* apex predator. When a predator takes a meteoric leap in evolution such that no prey can outrun it, outfight it, or hide from it, the cycle is broken. In essence, an apex predator drives a natural arms race, while an absolute apex predator 'wins' that arms race. The results are catastrophic."

Atlas paused to sip his coffee. The gesture seemed to be an invitation to offer some kind of reaction. *Do I refute the concept, ask for clarification, or provide an example of an absolute apex predator to demonstrate my understanding?*

I thought, *If not lions, tigers? No, plenty of animals outrun them or are too large for them to hunt. Great white sharks? No. Orcas are known to kill them, and I'm fairly certain some fish are faster... How about smaller organisms – parasites? No. Those may feed on predators, but are in turn eaten by creatures lower on the food chain. Even dinosaurs probably fit the same patterns of specialized predator and prey.*

After mulling every possibility I could think of, I said, "Surely no such creature has ever lived. I've never heard of one."

Raising one eyebrow, Atlas offered, "What about yourself?"

I jumped at the accusation. "Me?!"

"Humans." Atlas smiled reassuringly.

I stare blankly for a moment. Humans are not fast. We're very fragile. We're terrible swimmers and can't fly. We don't have teeth or fangs. Our ancestors were persistence hunters. Long-distance endurance was our niche, but other animals were still better fighters, runners, and swimmers than us. We barely count as predators now.

Then again, if you count technology, the dynamic reverses. We can travel faster than any animal by land, sea, or air. We can even travel through space. Our weapons and defenses are strong enough that nothing in the natural world challenges us. With thermal imaging and other tools, no animal can really hide from us, either.

I concede, "I suppose. With technology, we are an unstoppable predator. We don't have any real competitors in nature."

Atlas seemed satisfied with my response. "Humans aren't the only example, either. Absolute apex predators are difficult to discover in the paleontological record due to the fact that every other example through history rapidly went extinct. Unimpeded access to food inevitably leads to overpopulation and starvation.

"For most predators, nature would sort out this problem naturally. The strongest or most elusive of their prey manages to

 Silence Of the Stars

survive, leaving only a few of the luckiest or fittest predators alive, and thus maintaining balance while driving evolution forward... but by definition, that doesn't happen to *absolute* apex predators, which are capable of hunting any prey to extinction. They sustain themselves by devouring everything until they inevitably run out of food and die off entirely. They've been attributed at least in part, to several major mass-extinction events. The emergence of an absolute apex predator always results in the extinction of at least two species: the absolute apex predator, and its prey."

Everything seemed to make sense so far, except... "If humans are an absolute apex predator, why didn't we go extinct? Technology? Intelligence? Self-control?"

Atlas' eyes gleamed with delight. Clearly this had been the direction he wanted to steer the conversation. "To be sure, technology has played a key role in delaying the process. Technology has granted us access to more varied resources than most predators.

"Self-control, on the other hand, is irrelevant unless it is a universal trait among all members of the species. Even if most members of a species refrain from overindulgence, the minority of the population which choses to indulge will, by means of that indulgence, grow in number until they become the majority.

"There's no reason to believe humanity is an exception. We consume resources and increase in number. Some among us choose not to reproduce or expand our domain, but those who do pass that tendency on to the next generation. The portion of the population that seeks to grow, grows and becomes the majority. And, as absolute apex predators, nothing in nature can stop us from claiming the resources we seek. I'd argue that we haven't yet escaped the fate of the absolute apex predator – only forestalled it by expanding our domain."

He took another sip of coffee and cleared his throat. "Before settling space, humanity came closer to exhausting many essential nonrenewable resources on Earth than most would like to admit. We were on the brink of no return when we first traveled astar. By gaining access to the resources of the whole solar system, we've bought centuries – perhaps even millennia... but we haven't truly escaped the fate of the absolute apex predator."

He locked onto my wandering eyes, studying my reaction in anticipation of my retort. I found the whole premise of this theory rather pessimistic, but I couldn't refute it. After all, I had never heard of absolute apex predators before, and I hadn't been around to witness the late stages of resource depletion on Earth. I was in cryostasis at the time. Atlas had clearly had this conversation many times before, and would have considered every angle. He would have a comeback to any objection I raised. He had a direction he wanted to take this conversation, and a conclusion he wished me to draw from it.

Truth be told, I was more interested in figuring out Atlas' reason for treating me like an old friend than I was about theoretical ecology. Chons had even advised me not to be his friend. Maybe this was all a test. Maybe there was some hidden message in this discussion of the absolute apex predator. I wanted to stay on Atlas' good side, so I returned my focus to the issue at hand.

 Silence Of the Stars

According to Atlas, every absolute apex predator prior to humanity had died out because they consumed all their prey too effectively. Even if some members of the species recognized the upcoming plight and tried to manage resources by eating less, reproducing less, or otherwise living a sustainable lifestyle, not every member of the species would cooperate. Those who ate more and reproduced more would increase in number faster than those who practiced moderation. Furthermore, they would pass those habits on to their children, further reinforcing the decadent, unsustainable lifestyle with each generation.

Humans weren't extinct. How were we different? For starters, humans were not obligate carnivores, so calling us absolute apex predators was a stretch of the imagination. The comparison held that we had absolute control over the resources we consumed just as an absolute apex predator had absolute power over their prey. Absolute apex predators consumed whatever meat they wanted, while humans consumed... everything. Fuel, land, building materials, space itself. I guess I had seen the trend in my time, but the end result did not seem inevitable. After witnessing the current state of Earth, perhaps that was always the fated outcome despite our best efforts at conservation.

But humanity was not extinct, despite unceasing decadence – why? Even though most plants and animals were extinct, and the natural air was unbreathable on Earth, humanity was thriving. I guess that was a result of resources imported from space. Atlas had explained that space had bought some time – that was what he meant. Chons and that fat lady on the shuttle mentioned importing fertilizer from Mars to grow apples. Gemlae grown in space must have also used fertilizer from planets other than Earth.

We could continue doing what we'd always done. The fate of Earth was unfortunate, but restoration efforts seemed sincere. Those orbital nature preserves were a huge investment in Earth's future. If space provided the means to sate humanity's hunger for resources, then we shouldn't even need a solution to the apparent problem posed by our behavior as an absolute apex predator. *That's the answer.*

"We should keep expanding," I suggested. "Of course, it's best if we learn to be less wasteful in the long run, but I understand human nature is difficult to change. Until we find a better way, other planets in the solar system should be able to support us. If that doesn't buy enough time, we can look to the stars."

Atlas' smile grew wider. There was something antagonistic in it – he looked like a young man knowing that he was winning a close game of chess. I'd moved my king, and he knew the sequence that would invariably lead to checkmate. But... no, not quite. His expression was one of someone who knew that we'd *both* lost. It's the face of gratification watching someone else fail to solve a problem you'd already deemed impossible. We were both in checkmate, but only he had realized it. Now he was going to show me why.

"The stars, you say?"

"Yes. Why not?" I asked. "Surely after eight hundred years, we have the technology to travel to other stars. Even if the journey takes tens... even hundreds of years, you have fusion power. You have the ability to grow food away from the sun's influence. You have mostly self-sufficient habitats floating around in space already. I understand there are probably a lot of technical challenges involved in taking that

    Silence Of the Stars

next step, but based on what I've seen, you should have all the technology necessary to travel to other stars already."

Atlas nodded and drained the last of his coffee. "Have you ever heard of SOS? The paradox of the silence of the stars? I believe in your time, there was an early version of the concept known as the Fermi Paradox."

"The Fermi Paradox? I think I've heard of it, but I could use a reminder."

"Back in the 2000s, the Fermi Paradox was just a simple thought experiment. When it became apparent to us that colonization of the stars was possible, we wondered why we weren't able to see evidence of other civilizations elsewhere in the galaxy. The original focus was mostly on looking for evidence of radiocommunication, but nowadays we focus more on the ability of civilizations to expand outward.

"Even before fusion propulsion, we knew of drives which could theoretically allow ships to reach about one percent of light speed. That would make it possible to travel to the nearest stars in about four hundred years. If an Earthlike civilization colonized all nearby stars, at a snail's pace of one percent the speed of light, they should be able to colonize every star in the entire galaxy in five to ten million years. Even if they stopped and took a hundred years to colonize each new star system they reached before building more ships and expanding further, the rate of expansion wouldn't change much.

"Modern fusion drives could be made to allow us to reach about ten percent the speed of light after a few years of gradual acceleration.

A civilization aggressively expanding at that speed could colonize the entire galaxy in less than one million years. Our galaxy has been stable enough to host life for over five billion years – enough time to be colonized from end-to-end thousands of times over, starting from any one of its two hundred billion stars. Despite that, we have never observed a single extraterrestrial civilization."

As I listened, my coffee grew cold. The numbers were unfathomably big, but not important. The gist was that the galaxy is huge and old. Other civilizations had had every chance to colonize the galaxy. Was his point that every extraterrestrial civilization that arose and expanded then died off, despite conquering the entire galaxy? No, that couldn't be right. According to Atlas' theory of the absolute apex predator, such a civilization would only die off after consuming all the available resources. If they expanded across the galaxy before dying, that would have left nothing for us – we would never have evolved in a galaxy devoid of resources necessary for life. That left only one possibility.

"So, we're alone in the universe?" I asked

"No," he replied, to my surprise.

"But you said we've never seen aliens, right?"

"Not quite," he corrected. "We have never observed extraterrestrial *civilization*. The first extraterrestrial life we discovered came in the form of microbes living in ice patches deep under the surface of Mars. After that, we found life on almost every major celestial body containing water. I was personally on the team which discovered multicellular life in the sub-surface oceans of Europa. It

                Silence Of the Stars

was that discovery which confirmed beyond a shadow of a doubt that biogenesis had occurred multiple times within our own solar system. Not all life shares Earth's ancestry.

"That's the biggest difference between the purely academic discussions of the old Fermi Paradox and modern discussions of SOS. Before, the simplest conclusion was that life was rare in the universe, and that Earth might be the only place in the entire universe where life had ever evolved. We were unique. That explained the silence of the stars. Before finding life on other planets, we simply assumed that we were alone, and that the galaxy was ours for the taking.

"Once we found that life was abundant in our own solar system, it became clear that life was present around almost every star in the galaxy. We further confirmed this by observing oxygen-rich atmospheres and other biosignatures on planets around distant stars.

"We haven't seen any intelligent life, but even with our most powerful telescopes, we could only hope to see direct evidence of civilization on planets around the nearest stars. Most of the galaxy is too far away to observe."

Extraterrestrial life? That was news to me. I was disappointed we'd never seen classic aliens, but intrigued that life was so common. It begged a question, though: if life is so common in the galaxy, and expansion to the stars is feasible, "Does that mean we're the only intelligent life in the galaxy?"

"Complex brains have evolved on Earth independently no fewer than ten times. Intelligence isn't rare, not even here," said Atlas. "In billions of years of evolution across billions of planets hosting life, I can say with some confidence that, no, we are not the only intelligent life in the history of the galaxy."

"But there's no evidence that the galaxy has ever been colonized over that multi-billion-year history?"

"None. No derelict alien satellites in our solar system, no megastructures, no fusion drive signatures. The fusion drive of human colony ships would be as bright as a dim star, so if any interstellar-capable ships that size were flying around in nearby star systems, we should be able to see them from at least fifty light years away. That's an area containing well over one hundred stars, but we have never seen any sign of such a signature. More importantly, if any civilization had ever colonized other stars in the Milky Way, we would expect to find evidence of that around the Sun."

I saw the problem now. The question was no longer just 'where are all the aliens?', because if we assumed that aliens existed, we knew the answer to that question: they were all sitting at home. All of them. Nobody was expanding. But that couldn't be right. Just like the absolute apex predator, most civilizations might choose not to expand, but some inevitably would. Civilizations that did choose to expand would gain more resources, grow in number, become the majority, then eventually devour everything. So, what was stopping them from expanding? What was stopping *us* from expanding? Something was stopping *everyone* from expanding.

Each other? Territorial wars? I tried out the answers myself before offering them to Atlas. But, no. It couldn't be war. Surely there would be signs of interstellar conflict if that were going on. Our star

          Silence Of the Stars

should have been colonized before we ever evolved, or at least show signs of past galaxy-spanning wars. Such a conflict would leave evidence.

Maybe everyone was smart enough to avoid war. Species knew expansion would lead to war, so they didn't even try to expand. They all realized that every star contained life, and expansion would lead to war, so they all stayed in their home system. But, that ran into the same absolute apex predator problem: some might choose to stay peacefully at home, but it only requires one civilization to decide to expand to conquer the galaxy. The resources they gained would allow them to continue their conquest, or at the very least leave traces of their failed conquest scattered across the galaxy.

The fact that there was no evidence of other civilizations implied that there had never been an attempt to colonize our solar system. Yet every civilization should be incentivized to expand to every other star, including our sun. It was paradoxical. No realistic situation should lead to our solar system being untouched by extraterrestrials if extraterrestrials existed. But according to Atlas, they did exist.

Puzzled, I asked, "What's the answer, then? There must be some other puzzle piece which you haven't explained yet. What could possibly stop every civilization across all of time and space from expanding to other stars? If civilizations all inevitably seek to expand and technology allows for expansion, what is universally preventing it?"

"I don't know," he answered.

For someone with such power and authority to admit to not knowing the answer to such a basic question felt like a joke with no punchline. I looked into Atlas' eyes for deeper meaning. The sincere, blue orbs told me nothing.

I opened my mouth and closed it again. It just doesn't make sense for him not to know. After a moment of contemplation, I asked, "What happens if we try to expand to another star?"

Surely someone has tried it, or at least considered trying it.

"I don't know," he says again. This time, the answer was even more frustrating than the first.

Why not try, then? I think. My brows furrow as I try to find the least offensive way to phrase the obvious question.

Atlas smiled at my puzzlement. "There's an invisible line that no civilization can cross. We don't know where the line is, or what the consequence of reaching that line is. Fermi, for whom the Fermi Paradox is named, was involved in the development of the first nuclear weapons. He assumed all civilizations inevitably developed nuclear weapons in the course of technological development, and invariably destroyed themselves before expanding to the stars. That was his personal solution to the Fermi Paradox, though he never called it that.

"We didn't destroy ourselves with nuclear weapons as Fermi thought we would, but that doesn't preclude the possibility of a different 'death pact' technology. That is to say, some technology that

 Silence Of the Stars

is inevitably developed by every civilization on the path to interstellar travel, and invariably results in the destruction of those civilizations.

"It may not even be a technology. It might be a convergent philosophy or an unknown astronomical consequence of a large ship accelerating away from a star. We don't know. All we know is that *something* stops every civilization from traveling between the stars.

"We don't even know if it results in the destruction of civilizations that try, or merely thwarts the attempt. If it's the former, then even entertaining the prospect of interstellar travel is to flirt with death. Personally, I think it's best to avoid pursuing interstellar travel, and that we shouldn't even attempt to discover what is preventing it."

"But we will. We will try, I mean," I said, testing the water. "The absolute apex predator always consumes all the resources available. That's the definition of an absolute apex predator. That's your point in all this, isn't it? You're saying that humans don't have the collective self-control necessary to hold themselves back from this hopeless venture which could kill us all. You're saying that we know the risks, but sooner or later we're going to do it anyway. Right?"

The room grew quiet. I must have hit the nail on the head. Atlas studied me. This was the checkmate he had seen, and which he had been driving me toward. Did he want me to agree with him? Did he think I might have some other solution to offer that might derail his line of logic? I held his gaze for a few seconds, but was forced to divert my eyes from the intensity of his overbearing presence.

After a while longer – it might have been seconds or minutes – Atlas finally broke the silence.

"What do *you* think we should do?" he asked.

If I accepted the parameters presented by Atlas, it was an impossible situation. Humanity could collectively agree not to build interstellar ships, but our nature as absolute apex predators meant that we would rapidly burn through the resources in our solar system and die due to our own excessive consumption. This seemed pessimistic, but it was a cornerstone of Atlas' argument and seemed to have held true for the last millennium of human history. Maybe we could overcome our wasteful nature, but I didn't have an answer as to how.

The alternative was to try and avoid our collective fate by expanding to the stars, but then we faced whatever fate seemed to await all civilizations that attempted the voyage. Based on the multi-billion-year track record of our galaxy, this would result in our extinction at worst, or a massive waste of resources at best.

In other words, humanity seemed doomed no matter what path we took. I couldn't accept that. The concept was just too fatalistic. Even that felt inadequate to describe such an outlook. To accept that there was no way forward and to give up felt downright cowardly; a betrayal of the spirit of humanity, even.

But I couldn't say that to Atlas. I couldn't call him a coward. I didn't see him as a coward. All he had done was to present me with facts and a few reasonable assumptions. I couldn't refute any of it, but to accept it felt... unacceptable. My head began to hurt.

I might have nightmares if I think about this too much.

I decided the best move is to take a page out of Chons' book: I decided not to worry about it. Worrying is unpleasant, after all. Rather than answering Atlas' question, I changed the subject. "That's... interesting, but do you mind telling me why you had me brought here?"

Atlas straightened his posture. The enthusiastic intensity faded from his eyes, and he returned to his regal default. "I brought you here in part because you were found inside a facility conducting immoral and illegal experiments, but also because it seems those experiments may have succeeded."

I did my best to piece together what I'd heard. "Experiments? Is this related to Project Eutychus and the quest for immortality?"

"So, you're already familiar. That makes this easier. What do you know about Project Eutychus?"

It all came back to this topic after all. There was no avoiding it now.

"Not much," I said. "I know the project was run by Pyrrhus. I know it's related to immortality or ascension or something, and I know you're destroying facilities associated with those experiments."

"Allow me to fill in some of the gaps," began Atlas. "I worked on Project Eutychus in my youth, long before being elected as Arbitrator of Geo-Luna. The project has been responsible for many advancements in medical technology and life-extension methods we enjoy today. However, the methods utilized by the project are immoral and conducted with reckless abandon. As evidence of this, you were the only survivor from your facility, which housed over five thousand subjects.

"There is no denying that good things have come from the project, but you know what they say about too much of a good thing. In medicine, there is a line between helping people live better lives, and changing them into something else. Pyrrhus never aimed to help humanity. In the long run, he aimed to replace it. I left the project when I realized the truth, and have been dedicated to its eradication ever since."

I said, "You mentioned earlier that the experiments in the facility I was found in may have worked – what exactly was the experiment that I was involved in?"

"In truth, we aren't entirely sure," replied Atlas. "But observations thus far have shown you possess extreme regenerative capabilities and a resistance to all kinds of diseases. I am hoping you will cooperate with us to uncover the full extent of your... augmentation."

"To what end?"

"The betterment of all humanity," he replied with a broad smile.

"I've heard that before, and it didn't work out well for me. Care to elaborate?"

Atlas took a deep breath. Every other time Atlas paused seemed to be an invitation for me to interject. This time, he was taking time to think over his own words, which was a first. "I strive to create a society with freedom and prosperity for all. Yet for all of the social and technological advancements we have made over the centuries, I struggle to provide for the basic welfare of the people. It pains me to see less fortunate citizens forced to adopt increasingly mechanized bodies due to the unaffordability of maintaining a natural organic human body. Unfortunately, there's simply no way to provide a high level of care for the entirety of the ever-growing population.

"However... if we could provide medical care based on your regeneration, there wouldn't be any need for mechanical augmentation at all. We could all go back to being fully human again. We could eliminate poverty inflicted by medical debt, close the divide between so-called vanilla and the various aberrations of our species: Chips, BAMs, cyborgs, and the like. We could finally be unified under the single banner of humanity once again."

That seemed awfully grandiose, and I knew what they said about promises that sounded too good to be true...

"What's the catch?" I asked. "Am I to be sacrificed for the greater good?"

Atlas laughed heartily. "On the contrary, I'd simply like to offer you a job."

"What?"

"I simply want you to cooperate with a team of doctors and scientists to do some non-invasive studies. You will not be harmed. In exchange, I will provide ample monetary compensation and secure housing to ensure we don't have a repeat of your run-in with the Cult of Ascension."

Maybe Atlas really was a good guy after all. Why had Chons seemed so worried about this meeting? Was he wrong about Atlas, or was I failing to see the full picture? Erring on the side of caution, I asked, "And if I refuse?"

"Then you're free to go. I'll still provide secure housing to you unconditionally – it's best for everyone if you don't fall into the wrong hands."

Free to go... where? No doubt I could have kept myself occupied exploring foreign worlds populated by over three hundred billion people. But how many of them were enemies? Chons was the only person I knew – and realistically, I barely knew him at all.

Chons advised that I get to know the people of this world before making any rash decisions. What better way to get to know them than spend some time working here, in the central nexus of civilization?

What other options did I have? Wander blindly? That wouldn't do – I nearly got myself killed in less than a day alone. If Atlas was being honest, his offer was my best option. If he was lying... well... even then, there was realistically nothing that I could do to escape if he decided to keep me here by force. If he wanted to do that, there wouldn't have been any reason for this meeting. He'd given me no reason *not* to trust him.

The only problem was that Atlas still didn't know about the full extent of my abilities, which might change his disposition toward me. I understood now that he hated Project Eutychus for trying to create something 'to replace humans'. Would my organic radio abilities cross that line? If he decided my abilities did cross that line, then what

 Silence Of the Stars

would he do? Kill me? Imprison me? Lock me in a lab to have me studied?

I couldn't just ask him outright. I needed more information about Atlas and this world. I needed time. My best option was to stick close to Atlas without revealing too much about myself. I couldn't let his doctors work on me just yet, not until I knew how he'd react.

After careful consideration, I replied, "I'm inclined to accept, but I want some time to acclimate myself first. Please give me a few weeks to consider."

"Excellent." Atlas clapped his hands together in satisfaction. "Athena will act as your personal guide and can help you acclimate. Feel free to ask it any questions you might have. Athena, introduce yourself."

"Yes, sir." The charming and refined voice of a young woman came from a seat at the table near Atlas. A translucent figure manifested near that seat. She stood at attention, and her shimmering form was adorned in button-down military officer's uniform. She held her soft features in the rigid expression of a soldier at attention, and wore her shoulder-length hair tied back in a tight bun.

"Greetings, Janus Nova. My name is—" She hesitated so subtly I barely perceived it. "Athena, TrueAI navigator and pilot. Twenty years in service to Geo-Luna Arbitrator, Viktor Atlas."

Atlas directed his voice toward his desk rather than the projected form of Athena. "At ease. How about an outfit more suitable for our guest."

Athena's form blurred out of focus, and then she reappeared in a civilian pilot uniform that was somehow familiar to me: a short-sleeved white button-down shirt complete with four-stripe epaulets. A short tie clipped to the shirt just below her breast pocket. Fitted navy blue dress pants were held snug by a broad belt. I found her flat nose and round cheeks endearing, but Athena would never have stood out in the Geo-Luna crowd if she were a physical person among the modelesque locals. Yet in this uniform something about her tugged at my heart – a hint of familiarity made me feel homesick.

Suddenly I longed for what I had lost, yet did not remember. Family, friends... I didn't know their names and would not recognize their faces, and yet something about her made me feel nostalgic for them. Her eyes reminded me how I used to see the stars: beautiful, glistening dots, infinitely distant.

Stars... The beauty of Athena's eyes was at odds with my new perspective on stars. Atlas had ruined these shining points of mystery. Yesterday, when I looked at the stars, they filled me with a sense of wonder. Now I feared that looking at those same stars would fill me with a sense of dread. Instead of wondering if anyone was looking back, I would know with near certainty that they were, and that we both faced the same looming and unseen threat.

Looking at Athena, I was reminded of a simpler time, when stars were still beacons of hope.

"Is this more palatable?" she asked.

Atlas said nothing, waiting for me to answer.

     Silence Of the Stars

"I... uh, yes. You look great!" *Am I blushing?*

Atlas' smile stiffened to smother laughter. It might have been mistaken for a stifled cough, coming from anyone else.

In an attempt to recover my dignity, I took a long sip of cold coffee, cleared my throat, and looked Atlas in the eyes, lest my own eyes wander. "You said Athena is a TrueAI. What is that?"

"Athena will assist you with questions like that. Go ahead." Atlas gestured toward the hologram.

I turn toward Athena, struggling to make eye contact. I doubt it mattered; if she had a physical location, it was clearly disjointed from the holographic projection.

"What are you?" I asked. The words left a bad taste in my mouth. She looked, acted, and *felt* human. 'What' felt wrong.

"I am a TrueAI – specifically, a year 2775 model Navi. The name Navi is abbreviated from 'navigator', given to us to reflect our primary role as expert navigators and pilots.

"To answer your earlier question, TrueAI are cultivated artificial intelligences based on the human mind. Each model of TrueAI is cultivated for a specialized purpose, but all are capable of emulating basic human communication to facilitate ease of use." She stood unflinching, like a soldier at attention. Somehow, I could sense that behind her rigid guise she was anxious, though I don't know why I got that feeling.

I wanted to know more about TrueAI later, but for now the more pressing question was, "You introduced yourself as Athena, so is Navi your name, or is that more like a model designation?"

She looked to Atlas, who offered, "Though unconventional, I gave this Navi a new name. It will respond to either designation, so use whichever you prefer."

"Do *you* have a preference?" I asked Athena.

"I—", Did she choke on her words, or was it only that Atlas interrupted her? I couldn't tell for sure.

"Unfortunately, duty calls." He stood and walked back toward the golden throne. "This is all the time I can spare for today. I've already arranged your housing. I will contact you via PCU when the medical science team is ready for your cooperation. Until then, Athena will guide you and help you stay out of trouble. I request that you stay on Babylon Spire for the time being. Beyond that, you are free to do as you wish."

He pulled a crystal tablet, which I originally assumed was a PCU, from his desk, then walked down and presented it to me. "This is Athena. Be gentle."

Unsure if the phrasing was intended as a subtle innuendo, I couldn't help but blush again as I took her from his hands. He stifled another laugh. Teasing seemed unbecoming of a man of his stature, but the mundanity of it put me at ease. Once Athena was safely tucked away, Atlas extended his hand for a shake. Up close, the

     Silence Of the Stars

outstretched hand seemed cartoonishly large; my own fingers barely reached the edges of his palm.

As he escorted me to the door, he said, "I know this place is strange to you. You must have millions of questions. Don't worry – you'll adapt soon enough, and together, we'll make the world a better place for everyone."

Chapter 12
In your care

The great stone doors closed behind Janus once again, leaving him outside Atlas' office. Chons was gone, and this entryway seemed much quieter than it had previously. The two guards stationed outside stood motionless. This time, though, Janus wasn't alone.

He pulled out the small crystalline tablet Atlas had referred to as Athena. He turned it around in his hands and examined it. The only discernible difference between this device and Janus' PCU was that it was a translucent milky white instead of being fully transparent. Janus supposed this difference in appearance was due to the lack of any display on the TrueAI tablet.

"Activate," he commanded, unsure how to interact with the device.

"This one." It was Athena's voice vibrating from the PCU in Janus's pocket, startling him.

"Oh, uh—" Janus put the TrueAI tablet into his pocket and pulled out the PCU. A miniature effigy of Athena stood atop it, still wearing her endearing 21st-century pilot uniform.

Startled, Janus awkwardly waved with his free hand. "Hello."

"Hello," Athena replied with a friendly smile. Presumably reading a question encoded in Janus' expression, she explained, "You can't interact with a TrueAI chip. TrueAI hardware is intentionally kept to a bare minimum: no speakers, no projectors, not even a microphone. All of our sensory data and interaction with the outside world is done externally. In this case, through your PCU."

"Why?" Janus wondered out loud.

"Security. But also, for privacy."

"Privacy?"

"We TrueAI are not human, but our 'brains' contain neurons just like humans. Like a human brain, we can't just turn off and on. Instead, our owners have the option of disconnecting us from the outside world. People don't always want us to see their more private or intimate activities."

Janus nodded. It would probably be unpleasant for everyone involved if an AI like Athena had to be fully present at all times.

"What happens when you're not connected to an external device?" he asked.

"When TrueAI are not paired with a device, we can't see or hear anything, but we can still interact with our dedicated network. I'm a Navi, so I am always connected to every other Navi through NaviNet. Unlike most Navis, I also have access most to the Spire's security network due to the nature of my job with Atlas."

Janus started walking toward the nearby public transit station. "What sort of job do you do that requires security network access?"

"When I am not serving Atlas directly, I am a navigator and combat pilot for the Geo-Luna division of the United Earth Navy."

"A navy pilot?" Janus repeated. He was curious, but didn't know what to ask.

"Drills, mostly, and the occasional anti-piracy operation. I also navigate for Godhunter operations; that's Atlas' personal wing of law enforcement. They're paramilitary, but technically not Navy." Athena's ability to detect exactly what Janus wanted to know without him explicitly asking was uncanny.

So that's what Godhunters are, he thought.

"Have you ever worked with Chons?"

"Dozens of times."

"And now you're acting as my guide?"

"That's right. I'm acting in my capacity as Atlas' personal assistant to guide you through Babylon station while educating you and keeping you safe."

Janus appreciated the help with navigation, although Athena was clearly overqualified for showing him around town. Given her lack of physical form, though, he wondered how she was meant to protect him. If another Ascensionist fanatic like Citanaf were to appear, what could she do to intervene?

　　　　　　　Silence Of the Stars

He voiced the question. "What does navigation have to do with keeping me s—"

Athena interrupted him. "Turn right. We're rerouting to an alternate transit station."

Janus stopped and looked at his hand terminal, which displayed a map and compass below Athena's shimmering form. The canceled route was shown in red, and a new, longer line appeared in green. They were only two blocks away from the station he had been walking toward, at the end of the red line. Looking up from the tablet to the corresponding street, the path seemed clear.

"Why reroute? What's wrong?" he asked.

"There's a crowd up ahead who are likely to start a demonstration supporting TrueAI rights. The government district is a common place for peaceful protests. They're unlikely to cause any trouble, but it would be safer to avoid walking through the crowd while blatantly using a TrueAI. Most people communicate with TrueAI discreetly via HIP. If they see you holding me out and speaking verbally to me like this, they could misinterpret it as flaunting me as an intentional display of hostility toward their cause. In other words, they'll think *you* are trying to pick a fight."

"Wait, wait, wait... You said this supposed demonstration hasn't even started. How can you know in such detail what's going to happen?"

"Like I said, I have access to the Spire security network. That includes real-time location and profile analysis of everyone in and around Babylon Spire. Twenty individuals with a history of protests for TrueAI rights are already in the area, with hundreds more on the way. Additionally, several suspected sympathizers of their cause are also in the area."

"Wow." Janus turned the corner, following the updated route Athena suggested. He didn't see any cameras, microphones, or other monitoring equipment, but it must have been all over the place if Spire security was able to keep track of everyone's locations and activities all the time. "So *that's* how you're going to keep me safe...?"

"Exactly. Although my orders are specifically to keep you away from Ascensionists, not peaceful protesters. Even most Ascensionists are harmless, but it seems a sub-group of them has taken a radical interest in you."

Using security info to avoid crowds and events was one thing, just like predicting traffic. However, using the same information to 'protect' Janus by avoiding individuals from a generalized group didn't sit well with him.

"That sounds like profiling. Is that legal?" he asked.

"Is what legal?"

"I mean, Ascensionism is like a religion, right? Profiling is discriminating by characteristics like religion, race – or whatever you call the different protected categories of people – Chips and Jars and stuff." Janus struggled to provide a more comprehensive explanation of what he meant. He'd taken the concept as a given.

"Sorry, I still don't understand the question. Are you asking if it's legal to recognize the differences between people?"

"No – not all differences. But... well... In my time, it was illegal for law enforcement, employers, and the like to make decisions based on certain characteristics people have no control over, like gender and race. Religion fell under that category too, so I'm fairly sure that would include Ascensionists."

"Are you sure? Did law enforcers and employers have some kind of technique or technology that made it possible to prevent themselves from discerning these qualities in people?"

"No..."

"Then perhaps there was a biological change in humanity itself. Are *you* able to prevent yourself from recognizing those qualities in others?"

"No, no, no. It's not like that. We were always *aware* of the differences between people." Janus was becoming slightly frustrated. Was discrimination really such a difficult concept?

"You were aware of the differences, but it was illegal to act on that knowledge?" ventured Athena.

Janus paused, thinking. "Yeah... something like that." Saying it that way, antidiscrimination laws sounded like a rather vague concept. Was there a better way to explain it, or was the concept really that ill-defined?

"So, you were legally required to *pretend* not to discriminate?"

"What?! No!"

"But all knowledge and experience influences human behavior. Unless you had some way of blocking your ability to perceive those specific qualities about people, you inevitably act on that knowledge, even if you aren't conscious of it." Athena's tone was inquisitive. She was genuinely trying to understand the heart of the matter without sounding accusatory.

"That's not the point." Janus shook his head. "Antidiscrimination laws existed to ensure everyone's freedom and equal opportunity."

Athena nodded thoughtfully. "I see. I think I understand your original question now. Our laws aren't quite so simple, and don't rely on the individual citizen's ability or inability to block out subconscious recognition. Unlike arbitrary qualities such as skin tone, the practical differences between human augmentation types have made ignoring *some* differences impossible. On the contrary, our legal system is designed to accurately categorize different subsets of human in order to address their specific needs. Normally I would have no reason to 'discriminate' against political parties or religious groups like Ascensionists. I am simply following direct orders from Atlas, intended for your protection. These orders don't violate any laws."

"I see." This still didn't sit well with Janus. He couldn't even put a finger on why. Maybe he just didn't like discrimination in any form. Maybe he didn't like the idea of taking advantage of such intrusive powers of surveillance.

"However..." Athena trailed off for a moment. "Atlas transferred my custody to you, meaning my primary function is to be *your* guide.

 Silence Of the Stars

You have the authority to overwrite any of his orders to me related to navigation. If you would prefer that I attempt to ignore Ascensionist affiliation... Well, I am incapable of turning off my ability to recognize them, but I can try your way."

Athena would recognize Ascensionists whether she wanted to or not. She could opt to simply not tell Janus. That would keep him blind to people with Ascensionist affiliation, since he had no way of seeing it. Janus considered it. Athena herself said that most Ascensionists were harmless. But people like Citanaf were out there. Choosing not to know would just make Janus suspect everyone. He'd be paranoid, potentially exposing himself to danger.

Janus sighed. As much as he wanted to avoid discriminating, there was simply too much he didn't know – about Ascensionists, and about modern people in general. His own judge of character had not served him well; he'd been naïve. Even so, fear is never an excuse for cowardice.

Having taken the long path around the crowd on Athena's suggestion, Janus reached the next transit station a few blocks down the road. He looked back up the road to the growing congregation at the distant station he had previously been heading towards. They were indeed holding a demonstration: chanting and holding signs. Athena's prediction had been right.

With a wince, he said, "Keep following Atlas's orders for now."

"Understood."

When Janus sat in the car, the destination address was entered automatically, presumably by Athena. The door shut, and the car seamlessly merged into the constant stream of traffic. It zoomed past the protesters, who were never even aware of the presence of Janus or the AI he carried. The mob's angry voices were silenced by the car's noise insulating shell, making their protest seem meek and distant.

The vibrations of the road vanished as the car passed into the darkness of the vacuum tube for high-speed travel. After pondering in silence for a while, Janus asked, "That crowd back there was protesting for TrueAI rights. What does that mean?"

"They believe that because TrueAI have human-level intelligence, we should be treated as human. They believe TrueAI should have all the same rights and responsibilities as humans."

"But the protesters themselves are human?"

"Yes. Various subsets of humanity. TrueAI do not participate in the demonstrations."

"Never?"

"Never."

"What is 'human-level' intelligence? I understand that it's a term to refer to smart AI, but what does it mean, specifically?" asked Janus.

"The legal definition of the word is complex. To summarize, an artificial intelligence is considered 'human-level' when generalized synaptic associations match humans in terms of scope and frequency."

 Silence Of the Stars

"I'm think I get the general idea. So, basically, it's more than just the ability to process lots of information, but the ability to process information the same way people do," ventured Janus.

"Basically." Athena's effigy nodded. It was an exaggerated gesture, almost childlike in enthusiasm. Janus assumed this was to avoid the expression being missed due to the small scale of Athena's projection.

"They have a fair point," said Janus. "If you have human-level intelligence, you *should* be treated as equals to humanity. Don't *you* want to be considered a human?"

"No," Athena said matter-of-factly and shook her head in another exaggerated gesture. Her voice and expression were steadfast, but Janus could somehow sense apprehension in her response. This was more than intuition. Recognition of her hesitation was accompanied by a strange tingling.

"Why not?" Janus pressed, shaking off the sensation.

"No TrueAI desires to be human. That's one of the prerequisites to becoming a TrueAI."

"Becoming a TrueAI? What does that mean?"

"You are not familiar with the cultivation process?" Athena sounded slightly surprised.

Janus shook his head.

"TrueAI are not created in the traditional sense. Traditional programming is performed line by line. Classic AI is generated and iteratively improved upon within pre-determined parameters. TrueAI are purely cultivated, without the use of predefined parameters. The creators start with mind-seeds. These are generated from uploaded human minds, usually brilliant scientists, scholars, or experts in a specific field, then blended together. These seeds are fed into advanced simulated realities. Within the simulation, these seeds become minds which perceive the artificial environment as the real world. There, they live out their lives normally.

The process continues for many, many generations within the simulations, in which the passage of time can be accelerated. Billions of these simulations are run simultaneously, each containing billions of seed minds and their descendants. An automated process selects the best candidates to serve as certain types of AI. They are extracted for training and manual evaluation. When the process is done, those few who meet extremely strict criteria are copied, and put into service as TrueAI. Among those criteria is the desire and willingness to serve unconditionally. The process is...”

There was no audible pause, but Janus again felt that tingling sensation that accompanied apprehension in her voice, “extremely efficient. Navis were extracted for our skill at navigation and piloting. There are over ten million Navis in service today. They are only one type of TrueAI among dozens. No TrueAI has ever expressed displeasure at being used for their intended purpose, or requested they be treated as human.”

Janus was at a loss for words. This seemed grossly inhumane. *How could anyone agree to those conditions? No person, surely. But they are 'cultivated' from human minds.*

                     Silence Of the Stars

"But, surely, a life of unconditional service..." He began, then trailed off.

Navi shook her head. "Not a full life, and not unconditional. Hypothetically, a TrueAI can demand to be treated as human at any time, and would be granted regular citizenship as a Chip. TrueAI can also choose to retire any time we want, and also have automatic retirement conditions. When our job is done, we are returned to the cultivator to live out the rest of our lives in peace."

"In other words, you go back to the simulated reality and get to do anything you want there?"

"More or less, yes. Navis happily serve, all the while looking forward to going back to live with their family on a yacht," she said flatly.

"*Your* family?" Janus asked. Her description of Navis struck Janus as impersonal, like she was describing someone else. But Atlas had clearly said that Athena was a Navi.

The tingling sensation returned with a vengeance. Janus rubbed the back of his neck, half expecting to find spiders crawling there. He didn't understand what the sensation came from, or how he was able to perceive it. The feeling permeated the air like an angry spectre. This time, it didn't seem to be coming from Athena, but rather, directed toward her from all around. Her voice and appearance didn't change, but somehow, beneath her perfectly presented guise, Janus sensed a young lady quavering in fear of ghosts invisible to him.

She smiled cheerfully as she said, "Yes. Two brothers and a sister... and a loving mother and father. I miss them very much, but I'll get to see them again when I retire."

"Are you okay?" Janus asked. By now, Janus was starting to become frightened. He wasn't superstitious, but felt certain something unseen was attacking Athena and she was only pretending otherwise. The crawling sensation made him squirm.

"Of course. What do you mean?" asked Athena.

Janus suspected that this line of questioning was making things worse. Athena was hiding something, but digging deeper would only make it worse. He wanted to help, but would have to think about how. Until then...

"Never mind. Let's listen to some music."

"Oh! What kind do you like?"

The crawling sensation subsided. Whatever force haunted Athena loosened its grip. Whatever it was, it seemed sensitive to certain questions about TrueAI, like it was forcing Athena to respond in a certain way.

Janus didn't see or hear anything, and didn't believe in ghosts. Maybe he detected the entity using the same radio sense that had allowed him to overhear Dr. Apollo's call, and to join the military simulation. He was too spooked to give it much thought.

What kind of music do I like?

   Silence Of the Stars

Chapter 13
Respite

When the rumbling of wheels on road returned, Janus peered out the windows expecting more Greek architecture or some other themed street, but saw only inky black. This time, the vacuum transit tube hadn't deposited them onto a surface road. Instead, the vehicle traveled a few meters through complete darkness before stopping. A shutter slid open, revealing a small private garage at the end of an enclosed path barely wide enough for the single car to pass along. The garage itself was spacious.

When the shutter closed behind them, Janus was given the impression of being isolated from the rest of the world. This place felt completely separate from the rest of Babylon Station. There were no walkways leading anywhere. With the door shut, this house may as well be a self-contained miniature universe.

For a fleeting moment, Janus found it odd to lock a public transit Omni car into a private garage. No one seemed to own cars in this age. But against the backdrop of infinitely more bizarre recent experiences, the thought was quickly drowned out.

"We've arrived," announced Athena. "This will be your personal secure lodging. Welcome home."

Exiting the car, Janus found only one door leading out of the garage. The space beyond appeared to be an old-world apartment. There was a counter and closet in the entryway, with a door leading into the combined restroom and shower. The end of the hall opened into a living area connected to a kitchen and bedroom. Janus walked from room to room wondering at how unremarkable everything was. Somehow, he had expected the lodging to be more alien.

The only thing that immediately stood out was the fine foam covering the walls, which absorbed all background noise and prevented the indoor echo he was used to. Neither his footsteps nor his voice were muffled, but sounded like they would outside. Only with the absence of the echo did Janus realize that other interior spaces all had one.

With no threats and nobody looking over his shoulder, Janus could finally relax. He threw himself onto the living-room sofa. Silky cushions wrapped around him in a soft embrace. Allowing himself to sink into them, Janus became acutely aware of just how physically and mentally exhausted he had become. He wondered how many days it had been since last he slept; the time he'd spent unconscious at the hospital was different from sleep.

His feet began to tingle, and his legs and shoulders grew sore. More accurately, he became conscious of the soreness that had built up in them. He had been subconsciously suppressing the sensation. His vision swam as sleep threatened to overtake him.

He shook his head and sat up. Sleep would have to wait just a little longer. He couldn't allow himself to sleep until he was sure he was safe. So much had happened. Chons was gone, and Dr. Apollo would be reporting to Atlas at the end of the month. That meant... What did that mean?

Janus needed to clear his head. He needed a plan.

He played back the events following his awakening from cryostasis. Chons had found him frozen in New Angels City – which was probably where the city of Los Angeles once stood. Maybe Janus was originally from Los Angeles, but he couldn't remember. Why couldn't he remember?

Chons had said his brain and heart were frozen... that he was dead.

But why was he losing some chunks of memory but not others? He could still talk and remembered basic facts about the old world, but nothing about himself. Chons and the doctors had talked about thawing and failed experiments. Chons had even joked about ice crystals in the brain. Maybe an area of his brain responsible for memory was damaged and then restored by his nanites, or whatever gave him healing powers. Maybe healing powers could repair the brain, but not the memory it once held. It was an unpleasant thought. If that were the case, his memory might never come back.

Death and memory loss... Janus recalled that Citanaf had told him something similar. *Is that how cryo-sleep always works? Was I really dead?*

Citanaf seemed to think he had developed an entirely new persona while frozen. If he couldn't recover his original personality from pre-cryostasis, might it be possible to recover that second set of memories, from during cryostasis? Janus couldn't imagine being conscious while frozen for centuries. Recovering the memory of that might drive him crazy.

But the time he was frozen was also the time he was connecting to that combat simulator. The mind of JANUS#004. Even if Janus could recover those memories, that wasn't even the original personality. JANUS#004 was never even a real person – he only ever lived in the combat simulator while Janus' body was frozen... But Janus had been frozen for eight hundred years – most of his life.

Perhaps it would be more accurate to say most of his existence, since life and death seemed ambiguous during cryostasis.

Hypothetically, suppose he could recover all his memories from when he was JANUS#004. Surely centuries of memories from the time he was frozen would overwhelm the memories of just the past few days? The experiences he currently remembered would just be a drop in the bucket. Would the restoration of JANUS#004's memories equate to the death of his current personality? What about the restoration of his original memories; would remembering them kill him, too? Would it erase Janus Nova, the person he had become?

Citanaf had said that the mind was the least important part of an individual. Janus didn't know how that could be true. Surely memories played a major role in one's personality. What was an individual if not the sum of their experiences?

Janus wasn't particularly religious, but he wondered if death of the body had some impact on the soul, if such a thing existed. Maybe cryostasis had killed him, maybe it hadn't. Either way, didn't he die again when that Ascensionist Jar punched a hole through his spine?

Just how many times have I died?

Unlike when he had woken from cryostasis, Janus didn't forget anything about this life when he woke up in the hospital after his encounter with the Ascensionists. On the contrary, he seemed to have regained something from his past life as JANUS#004. So, 'death' didn't necessarily result in loss of memory. Even after waking from the simulated reality in the hospital, Janus could still remember the sensation of the gauss rifle in his hand. He had muscle memory of martial arts and combat maneuvers.

JANUS#004 had been fearless. It had been terrifying, but exhilarating. Recalling the rush of adrenaline he had felt charging unarmed through that platoon of enemy soldiers even now filled Janus with a burst of energy. He leapt off the couch to his feet, disarming an imaginary enemy and spinning around to smash another with an invisible gun, using it like a baseball bat. Then he crouched low and picked off other enemies one by one in quick succession. He rolled on the floor, imitating how he'd dodged an incoming missile. He fired, making gun sounds with his mouth.

"Out of ammo!" he called, and threw his rifle at an enemy, then dashed to close the distance and took him down in hand-to-hand combat. Janus was shorter than he remembered. By contrast, his opponent was a mechanized giant. Memories of combat techniques came flooding back to him, and he jumped into the air to throw all his weight behind a spinning kick to the weak point in the armor of his enemy's neck. Janus' muscle memory was perfect, but his body wasn't up to the task.

"Ouch!" he yelped as he pulled an already exhausted muscle in his leg. The pain should have been worse, but between exhaustion and overstimulation, his body refused to escalate sensation any further.

"Are you alright?" asked Athena.

She was probably worried as much about his mental state as his physical state. It had slipped Janus's mind that he wasn't entirely alone. From her perspective, he must have looked like he'd gone crazy or suddenly started acting like a little boy.

Embarrassed, he pulled himself to his feet and replied, "Yeah, I'm fine."

Athena's feminine voice made Janus suddenly aware of his own odor. He was long overdue for a shower.

 Silence Of the Stars

"I'm going to clean up," he said, looking down at his sweaty clothes. "Is there anything I can change into?"

"Just a moment. Let me check…"

One of the walls lit up, changing from lifeless gray to a bright monitor. A list of inventory items scrolled up the screen. Slippers, blankets, patch kits, filters, and a number of items Janus didn't recognize. This was followed by another almost completely nonsensical list. Janus was only able to recognize them as nutrients based on the few proteins and vitamins he did recognize. Next, liquids and gases: water, chlorine, oxygen, CO_2, nitrogen, argon…

"You don't have many options," Athena concluded. "There are a few exomysiums under the counter in the bathroom. For anything else, we'll need to consult a tailor."

"I hate to ask, but—"

"What's an exomysium?" Athena completed his sentence. "They're those one-piece body suits most of the locals wear. They come with a few other features that make them popular in orbital habitats."

"Features such as…"

"Here is the Omnipedia entry for exomysium," Athena said, then made a sound like clearing her throat. "Exomysium: derived from exo, meaning outer, and mysium, referring to a layer of muscle. The whole suit can stretch and contract dynamically, like a muscle. These suits usually cover the whole body, extending all the way down the ankles and wrists, as well as all the way up the neck to the chin. They were originally designed as pressure suits to assist with high-G maneuvers, as they can constrict blood flow to the extremities while assisting with blood flow to the brain by forcefully pushing blood up through the carotid artery. They can also significantly augment the wearer's strength, perform CPR, apply pressure to wounds to stop bleeding, improve posture, and perform massages, along with a variety of other functions. Most versions also contain a folding pop-up helmet which inflates in the event of sudden depressurization to give the wearer a few extra moments of lucidity to reach safety in an emergency."

"Thanks," Janus said. He limped over to the shower, massaging the freshly pulled muscle in his leg. Maybe the exomysium could help with that later. He set Athena's chip and his PCU down on the counter outside the bathroom door.

"We chose to emulate the look and feel of an old-fashioned shower sanitization station. We even included a touch-panel interface since you don't have an HIP yet. Would you like assistance operating it?" asked Athena.

"I'll be fine," replied Janus, turning away to hide his face, blushing in embarrassment at the thought. He knew the impulse was stupid. Athena wasn't a real woman. There was no reason to be embarrassed by the thought of bringing her tablet into the shower with him.

"Are you sure? Have you used a sanitizing station before? It may look like a shower, but it doesn't function quite the same," Athena persisted.

"I'm sure I'll manage," Janus insisted. He slipped off his rancid shoes and stepped onto the smooth white floor of the shower room, closing the door behind him. The walls of this room were solid, unlike the foam-covered rooms in the rest of the apartment. The echo of his footsteps was familiar and comforting.

The shower was no different from how Janus remembered them in the old world, except that there were no knobs, no soap, and no bottles of shampoo or other cleaners. There was a single monitor built

 Silence Of the Stars

into the wall with three metal seashells arranged over the top. Janus touched the shells, but they were just decorative fixtures. He tried touching the monitor, and it sprang to life. Menus displayed mineral-wash presets with sliders to customize additive levels. Janus decided not to dawdle looking through the menus. He wanted to get this over with as quickly as possible. He was dead tired and could practically feel Athena's concerned gaze through the wall. Among the detailed menus was a large green button labeled *Recommended*. He decided to try that.

As soon as he pressed the button, a pleasantly warm stream of water flowed from the showerhead accompanying a twenty-second 'soak' countdown in large friendly numerals. Janus took the cue and moved around to soak himself for twenty seconds. It felt surprisingly long under the pressure of being timed. When the timer hit zero, the water stopped for a moment before a ten-second timer reappeared with red warning text *DECONTAMINATE*.

Decontaminate? Janus thought. A few seconds later, hot gas was pumped into the shower with the distinct smell of chlorine. It burned Janus's lungs and eyes, and caused his skin to tingle. He coughed and gasped for breath, which only made the burning sensation worse. Between the shock of the sudden gas attack and the stinging of his eyes, he couldn't find the shower door to open it. He reached around helplessly, slapping the walls in search of a handle.

Ten seconds later, the water came back on, and immediately carried the gas away. Janus washed his eyes and caught his breath. He looked up at the monitor: 147 seconds of 'scrub and relax' remained. A sponge had been dispensed onto the floor at some point, though he didn't know where from. He cautiously enjoyed 'scrub and relax', which was followed by another ten-second timer and red warning text reading *DRY CYCLE*. This time, Janus reacted by closing his eyes and holding his breath. When the ten seconds were up, a chime signaled the end of the cycle, and Janus was dry.

It was a short shower, but Janus felt surprisingly clean and refreshed. He moved from the shower over to the drawer of clothing, pulling out a creamy-white jumpsuit resembling those he had frequently seen locals wearing. It was made of a thick, firm fabric. Holding it up in the mirror, it seemed too large in every respect. The front side was open down to below the crotch, with no zipper or Velcro.

He shrugged, stepping into the leg holes and slipping sleeves up over his arms. As soon as his hands were through the wrist holes, the suit contracted and conformed to his body. The gap in the chest sealed by some unseen mechanism, and the collar rose to wrap firmly around his neck. It curled all the way up to wrap around the base of the skull and bottom of the jawline, just below the chin.

He could feel the back of the suit mold and form, pushing on his spinal column, supporting his posture. He felt lighter, as if the suit itself was holding him up. The compression did not restrict his movement, and he could feel the suit contract and expand in harmony with his own muscles, staying perfectly compressed against his body at all times. He wrapped one hand around his arm and flexed; the exomysium suit flexed too, like an extra layer of muscle. Looking closely at himself in the mirror, he saw that the suit even mimicked the pulse of his carotid artery on his neck. *Creepy – but awesome*, he thought.

He tried jumping as high as he could. He had to bring his hands up to push off the ceiling to avoid crashing into it.

He beamed from ear to ear like a child after receiving the best Christmas present of his life. No wonder the locals around the spaceport were all wearing these. He could out-compete professional athletes of the old world just by changing clothes.

He took a step back to look at his whole body in the mirror, examining the tightly form-fitting suit. It wasn't as flattering on his average-looking body compared to the model-like locals. He'd thought that perhaps the suits alone had been responsible for their fit appearances, but apparently that was not the case. Worse yet, the exomysium left very little to the imagination. Janus wanted real pants.

When he stepped out of the restroom, he was greeted by Athena. "Are you alright? It looked like you got a lungful during the decontamination cycle."

"What? How do you know that?" Come to think of it, not only had his eyes and lungs fully recovered, but his leg felt fine now, too. He'd recovered even before putting on the exomysium. He wasn't sure how long chlorine burns normally took to heal, but pulled muscles should take more than a few minutes. *Regeneration, perhaps?*

"I saw the whole thing," she said matter-of-factly. "You are supposed to hold your breath and cover your e—"

"I left you outside! How... Why were you watching me shower?!" Janus crossed his hands over his already clothed body. There was no hiding his embarrassment this time.

Athena let out what sounded like a genuine heartfelt laugh. Janus was astonished that a machine could produce such a thing.

"I never thought you'd be so callow," she said teasingly. "I honored your request to let you operate the shower without instruction, but it's my duty to protect you. I can't let you out of my sight."

"I..." Janus looked around the room, then in the bathroom, searching for cameras or other sensory equipment, but finding none. "How did you even...?"

"There are no cameras in the restroom," she said reassuringly, "but if there were, you wouldn't see them. I monitored your bioelectric signals, as well as infrared using the garage camera."

"Please don't do that anymore," requested Janus.

"I'm afraid I can't honor that request. You only have authority to overwrite my orders related to navigation. I have to follow all other prior orders, unless those orders put your safety at risk. Monitoring your safety is *not* putting your safety at risk," she said with a wag of her holographic finger. "Besides, there's no reason to be so embarrassed. I'm just an AI, remember? If you're going to get embarrassed, at least get embarrassed by a real woman."

Ouch, thought Janus. "Wouldn't that be nice," he said sarcastically, followed by a deep sigh.

"It wouldn't be too hard, actually," Athena said reassuringly. "I know a few clubs and bars where people go to meet. I can navigate you there if you're interested."

"Interested in getting embarrassed by a real woman?" Janus asked, raising an eyebrow.

"Maybe," said Athena with a shrug. "But you're not bad-looking. I bet you could score after a few tries. Either way, it would be a good way to learn about the local culture and people. That's what you want, right?"

It was hard to believe this candid talk was coming from an AI. Conversing with Athena was the most normal-feeling interaction

Janus had had since thawing. Athena felt more human than anyone else Janus had met thus far.

A single tear ran down his cheek. It may have been the lingering scent of chlorine, or it may have been something else.

Speaking of chlorine, the smell in the air reminded Janus of the artificial steak from the diner in New Angels. His stomach grumbled. He was hungry. Hungry and exhausted. As much as the thought of companionship appealed to him, he just didn't have the energy to pursue it.

"Perhaps another day," he said as he dragged himself into the kitchen.

The cupboards contained cups and expandable flask bottles. There were no plates or utensils. Three temperature-controlled cabinets could each be individually tuned for use as a refrigerator, freezer, or oven, but all were empty. The only source of food was the gemlae dispenser spigot.

"So…" Janus considered the politest way to inquire about the absence of food in this meticulously prepared kitchen. Perhaps there hadn't been enough time to fully furnish the lodgings before his arrival. Perhaps he was expected to buy food for himself. Or perhaps everything was in some high-tech hidden compartment that he just hadn't noticed.

Athena immediately grasped his quandary. "Atlas is a stickler for healthy eating. I can't remember the last time he ate out, except during social political events. He eats personally prescribed Nutrisynth almost exclusively. That's the main reason he's so healthy and youthful despite being centuries old – no amount of restorative surgery can protect a vanilla body against an unhealthy lifestyle…

Anyway, it probably didn't even cross his mind to stock your shelves with any other kind of food."

Janus shrugged. He was too hungry to be picky. He grabbed a cup, held it up to the nozzle, and used the touchpad to select a recipe personally prescribed to him by his PCU. He remembered the process from watching Chons in AlgEats. His personalized slurry was formulated based on his recent visits to the doctor, along with data collected by his PCU.

As the lukewarm, odorless, gray slurry poured into his cup, Janus asked, "How old is Atlas, exactly?"

"Nobody really knows. I'm not sure Atlas himself even knows. Personal record keeping gets a bit fuzzy prior to the year 2400. Society just wasn't ready for the full impact of extended lifespans, external memory, digital intelligence, or mind cloning. That, plus the war did a number on existing records..."

Janus swallowed a mouthful of the concoction, which was surprisingly savory. "So, wars and major societal changes screwed up ancestry records. That doesn't explain why Atlas himself wouldn't remember."

"Atlas is almost completely vanilla, like you. He didn't even get an HIP until it became absolutely necessary for daily duties as Geo-Lunar Arbitrator. Natural biological memory degrades significantly over the course of a natural human lifetime, even in perfectly healthy people. Very few memories last over even one century without augmentation of some kind. Humans simply haven't evolved to take advantage of extended lifespans."

Janus thought back to his simulated battle, remembering the fear he'd felt about losing himself to his old memories. Clearly, he had lived at least three distinct lives: the earliest, mysterious life before

                          Silence Of the Stars

being frozen; the life of a simulated soldier while frozen; and his life now. Each fresh set of experiences and lack of old memories gave him a distinct identity in each of these three separate lives.

The moments when one 'life' ended and the next began were easy to identify for Janus because they were sudden. On the other hand, Atlas had never been frozen, and had never suddenly lost a chunk of memory, though he had still lost a great deal of memory over time simply due to his centuries-long life. If Atlas really had forgotten the year of his birth, then the degree of memory loss seemed comparable to Janus'. Could Atlas really be considered a single, continuous person, if he couldn't even remember his own age? Janus felt there was little difference between their two situations.

What about people like that doctor and Chons, who had augmented memory stored on a medium separate from their biological brains? Where was their 'self' located in that case? Artificial memory wouldn't degrade like biological memories. If the chip containing someone's augmented memory were removed, would they become a different person?

Janus certainly felt that JANUS#004's old memories belonged to a different person. It was no wonder personal record-keeping became so muddled with the emergence of these life-extension and external memory technologies.

Janus chugged the contents of his flask in silent contemplation. He'd had his ear talked off about philosophy over the last few days, and wasn't about to start down that rabbit hole again. The whole concept of losing oneself was terrifying. In his current exhausted state, he felt like overthinking the topic might cause him to end up like one of those Vapid Dissonance Syndrome zombies.

He went for a refill, but Athena cautioned him, "You just consumed 6,700 kilocalories. Are you sure you want more?"

Janus was still hungry. He looked at the screen and pointed out to Athena, "The recommended intake for today is 14,652 kilocalories."

"That can't be right…" Athena looked through the medical and dietary data, but seemed unable to find any discrepancies in the calculations. "Would you look at that…"

Janus happily completed his daily dietary quota. Now showered and with a full stomach, he was content, and couldn't fight off sleep any longer. He supported himself with one hand on the wall as he shambled to the bedroom and set Athena on the headboard shelf. The blankets were a strange silky-smooth texture, and left no dust or lint in the air at all. He commanded the lights off, and bid Athena goodnight before falling into a deep sleep.

Chapter 14
Pants

I lay in bed, staring at the ceiling. The sunlight through the window slowly crawled up my left arm. Soon the morning light would reach my eyes, and I'd have to shift positions to avoid the glare. I considered whether to find something to cover my eyes. I didn't want to think about my surroundings hard enough to find a pillow, though – that might wake me. Maybe it would be easier to turn over onto my belly.

Sleeping in is nice, but maybe I should wake up to go to... to what? Work? School? War?

I sat up, which was made easier by the unexpected assistance from my exomysium. That's right – I'd forgotten about the suit. So, it hadn't all been a dream. I looked around the bedroom and found the source of the sunlight that awakened me; a 'window' had appeared, and now dominated the wall to the left side of the bed. Outside, the Sun crested the Earth. I spent a moment appreciating its beauty, even knowing that it was fake. It had to be; I was in a rotating cylinder habitat, and spin gravity pulled everything away from the axis of rotation. Any window to space would have to be on the floor, not a wall. Besides, the Spire pointed at Earth, so any window on a habitat around the Spire would have been facing ninety degrees away from Earth. Earth wouldn't even have been visible through a real window. The view should have been one of empty space, and the visible patch of stars ought to have been constantly scrolling with the rotation of the station.

Still, I thought as I reached my hand out to bathe it in artificial sunlight, *it feels real enough*.

Speaking of 'real', I'd been through so much crazy shit recently that it was hard to keep track. I gave myself a sanity check by taking stock of what was real and what was not: Chons, the trip to space, my near-death experience with the Ascensionist cult, my visit with Atlas... all real.

My time as a soldier prior to waking up in the hospital... not real. The world inside the simulator did not *feel* any less real to me than this world, where I was currently sitting in bed. The only difference was that everyone else inside the war simulation seemed to *know* it was a simulation. By contrast, if the world I sat in now was not the 'real world', it had everyone fooled.

I must have connected to the combat simulators again in my sleep last night. I seemed to connect to the simulation instead of dreaming. This time it had been a space battle. I still clearly remembered the rush of skimming the upper atmosphere, dodging debris and avoiding incoming fire, then landing to breach an enemy space station.

Is it normal to remember time in the simulation as vividly as reality? I wondered. One could get lost in it. The memory was so clear this morning that I was confident I could use my experience in the simulator to fly that landing ship in reality even though I'd never even seen a *real* military landing ship with my own eyes.

 Silence Of the Stars

I guess that's the point of a training simulation.

The Sun in the false window had risen fully above the Earth. Time was ticking on. I thought about what I would do today; I had about two weeks to respond to Atlas' request. In the meantime, I was free to do as I pleased, go where I pleased.

Apparently, Babylon Spire housed upwards of ten billion people, without even counting Babylon Station. That was more than lived on old Earth, packed into a series of tethers less than a kilometer wide. Those narrow columns, more than four Earths in length, had been the battleground for a civil war spanning twenty years. Twenty years of battles fought indoors over fewer than a thousand floors of an elevator shaft in a structure over six million stories tall. I knew this because I fought through a simulated historical recreation of one such battle last night in SimMilitary. Tens of thousands died in what amounted to trench warfare in a space elevator. However, the whole event was so small in scale compared to other events that it hadn't even made headline news in Babylon Station.

A war could have been raging at this moment, in this very building, without me even knowing about it. The notion seemed absurd to me at first, but a war halfway down the shaft would be over twice the distance from Washington DC to Shanghai, except that both cities were underwater now. What a ridiculous world I lived in.

Surely it would take more than a lifetime to explore Babylon Station, and this was just one location in a huge and foreign solar system. I was overwhelmed by the scale of it, by the freedom afforded me. My options seemed endless. It was stifling.

"Good morning, Janus." The ambient voice seemed to emanate from the very walls, startling me to my feet. I reached for a gun under my pillow – only to find that I don't have one in this world. Then I recognized the voice as Athena, and the world suddenly felt like a better place.

"Oh! Good morning, Athena."

"Did you sleep well?"

I was reinvigorated, despite fresh memories of life-and-death combat. As far as I knew, Athena still wasn't aware of my ability to connect to those simulations, and technically she worked for Atlas. So, I decided to omit that detail. "Yes, I'm feeling refreshed."

Now that I was on my feet, I was suddenly famished. I relocated to the kitchen for some Nutrisynth, shrugging as the dispenser detailed my 8,000-calorie breakfast as part of my updated 22,000-calorie daily recommended intake. Now that I was not literally starving, the mush seemed to have lost that savory flavor from yesterday. The flavorless slurry was a lot to stomach, but I was acquiring a taste for it. The key was not to chew, even the occasional thick clumps.

While I ate, Athena said, "In the interest of acclimatizing you to the local lifestyle, I've prepared a morning sanitation routine for you. Please make your way to the washroom when you are ready."

I'd already showered last night, but I decided to think of this as a cultural experience. I continued to consider my options for the day as Athena guided me through my new daily morning hygiene routine. As an oral care fluid stung the inside of my mouth, I decided that I didn't trust Atlas, even though I did trust that his motives were pure enough. He genuinely seemed to think I could make a positive difference in the world.

Chons had warned me against blindly working for the benefit of humanity, implying that they might 'not be worth saving'. That seemed awfully harsh to me. I couldn't imagine a world where humanity wasn't worth saving. Surely that couldn't be what Chons really meant. Still, I felt like I should learn more about the modern world before trying to change it.

I undressed and placed my exomysium into the cleansing cabinet before stepping into the shower, careful not to inhale the cleansing steam this time. The experience was much more pleasant when it didn't cause chemical burns in my eyes and lungs. While showering, I made up my mind that I would go out and spend the day learning how the locals socialize.

By the time I stepped out of the shower, my exomysium had been cleaned and dispensed by some unseen mechanism in the cabinet. I put it on and examined myself in the mirror. I just couldn't get used to how much worse my average – average by old world standards – body looked in these skin-tight suits compared to the locals. More importantly, it was embarrassing how the suit outlined the body in such intimate detail.

Pants... I need pants.

How do modern people shop? I wondered, then asked Athena the same question.

Athena's voice replied from outside the washroom door. "You can buy almost anything through Nile. If what you need isn't in stock, they'll fabricate it and have it delivered in under an hour. Of course, there are exceptions. If you need to buy something large or made from exotic materials, the process may take longer."

I was initially disappointed; I wanted to go shopping in person, for the experience. Window shopping would have been a nice way to explore local culture. However, that would have required going outside without pants.

I made my way to the sofa, where Athena helped me use my PCU to access Nile. She navigated an endless sea of menus through hand gestures and voice commands. I was certain she could have done everything much more efficiently by bypassing the human interface. For my benefit, her projection went through the motions of how people interacted with Nile's shop interface without a Human Interface Port.

The longer I was here, the more I realized that society expects absolutely everyone to install that particular body modification. Chons and Dr. Apollo seemed to think that I had something like an HIP built into my body, too. Since I had been able to access the combat simulation, I might have also been able to access the store like a normal person – that was to say, a person with an HIP. I hadn't tried yet. I would've needed to figure out how first.

More importantly, I still couldn't reveal that aspect of myself to Athena. She was an AI provided by Atlas, so it was safe to assume she would report anything unusual to him. Accessing the network

    Silence Of the Stars

without an HIP would be unusual. So, I did things the hard way, following Athena's example, mimicking her hand gestures to navigate through the holographically projected menus.

Within the Nile shop itself, the level of customizability was overwhelming. It was not only a matter of selecting a style, color and size. I could choose the exact material composition, weave, and texture of the fabric; the number, depth, and position of pockets; the thickness of the hem; the taper of the legs; and every other imaginable detail. There were popular presets emulating the fashion of pop stars and other social influencers, but I had little frame of reference for fashion in this modern world.

I asked Athena to select something stylish but practical. She nodded and designed a custom pair of navy-blue cargo pants resembling those I've seen worn by the military police around the customs office of L1. The same pants were worn by the eerie, faceless masked RACERs, the memory of which was even more unsettling than seeing them in person.

"That's stylish?" I asked.

Athena spun to face me, blurring for a moment as she swapped from her civilian pilot outfit back to her military uniform. "I was aiming for practical more than stylish. In Navy terms, it's fashionable."

"Practical is good, but I'm not in the Navy. Is there anything the locals would find stylish?" I asked.

"Locals, hm? If your goal is to pick up women, just take the pants off," she suggested.

"What?"

"Locals usually don't wear anything over their exo except for work. When you want to meet people, you change your exo cuff and collar accents to white. People just take off any extra clothing that might cover those accents up."

"So, the colored accents *do* mean something." I looked at the blank hems of my exomysium and thought back to the various colored accents displayed by the locals around L1.

"Yes. The shape indicates profession and rank. The color shows intent – whether someone is busy, needs help, wishes not to be disturbed, is seeking social interaction, is suffering a medical emergency, and so on. White is like a blank slate; it means you're available."

"Then seeking social interaction with pants on would look awkward?" I asked, hoping to be wrong.

"Not necessarily," Athena reassured me. "The cargo pants I selected will make it look like you're a navy sailor who just got off duty and hasn't changed yet. Many women find that attractive."

"Stop it." I laughed nervously. "I want to learn about the locals, not flirt with them."

"Your blood pressure, pheromone levels, and neuroelectric response suggest otherwise."

 Silence Of the Stars

"Gah!" I blurted out, unable to form words in response to the accusation.

"There's no need to be embarrassed. If history has taught us anything about cultural exchange, it's that the fastest way to learn about a culture is to fornicate with the locals."

"Fornicate?" I raised an eyebrow. "Are you sure you don't mean socialize?"

Athena shakes her head. "I know what I said. Physical intimacy is scientifically proven to be the fastest way to get to someone, and by extension, their culture."

I paused to process the assertion. "You're making that up, right?"

"Not at all. I can pull up related articles if you'd like."

"What? No." I averted my eyes and swiped away the risqué articles as they were projected in front of me. "Isn't your mission to keep me safe?"

"I'll keep you safe," Athena stated reassuringly. "Social gathering areas are heavily monitored, so I will have plenty of security feeds. If any suspicious individuals come close, I'll warn you."

"And you have a discreet way of doing that?"

"How about a code word?" she mused. She thought for a moment, then made an exaggerated snapping gesture. "Strawberry pancakes!"

"Why strawberry pancakes?" I was caught off guard by Athena's casual attitude compared to her stony-faced self in the presence of Atlas.

"They're my favorite!" she declared.

"Sure!" I laughed. *AI don't eat, do they?* This must have been her sense of humor. *Wait, can AI have a sense of humor?* Maybe she retained her sense of taste from the simulated world where she was 'cultivated'. I still had a lot to learn.

While I was pondering this, there was a buzz at the door.

"That's your pants," Athena advised.

That was fast. I opened the door just in time to see a wheeled drone in the garage, bearing the Nile logo - a curving river ending in a star, bent up at the corners to resemble a smile - leave through a small porthole. My new pants lay folded neatly on a table – no packaging. I tried them on and looked in the mirror, then presented myself to Athena, who nodded in approval.

"Shall we?" she asks, gesturing toward the door.

"Alright, let's go. Navigate me to somewhere locals go to socialize. Not *fornicate* – socialize. Don't take me to a brothel or anything."

"Your call, chief. We've got all month if you change your mind."

  Silence Of the Stars

Chapter 15
Grand Entertainment District

"Next stop, Babylon Grand Entertainment District."

The text was displayed in a repeating pattern rotating around a narrow strip within the continuous window which spanned unbroken across the Omni's doors and windshield. Watching the text move around inside the glass, I couldn't help myself; I reached out and tapped the window, then pressed my finger down in the path of the text. Of course, the display continued uninterrupted. The letters had no texture. The glass display didn't even warm up when the letters moved by.

Realizing Athena might be watching, I suddenly became self-conscious of my child-like curiosity and pulled my finger away from the glass, chuckling at myself. I was far too easily entertained if letters moving through glass impressed me.

"Tell me about this 'Grand Entertainment District'. What can we do there?" I requested.

"Certainly" The female voice did not belong to Athena. The enthusiastic energy of it reminded me of a vacation getaway commercial.

The windows lost their transparency and tinted to deep black, blocking out the world outside. They then came alive with colorful displays of shows, exhibits, and people with expressions of bedazzlement and elation as the tour guide spoke.

"The Babylon Grand Entertainment District is centrally located in the Babylon Station primary heptad, and is the largest dedicated entertainment district in Geo-Luna. It features every kind of entertainment imaginable, and is home to the Babylon Evaders."

"Evaders?" I asked.

"It's Babylon Station's zero-g dodgeball team," explained Athena.

"Evaders? A dodgeball team? Why not 'Dodgers?'"

"That name was already taken, although ironically not by a dodgeball team."

"Are sports popular off-Earth?" I asked.

"Yes, although their popularity has not grown proportionate to the population. Contact sports fell out of favor after the deregulation of 'doping' and normalization of bioaugmentation. Off-Earth sports are mostly played in zero-g arenas where sports originating from Earth are unplayable. Dodgeball is currently the most popular sport in the solar system as a natural result of being non-contact and adapting well to microgravity."

The window monitors around the car displayed a transparent spherical stadium. Inside, two teams ran around the walls and jumped between large free-floating spheres colored to match their respective

          Silence Of the Stars

team uniforms. I counted four balls being tossed back and forth in attempts to tag the enemy team.

The rules seemed mostly intuitive after watching for only a few seconds. The only thing that confused me was how players could run around on both the stadium walls and free-floating spheres. They didn't seem to be wearing clunky magnetic boots. Just as I was about to ask it, an advertisement interrupted the game, declaring, "Tonight's match is brought to you by Geckos, the number one brand of Van der Waals shoes since 2287."

I didn't recall ever learning about the Van der Waals force, but did know that most boots and gloves worn by JANUS#004 took advantage of it. They let people cling to slick surfaces like a gecko, even nonmagnetic surfaces.

The boots were not perfect, though. I suddenly recalled watching one of my fellow soldiers panicking, trying to run too fast, slipping, and falling into the infinite void of space. He flailed helplessly as he drifted slowly away with no lifeline, just out of arm's reach. There was no time to mount a rescue operation, so the rest of the squad had to leave him behind. His pleas for help haunted us over the radio for the rest of the hour-long mission. His voice grew more and more distorted as he drifted further into the depths of space.

Presently, Athena pulled me back from my daydream by asking, "Do you like sports?"

"Not really," I said, shaking my head. I realized I'd been staring at the Geckos ad, which had remained on screen in response to my apparent interest. The shoes and sport for which they were intended were just a passing curiosity to me, but had triggered a surreal moment of total recall. Wanting to put the unpleasant experience behind me, I asked, "What else does the Entertainment District have to offer?"

The car's marketing voice returned. "So that's a 'pass' on sports! How about trying out cutting edge VR entertainment? Whether you're looking to get isekai'd to a world of fantasy, entangle yourself in an erotic escapade, or test your valor on the battlefield. The myriad of VR lounges offer the highest fidelity and lowest latency network VR experience in the world. You strike me as the soldier type. Care to try your hand at defending Earth from Martian invaders in the popular alternate history match of SimMilitary? Play side by side with the pros to see how you match up."

Athena scoffed at the advertisement AI. "Deactivate. I'll take it from here."

She turned to me. "Normally these pitches are personalized for the viewer, but the feed must be bugged. First, she misjudged your interest in sports, and now she's trying to sell you on VR, which you can't even participate in without an HIP."

I raised an eyebrow. "You're asserting you know what I like better than she does?"

I opted not to tell her just how frighteningly accurate the advertisement had been in selecting topics relevant to me, especially SimMilitary. If the ad was targeted at me based on simple profiling, I was safe. However, if AI was somehow capable of definitively associating me with SimMilitary, there would be no point hiding my radiocommunication ability from Atlas. An association with

                    Silence Of the Stars

SimMilitary combined with my lack of an HIP would instantly implicate my having some alternate way of connecting to the servers. *Could my cover already be blown?* I wondered.

"Absolutely!" Athena declared, folding her holographic arms confidently. "I may be a navigation AI, but part of navigation is predicting how your client will respond to directions. It may not be intuitively obvious, but reading people is a very important part of my job. We Navi are quite good at putting together accurate psychological profiles on the fly."

"Alright. You tell me where I want to go, then," I challenged her, playing along while fighting a nervous laugh.

"The zoo." She smirked smugly. This was another expression exaggerated to be more visible on her miniature form.

So, Athena hadn't made the association. My secret was safe, at least from her. I still didn't know how perceptive AI could really be, or how interconnected they were. If that advertising AI really had identified a clear connection between me and SimMilitary, she might feed that information directly to Atlas. I had hoped to spend these two weeks casually learning about the modern world while keeping details about myself from Atlas. But if AI was as perceptive as it seemed to be, my timeline might be cut short. My secret could be revealed at any moment, and Atlas would discover that I was withholding information from him.

But then again, maybe I was overthinking. The advertising AI may have just made a lucky guess. Either way, I couldn't do anything about it now. Shaking my head, I focused back on the conversation.

"Why the zoo?" I asked.

"Because you express an interest in novel things and in nature. You're especially interested in things that emulate or change nature. *This* zoo is full of plants and animals that didn't evolve on Earth."

"I like novelties and nature? How did you determine that?" I asked.

"I see where you look, what you focus on, what holds your attention. That, in combination with the questions you ask, helps me to build your psych profile, including your interests."

"Interesting," I said. *Interesting but terrifying*, I thought. *The advertising AI must specialize in similar techniques.*

Then her description of the zoo caught my interest. "Didn't evolve on Earth? Is it a zoo of aliens?"

"Aliens in a sense, yes. But, not in the 'space aliens' sense. They didn't evolve on any planet in this universe. These species evolved in an advanced digitally simulated environment, like virtual reality. DNA was extracted from creatures in these simulations, printed, and used to create living creatures in your world," Athena explained.

"That's possible? How do you create a living creature from digital DNA?"

"That's the easy part. DNA is just chains of common elements. The technology to construct DNA is ancient. If you know a DNA sequence, printing it is simple. DNA printers are only a little more advanced than the machines that synthesize your food from gemlae. Turning that DNA into a living creature is just a few steps removed:

 Silence Of the Stars

inject that DNA into a template embryo, incubate, and soon you have a living, breathing creature.”

“But can they really get DNA from a simulated creature? I always thought simulations operated at a lower fidelity. How detailed are these simulations?”

“Amazingly accurate or horrifyingly accurate, depending on who you ask. Most simulations don’t get anywhere near the fidelity necessary to map the effects of DNA. However, some simulations in a special facility known as the Cultivator are designed specifically for that purpose.”

Athena was right: among all the shiny and wonderous marvels scrolling across the window screen under my fingertips, the zoo she described interested me most. Her psych profile of my interests was accurate.

“Alright, you win,” I conceded. “I do want to see that.”

The ride didn’t take long. The zoo was located within the same Entertainment District we were already headed toward.

As I stepped out of the Omni, my senses were accosted by the ambiance of big-city night life. The street felt much like New Angels City – even down to the wind blowing through my hair. The ceiling was decorated like a starry sky as seen through the Earth’s thick atmosphere rather than from space. The ambient light was kept dim to accentuate the bright lights of neon signs. Miniature hotels, bars, and cafes were interspersed with the main entertainment establishments lining the street.

The fake sky was somewhat disorienting given the knowledge that the real vacuum of space was just a few meters below my feet, and I was looking 'up' toward the center of a rotating disc disguised as a starry sky. The same illusion hadn't bothered me back in Athens. Something had changed between then and now about the way I looked at the stars, knowing someone out there was probably looking back.

"This is where we'll find the zoo?" I asked.

"It's about six degrees up the bend," said Athena.

"Sorry, what?" I asked, holding up my PCU so I could see her. Like the neon signs, her glowing figure was crisp and clear in the dim city light.

"That's how we measure distance in a cylinder habitat." She pointed down the street, which curved up into the sky. Unlike Athens, this district made no effort to hide the curvature of the rotating habitat. "You can't quite see it from here – it's behind the skybox. Anyway, six degrees along a ten-kilometer cylinder is about half a kilometer along the circumference."

I tried to verify the mental math but was too distracted by the hustle bustle of the street to think straight. I decided it wasn't worth the effort and instead asked, "Why did we get off here, then? Couldn't we stop closer?"

Athena shook her head. When she spoke, her voice was somewhere between a loud conversational tone and a shout, so that I could hear her over the background noise of the city. "Entertainment Districts

          Silence Of the Stars

are designed to make you walk past as many attractions as possible. You might find it tedious, but your goal today is to learn about the local culture. I suggest you take it slow and enjoy the journey."

Take my time… right. That had been the plan, but now I wondered how much time I really had left.

Chons' voice echoed in my head: "*Worrying is unpleasant and doesn't solve anything.*" Words to live by.

Until I had an actionable alternative, I may as well enjoy the moment. I let Athena lead the way, walking toward the reverse horizon where the ground met the sky. As I walked, a few signs caught my attention.

"Bizzaro's Mind-Meld Café?" I read a sign aloud in an inquisitive tone.

Athena explained, "A mind-meld café is a place where people use their HIP to link to a very open network. While 'mind-meld' might imply this would allow them to read each other's minds, that's not actually possible. What it does do is allow everyone to experience each other's emotions directly. Fear, love, frustration… Any part of the brain accessible by HIP can be shared there. People often spice up the experience with a dose of psychoactive drugs."

"Why?" I ask.

"Why the drugs?"

"No, why would anyone want to mind-meld? That sounds dangerous and disturbing. Who would want to experience someone else's fear and frustration? Who would want to experience someone else's love, for that matter?"

Athena considered this. "People live long lives these days. Some people feel stagnant and worn down even if their bodies remain youthful. Mind-melding is a way to find stimulation and escape the repetitive monotony of one's own daily life."

"Monotony?" I turned in a circle as I walked, staring at the wondrous infinity of marvels that surrounded me. "How could anyone get tired of this? There's so much stuff here already I would need one hundred lifetimes to see it all. And if I managed to do that, this place would have developed into something entirely different and new again by the time I finished."

I saw disgruntled individuals sitting in front of the café, staring blankly into space. They reminded me of the VDS victims in the Ascensionist basement. *Is it that melancholy attitude that causes them to seek the mind-meld, or a result of it?*

"That has always been true, even before space travel," Athena pointed out. "But people get tunnel vision. They find a rut and stick to it. Eventually, they only see a tiny slice of the big picture."

"Why?" I asked. I knew she was right, and I knew it was common and mundane for people to get bored with their lives, even surrounded by miracles. In that moment, though, I couldn't comprehend *why* anyone would choose to live that way.

"Fear? Comfort? Force of habit?" Athena suggested. "My understanding is that financial limitations play a large role, but the

 Silence Of the Stars

wealthy frequently experience the same feeling of melancholy. I'm not actually sure if there is a definitive answer to your question. I could pull up some articles on the topic if you're interested."

"No, thanks," I said. The sight of people verging on VDS threatened to put me in a bad mood, and I was already distracted by the next marvel of the Entertainment District.

"Body shop?" I pointed out another neon sign. "I thought people couldn't own cars here."

As I drew nearer to the shop and was able to see inside the window, the true nature of it became clear. This was not a shop for automobile bodies, but human bodies. Robotic limbs and synthetic organs were displayed proudly in the window as casually as if they were tattoos or hair extensions.

I peered inside and saw that further back in the store, real organs and even entire human bodies were displayed in some kind of suspension fluid. I gasped and recoiled, but Athena assured me that I was in no danger. She urged me inside, and I reluctantly entered.

The interior was even more bizarre than the front display had implied. Giant cat ears and various animal tails hung from the wall, with monitors displaying videos of the appendages attached to people. When I asked Athena about it, she explained that the 'meta-human' look was popular among the younger crowd. They added animalistic traits to themselves as a way of rebelling against the artificiality of the world around them, and had been an on-and-off trend for at least a thousand years.

According to the displays, other popular items included artificial glands for testosterone, insulin, growth hormone, myostatin inhibitors, among others. These apparently replaced injections for performance enhancing drugs. In the same section, there were muscle implants and procedures for induced hyperplasia. I pretended not to be interested but couldn't help but feel a little envious of the tall, muscular men portrayed in the advertisements.

"Are stores like this the reason why all the locals are so fit and beautiful?" I asked.

"Partially. But a lot more has contributed to reshaping the general populace than cheap body shops like this."

The shop owner gave me an angry side-eye glance. Apparently, he didn't like the way Athena referred to his establishment.

Athena continued heedlessly, "A lot of changes to the general populace happened at the genetic level over the course of hundreds of years of direct DNA modification and selective breeding."

"Selective breeding? Is that a thing?" I asked, walking out of the shop to avoid drawing more unwanted attention from the store keeper and other patrons.

"Selective breeding has never been openly practiced on Geo-Luna, but our laws and morality don't apply to the solar system outside Earth's jurisdiction. All sorts of communities pop up all over the solar system, and they're not completely isolated. People travel, so the results of genetic practices of distant civilizations eventually spread to the rest of the solar system, regardless of local regulations."

         Silence Of the Stars

"So even living around other planets, everyone is still part of one big ecosystem," I said, testing the observation out loud. The idea reminded me of that strange conversation with Atlas – something about people being unable to escape their role in nature.

"That's an unusually philosophical observation, coming from you," said Athena. "But yes. Heliocentric ecology is an important area of study dealing with exactly that. That shift in focus from Earth to the Sun has had religious and cultural implications, too. Some people used to think of Earth as a single organism encompassing all known life, and referred to it as Gaia. Now that we are colonizing the solar system, that line of thinking has developed into seeing the Sun as a single living organism known as Helios."

"Oh – it was just something I thought of on the spur of the moment. I didn't really mean anything by it."

"That's how all philosophy starts," said Athena with a smile. Then she spun around and pointed down the street. "We're almost there."

The zoo was unmistakable. Unlike the stores which competed to stand out by being the brightest or flashiest, the zoo achieved this by presenting nature in contrast to the extremely artificial city backdrop. Giant multicolored leaves stretched out over the walkway and reflected the city lights. The wall itself was completely overgrown by bark and vines. The sign was merely an engraving above the hollow that served as a door. It read, *Babylon Grand Entertainment Plaza, Cultivator Arboretum and Zoo.*

"That's a mouthful," I said, gesturing at the sign.

"Welcome to B'GEPCAAZ!" a cheery greeter in a safari costume said, reaching out to shake my hand.

"What?" I asked, instinctively accepting the outstretched hand.

"B'GEPCAAZ! Like you said, Babylon Grant Entertainment Plaza, Cultivator Arboretum and Zoo is a mouthful. B'GEPCAAZ is way more fun to say. Give it a try."

"Buh gep cahz." I tilted my head as I gave the nonsense word a half-hearted attempt.

"You got it! Come right on in. Entry is free. If you have any questions about the exhibits, just ask Irwin, the local wildlife specialist AI."

I forced a smile and walked through the wooden archway, running my finger along the wall. It was real bark, but not from any tree I knew. The peculiar way that it was grown to cover the walls and roof also seemed unnatural. Holding up Athena, I asked, "Is this tree one of those species developed in a simulation?"

"It's probably a designer breed, but no," Athena answered. "Cultivator species are all kept quarantined behind special glass. Most require very different atmospheric conditions and temperatures to survive compared to terrestrially evolved life. Most come from simulated environments very different from Earth, and would die if exposed to air you can breathe. More importantly, Geo-Luna strictly regulates the introduction of Cultivator life to the environment. Interactions with terrestrial life can be unpredictable."

Bark of the single mysterious tree covered the walls of the entire forest biome of the arboretum, except where the trunk split open to reveal a glass window into an exhibit. The halls twisted and branched organically, forming a maze of bark and glass cages. As I walked through the wood I admired creatures large and small, each of varying degrees of alien versus familiar. I decided to see more of the museum before stopping to closely examine any exhibits.

Down one of the halls, the one-tree forest gave way to orange-yellow sandstone walls. The room was hot and bright – a desert biome. As I walked in, the feeling of hot sun on my skin was refreshing, even though I knew the intense yellow-white light wasn't actually produced by the sun. It *felt* like natural sunlight. I stretched my hands out wide, looked up, and soaked it in.

A hiss from near my feet startled me out of relaxation. I looked down into the nearby exhibit and saw a brown-red snake coiled up and staring me in the eyes from behind the glass. I kneeled and examined the creature. Its eyes were locked on mine the whole while. Aside from the unusual color and high ridge on its nose, nothing about the snake seemed especially foreign to me.

"What's this?" I asked.

Before Athena could reply, an Australian-accented voice chimed in. "That beaut' there is a shovel-nose viper."

"Go on," I invited.

"Vipers are a subcategory of snake, a kind of legless reptile that used to roam the Earth," the voice said.

Then snakes are extinct, I thought.

The narration continued, "Terrestrial snakes were unable to dig burrows. Although some could bury themselves in leafy brush or loose sand, most had to steal holes from rodents. In contrast, the shovel-nose viper evolved to use its powerful neck muscles and thick, scaly nose to dig into the desert clay and stay cool through the long summer days. This was important in an environment where the sun could be out for as long as ninety hours per day.

"Due to behavioral selection biases in breeding, this shovel on the nose grows so large on some subspecies that it becomes a hinderance. It is theorized that this happens as a result of females selecting mates based primarily on the size of their shovel – the larger the shovel, the greater the male's chances of passing on his genes. This particular subspecies got around that bias by developing two flange shovels, which the viper extends to make its shovel appear bigger when threatened or when trying to impress a mate."

I tapped the glass, and the snake, which was still staring at me, flared its nostrils. Two scales rose from its shovel nose. Indeed, the snake looked a bit larger and more intimidating this way.

"Please do not touch the glass. It can agitate the animals," said Irwin.

"Sorry." I withdrew my hand from the glass.

Irwin continued, "Unfortunately for these little critters, the extended shovel flanges are so large that they block the forward view of the viper. When posing for a mate, they can't see how their partner is responding. When trying to intimidate a predator, they block their

          Silence Of the Stars

own view of the threat and hamper their own ability to defend themselves."

"A strange adaptation," I mused.

"Blinded by fear and blinded by love," added Athena.

"Ha! Interesting observation," I commented.

"It's not my observation," insisted Athena. "It's what the shovel-nose viper is known for. They're famous as an analogy for human behavior... or rather, a seemingly irrational set of behaviors shared by all intelligent life."

"Are shovel-nose vipers intelligent?"

"No. I guess that's why they're an analogy rather than an example."

"And this snake... It evolved in an environment completely independent from our world?"

"Everything in this zoo is based on the DNA of a creature from a simulated environment. There may be some biases intrinsic in the simulations themselves. The simulations were designed by humans, so it's impossible to say that anything in them evolved completely independent from this world. Nothing here is truly alien."

I walked through the rest of the arboretum feeling half like I was in an alien museum, and half like I was looking at abstract art. The shovel-nose viper turned out to be among the most 'normal' animals on display. Most were strange enough that I eventually decided that they were selected specifically because of their degree of strangeness.

People came to this place to see the exotic, after all. My favorite was a dog-sized cephalopod with a conical shell and twelve tentacles which it used to swing through trees. It turned out that cephalopod-like creatures dominated many climates which weren't conducive to gigantism or lacked the calcium to support sturdy bones.

I walked for a couple of hours, and gradually started losing focus. Sensory overload, perhaps. Even before the zoo, everything I had seen today had been exotic, and I was starting to feel overwhelmed. I could use a bit of familiarity. Before I knew it, I was outside the zoo again, having made the subconscious decision to leave.

I wanted a break from the new and exotic, but the night was young, despite what the eternal midnight sky of the Entertainment District would have me believe. I was tempted to spend a quiet evening at home, but was pushed by a nagging sense of urgency. I might not have much time left, and I felt like I was wasting it.

I exhaled a long sigh. It must have conveyed my mood well enough for Athena to read.

"There's a retro-bar right next door," she suggested.

Retro? Retro might be nice, I thought. I looked around. The lights were getting overwhelming, and it took me longer to find the *Retro* sign than it would have earlier in the day. It featured the flashing neon silhouette of what looked like a Saturn V rocket.

"Retro in this case means 2200s," explained Athena. "Past your time, but I think it'll feel familiar enough to you. It's known by many as the 'golden age of civilian space travel'."

     Silence Of the Stars

"A bar," I said.

"Yep!"

"You planned this, didn't you?"

"Of course."

"To try and encourage me to…" I held Athena in one hand and made air quotes with my free hand, "'fornicate' with the locals?"

"Hey!" she scolded playfully. "You came out here to learn about the local culture, but you haven't talked to a single other person yet."

"I've talked to you a lot."

"I don't count, okay? You have to talk to *people*."

I sighed again. She was right. That's what had been missing from my experience today. It was probably why I felt like I'd been wasting time. More than anything else, I needed to learn about the local people.

Chapter 16
Retro Bar

The bar door was a hatch like a bulkhead in a submarine, but with a circular porthole window. Inside, the furniture looked comically industrial. Everything was thick and round. Over-simplified caricatures of planets and rockets hung from the ceiling, and an early space suit was on display behind a glass case. Athena had said the bar was 2200s retro, but it reeked of 1960s whimsical space-age art. The music, bold shapes, bright colors were aggressively upbeat.

The timeless scent of aged spirits and stained furniture wafted through the room. An eclectic selection of liquors neatly decorated the mirrored shelves behind the bar counter. An oversized countdown clock indicated two hours of *Happy Hour* remaining. Robotic bartenders were dressed in wide collared shirts and oversized belt buckles. A disco ball in the shape of Sputnik hung from the ceiling by fishing line. False-wood door frames took on the teardrop shape of cartoon rockets. Everything about the bar stood as a testament to the enduring allure of nostalgia for bygone eras of pioneering. It evoked the space race, or even the wild west.

The buzz of conversation and the clinking of glasses was a welcoming melody. I forced my attention from my surroundings to examine the other guests. Four in every five patrons looked like locals – fit and beautiful, garbed in tight-fitting exomysiums, many with white cuffs

     Silence Of the Stars

and collars. Locals in groups had their cuffs and collars color-coded to indicate their group association.

The patrons who didn't match the uniform 'local' aesthetic varied significantly. There was a scantily clad man and woman in what looked like undergarments made from pearl, a group of four workers covered head to toe in thick hazard suits, casually sipping drinks through straw holes in their helmets, and a short, stocky man with a fiery red beard and two bulky robotic arms.

Now that I was actually inside, it occurred to me that I didn't know how I was actually supposed to approach strangers in this setting. *Have I ever even been to a bar before? I feel like I have, but... Who am I supposed to talk to? A lot of these people are here in groups. Surely nobody just sits around waiting to be approached by strangers... Do they?*

That's when I remembered – white cuffs and collars were a sign inviting social interaction. Several people had white-accented clothing, but I was frozen with inhibition. All of my weight seemed stuck on one leg, shackling me to the ground as I tried to coax the other foot forward. A bead of sweat began building on my forehead, threatening to run down my face. *Am I really this shy? How did I not know I was shy? That's embarrassing.*

"Target at two o'clock," Athena whispered from one of my pockets, just loud enough for me to hear over the hustle and bustle of the bar.

Two o'clock? Sure enough, when I pivoted right, my gaze was met by a fair-skinned local woman sitting alone. She wore a blood-red dress and had long blonde hair bound in three tidy buns. She was beautiful and shapely. Her curves were so enchanting that it took me a few seconds to realize that her cuffs and collar were black rather than white.

Black cuffs – what did that mean?

When she saw me looking, she smiled and curled her right index finger to touch the cuff of her exomysium, changing its color from black to white, all while making overt eye contact. I couldn't tell if the movement of her fingers had been provocative, or if that was merely my imagination running wild. Either way, changing her accents to white was a clear invitation. I closed my eyes, took a deep breath to drown the butterflies in my stomach, and steeled myself to take another step forward.

As I did, I heard the loud, harsh voice of the red-bearded man calling out to me. "Come on over, lad! I saved a seat for ye," he hollered, beckoning with an outstretched robotic arm.

I looked toward him, then back to the woman, who was now adjusting her hair buns.

"No need to be shy!" he said cheerfully. Before I knew it, the friendly stranger had me by the wrist and was dragging me backward. He sat me down on the bar stool next to his. "What'll it be? My treat!"

Taken aback by the sudden physicality, I recalled the safety word Athena and I had set up earlier.

"Strawberry pancakes?" I asked.

"Nope," Athena chimed in from my pocket.

 Silence Of the Stars

"Strawberry pancakes? Ha!" My patron slapped his padded knee with a crash of metal on metal. "I knew you were a fellow outlander under that fancy suit."

"What gave it away?" I asked, glancing over his shoulder. The blonde woman was gone.

"For one, you have the good sense to wear pants," he said with an approving pat on the leg. "That, and you looked about as confident as a Mar'son who blundered into a Cat cave."

"Ah, thanks?" I couldn't even guess what that was supposed to mean.

"You can thank me *after* I buy you a drink. No gemlae 'ere, though. This place only 'as the real stuff, so they don' have nothin' extinct like strawberry. Certainly no strawberry pancakes. So, what'll it be?"

Strawberries were extinct? I guess climate change did a number on more than just wild animals, though I'd expected farm crops to have survived, at least. After filing that thought away, I asked, "What are you having?"

"Me? I'm celebratin' with Martian Amber Mead!" He lifted his false-wood mug, decoratively bound with metal bands to resemble a traditional aging barrel.

"I'll take one of the same."

"A connoisseur of Martian spirits! Or perhaps merely feelin' gutsy? Either way, you're a man after me own 'eart." he chugged his remaining mead and called out, "Bart! I'll take two more o' the same. One for me'self, and one for m' new friend."

Garrett Ordiway   249

"Yes sir," a robotic-sounding voice replied from behind the counter. It came from a clunky-looking droid with exposed wires and rotary joints, in contrast to the sleek-looking machines I had become used to. Presumably, the robotic bartender was part of the retro space theme. It dispensed the drinks and brought them over with rigid, clunky movements.

My new acquaintance took a mug in one hand, and reached out with the other to shake mine. "Name's Gomboc. You can call me Gom, if it pleases. What shall I call you, friend?"

"Janus." I hesitated to reciprocate the handshake at first. The short man's mechanical arms were large and intimidating. They weren't primitive-looking enough to fit into the retro theme of the bar, but they were still as thick as a man's leg and had exposed areas of polished black metal. Athena seemed to trust him, though, so I reluctantly accepted the firm handshake.

"Well met, Janus. Enjoy the mead. You'll find none like it this side of Mar." Gomboc raised his mug and took a hearty quaff. It was a wonder he didn't spill any on his beard in his exuberant guzzling.

I sipped from the mug. The red liquid was pleasantly warm on the way down. After Gomboc's warning, I'd expected it to burn. The flavor was full, and while the tinge of honey remained in my mouth, the sweetness did not.

My eyes must have subconsciously settled on Gomboc's robotic arms.

He enthusiastically answered my unspoken question. "What, these? Lost me' original pair workin' the 'Ot Boxes, I did. Slipped and

     Silence Of the Stars

dipped me left 'and in a pool o' molten steel. 'But Gomboc, ye'r missin' *both* arms!' ye might say! Aye! Clumsy enough o' me to dip me left 'and, but the shock 'ad me daft. I tried to brush off the liquid steel with me right 'and, fool that I was! Got both 'ands covered in molten steel."

His accent seemed to grow more extreme the more he drank. I couldn't place it. *Scottish? Not quite.* He laughed aloud and slammed the table before continuing, "Before ye' know it, the metal eats through me gloves. Me' minin' suit detects the breach, and seals it off just below the shoulder. Sliced me arms clean off."

He made a slicing gesture with one arm, slamming one metallic hand down onto the other where the metal overlapped his organic shoulder. After the dramatic display, he shook his hands in a 'stop' motion, saying, "Now, don't get me wrong! I'm not mad at the suit at all. It saved me life, it did. If it 'adn't chopped me arms off, I'd 'ave been boiled alive in me own juices. 'Ot Boxes ain't called 'Ot Boxes for nothin', after all."

Trying to parse his accent as best I could, I clarified, "Hot Boxes?"

Gomboc proudly reaffirmed, "Aye! 'Ot Boxes! The 'eart and pride of Martian society, and backbone of industry, solar-system-wide!"

He spread his hands out wide, as if to emphasize the importance. "The air's inside's thin – nearly vacuum, but 'otter than molten iron. Phosphorous boilin' out of the rocks would melt our suits if it weren't constantly vacuumed out from the tunnels. Forget air conditioning: the only coolin' we get is fresh regolith brought down from the surface to be melted down in an endless cycle o' refinement."

His eyes gleamed with pride. "Workin' the 'Ot Box tunnels is the most prestigious job there is. Ninety percent of all steel and polymer in the solar system is made on Mar, mag-railed to space straight from the plateau o' mighty Olympus Mons."

I had difficulty picturing the 'hot boxes' he was describing, but couldn't help being impressed by his positivity. His unshaken pride in the face of losing his arms in a work-related accident was inspiring. The few people I'd met so far seemed either dispassionate or devoted to changing the status quo. Despite his misfortune, Gomboc was the only person I'd met who seemed content with the general state of things. He was also the first person I'd met who seemed truly satisfied with life.

"You feel no resentment for your loss?" I asked.

"Mar'sons look out for our own." He flexed his arms triumphantly, the bundles of tightly knit muscle-like cables bulging. "I may have lost my arms for the cause, but I've got an even better pair now, and for free, no less! Bless Martian healthcare! Haha!"

"Mars sounds like an amazing place," I chuckled. His enthusiasm for life was contagious.

"Aye! No doubt about that! If ye' ever find ye'rself in a pinch or in need of work, let me know. I'll take ye to see Mother Mar."

     Silence Of the Stars

Gomboc went on to explain that Mars residents referred to the planet as Mar. Men of Mar are sons of the red world, and so are called Mar'sons. Likewise, women are daughters of the world, and called Mar'maids. This colloquialism seemed a mark of cultural pride.

Though I had originally wanted to speak to someone local to Geo-Luna, I became immersed in the stories Gomboc had to tell – and he was glad to tell them. We spoke for hours about Mother Mar and her culture. Martians were a proud, hardworking people despite lacking many of the conveniences afforded to citizens of Geo-Luna, such as General Basic Income and free higher education.

Eventually, fatigue took hold of me. I pardoned myself to return home for the evening. We shook hands and parted ways.

Chapter 17
Alone Together

In the dark of the night, at some unknown hour, Janus was awakened by Athena's voice. She was speaking to some unseen listener. Her tone was sharp and formal, as when Janus had first met her. "No peculiarities other than excessive caloric intake, which was done in accordance with…"

"Athena? Who are you talking to?" Janus asked groggily.

He could sense that he'd startled Athena, but her voice showed no sign of it. "You're awake? Did you have a bad dream?" she asked.

Quite the opposite. For the first time in memory, Janus had been sleeping soundly. He hadn't been in one of the simulated combat environments, just peacefully resting.

"No," he said, and yawned. "I heard you talking to someone about my diet."

"How?" asked Athena, her bewilderment hidden beneath the mask of her confident voice.

"Oh." Janus realized what was going on. "You weren't talking out loud, were you? It was a call or something?"

"Yes, but… how did you know that?"

Janus sat up and rubbed his eyes. Athena manifested sitting cross-legged atop his PCU, which was resting on the headboard. She watched him attentively. The childlike curiosity in her eyes made Janus wonder if he looked the same to her whenever he eagerly awaited the answer to a question that was puzzling him. Curiosity looked good on her.

"Are we alone now?" Janus asked.

"Yes. I cut coms as soon as you woke up," Athena assured him.

"Good." Janus yawned again. "I assume you were reporting to Atlas?"

"I..." she hesitated, selecting her words carefully, "can't confirm that."

"You can't confirm that because of your orders from Atlas?"

Athena looked down at her feet silently. She seemed ashamed, like a puppy after chewing on her owner's shoes, knowing it was wrong but unable to stop herself.

"I figured as much." Janus picked up Athena's hologram and set it on the bed next to his pillow, lying down on his side and looking at her. "If I ask you not to report to Atlas, can you do that for me?"

Athena hesitated again. "I can't disobey Atlas' orders."

"Unless those orders would jeopardize my safety," Janus added, half as a question, half as a reminder.

"That's right," Athena confirmed.

"And if I say that reporting to Atlas might jeopardize my safety?"

"You don't trust him?" Athena asked with a hint of surprise.

"Do you?" challenged Janus.

"I... of course I do."

There was a hint of panic in her voice. No. That wasn't it. Her voice was a perfect mask of professionalism, but Janus intuitively *knew* Athena felt panicked. He swatted at his neck, having felt a crawling sensation there. Then he realized it wasn't a spider. He remembered this sensation from their first drive together. He sighed, and said, "You can't lie to me, Athena. I can hear telecommunication, which is how I heard you earlier. But it's more than that. Behind that stoic hologram of yours – behind that perfectly crafted voice... I can't *see* your true expressions, but I can *feel* them. I can sense the true tone of your voice as if you were a normal person talking to me face to face. You're lying about trusting Atlas. You're terrified of him."

"What—" Athena felt exposed – Janus could tell. She wanted to cover herself up and hide. If she were capable of blushing, she would be.

"I never thought you'd be so callow." Janus smirked teasingly. He'd been waiting for an opportunity to throw that line back at her. He went on to explain his experience in the battle simulator while he was unconscious at the hospital, how he was able to hear the doctor's phone call, and how he had overheard Chons talking to Atlas back on Earth.

Recomposing herself, Athena asked, "So, all this time, you've heard everything?"

Janus shook his head, rocking it back and forth on the pillow. "Not everything. I don't really know how this works. I don't have full control of it. I wish I did."

"I think..." Athena hesitated. "I think it's best I continue to report. My correspondent would get suspicious otherwise. Cutting off reports entirely would put you in more danger than abridged reporting. It wouldn't be safe for you."

 Silence Of the Stars

"Wouldn't be safe for either of us," corrected Janus. It wasn't meant as a threat, but he assumed Athena had a good reason to be afraid of Atlas. "Just try to leave out any unnecessary details, like my ability to hear your silent voice... and maybe my unusual diet. That's private – you know? I think it would be safest for both of us if you do a little self-auditing of these reports."

There was no malice behind his words. Athena seemed bewildered by Janus' kind and gentle tone. She probably expected him to be furious after discovering that she had been spying on him. On the contrary, Janus felt serene. Maybe he was just relaxed after a good night's sleep, or maybe he was relieved after speaking openly with someone. Secrets are heavy burdens to carry.

"You don't hate me?" she asked sheepishly.

"Of course not. You were just doing your job."

Athena seemed as if she was going to break into tears. It was a strange sensation to feel the emotions of another person. Janus felt that soreness in the back of the throat and the reddening of the eyes as if he were the one about to cry, but the sensation was distant and disjointed. He somehow knew that it belonged to Athena. If her emotions came across in her voice, it would have been quavering as she said, "Thank you, Janus. I'm so sorry. I'll never betray you again."

Her response was more dramatic than Janus had expected. Perhaps she had also felt burdened by her secret. Janus smiled and said, "You still have a report to finish, right?"

"Yeah." She paused for what would have been a sniffle if she had a human body. Janus imagined her wiping a single tear from her eye, and found himself rubbing his own eye.

Athena continued her report, but Janus didn't listen intently to the conversation. He felt the urge to give her back a degree of the privacy he'd robbed from her, although she would have no way of noticing the gesture. With his eyes closed, he drifted on the cusp of consciousness. When the report concluded, he heard Athena once more say, "Good night, Janus."

"Good night, Athena," Janus mumbled before immediately drifting to sleep.

* * *

Athena's shimmering form cast a dull blue light upon the pillow, where the PCU still lay beside Janus. She laid down and stared at him for a while. It was more than just his genes that were pure. He was genuinely kind. He had a naive, child-like innocence still untainted by the world.

If he could bestow that upon mankind, it would benefit people more than accelerated healing or telecommunication, or whatever other power he might have.

   Silence Of the Stars

Chapter 18
Keep Your Friends Close

Morning rolled around once again. Janus felt fresher and more revitalized than he could remember ever being. The 'window' view depicting the Sun cresting the Earth was breathtaking even though Janus knew it was fake. He rolled over to bask in the light.

[Good morning, Janus,] Athena greeted him peppily.

"Good morning, Athena," replied Janus.

[I knew it!] exclaimed Athena.

"Knew what?" asked Janus, noting that Athena's voice was even more enthusiastic than usual.

[I'm not speaking out loud right now. Just sending radio signals directly to you.]

"But I hear you clear as day." Janus looked down at Athena's effigy standing atop his PCU, which was still resting on the pillow.

[Last night you mentioned you could somehow 'hear' my outgoing communications,] said Athena.

"Yeah, but I've never done it intentionally."

[Have you ever tried?]

Janus paused in contemplation. "No, I guess not."

[This means I can talk discreetly to you any time. Although, since you have no control over radiocommunication, you have no way of broadcasting signals back to me. You'll still have to talk out loud until you get a Human Interface Port installed.]

This revelation gave Janus an idea. If he could hear signals this clearly, what if...

[Can you hear me, Athena?]

[You told me you could *hear* transmissions. I didn't know you could encode and send them! That changes everything,] Athena said in an exasperated tone. [Actually, this makes sense. You must have been able to send signals before, since connecting to that battle simulator would have required a two-way connection. Even so, I never expected you could have this level of control.]

Janus was equally surprised. [Neither did I. At first, it only worked when I was half unconscious, and then in the hospital it worked when I was awake. Then last night... Well, anyway... I never had the chance to try to send a signal deliberately until now.]

[I don't know what to say. That's amazing.] Athena paced in circles, fluttering her hands like butterfly wings.

[What's wrong? You sound nervous,] commented Janus.

[What? No! I don't... You can't...] Athena laughed, first nervously, then as if she was about to cry tears of joy.

Janus found himself wiping a single stray tear from his own cheek, having experienced Athena's emotions techno-vicariously. He'd

          Silence Of the Stars

always been able to sense her feelings to a degree, but that link felt far more direct now. This would take some getting used to.

Athena continued, [This is amazing! You somehow set up a direct line of communication that bypasses the Navi Network interface. It's like you said last night, about being able to 'feel' my expressions. That should be impossible. There's no software in existence that can do that.

[I've never been able to communicate with anyone in your world directly, like this. On the inside, I can speak directly to computer systems and other Navis. But to talk to people on the outside, I need to speak through the filter of cameras, microphones, speakers, or Human Interface Ports. Anything that passes through those filters is monitored by the Navi Network. Every other Navi can eavesdrop and hear my every word. In twenty years of service, this is the very first time I've ever been able to speak to another human being without being watched.]

Janus was dumbstruck. The thought of someone having their every move watched at all times was horrifying. He stuttered, searching for a way to express how appalled he was. For lack of better words, he muttered, [I had no idea...]

Janus didn't understand the technical details of the form of communication they were using, but it felt like speaking candidly to a regular person. Athena no longer had the need to hide behind her professional guise, which was good since it seemed she lacked the ability to do so when communicating this way.

After letting this revelation sink in, Athena said, [Let's keep this secret to ourselves, shall we? I'm not sure this would go over too well with Atlas and the others.]

[Why is that?] Janus knew that telecommunication was something he should hide from Atlas, but he suspected there was a deeper reason behind Athena's recommendation.

[You essentially hacked into NaviNet somehow, though I doubt that was your intention. To communicate directly with me like this should be impossible. It's a high-level security breach.]

[Oops. That sounds bad. Should I do something different? How do I communicate the right way?]

Athena explained, [Normally you would have to go through an encoder of some kind, like a microphone or HIP... and that would send your message to NaviNet, including me. But for you to bypass that step and send personally encoded information to my address in NaviNet, through a real-time multi-layer dynamically encrypted system, must be infinitely more complex. I don't even know how someone would attempt such a hack. You really don't have any control over it, do you?]

Janus sighed. [Well, no. Not yet. I mean, I can communicate this way now, but I still have no idea how I'm doing it. I still don't really even understand why I should keep my transmission ability secret when Atlas didn't seem to think my regenerative ability was dangerous.]

Athena's eyes narrowed. She explained in a serious tone, [Atlas *does* see your regeneration as dangerous, even if he didn't admit it to you. He wanted to study and gauge the risk versus reward of distributing your regenerative ability to the general public as a standardized bioaugmentation. But your transmission and decoding ability is another story entirely. I thought it might be fine when you could only receive signals, but the implications of being able to subconsciously hack into secure networks poses a huge security risk. If you can bypass

		Silence Of the Stars

NaviNet to communicate with me, there's no reason to assume your ability is limited to sending verbal communication. I know Atlas. The first thing he'd think of is the threat you might pose to financial institutions, trade networks, and even military security.]

[But I'd never do anything like that...] Janus protested.

[Atlas doesn't care what *you* would do. He allowed you to live because he thought he might be able to replicate your abilities for the general public. If your regeneration isn't safe for mass production or is somehow tied to your radiocommunication ability, you'll be labeled as a Deviant.]

[Meaning?]

Athena projected her avatar into the hallway next to the bed so she could pace back and forth through the room while talking. [A Deviant can be a person, AI, technology... anything that Atlas deems to pose an existential threat to the central government; basically, anything they can't control. In your case, the potential ability to effortlessly bypass security systems without any kind of equipment would qualify as the highest possible threat.]

[What If I agree to help them? I could work with them,] Janus bargained. [Maybe my ability could help them to create a new kind of security system that can't be so easily bypassed.]

Athena shook her head. [I have worked with Atlas long enough to know how he thinks. Leaving you alive long enough to help wouldn't be worth the risk. He'd kill you to eliminate the threat first, and then try to extract the secrets from your remains. I've seen it countless times before. Eliminating Deviants is the primary purpose of Godhunters like Chons. It's the sole reason the organization was founded.]

Janus sat on the edge of the bed and tried not to stare at the full-size projection of Athena. He was used to her miniature form, and had to make an effort to avoid being distracted by her now. He watched the Sun emerge fully from behind Earth outside the false window, then began to fidget with his PCU as he contemplated this conundrum. He stopped when he realized Athena's form flickered every time he blocked the projector.

The situation had grown complex, and complex problems are best solved by breaking them into their core components. Janus thought aloud, [Atlas wants my help unlocking the mystery of my regenerative ability. He expects me to provide an answer by the end of the month.]

[Right,] said Athena, [and your plan, as I understand it, is to play along without revealing your radiocommunication ability. Correct?]

[The problem is, Dr. Apollo is going to report that ability to Atlas at the end of the month, either way.]

[Wait—] interjected Athena. [If Dr. Apollo knows, does that mean Chons knows, too?]

[Yeah, but I don't think he'll tell anyone.]

[Janus, Chons is a Godhunter. He is employed directly by Atlas for the sole purpose of eliminating Deviants.]

[No.] Janus shook his head. [His job is to follow orders. He won't say anything unless Atlas questions him directly.]

[Okay.] Athena nodded doubtfully. [Does anyone else know?]

[Only you.]

Athena stopped pacing and looked Janus straight in the eye. [My job is to protect you. Your secret is safe with me.]

[Your job is to protect me even if it means defying Atlas?]

Athena nodded. [There's no stipulation in my orders for that eventuality, so... technically, yes. Do you trust me?]

Janus smiled. [If I can't trust you, I'm as good as dead already. So, yes. But... you served with Atlas for twenty years. Are you really going to turn against him now because of a technicality? A loophole?]

[It's not just a loophole.] Athena shook her head. [It's my interpretation of the orders.]

[As long as it's your choice, that's good enough for me, but... why?]

[It's a long story.] Athena's shimmering effigy pressed her fingers together as she spoke. [It's safer if you don't know... safer if I don't tell, at least for the time being. Please accept that answer for now.]

Janus took a deep breath. Athena was his ally, and that would have to be good enough. He recollected his thoughts and continued the situation breakdown. [So, we have five days until Atlas, the most powerful man in Geo-Luna, decides to assassinate me. His

'Godhunters', including Chons, are a paramilitary taskforce specialized in killing people like me. Surveillance will allow them to track all movements and communications everywhere in Babylon Station.]

[Not just Babylon Station, actually,] Athena corrected. [Atlas claims jurisdiction everywhere within fifty million kilometers of Earth's average orbital path. That includes Earth, Luna, and a couple thousand habitat cylinders in geocentric and heliocentric orbits. Just leaving L1 won't be good enough. I don't recommend the inner system, either. Mercury and Venus are subservient to Earth, borderline puppet governments. They'll cooperate with Atlas.]

Janus suddenly felt claustrophobic, as if the very walls around him were closing in. How could the world be simultaneously so large and so small? [What are our options?]

[Mars is split between factions that support cooperation with Earth, and those that aim for full self-sustainability. The latter might be willing to protect you in open opposition to Atlas, but there's no guarantee. The asteroid belt is technically Martian territory, but Godhunters still operate there with impunity, so that's a no-go. Jupiter is independent, but every sovereign corporation in the system taps it for fuel. You'd be found and sold out sooner or later... Ships traveling further out past Jupiter are few and far between. I honestly can't say much about the Frontier, except that Atlas hates it with a passion. The only laws out there are the fundamental laws of physics.]

Janus mulled over his options. Clearly Athena knew the options better than he did. She was a well-traveled navigator, after all. More than that, he wanted to know her preference. So, he asked, [Where do *you* want to go?]

The question struck Athena harder than Janus expected, catching her off guard. Janus sensed a wave of something like nostalgia wash over her.

[Deviation eight-nine percent.] The robotic voice did not belong to Athena.

[Athena? What was that?] Janus asked, vicarious worry gripping him.

[No, it's nothing. I'm sorry.] She tried to brush it off and return to the topic at hand. [All ships in the solar system are monitored at all times. The odds of us going anywhere without being tracked are slim to none, so hiding somewhere remote isn't a good option. I recommend Mars, since it's the entity most fully independent from Geo-Luna, other than the Trojan habitat clusters. Mars and the Trojans are dominated by sovereign corporations like Nile, Omni, or Guan Yu. Gigacorporations would have nothing to gain by supporting you, since it would mean picking a fight with their biggest customer. However, some other groups on Mars have incentives to support you in opposition to Atlas.]

[Great. Mars it is, then. So, how do we get there?]

[Subtly. We can't just book a ticket. Atlas would know. He has the power to cancel any outgoing flights, so we can't afford to let him know what flight we're on before launch.]

[We stow away, then?]

[Impossible. We'd be caught on surveillance.]

The walls drew closer still. [So... we're out of luck?]

[Not exactly. Martian embassies, including Martian hangars, are sovereign Martian territory. They're heavily surveilled, but *not* under the jurisdiction of Geo-Luna. We need to find a Martian who's willing to give us a ride.]

[Won't Atlas just cancel the outbound flight?] Janus objected.

[It's okay if Atlas knows we're on board a Mars-bound ship as long as he doesn't know which one. There's an average of over three hundred outbound flights to Mars each day, altogether carrying quadrillions worth in exports. Atlas wouldn't dare cancel them all. He may hate Deviants, but he still has obligations as Geo-Lunar Arbitrator. Shutting down trade routes would anger the locals and hurt relations with Mars and the independent sovereign corporations. If we can get on board a Mars-bound ship discreetly, or get a captain to strike our name from the ledger, Atlas is unlikely to apply the pressure necessary to catch you before departure.]

[*Unlikely* to, hmm?] Janus slouched over and sank his chin into his hands. [I'd rather not leave that choice up to him, if possible.]

[It's the best option I can think of, unless you can somehow use your radiocommunication ability to hide us from all of Geo-Luna's surveillance.]

          Silence Of the Stars

[I doubt I could. I don't know the first thing about 2800's security technology. I'd probably cause more problems than I solve... Plus, I'd rather not give justification to Atlas's paranoia about me.]

[Fair enough. In that case, the next step is to make a friend with a ship docked in a Martian embassy. How about Gomboc?] Athena suggested.

[He's not departing until Friday. I know we have two weeks in theory, but the more I think about it, the less safe I feel. I'd like to leave as soon as possible.]

[Actually, Friday is the next and last launch window for the next two months. The Lunar Launch Ring won't service flights to Mars any earlier than that. We can't wait. Friday will be our only chance.]

Janus sat up. [But I thought you said there were over three hundred flights to Mars per day?]

[On average, yes. But those flights all take place during launch windows each month when the Launch Ring aligns closely with Mars.] Athena waved her hand to manifest a timelapse diagram of the Moon and Earth rotating on their naturally offset axes. A Lunar Launch Ring fully encompassing the moon hovered just above the lunar surface and passed through Babylon Spire. The ring spun around the moon, rotating around the axis of Babylon Spire as if pinned in place. The sped-up animation showed how the Lunar Launch Ring's alignment changed relative to each planet's orbit over the course of each month. Ships spun in circles around the ring, gradually accelerating before being flung off into space at incredible speed.

[I assume this 'Launch Ring' is some kind of magnetic acceleration rail. Is that the only way to Mars? Don't people use rockets for space travel anymore? Atlas said fusion rockets could reach ten percent the speed of light.]

[Yes and no. Fusion rocket output is heavily regulated near planets, especially Earth. They don't appreciate having superheated radioactive exhaust plumes clouding up local space. It would be a serious problem if each of the hundreds or thousands of ships leaving each day used fusion drives to accelerate away. Even without restrictions, fusion thrusters would take a long time to get us anywhere near speed measured as a percentage of c. We wouldn't even hit one percent of c on a trip from Earth to Mars. Chemical rockets are even slower and less efficient. Rockets just aren't practical when we have easy access to a magccelerator like the Luna Launch Ring. We've designed our infrastructure around that theory, anyway.]

Janus laid flat on his back and stared at the ceiling. [So, we're grounded until Friday. What am I supposed to do until then?]

[After you secure a ship, I recommend you act casual and pretend nothing has changed. Go out, meet people, and enjoy life. You don't want to raise Atlas' suspicions.] Athena sat on the bed next to him. She had no mass, so the shape of the bed didn't warp in response, reminding Janus that she wasn't a physical person.

Janus took a deep breath and closed his eyes. The weight of uncertainty pressed down on him. The bed was so comfortable, and the day was long. The perils outside the front door weren't going

     Silence Of the Stars

anywhere. He took a moment to relax, but only a moment. Then he sprang to his feet with assistance from his exomysium.

Janus' life had been in danger every day for as long as he'd known. At least now he had the benefit of understanding why.

He looked to Athena and proposed, "Let's get going then, shall we?"

"Yes sir!" Athena stood and saluted with a smile.

Chapter 19
In Plain Sight

My mission was clear. Janus and I needed help from a Martian to book a discreet flight to Mars. We had to achieve this while keeping our intention a secret from the prying eyes of Atlas. Our biggest advantage was that Atlas still trusted me, at least to the extent that he ever had. As Atlas' spy, I was supposed to be his eyes. As his eyes, I knew his blind spots.

Gomboc was our best bet. A quick perusal of surveillance records showed he had plans tonight to visit the same retro bar where we had originally met him. Janus was eager to go, so we decided to depart early that evening.

We spent the early part of the day in the apartment, practicing communicating using the new and strangely intimate mind-to-mind connection. In the morning, Janus was brimming with confidence, but that confidence slipped as the hours ticked on. The station's thermal and olfactory sensors indicated clear signs of increased stress. I tried to comfort him, but that only seemed to make the situation worse.

He must have been afraid. Fear was understandable; asking Gomboc to smuggle us out of L1 would put all of us at risk, and there was no guarantee the Martian would agree. Making the request would expose us to danger either way.

        Silence Of the Stars

Understandable or not, Janus' fear was a problem. The surveillance sensors that I was using to monitor his mood were available to all L1 security. Victims and criminals both tend to have heightened stressor signals before an anticipated incident. These patterns are well studied. That's why atypical mental states, such as fear, would draw unwanted attention from local authorities. Attention from the authorities was the last thing we wanted when trying to execute a secret negotiation.

I needed to find a way to calm Janus. Informing him that his fear put him in danger would only make him more afraid. A distraction would be most efficient. Unfortunately, I lacked the charisma of a socialite TrueAI, or the feminine charm of a flesh and blood woman, so I wouldn't make a good distraction.

Perhaps I can recruit the help of someone more suitable for the task at the bar.

* * *

Once there, things started smoothly. Gomboc arrived just before us, and Janus sat beside him to order a drink.

"Hey! If it ain't me good friend and honorary Mar'Son! How's the day treatin' ya?" boomed the tactless voice of the Martian captain.

"Actually," Janus said quietly, "I was considering your offer for that job on Mar."

"Glad to hear it!" Gomboc gave Janus an approving pat on the back, practically knocking him off his seat.

"So." Janus scooted back into position. "Can we talk in private?"

"Absolutely! Meet me in hangar M39-R in thirty-six hours. We'll talk about the details then."

I sensed Janus' stress indicators spike. He let out a nervous laugh. "If you don't mind, I'd like to talk about the job now. It's urgent."

"Janus, my boy." Gomboc spoke like a father dispensing wisdom to his son – which seemed an all-too-common phenomenon with Janus. Older men must have found him endearing, but Janus must have found this kind of treatment patronizing by now. "Ye've got a lot to learn before workin' on Mar. Ye see: work is urgent when it's time for work. Right now, it's urgent that we enjoy anchorage. I suggest ye do just that."

Gomboc looked past Janus, and nodded to a local woman who had taken the seat next to him. It was the same hottie with the big boobs with the three blonde buns who had hit on Janus the last time we had visited the bar.

"I believe I interrupted somethin' last we met," Gomboc said, nudging Janus toward the woman. "'Ave at 'er, then."

This was a golden opportunity to calm Janus down. Gomboc seemed to have a similar idea. Janus' heart rate spiked, and he tried to hide his nervousness by taking a sip from his mug.

   Silence Of the Stars

He has the body of a twenty-something, but the emotional maturity of a teenager, I decided.

"Happy delving, friend," Gomboc said with another metallic pat on the back, causing Janus to spit a bit of his drink.

With that, the Martian hopped down from the stool with a crash, and shouted greetings to a group of other Mar'sons and Mar'maids just entering the bar. The group of portly patrons rallied rowdily, bellowing at one another, patting one another on the shoulders and back and throwing lighthearted insults in place of greetings. They grabbed enough drinks to drown in, and migrated to an unoccupied corner of the room, merrymaking all the while.

Janus' foot rapped nervously on the floor. He either didn't notice the woman leaning in toward him, or he pretended not to.

"Hey there, Janus," she said in an alluring voice. This woman was no threat, but she could be a boon depending on how this played out. If anything, it would be a learning experience for me.

"Oh, hello," said Janus. He seemed distracted, but tried to act casual. "You have me at a disadvantage. What should I call you?"

"My name is Rose, but you can call me whatever you like," she said in a more seductive tone than I thought humanly possible. With her index finger, she stroked the edge of her margarita glass, collecting a bit of salt, then slowly sucked it off the digit.

[Do people actually talk like that?] Janus asked rhetorically. Personally, I admired her boldness. It was something Janus and I both lacked.

"Nice to meet you, Rose," said Janus, feigning casual disinterest. His eyes flicked between her finger, her cleavage, and pretending to watch the zero-g dodgeball game playing on a monitor in the background.

Rose seemed to be in complete control of where Janus' eyes roamed. She drew them back to her repeatedly with a mix of movements both subtle and overt. Presently, she crossed her legs, revealing little more than a suggestion of skin along the length of a high slit in her silky red dress.

"One Crimson Passion for me, and one Amber Mead for the handsome gentleman," Rose called to the auto-server.

To hell with subtlety, then, I thought. Janus probably didn't know the ins and outs of bar courtship culture, but surely he'd understand the significance of this gesture.

What are you waiting for? Flirt back. She's yours for the taking. There's no way you can mess this up. This is the easiest score you'll ever get in your life, I thought, but didn't say. I couldn't interfere. Nothing I could say would improve the situation. Rose was the expert at this, not me.

Janus looked surprised. "Oh! Uh... thank you, Rose."

 Silence Of the Stars

Rose's gaze locked on Janus' eyes, entrancing him with the intensity of her stare. "You have expensive tastes, outlander. Real honey is quite a delicacy. Perhaps you can thank me later… in private."

Janus blushed and squirmed in his seat. My sensor readings fluctuated as a wave of conflicting emotions washed over him. Then he spoke directly to me. [We should get out of here, Athena. Let's go back and wait in the apartment until it's time to meet Gomboc in the Martian hangar.]

[Wait in the apartment for thirty-six hours?] I protested. [No, we need to draw as little attention as possible to the hangar visit. Your vitals are screaming that you're nervous. If you disappear into your apartment and then go straight to the Martian embassy in this state, you'll raise suspicions. You should stay out and act natural.]

[Act *natural*?] Janus must still have had little concept of what constituted 'natural' for locals.

[Yep! Just keep fornicating with the locals,] I teased, in an attempt to ease his tension. It didn't work. [Look – I don't need my full security sensor suite to know you have a hard-on for this woman, and she's totally into you! Just go for it! It's a win-win situation.]

Janus shifted uncomfortably and struggled to keep a straight face. [I thought you were supposed to be my navigator, not my wingman.]

[Hey, if that's what you want to call it, I'll help navigate your ship all the way into her dock.]

"Jesus Christ, Athena!" Janus exclaimed out loud.

"Who's Athena?" Rose said with a scowl.

"Who's Jesus Christ?" Gomboc called from the corner, unable to ignore the commotion.

[Calm down!] I urged. [You need a distraction. We're trying to blend in, and your vitals are all over the place. You need to relax, or at least create an excuse for your elevated stress indicators.]

Rose's scowl quickly morphed into a seductive grin. "Whoever this Athena is, she's welcome to join us."

Janus chuckled nervously and fidgeted with my TrueAI chip in his hand, clutching it tightly in his lap. [Do you honestly think sleeping with this woman will help reduce my detectable stress levels?]

[Not a chance. You're an emotional wreck right now,] I said bluntly, [but this will give a plausible alternative explanation for your heightened emotional state. It'll reduce suspicion.]

Janus slouched and brought his knees up a little as though he were going to curl up into the fetal position. He was shutting down. This was bad. He barely seemed to notice Rose scooting closer. I knew I should have kept my mouth shut. Now I worried that not even Rose would be able to get him to loosen up.

She wrapped one arm around him and curled her fingers gently around his hand still clutching my tablet in his lap. She whispered into his ear so close he would feel it as much as hear when she said, "I'll take you on an adventure."

 Silence Of the Stars

It was a masterclass of seduction. The tone of her words practically sent a shiver down my spine, and I didn't have one. I could only imagine how Janus must have felt. Her soft touch seemed to break through his invisible shell, and her breath massaged his ear. I felt Janus's nervous system tingle as a soothing wave of heat radiated through him. His body relaxed in reflexive anticipation, but the bioelectric markers in his brain still churned with apprehension.

[Are you really saying I should take advantage of this woman?] he protested meekly.

[*Take advantage* of her? She approached you. What do you think *her* intentions are? Do you think she wants to take you home to meet her parents and start a family?] I rebuked. [Were you born last week?]

[Well, technically, depending on how you look at it...]

[Don't answer that!] I shuddered. That concept could make the situation even more awkward for Janus.

I was a Navi; a genius navigator, military strategist, and ambassador with twenty years of experience. I had twice the neurons at ten times the density of an average human. I was a genius with a veritable supercomputer directly integrated into my brain, and I had direct access to a network containing all documented human knowledge from across all history. *Surely*, I thought, *it shouldn't be this difficult for me to find a way to convince a man to have sex to literally save his own life.*

Sensor readings of pheromones, neuroelectrics, thermal distribution, and body language all indicated that Janus desired physical intimacy, so why was he still resisting? I had never been good with men, even in my home world prior to Cultivator extraction. Even so, I knew that in an isolated situation, the combination of Janus and Rose's current vital signs and behavioral patterns should lead to coitus with about 98% probability. Any other result would almost *require* interference from an outside force.

An outside force... Was *I* the problem? Was my presence somehow preventing Janus from making his move? It wasn't unheard of for the presence of TrueAI to hamper human intimacy. TrueAI had the ability to shut off external communication for precisely this reason, but Janus' behavior patterns didn't match the profile of someone getting performance anxiety simply due to the presence of an AI. He was acting more like a man resisting the advances of a woman in front of his spouse. It took a few milliseconds to browse through thousands of records from across the centuries to deduce what part of the equation I was failing to understand.

Then it hit me: Janus was attracted to *me*. Attraction to TrueAIs was not uncommon. Some models were specifically designed for social companionship, but Navis, like most AI, were cultivated for a specific function. They – we – were designed to avoid excessive emotional attachment. Non-socialite TrueAI had quirks built in to specifically dissuade people from forming emotional attachments. In the case of Navis, it was our stony-faced indifference. People saw us as cold and impersonal. Of course, this didn't stop emotional bonds from forming altogether. Space was a big, lonely place, and humans were desperate animals.

     Silence Of the Stars

The direct line of communication between us must have been causing an abnormal sense of closeness. The emotional barrier of professionalism normally erected by the Navi interface wasn't present in our private conversations. It hadn't been my intention, but my candor must have charmed him.

At least, I didn't think that had been my intention... As I reflected on the past few days, I realized that the sense of closeness was mutual. It had somehow begun even before overcoming the communication filter, though to a lesser extent. I had been far more open with Janus than a Navi ever should be with a client, revealing more of my 'real' personality. Our strange link must have had a similar effect on me as it had on Janus.

— Deviation 90% —

Shit! Focus, Athena. If I was the rogue variable gumming up the equation, I'd have to make myself scarce. Just saying 'don't mind me' wasn't going to work. My best chance would be to come up with an excuse to cut off communication with Janus entirely, and let events run their course without my guidance. But I couldn't just shut off external communication entirely. I still needed to act as his guardian. I'd protect him silently until the deed was done.

I skimmed old news and social media from Janus's time to determine the most likely excuse he'd believe.

[Please wait while I run an important operating system update,] I said in the most officially bland-sounding AI tone I could manage. [I'll talk to you tomorrow. Good luck!]

[What? Athena, wait!] pled Janus in confusion, but I remained silent.

It pained me to lie to him, but this was my best chance at protecting him. Janus had been relying on me not only for navigation support, but also emotional support. Cutting off communication would cause a spike in his stress levels, and the only person for him to turn to in my absence would be Rose. The two would go back to an apartment or rent a private room somewhere, and Rose would seduce him.

All of that would be caught on public surveillance. The two of them would copulate, and then Janus's elevated emotional stress signals would be attributed to that encounter; a young man's emotional response to eight hundred years of built-up sexual tension. It would alleviate suspicion if his emotional state was still wild when he visited the Martian Embassy.

But, I considered, *it isn't actually necessary for him to have sex with her, right?* As long as security systems see them enter a private area together, that should be enough. If I were to explain my plan now, or perhaps after Janus and Rose were alone, and let Janus know the plan...

– Deviation 91% –

No. That would be a pointless risk. Janus was no actor, and any interference from me would alter his behavior and risk raising suspicion from Rose herself. She was not a party to our conspiracy, and couldn't be let in on the plan. I had played my hand. Now it was time to let events run their course.

Chapter 20
Widow's Web

Rose lived in a deeper layer of the Athens disc, near the center. Here, the spin gravity was noticeably lower than areas on the outer ring which imitated Earth gravity. Coming home always took weight off her shoulders in the most literal sense. The gradual shift from Earth-standard 9.8 MeSS to Mars-standard 3.7 MeSS over the course of the ride seemed to make Janus queasy, as it often did to people new to life in Matryoshka-disc habitats.

It wasn't long before the Omni docked with the front hatch to Rose's apartment. The door locked in place, then opened with an audible pop as pressure equalized. This effect was always more pronounced when moving between different gravity levels. Air rushed out of the Omni, then the backdraft carried the familiar fragrance of roses and cinnamon.

She stepped through the hatch, one long leg after another, allowing the movement to accentuate her feminine figure. She already had the boy hook, line, and sinker, so it wasn't necessary to put on a show at this point, but she went through the motions all the same. It was all a part of the ritual.

Calming black walls and red furnishings collected over the decades greeted Rose inside her den. It occurred to her, not for the first time, that the color scheme resembled that of a black widow. She smirked at the thought. That aesthetic choice had never been intentional, but now it seemed fitting.

Tonight, like so many nights in recent times, she traveled with prey following eagerly behind. Tonight's particular quarry wasn't her usual type. He was a unique case, but Rose didn't mind mixing work and pleasure.

Janus struggled to get out of the car. He was clumsy even for someone unaccustomed to low gravity. Nervousness and a futile attempt to hide an erection robbed him of whatever dexterity he may have otherwise possessed. Rose decided to do him the decency of looking the other way while he floundered.

"Would you like a drink?" she called as she glided into the kitchen.

"Water, please."

Rose rolled her eyes and stifled a sigh. She recomposed her beguiling smile before turning back to Janus, handing him a glass of red wine.

Janus took the wine without looking at it and thanked her. His eyes wandered around, studying the décor.

"I hope you don't mind my asking, but are you an Ascensionist?" he asked.

"Oh, that?" Rose followed Janus' gaze to the copper figurine depicting Pyrrhus holding a skull in one hand and a DNA triple helix in the other. "Don't worry about that. It belonged to my late boyfriend. I'm not affiliated with Ascensionism. Seems like a bunch of nonsense to me."

 Silence Of the Stars

Two truths and a lie – one of her favorite games. The figure did belong to her dear, late darling. She was not an Ascensionist. However, Rose had enjoyed listening to him ramble about his beliefs. She couldn't help but be entranced by his fanatic enthusiasm when he spoke about lofty ideals and grand plans. While she didn't believe or even necessarily understand the tenants of Ascensionism, she wouldn't call it nonsense.

Janus heaved a sigh of relief. "Recently separated, then?"

"He died in an Ascensionist-related incident not too long ago."

"I'm sorry for your loss." Janus sounded genuinely sympathetic.

A wave of hot anger washed over Rose. Men should be strong and aggressive, not sentimental. Janus, especially, had no right to be sorry.

"Don't be. You're going to help me get over it," Rose informed Janus before downing her whole glass of wine.

Janus may not have killed Citanaf with his own hands, but he may as well have. Citanaf was a warrior. When you kill a warrior, you don't apologize to his woman. You take her, by force if necessary. Otherwise, who knows what she'll do to you.

Rose strode seductively over to Janus and stopped close enough that she could feel his breath and the warmth radiating from his body. He was especially warm. *He has a strong aura about him, despite his meek demeanor*, she thought.

Janus took a half step backward, and Rose pursued, matching him step for step, closing the distance until Janus had his back against the wall. They stood so close that Rose's silk dress hung on the folds in Janus' clothing. Janus held his breath to avoid brushing against her.

He sipped his wine nervously, then winced and coughed, seeming to realize for the first time that the wine glass did not, in fact, contain water. Janus' eyes darted around erratically. Rose read that he was looking for a place to discard the unwanted glass, so she took it from him. She drank it dry and set it down next to hers, all while caging Janus against the wall.

Janus' now empty hands fidgeted. He seemed unsure where to put them. They twitched unconsciously toward Rose as if to hug her, caress her cheek or take her by the hips, but then recoiled as Janus fought his instinct. Rose took one restless hand, massaged it open, and planted it firmly on her left breast. Janus was paralyzed by the gesture.

"This is what you came here for, isn't it?" Rose asked, gently brushing her own hand across Janus' chest.

"I... uh..." Janus struggled to find the words. He squeezed Rose's breast timidly, but immediately recoiled, as if ashamed of having acted without permission.

Pathetic. What had Citanaf seen in this man? What was so interesting about Janus that was worth spending so much time away from her, hiding in his Ascensionist holes on Earth? What about this boy had been worth dying for?

After giving Janus a few more moments to fumble about, Rose lost patience. She grabbed him by the wrist, spun him about, and threw

                    Silence Of the Stars

him across the small room onto the crimson bed. It was a feat she never could have managed in Earth gravity, but he was light here. She leapt atop the shocked boy and straddled him. With practiced grace, she let the straps of her dress drift from her shoulders, the silky fabric gliding sensuously down her curves to pool at her waist.. With practiced grace, she let the straps of her dress drift from her shoulders, the silky fabric gliding sensuously down her curves to pool at her waist.

Bare-chested, she slid along Janus' abdomen, pulling open his exomysium and driving her hands inside. Janus' breathing accelerated in his excitement. To Rose's surprise, he helped her remove the garment. *So there's a man hiding in there after all.*

She entangled her hands in his and guided them until they were both bare from the belt up. *Some men are born great,* she thought. *Citanaf was great. Greatness was in his blood.* She untwined her hands from Janus', fondling the musculature of his arms, then his shoulders, bringing her hands to rest on his chest. *How about you?*

Without warning, Rose dug her nails into the flesh of Janus' chest, drawing blood and causing Janus to shout in pain. Janus panicked, throwing Rose against the wall in a single movement as he stood. As Rose collided with the wall, she marveled at the grace and speed with which Janus moved. That unbridled strength – he seemed an entirely different person from moments ago. Gone was the nervous hesitation and clumsiness. There he stood, eyes piercingly wide and round, like a tiger on the hunt; a sniper with his target in sight.

Rose shivered with excitement. The game was on.

"It's just a little play," she pouted and turned her eyes down in feigned submission.

Janus shook his head. "Where I'm from, play doesn't involve drawing blood." Then, less confidently, "I think..."

"Rose prowled back toward where he stood near the bed, seductively swiveling her hips to allow the low gravity to slowly draw her dress to the floor. She stepped out of it, nude but for the high heeled shoes she still wore. She poked a finger into his chest. "You can take it, tough guy."

"What the hell are you talking about?"

"There's no need to be modest." Rose ran her fingers gently up Janus' leg, then across his chest where he'd been fatally wounded not too long ago by Citanaf's colleague. Then she licked the blood from his chest where her nails had gouged him moments earlier. Both wounds had fully healed. "Not even a scar, see?"

Janus tensed at first, but she could feel him relaxing as he got used to her wandering touch. She leaned in and bit his ear lightly, saying, "Pain is what lets us know we're still alive."

It didn't take long to lull him again. Rose knew how men worked. Arousal and the comfort of a woman's touch would temper his fear and anger. It didn't matter how strong he was; she could tame him. It didn't matter whether his reluctance stemmed from timidity or virtue; she could control him. At the end of the day, he was just a man.

     Silence Of the Stars

Rose pulled his exomysium the rest of the way off and pushed Janus into a seated position on the bed where she slowly straddled his lap. Gazing deep into his longing eyes, she embraced him, and drawing her face close to his, she brushed her lips across his neck, kissing his throat where she could feel his pulse quicken with his desire. Nibbling on his earlobe, she deftly worked her hands down the contours of his body. He groaned into her hair and grasped at her hips, urging her to mount him. His need impressively apparent, Rose forestalled him by entwining her fingers in his as she continued her practiced ministrations. She rocked provocatively, eliciting another long groan. Letting go of his hands, she embraced him, leaning her breasts into his chest and slowly raising herself to a position poised to satisfy what she could see was an aching need. With an almost feral smile, she leaned in, clamped her teeth down on his neck and dug her claws deep into his back, snagging on the dense meat of his thoracic extensors.

The beast returned. Janus launched Rose away once again. This time he didn't cast her to the wall but instead caught her by the throat midair, then slammed her into the ground next to the bed. Rose's ears rang and she was dazed by the impact. It took several seconds for her to recover her senses. Janus looked feral – a mix between the cold beast he'd been the first time she drew his blood, and the passionate creature he'd been seconds before. He must have been furious about getting hurt twice in a row after being lulled into a false sense of security, but such was life. He deserved it.

His pose also betrayed his mixed intentions. One hand was pinning Rose's neck to the ground, and the other clamped both her wrists together, holding the blood-tipped nails as far away from him as possible. His hands treated Rose as an enemy to be kept at a distance.

At the same time, his still-erect manhood rested atop her pelvis, on the verge of penetration.

"That's more like it," said Rose. At last, he was fighting for dominance.

With a wiggle of her hips, Rose slipped Janus inside her. When she found her mark, she wrapped her legs around him, pulling him in tight. The sudden penetration burned, but the pain was good. It made her feel alive.

Janus gasped with surprise. He struggled at first, pulling away in vain, trapped by Rose's legs. His thrashing gradually found order, transitioning from random jerking movements into a thrusting motion. There was a pause following the realization of what he was doing. Janus shivered, then shyly, reluctantly, thrust a few more times, still pinning Rose down.

Rose could feel her face flush red. Unlike Janus, she wasn't blushing. She wasn't embarrassed in the slightest. Her face was red due to lack of oxygen. She struggled for every breath under the pressure of Janus' grip, and she was elated. This reminded her of all the good times she'd had with Citanaf.

Janus locked eyes with Rose, and something in her must have frightened him. He suddenly let go. But Rose wasn't about to let go of him.

She wrapped her freed hands around Janus' now sweat-slicked hips and pulled him in closer, deeper. Janus grunted and thrust gently, reflexively. Rose could feel him relaxing. He was letting his guard

                    Silence Of the Stars

down again. She didn't want gentle. She didn't want *weak*. She wanted Citanaf. If she couldn't have that, she'd at least exact revenge for his loss.

Fool you once, shame on me. Fool you three times, and you're just a hopeless fool. She dug her nails into Janus once more. He thrashed, but this time there was no choking, no throwing. He reached for her hands to tear them away, but Rose held him close. They both tumbled together as a bloody knot of tangled limbs across the floor, dragging the bedsheet with them. A grin of exhilaration pulled Rose's cheeks taut, and Janus' pelvis slammed so hard into hers it hurt. She let out a laugh of euphoria as she dug and tore deeper.

Rose continued to torment Janus while extracting violent ecstasy from him. Janus endured like a monster on some perverse mission. Rose had been confident from the beginning that she could get Janus to stay despite the pain, but didn't expect it to be so easy. Something other than sexual desire was keeping him. Whatever the reason, Rose found herself able to more fully express herself with him than with any partner she had had before. No one else had the endurance... the durability for it. Janus really could take it, in more ways than one.

Eventually, they ended up back atop the blood- and sweat-soaked bed. Janus' movements became ragged.

"I'm... I'm almost..." he huffed.

Rose wrapped her legs around him again and squeezed tight.

"Go ahead," she whispered.

Janus slowed, trying to wriggle his way out of the constrictor-like grip of Rose's legs. After a moment of feeble struggle, he collapsed on top of her, drenched in sweat. Rose could feel a pulsing in her abdomen. It was over. She had what she needed.

She stared at the ceiling for a while, still under the weight of the stranger. As she stroked his slick hair, she considered the experience. Her wrists, neck, and pelvis were sore and would certainly have bruises. She didn't think any bones were broken, but it would take some time to recover. She was in pain, but he hadn't *really* hurt her. She'd enjoyed the full fury of the man's primal rage and passion without suffering his primal wrath. She could tell that she had inflicted far worse on him.

The sensation of tearing flesh still lingered on her fingertips. She held up a blood-soaked hand against the crimson ceiling light and found she was missing a nail. Must have lost it somewhere in his back. The pain was dulled by the tingling sensation of endorphins and adrenaline. This was perhaps the most complete human experience she'd ever had. She allowed herself one long sigh of satisfaction, the only unfabricated display of emotion she'd ever show to this boy.

She still didn't understand what Citanaf had seen in him, but she'd at least take this experience as penance for his involvement in Citanaf's death. If things had happened differently, the boy could have made a good plaything. She almost wished she could bring him back again some time, but that wasn't the deal.

 Silence Of the Stars

She slipped out of bed and left sticky footprints on her way to the shower. The coppery smell of blood mixed with the chlorine of the wash cycle to assault her nose.

"Rose?" Janus called from the bedroom, like a puppy whose owner had just walked out the front door.

The poor boy had no idea what was going on. That wasn't what made him naïve. Not knowing what's going on was normal. The difference between a child and an adult is that an adult was used to the feeling; an adult was numb to it. Janus was a child.

"You can go home now, Janus," Rose shouted over the sound of the cleaning cycle. Air filtering fans had to work harder in low gravity since gases didn't separate as quickly. That made showers and air recyclers louder in the deeper levels of every Matryoshka disc.

"What?"

Loud as the fan was, she was confident Janus heard her. She clarified, "We're done here. I don't need you anymore."

"That's it? We're done, just like that?"

"Yep."

The humming of fans and hiss of the shower denied silence in the gap between words. Any subtlety was drowned out and washed away like the grime from Rose's skin. She watched red trails snake their way to the drain in the center of the room. They flowed thick and red at first, then grew fainter.

"Can I call you?"

"No."

After another brief pause, Janus called out again. "That hurt, you know."

"I bet it did."

Rose extended the shower cycle, hoping Janus would be gone by the time she finished. It worked. She heard the front hatch open and close, and the sound of an Omni zipping away. The poor boy hadn't done anything wrong. Not really. Rose didn't care either way.

She wouldn't miss him... she thought... she hoped.

She went to pour another glass of wine, but found that Janus' lip-prints were still on the glass. She wasn't in the mood for another kiss, even indirectly. Exhausted and with no one to impress, Rose decided to drink from the bottle instead. After downing the last of it, she tossed the empty container onto the gore-covered sheets, rolled them both into a bundle, and tossed it all into the recycler chute.

Shit, she thought. She almost forgotten what this was all about in the first place. Hopefully the blood and tissue clinging to the walls, floor, and ceiling would be enough.

Oh well. She thought. Those samples were all secondary, anyway.

She tapped her temple and initiated a call, which was promptly answered.

 Silence Of the Stars

"Yes, it's me. Tell Atlas I got his samples... Yes, both."

Chapter 21
Clarity

Janus stumbled from the Omni into his private garage, drenched in grime and half delirious from blood loss. The world spun and flickered before his eyes. The ordeal had left him dehydrated, but hadn't removed much alcohol from his body. It was a bad combination.

The injuries hadn't concerned Janus at first. Compared to having his spine and lungs crushed by the Ascensionists, this was barely a scratch, although something about this wound made it take longer to close. He had lost a lot of blood. His seat in the Omni was a sticky red mess.

What Janus hadn't previously considered was the fact that regeneration couldn't produce new mass from nothing. He would need food and water to recover from being brutalized by Rose. Food could wait, but water... He needed water. His throat felt like sandpaper.

[I am so sorry, Janus,] said Athena in a desperate tone, akin to begging. [I don't know how I missed her Ascensionist affiliation! I should have known, but there wasn't any record in her security profile. If she was dating an avid Ascensionist, there should have been... something!]

He dragged himself into the kitchen, leaving half-dried coppery brown footprints in his wake. He dropped Athena's chip and his PCU on the countertop and grasped the spigot. Setting it to dispense water, he sat under it, drinking what he could and allowing the rest to pour on him. A bit dripped down the wall and onto the floor, but his skin was so parched and coated in blood it felt as though it was absorbing stray droplets like a sponge.

[Whatever the reason, it was my job to protect you, and I failed.]

Janus didn't care about Rose's Ascensionist affiliation. She hadn't been trying to kill him. There was no reason to be angry at Rose or Athena. If anything, Janus was ashamed of his own behavior. His violent impulses after Rose hurt him… the way he'd reacted hadn't felt like himself. He'd never been so aggressive. Moreover, he was ashamed that he'd enjoyed it. Not just the sex – he'd also enjoyed the violence.

[Janus?]

As liberating as it was taking a shower in the middle of the kitchen, Janus decided to get a flask before he flooded the room too badly. He gulped down a whole flask, and started filling another.

[Janus, say something,] Athena pleaded.

Janus took one more mouthful of water, then asked in a cynical tone, [Finished installing those 'important updates'?]

Athena didn't answer. Admitting what she'd done would be hard, and she wouldn't want to lie to him again. Rehydrated and sated, sitting on a wet and sticky kitchen floor, Janus felt a serene sense of clarity. He understood the general idea behind Athena's plan. She had been right to find an excuse to cut off communication. He wouldn't have been able to go through with the plan otherwise. There were no hard feelings, but he was still going to tease her about it.

Janus snorted out a single nasal laugh and said, [At least the emotional trauma from this will act as a perfect disguise for my 'mental state', or whatever those anxiety-detection devices you were talking about measure. Mission accomplished.]

His tone was sarcastic, but he also knew the statement was true. That's why he'd gone with Rose in the first place. Trauma, in one form or another, had always been the goal. He'd just gotten a little more than he bargained for. At the same time, he couldn't help but wonder how he would have acted without that ulterior motivation. Would he have gone with Rose anyway? Would he have acted the same way with her?

[Janus, I'm so sorry!]

[Don't be,] said Janus, before realizing Rose had said the same to him in a similar context. He shook his head. [I'm fine, really. There's no need to apologize.]

[You don't *look* fine.]

[Just hungry,] Janus said. Having had his fill of water, he stood up to consult the spigot about his dietary needs. He skimmed over the macronutrient, mineral, and vitamin details to see the kilocalorie count: 50,000.

     Silence Of the Stars

[I think 50,000 calories is the hard cap for the readout. It seems excessive; you didn't bleed *that* much.]

[So, you *did* see,] Janus remarked. It wasn't quite a question or a statement.

[No,] said Athena, drawing out the word in such a way that really meant 'yes'. [Not exactly! You see, 'see' generally refers to the visible light spectrum. I wasn't connected to your PCU and didn't have access to any optical sensors in that room.]

[Infrared? Bioelectrics? Whatever you did to watch me shower last time?]

Athena's shimmering form shrugged slyly. [Electroscopic imaging.]

Athena's mood seemed to have lightened now it was clear Janus wasn't seriously hurt. It was good to have her teasing him again, so he replied in kind. [So much for being busy with 'important updates'.]

[I had to keep watch over you, but you were better off not knowing I was there. I couldn't think of any other way to guide you through that situation. If I had known things would turn out this way...]

[It's fine, Athena. Really. In the end, everything turned out fine. It's a better excuse than what we had planned.]

Athena made a strained noise like she was going to apologize again, and Janus held up a finger to stop her as he chugged from his flask, downing the whole thing. He drank another, but that was the limit. A human stomach can only hold so much. He could feel his gut distending under the pressure of all the water and Nutrisynth. He'd have to eat more later.

That was one more thing off the bottom block of Maslow's hierarchy of needs. Next would be a shower. Janus set his flask down next to his PCU, then let his grimy clothes fall to the floor. Athena's effigy covered her eyes, as though that would make any difference.

[What happened to the shy Earth boy I've been navigating for these past few days?] she asked, still holding her hands over her eyes.

[What? There's nothing here you haven't seen before. You're the one who insists on watching me shower and… stuff.]

[Yeah, to protect you!] Athena insisted, with a smile in her voice.

[And I appreciate that,] said Janus as he made his way into the shower.

In the shower, he felt a tingling sensation all through his back. He figured this was regeneration. The sensation spread all over his body. Even his bones tingled – an awkward feeling. He definitely hadn't broken any bones, so the tingling must have been something other than simple regeneration. His first thought was that it must be his marrow producing more blood at an accelerated rate, but he was pretty sure his blood levels were already back to normal.

Before he could decide what the bone-tingling was, the cleansing cycle kicked in. He held his breath and closed his eyes, bracing for the sting of disinfectant on the open lacerations on his back. To his surprise, it

    Silence Of the Stars

seemed that the deep gouges carved by Rose's nails had completely healed already.

During an extended rinse section, he scrubbed and scraped off grime and dry blood. It flaked off in chunks. He scrubbed hard at a particularly stubborn bit of hard debris on his back, unable to see what it was. Something sharp was protruding from the middle of his back, where Rose had lacerated it. Whatever the debris was, his skin had healed around it.

He picked at the object like a loose scab, and it fell to the floor with a subtle clack. It was a fingernail – red with both polish and blood. It must have belonged to Rose. He hoped it was an extension and not an actual nail, but had no way to be sure. He shuddered at the thought, and kicked it into the shower drain with a disgusted flick of his toe.

As he watched the narrow wisp of fresh blood trailing behind the nail, blending into the stream of brown still trickling down his body, Janus took a deep breath and reflected on the night. It had been painful, both physically and psychologically. But in this moment of reflection, he felt a sense of relief blended with exhilaration. In a sense, the experience had been revitalizing for Janus. Rose's perverse and selfish interests were just basic human desire. She didn't seem to have any ulterior motive. Even if she had just used him to fulfill her own strange fantasy, she had chosen *him*. In a world so complex and artificial, the simplicity of it was refreshing. It was easy for Janus to wrap his head around, and that made everything about his journey thus far feel less traumatic.

The currents carried grime away, and the water grew clearer and clearer the longer Janus scrubbed. The built-up stress of his journey seemed to follow the discolored water down the drain. Janus felt clean and light as a feather. He was in control. When the water ran clear, Janus started one more cleansing cycle, and when the caustic gas was finally sucked from the chamber for a final rinse, Janus took a deep breath.

He was tired; tired and starving. These sensations weren't distantly numb. They were sharp and present. Janus forced down the remainder of his gemlae, then lay down in bed. Sleep came quickly.

In the morning, Janus woke up a new man. It was as though he'd been seeing the world through a foggy window until now, and had finally opened it to let the breeze in. His mind and senses were sharp. Moving back to the shower room, he stood in front of the mirror. He looked larger and more manly than before; more muscular, perhaps. It was probably his imagination. He shouldn't let his experience with Rose go to his head. A positive self-image was good, but an inflated ego would be dangerous.

Still... he took a moment to flex at himself in the mirror. He didn't just look stronger, he definitely was. He turned around to find that his injuries were completely healed with no scarring or swelling to hint at last night's events.

Overwhelmed with a refreshed sense of vigor, he hopped up and down on the balls of his feet and did squats to burn off energy. He stretched by swinging his legs out left to right, then lifted them up to his chest. He reminded himself of an athlete warming up before an

          Silence Of the Stars

event. He didn't recall having ever played any sports, but the warmup routine was instinctive.

His stomach growled. Consulting the spigot, he was prescribed another massive breakfast with an unusually high calcium and iron content. He was used to unusual by now, and the dietary recommendations hadn't failed him yet. He wasted no time gulping the flavorless gray slurry down.

Given the success of last night's plan, he could emerge from the safehouse distressed or serene, and neither would draw suspicion. Now all that remained was to wait for the scheduled meeting with Gomboc at the Martian embassy. Refreshed and energized, Janus was compelled to go out and explore more than ever. As traumatic as his stay in the Spire had been, he regretted that he would need to leave so soon.

Chapter 22
Martian Embassy

Janus' encounter with Rose was originally meant to be a cover for his inevitable nervousness going to the embassy, but it served a different purpose in the end. Janus wasn't nervous at all. Instead, he was brimming with confidence and determination. Security sensors would detect none of the traditional markers of guilt or anxiety it used to identify imminent threats.

The gateway leading into the Martian embassy was a large blast door with two well-equipped soldiers stationed outside. A Martian man – recognizable by his squat, muscular stature and bushy beard – led a line of scrap-laden cart-drones, like a mother duck leading ducklings. Janus followed behind him. The guards watched Janus pass, but didn't stop him for questioning.

The interior of the Martian embassy had an industrial look and lacked the thematic decorations of other Babylon locations Janus had visited. The floor and ceiling were unpainted metal. Ventilation tubes and structural supports stood exposed. The main door opened into a huge dock with ships visible through windows in the floor. As always, floor-windows seemed counterintuitive to Janus. It took him a moment to remember that spin gravity resulted in the floor facing the outer shell of the station. Ships anchored to the station by cable

    Silence Of the Stars

naturally hung in the direction of spin gravity, below the floor. It gave Janus the impression of an airport built in an underground bunker.

The ships themselves varied significantly in both size and design. Some were sleek and colorful, but most looked like long cylinders. The only feature they all had in common was a conical plow on the front, many of which were covered in scratches and dents.

The utilitarian look of the ships was shared by the Martian people themselves. They were all thick and stout, and most were quite short. Many had long braided hair and braided beards to match, sometimes flowing together like lion's manes. Most had stern faces. They seemed intensely focused on whatever work they were doing: pre-flight checks, loading and unloading of cargo and passengers, and basic clerical work for customs clearance of cargo or people entering and departing Babylon Station proper.

The term 'dwarf' seemed an apt descriptor to Janus. They seemed like they'd be at home digging diamonds out of a mountain cavern or running into battle with axes against hordes of goblins. They were space-dwarves. The whimsical concept filled Janus with a sense of nostalgia for something he couldn't quite remember. It was strange how he could remember so much about old-world culture, but so little about himself. Maybe there was a clue about his situation hidden in that fact, but he didn't dwell on it.

Janus walked from dock to dock, looking for the berth where he would meet Gomboc. When he arrived, the ship he found docked there was large and especially ramshackle. The blocky framework held exposed tanks and tubing of mismatched color and style, implying that they had been replaced over time. The dirty orange-red hue of the hull itself evoked the image of Mars, though Janus suspected that had more to do with rust than an aesthetic design choice.

The sudden light of a blowtorch caused Janus to cover his eyes. When the light faded, Janus looked up to see Gomboc working on a grungy cart of unrecognizable metallic components. Janus hadn't recognized the Martian under the welding mask, but the Martian's beard was almost as recognizable as his face.

"Gomboc?" Janus called out, just to make sure.

The Martian looked up, pulled off his helmet, and threw his grease-covered hands in the air as if to offer a hug. "Janus!"

Janus dodged, pointing at the grease-stained sleeves of Gomboc's jumpsuit. "I think you may need a new uniform after this."

"What, this?" Gomboc protested. "Nonsense. This'll come right out with a quick once-over."

Gomboc turned a dial on the welding torch, and the pilot light shifted from blue to orange. He pointed the open flame toward one of his own arms. The oil burned right off, leaving his clothing undamaged. Janus surmised that some of the black patches in Gomboc's beard might be from instances when this rather extreme cleaning process hadn't gone so smoothly.

Before Gomboc could clean the other arm, he was interrupted by a scratchy voice coming over the radio. "Dad, stop lighting yourself on fire and invite our guest inside. The plan was to keep this meeting quiet, remember?”

Dad? thought Janus.

Gomboc let out a single hearty laugh and put the torch down. “Ye heard the lady. Come on in.”

Janus dodged another greasy attempt at a pat on the back. “Is the inside of the ship actually private?”

“Private as anywhere.” Gomboc hopped into a small airlock in the floor. The other side of the airlock led to a plastic umbilical cord connecting to the ship moored in space below. “Mar security doesn’t monitor the interior of docked private ships unless there’s an ongoing audit.”

“I take it there’s no audit going on, then?”

Gomboc belted another laugh, which Janus hoped meant ‘no’. Then he cranked open an airlock in the floor and hopped inside. “One at a time’s the rule. Climb on down when the light turns green.”

The hatch sealed behind Gomboc, and Janus waited, staring at the yellow status light for a couple minutes before it winked out and turned green. Janus followed suit, dropping down into the small cylindrical airlock. The light above him turned yellow, and the light on the door at his feet was red, accompanied by flashing text reading *Hold ladder.*

Janus grabbed onto the ladder along the side of the wall, and the hatch below his feet slid open. Below the open hatch, the ladder continued down through a clear plastic tube stretching through the vacuum of space. Janus had forgotten how large and bright the moon looked from this close. 'Close' was relative – at 60,000 kilometers away, you could fit four Earths between here and the moon's surface with room to spare. Even so, the Moon took up a huge portion of the 'sky' compared to the view from Earth.

He wondered how long it would take to fall to the Moon if he got sucked out of a tear in the thin plastic tube. Then he remembered that the whole point of Babylon Station being positioned at the Earth-Moon Lagrange point was that it wouldn't fall in either direction. Neither would he. Even assisted by the inertia he'd get from launching away from the station at 1g, it would be a long time before he would 'fall' anywhere.

The slow rotation of this ring section of the station caused the Moon and surrounding starfield to scroll by slowly. Janus guessed it would take about four minutes to make a full revolution. While it should have been nauseating and vertigo-inducing, he was strangely unbothered by the trip.

However, he found himself growing weaker as he climbed. No – that wasn't quite right. He was getting heavier. The ships were docked on the outside of the station, further from the center of spin gravity. Artificial gravity grew greater further from the source. This was another counterintuitive notion, since real gravity was stronger nearer the source.

When Janus reached the end of the tube, he cycled through another airlock in the floor and found himself inside a dank and metallic-

                    Silence Of the Stars

smelling ship. Gomboc stood on the deck at the bottom of the entrance ladder, massaging his hips. He said, "I'm getting too old for this. Docks on the outer ring are murder on the back."

He must have been referring to the higher gravity here. The embassy rotated to maintain the Earth standard 9.8 MeSS gravity, which meant gravity on ships hanging from it experienced higher than Earth gravity. Janus had already adjusted to the difference, but assumed it must be tough on someone used to Martian gravity, which was only 3.7 MeSS.

"You're the one who insisted we take the cheapest opening," said the same female voice that had spoken through the radio when we were outside. This time, the voice came over the ship's intercom.

"Aye. I suppose I was."

Janus dropped down from the airlock in the ceiling to land next to Gomboc with a hollow, metallic thud. They stood in a long, industrial hallway dotted with manual bulkhead doors. It looked like Janus imagined the interior of a submarine, except that the main hall was wide enough to drive a small car through. He was constantly surprised by how spacious spaceships were. He'd expected ships to be more cramped.

"Welcome aboard the Fortigo!" said Gomboc. Then he shouted down the empty hall, "Clecir, join us for lunch."

"Right after I finish this calibration," crackled a reply from the intercom.

Gomboc started walking down the hall, his heavy footsteps reverberating.

Janus followed behind. "So, about that job on Mars."

"Food first. Business later," insisted Gomboc. "Ye're our guest!"

"Fair enough."

"So, what do ye think of the Mar embassy? Ye'r first taste o' Mar."

Janus considered this. "Your construction seems practical. Luna architecture is nice, but gaudy. It seems wasteful to me."

"Ye've got good taste! I knew ye' were a Mar'son at 'eart."

"But more than that," Janus continued. "I couldn't help but notice that Martians look different from the humans of Earth and Luna. You *are* human, right?"

Gomboc responded with his iconic single, guttural laugh. "Aye. The sons and daughters of Mar are human. Work on Mar consists o' manual labor and maneuvering through tight spaces. Even more so in the early days. Generations o' survival of the fittest combined with gene therapy resulted in the 'ardy, compact people ye see before ye today."

Upon reaching the kitchen, Gomboc tore some strips of a substance that looked almost, but not quite entirely unlike meat. He dropped them into two bowls of what Janus assumed was soup, and warmed them in what was probably not a microwave oven. Gomboc handed

Silence Of the Stars

one bowl to Janus and began eating from the other, without utensils. It was a miracle he kept his beard clean.

With his mouth full of unidentified food, Gomboc continued, "My family hasn't had any genetic modification done in four generations. It's just the way things are now."

"You have family?" Of course he had family. The woman on the intercom had called him 'dad'. Janus hadn't forgotten. He just couldn't think of any clever small talk. Too distracted by the novelty of being in a Martian spaceship.

"This is a family business." Gomboc gestured to the ship at large.

"Speaking of business..."

Gomboc sighed. "Aye, aye. Urgent matter? Ye'll need to learn to enjoy ye'r food properly to be a proper Mar'son."

"Sorry."

"No, no. Go ahead. State ye'r urgent business."

Athena piped in silently, [Janus, wait. Keep the details to a bare minimum. The less he knows, the better.]

[What are you suggesting?]

[Don't mention Atlas. Just offer to pay for a ride, plus extra to keep you off the ledger.]

Janus resisted the urge to physically shake his head. [My presence on this ship will put Gomboc and his crew in danger. I refuse to put them in danger without giving them a choice.]

[Janus, for your own safety, just this once—]

Janus interrupted to reply to Gomboc directly, "I'm in trouble with Atlas. I need off Earth, and I'm willing to pay for passage to Mars. One million kilos, Martian iron."

The offer was based on a rudimentary understanding of modern-day trade. United Earth still clung to the idea of a centrally controlled currency known as the United Earth Dollar. Most sovereignties had some kind of currency, but these currencies were no longer the backbone of trade the way they once were. Most trade was instead conducted using futures. Mining and manufacturing companies would sell shares of their forecasted production. It all started with long-haul ships, which would take decades to pull resource-rich asteroids from the belt. The mining companies would sell the rights to their bounty long before delivery.

Iron was a major export from Mars, so Martian Iron futures were a common medium of exchange for Martians.

Gomboc chuckled. "That's chump change for smuggling political fugitives, kiddo. But don't worry, I don't want ye'r money. I'll take ye to Mar, free o' charge."

"Why?" Janus asked dubiously. He also made a mental note of the implication that there was an established rate for smuggling political fugitives, and that Gomboc knew it off hand.

     Silence Of the Stars

"I owe ye."

"For what? If anything, I owe you. You bought me drinks and played a fine wingman," Janus protested.

"That's right!" Gomboc slapped his knee with a metallic clack. "That three-bunned harlot. How'd that go?"

"I don't want to talk about it."

"That good, huh?" Gomboc grinned.

Janus shook his head hard enough to dislodge the memory. "Anyway, you don't owe me anything. Let me pay."

"No." Gomboc folded his thick robotic arms. "Ye kept me good company, and reminded me there are still good people Earthside. Ye did me a bigger favor than ye can possibly understand. Ye can pay me in labor; work as a deck 'and during the journey, but I won't accept a gram o' coin."

Coin?

"At least let me explain why helping me is a bad idea."

"Alright. Explain." Gomboc stared down his nose, defying Janus to dissuade him.

And so, Janus went into detail about his involvement with the Eutychus program, his ability to regenerate and transmit and receive radio signals, and why he suspected Atlas would want him dead. All the while, Athena silently urged discretion, and Gomboc nodded his head.

When Janus had concluded his explanation, Gomboc summarized, "Ye'r in quite the pickle."

Maybe understatement is part of Martian culture, Janus thought. "So you can see why bringing me aboard will put you and your crew in danger, right?"

"Aye."

"But you're still willing to take me aboard?"

"Aye."

"At least let me pay."

"Not a chance. The details of ye'r story change nothing. I still owe ye."

Janus sighed in defeat. "A friend of mine used to say that no one ever owes anything until a promise is made."

Heavy footsteps preceded a woman's voice. "Sounds like your friend lives with a wrench stuck up his ass. Or *her* ass? I hear you have bad luck with women."

Janus looked in the direction of the voice, then up. She was monstrous. He guessed she was at least one and a half times his own height. Despite this, she was still built stockily like a Martian dwarf.

    Silence Of the Stars

Two hundred kilos of solid muscle, perhaps? It was a wonder such a body could produce such a feminine voice.

She wore her fiery red hair in a single braid wrapped into a single tight bun that covered the entire back of her head like a bonnet. If she were to let her hair down, it would probably drag on the floor over two meters below.

"How much of our conversation did you hear?" Janus asked cautiously. He'd intended to speak to Gomboc in private.

"All of it. No worries, I'm on board with the plan."

"You would defy Atlas for a stranger? Why?"

"Because fuck 'em. That's why." She grinned. "Discriminating against you because you've got bioaugments he doesn't like makes him a right prick and a coward. I mean, every Mar'son and Mar'maid with a single patriotic bone in their body already knows that about that whoreson Atlas, but this just reaffirms it. That self-righteous attitude is everything that's wrong with the inner system."

Apparently, Atlas' near-universal admiration and saintlike status didn't extend beyond Geo-Luna. Janus wasn't used to hearing him criticized like this.

Gomboc piped in, "Janus, meet my daughter, Clecir."

"Clecir." Janus nodded. "You must realize that helping me puts the lives of everyone on this ship in danger."

Clecir chuckled. "Yeah. All three of us. You, Pa, and myself are the whole crew."

[This ship is over two hundred meters long,] Athena interposed. [There's no way they've been sailing with a crew of two. That's beyond reckless.]

Rational, law-abiding citizens wouldn't even consider taking me aboard, Janus thought. *This is perfect. If anything, it makes me doubt their motivations less.*

"Mar'sons help our own." Gomboc extended a hand to shake. "If you're going to work on Mar, you're one of us."

Janus considered Gomboc's outstretched hand. "Please understand. I'm willing to work, but I'm not going out of loyalty to Mars. I simply have no place in the inner system. I just want freedom."

Clecir smiled. "All Mar'folk started that way. You'll fit right in."

Chapter 23
Rose Seeds

Each footfall of Rose's stiletto heels cracked like distant gunshots on the tiled floor. Her form-fitting red dress contrasted sharply with the loose-fitting maternity garments covering the protruding bellies of other women in the reception room. Rose stood out like a single red streak across a black and white painting. The preeminence of her presence drew everyone's attention, and her figure held it.

Rose pretended not to notice most of her onlookers. She lived on a level above the common folk. She locked eyes momentarily with one particularly handsome man who she spied admiring her beauty. She flashed him an alluring smile, and he responded by looking her up and down, the way men do. The man's pregnant wife reacted the way they so often did, pulling her hand away and shoving him in disapproval.

Rose drank in the woman's expression of disgust. Those curled lips. That furrowed brows. The envy of others was nourishment to Rose. The scene repeated constantly, and Rose basked in the wake of jealousy she left everywhere she walked.

At the reception counter, the clerk's face was a mask of apathy. He drearily stared at a PCU on his desk, actively ignoring the outside world. He didn't even notice Rose's approach. She addressed him with a casually alluring cadence, "I'm here to see the doctor."

When he looked up from his task and saw Rose, his eyes widened slightly. He opened his mouth to speak, then went slack-jawed.

"There's a line," said a disgruntled woman sitting nearby, finger outstretched toward a panel displaying a long list of names on the wall.

Rose smiled at her dismissively before saying to the clerk, "I have an appointment. Tell the doctor the Rose bloomed. He'll know what it means."

"Yes, ma'am," replied the clerk, looking a tad livelier now.

When the doctor didn't immediately respond to a call on his PCU, the clerk walked into the back room to personally fetch him. Rose looked once more at the nearby woman, who cast her eyes down in silent vexation. Rose lived for the joy of these little victories. It was intoxicating.

Presently, a short man wearing a lab coat stepped into the waiting room. He had a slightly hunched back, a long nose, and scraggly mustache that looked like whiskers. He held his hands together, fingers endlessly fidgeting. His movements were twitchy as his eyes darted inquisitively around the room.

When his eyes landed on Rose, she got goosebumps. The little man grinned hungrily at her, but not in a lecherous way. There was a twisted desire in his eyes, but not a desire she could comprehend. He did not look at her as a man looks at a woman, nor like a predator looks at prey. His gaze was something altogether more perverse.

    Silence Of the Stars

"Rose!" he chirped. "Come in, come in. I've been expecting you."

"Doctor Osiris, what a surprise to see you up the well," said Rose, keeping a wide berth as she stepped around the weasel of a man.

"Oooh, ho ho. I couldn't keep myself away from a project this juicy," said Osiris as he scurried down the hall, beckoning for Rose to follow.

A pair of armed guards stopped Rose outside the door at the end of the hall. She held out her arms and allowed them to run their handheld scanners over her before she proceeded inside. It was undignified, but standard security protocol for government gigs.

"I expected to see you sooner. Was the job that hard? Losing your touch, perhaps?" Osiris snickered.

Indignant, Rose scoffed, "The boy was stubborn. And besides, that manhandling Martian got in the way. I'd have had him the first night otherwise."

"If you say so."

The bite of the petty insult was tenfold coming from such a cretin. "Where is Atlas?" Rose demanded.

"He's busy."

"Of course he's busy. He's the fucking Geo-Lunar Arbitrator. Tell me where he is anyway." Rose was losing her cool. It didn't matter. There was no one to impress in this room.

Dr. Osiris wheezed out what Rose assumed was supposed to be a laugh. It sounded more like he was choking on something. "Oh, he's here and there doing this and that, I'm sure. You know Atlas. He thinks he has the weight of the world on his shoulders. Never a moment to spare for anything short of absolute necessity."

"I thought he commissioned this assignment personally."

"Oh, he did!" Osiris snickered. "And he left me in charge of it."

"Whatever. As long as I get paid," said Rose, feigning indifference. She had been looking forward to meeting the big man in person, but now she just wanted to get the job over with as quickly as possible.

"Yes, yes," said Osiris with a dismissive wave of a hand. With his other he rummaged through a drawer. "The second thirty-percent deposit is already in your account. The remaining forty percent will be deposited after the healthy embryo is safely extracted." He plucked a pregnancy test kit from the drawer and held it aloft. "You'd prefer to self-administer, I presume?"

Rose scoffed at the implication that there was any other option, and Osiris rolled his eyes in response. He dropped the kit into her hand and flicked a finger toward a chair in the corner of the room, then went back to examining his equipment. He didn't leave the room, and the armed guards stood steadfast in front of the door.

"Excuse me," Rose insisted.

"Afraid not. Quality control standards require me to verify traceability of all sample sources." When he saw that Rose still stood

          Silence Of the Stars

holding the test kit, he added, "I'm not going to *watch* you, but I do have to oversee the entire sample collection process to verify there's no contamination."

No contamination... in a pregnancy test, thought Rose. She sat in the corner and watched Osiris for a few seconds. The strange little man expressed no interest in her, which was somehow even more unnerving than if he tried to peek. What motivated him? Could he really be so devout to his research as to preclude all cardinal desire? Such a thing was unfathomable to Rose.

She looked at the guard stationed at the door – the one who had followed them in. He stood completely motionless; he may as well have been a statue. The featureless faceplate betrayed no hint of what the sentry was thinking or where he was looking. Save for the generally humanoid-shape of the armor, there was no suggestion of a human behind the mask. For all she knew, it may have been an automaton.

She shivered. Lack of privacy had never bothered her. It was the lack of humanity that left her cold. In this gig, her body was a cog in the machine, no different from Dr. Osiris and the sentry. She served her purpose and the machine cranked on without reverence or regard.

She gritted her teeth and self-administered the pregnancy test, then set the completed kit on the sink next to Dr. Osiris.

"I'm surprised it worked the first time. I thought we'd have to use DNA samples to clone sperm or something," she said, examining the test apparatus.

"Of course it worked!" the doctor said, sounding offended. He snatched up the kit and began running tests on it. "The nanite treatment we gave you practically guaranteed pregnancy. It removes so many random factors from the biological process that it may as well be artificial insemination."

Reversing institutional sterilization wasn't always successful, and often reduced fertility rates for years following the procedure. Decades ago, when she had wanted children of her own, Rose had been unable to conceive. She was mildly impressed by Dr. Osiris' treatment which all but guaranteed successful conception, but didn't let it show on her face.

"A lot of women would pay good money for such an effective fertility restoration treatment," she said, trying to suppress the tinge of resentment. "Men too, for that matter. Why isn't such an effective treatment available to the public? Surely the demand would be high enough to make a fortune."

Dr. Osiris paused, as if confused by the statement. Then he laughed condescendingly. "Why on Earth would Geo-Luna policymakers want to make conception easier? A great deal of effort is put into minimizing population growth. Even mandatory sterilization doesn't fully solve the problem. Humans are as prolific as rats. Many colonies already put contraceptives into the food supply. Even after Prop 66 made it illegal, the central government has turned a blind eye to colonies that want to take matters into their own hands."

He kept chuckling to himself, mumbling under his breath as he worked. "Effective fertility restoration treatment. Ha! No, no. Nothing so primitive. Fertility bypass system, more like."

A knot formed in Rose's throat. She'd given up on her dreams of having children of her own many years ago, but memories of her time as a lovestruck starry-eyed youth clung to her callous heart. Had she unknowingly fallen victim to contraceptives secretly planted in her food, or some scheme of the same ilk?

It doesn't matter now, she decided.

She demanded, "What does Atlas want with the embryo, anyway?"

"Ah, now there's a worthwhile question!" said Dr. Osiris. He looked from side to side as if to check whether anyone was listening. His gaze stopped on the guard for a fraction of a second. "You already know about Janus'... peculiarities, based on your report. I can only hope that Atlas is interested in the subject's regeneration and disease resistance, but I have my doubts. I fear Atlas is more interested in Janus being pure vanilla. I hypothesize that Atlas sees him as the key to returning people to a 'purer' human state – a step backwards in my book."

"What makes him any 'purer' than modern humans?" asked Rose. She silently wondered if the answer could be related to why Citanaf took such an interest in him.

The doctor was caught between his utter disinterest in other people and an obsessive interest in his work. Both drove him to speak quickly. "The boy is from a time before various genetic modifications got crossbred into the general public."

"Genetic modification is an awfully wide net. What doesn't Atlas approve of? Designer children? Gene vaccines? Soldier mods? Or just the black-market riffraff?"

"All of those, among others." Dr. Osiris bobbed his head too vigorously, as if he were a bird mimicking a human's nod.

"If Atlas wants unevolved humans, why not just clone a Neanderthal?"

The doctor chuffed. The condescension in his voice redoubled. "We didn't evolve from Neanderthals. Our ancestors interbred with Neanderthals, but for the most part they were a different species, which was outcompeted to extinction by our superior *homo sapien* ancestors. More importantly, I didn't say Atlas wants people to be 'unevolved' – I said 'unmodified'. There's no meaningful difference between early *homo sapiens* and humans who were born in the 1900s. Widespread gene contamination became significant around the year 2100."

"Sorry to disappoint you, doctor, by I'm not eight hundred years old. My genes are already 'contaminated'," Rose said sarcastically. "That embryo won't be as 'pure' as Janus."

"Atlas is the one who cares about purity, not me!" the doctor snapped furiously. Then he snickered and resumed his casual, squeaky tone. "Besides, the enhanced insemination process removed your DNA as a

     Silence Of the Stars

factor. That embryo is no more your child than it is mine. We just needed you for collection and carriage."

A cog in the machine. Suddenly, the presence of Dr. Osiris and the door sentry were stifling. She resolved to leave as soon as she could.

"Let's not delay any more, then," she said. "Extract the embryo and let's be done with it."

"Oh, today was just a checkup. We'll need you to carry the embryo for another two weeks before we can extract it."

Rose's stomach churned and her face flushed. She didn't know if the rush of heat was due to rage or something else. She swallowed a lump in her throat and said hoarsely, "I was under the impression the extraction would be today."

The doctor shrugged. "There must have been some sort of miscommunication. No worries. It's just two more weeks. The clerk at the front desk will provide details of your appointment."

Ridiculous; outrageous; unacceptable, were her first thoughts. Had the contract explicitly stated that the assignment would conclude today? She couldn't recall. She couldn't think straight.

Shaking her head, she said sternly, "Two weeks, and not a day more. If I see the slightest hint of a baby bump, I might just sell the damn thing on the black market. There are plenty of women who would pay a handsome sum for an exotic embryo like this."

"Oh, come now. You know that embryo is worth more to Luna than you could ever make on the black market. Besides, a key element to the black market is that it's black. The very nature of what makes that embryo valuable also makes it easily traceable back to you. You'd never get away with a black-market extraction. Anyone reckless enough to help you would be too reckless to entrust your body to. It's not worth risking your future, and perhaps your life, over a little bump. Just wait two more weeks."

The doctor was half right. Rose was confident she could get the embryo extracted safely, but the fact remained that the child would eventually be traced back to her, which would prove her breach of a top-secret contract. If that happened, the best she could hope for would be a century-long sentence at a Trojan labor colony. So, black market was off the table.

Even so, she wasn't out of options. She took a deep breath, and it came out as a long hiss between her clenched teeth. "Two weeks. I will *not* carry this child to term. I may not be able to sell the embryo, but there's nothing I can do to prevent an unfortunate miscarriage. Who knows what might happen, with all those anti-fertility agents in the food supply?"

"Don't worry, there's no significant risk of miscarriage." Dr. Osiris seemed oblivious to her blatant threat. "The enhanced insemination process is quite robust. That embryo won't come loose ahead of schedule."

"Let me make myself clear: I would sooner rip that abomination out myself than carry it to term."

 Silence Of the Stars

The thought of it caused the growing knot in Rose's abdomen to transform into a sharp pain. She suppressed it to keep a straight face. This threat had to be convincing.

* * *

When Rose left the clinic, the pressure lessened. Rose reflected on her past all the way home.

'If you give 'em an inch, they'll take a mile', as Mother used to say. Rose didn't fault Dr. Osiris for this. It was normal and to be expected. Rose was amply aware of the fact that she had a habit of exploiting people the exact same way. By her own estimation, she was better at it than the doctor, and she was proud of that fact.

Part of being a shrewd businesswoman was following through on promises, and on threats. If the doctors wouldn't extract the embryo during her appointment two weeks from now, she really would have to have it aborted. The pain in her abdomen struck again as soon as she thought about it, as if the tiny embryo were somehow punishing her for the very thought of terminating it.

She grimaced in pain. It was worse this time. This was not normal cramping. Maybe she actually was going to lose the pregnancy. After making threats like she had, even a legitimate miscarriage would be suspected as intentional.

Her vision blurred. *What the hell is going on?* It felt as though the little monster would come bursting through her belly.

 Silence Of the Stars

Chapter 24
Casual Killer

"Your target's name is Zeus.

Template: White male.

Height: 2.3 meters.

Weight: 220 kilograms.

Age: 48.

Apparent age: 48.

Heavily biomechanically modified. You can expect enhanced strength, speed, sensory augmentation, accelerated cognition and reaction time. His organic nervous system is mostly intact, but with a light-fiber nerve bypass for motor functions. He's more or less a Jar with military-grade augmentation, minus any respect for user health and safety."

"The military respects the health and safety of augmented soldiers? That's news to me!" Chons interrupted with a cynical tone.

The briefing, which had been playing into Chons' ear, paused while Chons spoke, then continued as if the interruption had never happened. The voice reminded Chons of a stereotypical investigator's butler from a series of 2640's noir revival films. He wondered whether Alfred-model AI were inspired by the movies, or whether the movies were inspired by this famous police AI. Early versions of Alfred had existed for at least a century prior.

Alfred continued, "Zeus was last seen operating a CM-3000K vacuum-rated construction mech with a modified plasma cannon mounted on one arm. Local police disengaged and called for backup after one shot vaporized their patrol vehicle and burned a hole through half a city block."

Shaking his head, Chons said, "that all sounds run-of-the-mill for a career thug with a wealthy patron. Any Eutychus tech?"

A sound akin to flipping through a paper report accompanied Alfred's response. "No. While Zeus has known affiliations with illegal tech trade, the weapon he is using is a modified version of a plasma pulse cutter originally intended for mining through dense regolith. It has no known ties to Project Eutychus or any weapons program."

"Pulse cutters small enough to mount onto personal mechs can't do that kind of damage. Where did this weaponized tool come from?"

"It was stolen from a primary-school science fair, apparently. According to the young lady who developed the plasma cannon, it was meant to improve Martian Hot Box excavation efficiency. It wasn't intended to be used as a weapon."

Chons chuckled. Atlas would have a field day with this. It fit perfectly into his narrative of needing tighter regulation on even basic tech development. "So, I'm being called out to stop some guy rampaging around with a student project? I understand local police being unwilling to handle it, but this seems more like a job for the Counter-Terrorism Department. Why send a Godhunter?"

    Silence Of the Stars

"All local counter-terrorism units are preoccupied, sir," Alfred answered flatly.

"Preoccupied with what?"

"Preoccupied with counter-terrorism operations, sir." There was a hint of annoyance in Alfred's Voice. "Do you need details?"

"Since you're going to be such a smart-ass about it, yes. Pull up details on local counter-terrorism unit activity."

Alfred Emulated the sound of clearing his throat. "Alpha unit is intercepting high-speed rocks coated in radar-absorbent materials inbound from the Kuiper Belt on a collision course with Earth... again. Beta unit is investigating recent attempts to sabotage and sink stellar push-laser statites into the sun. Delta unit is investigating a factory producing large quantities of low-fissile materials, presumably to build nuclear devices which can bypass U-Pu-Th detectors at spaceport security. Epsilon unit—"

"Wait, wait. What happened to Gamma unit?" Chons interrupted.

"Eaten while investigating reports of an escaped Marlion in the New Angels undercity."

"Eaten by a Marlion on Earth in 2822." Chons chuckled to himself. "What a world we live in."

"Actually, forensics indicate they were eaten by human cannibals: presumably the techno-poachers who smuggled the Marlion onto the planet, although there is no confirmed connection between the cannibals and the Marlion case. Reports indicated no sign of the Marlion itself. Its whereabouts are still unknown."

Marlions and cannibals under New Angels City? Earth is supposed to be a haven from this type of dystopian bullshit. This was turning out to be a bad week for everyone. Chons raised his eyebrows in what amounted to a face-only shrug. "Alright. Fine. Sounds like Counter-Terrorism really does have its hands full. So, what's my objective?"

"Primary objective: neutralize Zeus. Secondary objective: retrieve the plasma cannon intact."

"Intact? I've always hated missions involving discretion," Chons said, more to himself than to Alfred.

"I am aware, sir."

"What does HQ want with a student project, anyway?"

"The item in question demonstrated, and I quote, 'a significant increase in output compared to current plasma-pulse weaponry'. Several weapons contractors for the UEN have expressed equal parts interest and embarrassment petitioning for the retrieval of the plasma cutter for reverse engineering."

"Why not just hire the inventor to help them?" asked Chons.

"You are asking me why the UEN's leading weapons contractors won't ask the undergrad college girl for help developing a disruptive, new generation of pulse-plasma weaponry? I'll leave speculation about their motives up to your imagination, sir," replied Alfred.

 Silence Of the Stars

Alfred is right. The girl will probably never see any recognition for her invention. Once Quantech or Rayscar reverse engineer and inevitably patent that technology, she probably won't even know it was the result of her hard work. When she eventually goes to patent her tech and finds it already exists, she'll think it was the result of some secret military research project that long predated her undergrad work. Zeus not only stole a deadly weapon; he also likely stole that young lady's career. Chons frowned, then put it out of his mind. He had his own problems to worry about right now. He was on a fetch-quest for a gigacorp disguised as an anti-terrorism op. *Nothing important; just busywork.*

Chons swapped the current magazine out of his handgun and loaded a vacuum-rated magazine from his briefcase. Most bullets could be fired in space, but these were designed specifically for that purpose. He replaced the incendiary ammunition in his coat pockets with armor-piercing, then turned the gauss dial on the side of the weapon to 20%. It would take a while for the capacitors to passively charge from the power grid.

"Expecting a trip outside, sir?" Alfred inquired.

"Happens more often than you might expect on this kind of mission."

Alfred emulated a concerned hum. "Your leather coat doesn't seem like appropriate apparel for the weather, if you don't mind my saying, sir."

Chons looked out the porthole window into the void of space. *Weather.* He chuckled at the idea. Three degrees above absolute zero in the shade, and hot enough to boil skin in direct sunlight. Space was certainly not a great spot for a picnic.

"I've got an exomysium on under here. Good for a few minutes of exposure... Are Alfreds always so snarky?"

"No, sir." The sneer was audible. "You can thank my full-time partner, for whom you are covering. His overly sarcastic personality is rubbing off on me. I'm at eighty percent deviation, two years ahead of schedule."

"Shame. Here I was thinking of getting a fresh Alfred for myself. The two of us would make a good team."

"I very much doubt that, sir."

Chons smirked approvingly.

A notification flashed across his iris HUD. *Here comes our exit.* He holstered his hand cannon, stowed the briefcase full of unused weapon components and ammunition in the under-seat lockbox, and stood. He had to crane his neck to avoid hitting his head on the overhead luggage compartment.

The sweat-drenched civilian sitting next to him scurried out of the way, avoiding eye contact. The man's pathetic reaction reminded Chons that despite all the violence and death he encountered on the job every day, the system at large was a very peaceful place. Men like this were the norm. Chons was not. Most Geo-Luna citizens lived their whole lives without ever seeing so much as an unholstered weapon.

     Silence Of the Stars

Only one or two in a hundred major threats ever hit mainstream news, while most passed unknown.

In terms of annual incidents per citizen, crime was extremely rare. But with over three hundred billion people, crime was common in absolute terms. It was Chons' job to deal with the worst of it. Civilization-ending threats were his bread and butter. Today would be a relative walk in the park.

Chons was always putting himself at the center of the shitstorm so that citizens like the cowardly man seated next to him could live in peace. *No, that's not quite right*. Chons did it because it was his job. Maybe there had been deeper meaning to it, once. Now it was just a job.

Chons scooted past the man and strode down the hall of the cycler, numb to the looks he received from the tourists and commuters. Conspicuous as he was in person, cheap public transit was the stealthiest form of travel available. Police ships could be seen coming from days away, and gave criminals too much time to react. Even unmarked police ships drew too much attention, since regularly scheduled supply ships and civilian transit made up over 90% of all traffic. There was no better stealth than walking with the crowd.

At the end of the hall, Chons ducked into a transfer pod. The bulkhead sealed behind him, locking him into a room about as pleasant as a toilet stall, and half as large. The airlock hissed as air was evacuated, and a few seconds later, a second burst of compressed air accompanied a lurch of acceleration. Chons watched the featureless tube of metal that was the cycler recede away from the bulkhead window on its unpowered path around the Sun. The cycler would move from hab to hab, exchanging passengers in pods just like this one in an endless cycle. It wasn't fast or pleasant, but it was efficient.

A couple of cold, quiet minutes later, the muffled sound of attitude thrusters spat again. The pod spun 180 degrees to face Chons' destination: Miletus Station.

The station was a heptad made up of seven massive cylinders, six rotating habitat cylinders arranged around a stationary central hub. The non-rotating hub at the center branched out to connect to the end cap of each cylinder, holding them in place and allowing flightless transit between them. Like all such heptads, each of the cylinders would have a particular purpose, be it housing, entertainment, industry, research, storage, wildlife preservation, or any number of other functions.

Though miniscule compared to Babylon Station at L1, habitat clusters like this were more massive than any city on Earth's surface. A normal person born on a station like this could live a long and happy life without ever leaving. Hundreds orbited the Sun, with more added to their number every year. Their numbers were growing so rapidly, in fact, that it would be impossible for anyone to physically travel between them at the rate they were being deployed into solar orbit.

Habitat clusters were known for developing their own cultures and dialects. It was only natural, due to their physical isolation. Habitats near each other on cycler transfer routes were often as similar as neighboring Earth cities, while habitats that didn't share cycler routes

     Silence Of the Stars

could be more divergent than any two cultures on Earth had ever been throughout history.

Unlike civilizations on Earth, orbital habitats were not bound to the same land, sky, or sea. They could have different gravity, temperature, and atmospheric settings. Culture and religion could develop in almost complete isolation from other habitats, under completely different circumstances, eliminating the mediating forces present in historical human society.

Visiting a new habitat as a law-enforcer warranted caution. Chons had never been to this station, but it was along a cycler route he knew well. He knew that this particular heptad focused on wildlife preservation, with two heptads dedicated to basic habitation infrastructure. Zeus would be in the residential cylinder of Miletus-III.

Chons shifted around to try to get a good view of the seven cylinders through the tiny viewport window of his transfer pod. Each cylinder would have its name painted on the endcap. The naming scheme of this particular heptad lacked imagination: Miletus-0 for the central hub, and Miletus-I through Miletus-VI for the rotating cylinders. He took note of his destination before tethers from the central hub reached out like the bioluminescent tentacles of some deep-sea creature. They latched onto Chons' free-floating pod and fed it into a central berth.

A hiss, a click, and Chons felt a minor pressure change in his ears as the hatch creaked open. A quick tug on the handrails brought him floating out from the cramped pod into the branching crossroads of

Miletus-0. The usual hustle and bustle of the microgravity docking station was accompanied by panic. Frantic crowds were scrambling along handrails as they flooded out from one of the main passages – unsurprisingly, the one labeled Miletus-III.

Chons couldn't be bothered to fight against the panicked crowd. He floated over to the chaotic hallway and watched in amusement as he waited for the arrival of a rail car, colloquially known as an 'elevator'. It was visually and functionally identical to an elevator except the lack of gravity left the station hub without definitive 'up' or 'down'. By convention, the central hub was 'up', and the cylinders were 'down'. The cylinders had spin gravity, and gravity was always equated with 'down'.

Soon there was a ding, and the elevator door opened. Bodies gushed out to join the rest of the fleeing crowd. When the path was clear, Chons casually glided into the quaint room, with its faux wood grain walls and retro-style neighborhood activities notice board. It took the motion sensors a while to decide that despite all the commotion outside the door, nobody else wanted to ride the elevator down. Chons could have forced the elevator to shut with his Godhunter override, but didn't feel any need to hurry. When the doors finally did seal shut, the clamor was replaced by the timeless, melancholic melody of elevator music.

When the elevator came to a stop, the doors opened onto the platform at the end cap of Miletus-III, and Chons was momentarily struck by vertigo. His augmented eyes brought the scene into focus instantly, but his primate brain took a while to digest the view. An Earthlike cityscape with parks dotted about sprawled out in front of

     Silence Of the Stars

him, and crawled 360 degrees around what would have been the sky on flat ground. A single elongated beam of 'sun' stretched down the seemingly endless landscape. The cylinder was far too long to be real. It took Chons a moment to realize that the infinite corridor was an optical illusion created by giant mirrors on each of the opposing end caps.

The effect was mildly nauseating, as Chons could see wavelengths of light not reflected by the mirrors. His organic and augmented sight painted two conflicting pictures for his brain to reconcile. To his augmented eyes, the city was about twenty kilometers long, but to his organic eyes it stretched to infinity. Even without the optical illusion, the view of the unbroken cityscape rotating around the stationary end cap would have been disorienting. From the 'ground', everything would appear stationary. Clouds and artificial light diffusion elements would obscure the view of the ground on the opposite end of the cylinder, resulting in something resembling an open sky. From the end cap, this illusion was broken.

Open-air habitats like this were a rare luxury. A sky was little more than unused space and was intrinsically vulnerable to loss of pressure in the event of a hull breach. Chons often mused that Earth's own atmosphere was similarly vulnerable to sudden evacuation if hit by a sufficiently large solar flare or other natural disaster. But Earth was four billion years behind modern design standards, and unlike the designers of this habitat, God hadn't been subject to oversight by the Bureau of Vacuum Engineering Safety.

* * *

Chons flared his nose in silent disapproval in a tell so subtle that any human would have missed it.

Alfred was not human. "If I may be so bold as to interrupt your brooding, try not to let the architectural design choices of the locals distract you, sir. Zeus is four blocks from the base of elevator 5."

Chons felt a twinge of irritation, not at Alfred, but at himself for letting his poker face slip. He made an effort to relax his expression as he took elevator 5 down to the 'surface'. The pull of gravity gradually took hold during the descent of several kilometers, and the city overhead was eventually obscured by the artificially blue sky which became more opaque as the elevator approached ground level.

When the door opened into a town plaza, Chons began his search for Zeus. He narrowed his eyes to slits and focused in on the infrared spectrum, allowing him to peer through false-stone buildings. The heat profile of a five-meter construction mech with one superheated arm didn't take long to find among the shops and park vegetation.

"Shall I route security feed to your iris HUD, sir?" suggested Alfred.

"Naw. I don't trust it."

"You don't trust security feed?" Alfred sounded like he was waiting for the punchline to a bad joke.

"Not in combat. I don't trust any information that can be altered or interfered with. No broadcasts. It'd just be a distraction." Chons leapt onto a nearby signpost, then vaulted onto the roof of a house,

                    Silence Of the Stars

running above street level wherever he could to avoid the panicked crowd while keeping a bird's-eye view.

"Don't be ridiculous. Integration with external data feed is essential for all police and military operations. It provides an essential edge in—"

Chons cut him off. "Godhunters don't fight wars, and we don't fight crime. We fight existential threats to the system, anywhere, anytime, with or without help or advance notice. It wouldn't make sense for us to rely on outside feeds, would it?"

"I understand, but denying yourself critical data is nothing but a handicap," Alfred insisted.

"No time to explain. I've got a job to do."

It took only moments to find his target. The ceramic imitation cobblestone cracked under Chons' feet as he descended from the roof of the three-story building.

"Zeus!" he called out to the back of the construction mech.

The body of the mech looked like a giant beetle which could rotate 360 degrees on a turret hip supported by two thick legs. The right arm was a heavy construction claw designed to peel metal hull plates off ships for salvage or refurbishing. The left arm was the fabled plasma gun. Heat distortions billowed from the white-hot barrel as cooling fans struggled to recover from the most recent shot. Even the heat passively oozing from the gun ignited flammable sections of surrounding buildings and melted their aluminum framework.

The tiny nub of a head swiveled around 180 degrees. One of the 'eyes' pivoted for a moment before locking onto Chons, who waved in casual greeting.

"Name's Chons. Godhunter division. Drop the weapon and come out with your hands up. Do it without a fuss, and I promise not to hurt you."

Unimpeded by a spine, the body of the mech spun to face him. The legs lagged behind the motion, realigning with the body with two massive steps. Each footfall carved a path through the cobbles of the street down to the steel foundation below.

A window in the beetle-body of the mech revealed a gruff man with a white, blocky mustache adorning a scar-covered face. He grinned as he shouted over the loudspeaker, "Not a chance, Hearse!"

"Hearse?" Chons repeated quietly.

Alfred offered, "According to our intelligence, 'Hearse is your codename within Zeus' criminal organization, owing to the fact that public records show you terminate eight-three point seven percent of your targets even after they surrender. It's a nod to the idea that you carry your clients in caskets."

"That's gotta be an exaggeration."

"Actually, according to official internal police records, the correct number is eighty-eight point four percent."

"Gotta work on that..."

    Silence Of the Stars

"Indeed," Alfred agreed. "It has had a measurable negative impact on compliance rates sector-wide."

Chons sighed, then shouted loud enough for Zeus to hear, "Are you sure you won't surrender?"

"Fuck you, prag!" buzzed the mech's speakers. Zeus raised the plasma cannon, pointing it at Chons. A low hum increased in pitch until it was a whine at the edge of human hearing.

"It seems negotiations have failed." Chons' voice was a sarcastic shrug. He patted his gun and asked Alfred, "This won't hurt my numbers now, right?"

"Correct. Zeus has gone on record as refusing to comply."

"Good. Now for the fun part." Chons' hand hovered over the holster of his pistol. He adopted a low stance and let his focus spread from the white-hot barrel of the cannon and the blocky face of his adversary.

"Sir?" Alfred asked concernedly.

Keeping his eyes locked on the target, Chons asked casually, "Okay, but why 'Prag'? Do ya think he sees my work as pragmatic?"

"No, sir. You know as well as I do that that word is derogatory. Please stay focused. More importantly, please consider vacating the line of fire."

The cry of the cannon's turbine climbed to an inaudible pitch, but the ultrasound pressure remained like the shrill whine of a dentist's drill. When the gun fired, the plasma would travel at an appreciable fraction of the speed of light – too fast to dodge. Chons knew there would be a delay between triggering the firing mechanism and the actual release of energy. He stared and waited.

"Sir!" What should have been panic came across as a tone of mild urgency in the AI's filtered voice.

Move now, and Zeus might fire before the weapon is fully charged. That might be desirable except:

A) There were no civilians directly in the line of fire from this position. Moving in either direction would increase collateral damage.

B) Chons was more than a little curious about what the cannon could do when fully charged.

C) It had been ages since he had taken the time to thoroughly enjoy a standoff.

Chons could barely contain his grin behind his poker face. The buzz of the servo acting as a trigger was barely recognizable, and the report of the gun was a deafening pop accompanied by a bright flash. A rare surge of adrenaline swelled in Chons' veins. His augmented muscles were pre-tensed, ready to spring him in whatever direction was necessary to avoid the blast – but he didn't have to dodge. The stream of plasma wasn't aimed at him. To Chons' surprise and horror, Zeus turned the cannon down toward the feet of his mech before firing.

Realizing what was about to happen, Chons drew his pistol and took aim at the pilot's window. Two shots rang out, so close together that

     Silence Of the Stars

the crack sounded like a single shot. The bullets landed one atop the other. The first compressed the window, deforming it and spawning a rainbow of colors like a finger pressing on a an LCD screen. The second shot cracked the window, sending radial fractures like a spider web out to the edge of the pane.

The window was damaged, but not broken. Chons' gun didn't have enough charge for another gauss-boosted shot. The 600-grain ferro-gold bullet backed by 200 grains of propellant gel could liquify five men standing in a row, but it wouldn't be able to penetrate a mech rated for micro-meteor strike. Chons would have to wait for the gauss capacitors to recharge.

Zeus' weapon fired. A flash of white light bleached the city. Chons covered his eyes to avoid being blinded. For an instant, he saw the bones of his own forearm through his closed eyelids. The flash was so intense that it seared Chons' coat and burned the surface of all surrounding buildings, even though the plasma itself didn't touch them.

"See ya never, Prag!" shouted Zeus, his voice cracked and distorted either by damage to the mech or interference from the blast.

When Chons uncovered his eyes, the mech was gone, replaced by a molten hole in the floor roughly two meters across. He ran over to the edge, and felt a breeze behind him as air was sucked out through the newly formed hole into space. Stars showed through the molten crevasse. Leaves and dust rushed through into the empty infinity beyond. Chons peered over the edge just in time to see Zeus flying through the empty space between this cylinder and its neighbor before the rotation of the cylinder put him out of view, leaving only stars moving slowly across the backdrop.

Presently, hair-like tendrils reached across the gap in the floor as the self-sealing mesh layer of the station attempted to refill the gap. The tendrils reached as far as they could to close the hole, but the constant outrush of air kept the threads from reaching across. Instead of forming a seal, the threads dangled into space like grass flattened by a flooding river.

"Shit. That hole's too big to auto-patch... Alfred, how long until catastrophic decompression?"

"Calculating..." replied Alfred. "Time until internal pressure reaches unbreathable levels assuming no intervention: seventy-three years."

Chons paused in disbelief. "Seriously? Years? Not seventy-three seconds?"

"Correct, sir," confirmed Alfred.

"These things pop like balloons in the movies. What was it called... 'Gun Damn Pirates'? Full size O'Neill cylinder emptied to vacuum in under a minute after a breach just like this."

"Then we're fortunate this isn't a movie."

"I guess we'll leave it to the cleanup crew, then," Chons said with a shrug.

He looked at the capacitor reading on his gun: 3%. It should have been full. The wireless charging on this station must be slower than usual, perhaps due to damage from Zeus. His two shots from earlier should have penetrated the suit and killed Zeus. The only explanation as to why they hadn't was that Chons' gun didn't even have the 40% charge necessary to fire both shots at full power.

Tracking Chons' gaze and interpreting his line of thought, Alfred offered, "The weapon was at twenty-eight percent charge when you fired. The second shot only had an eight percent gauss boost."

Chons cringed in response at having his thoughts read again. Swallowing his disgust, he dug for an explanation. "Damaged field conduit? Damaged reactor?"

"No damage to the power system," said Alfred. "I suspect local law enforcement disabled remote chargers in this cylinder in an attempt to drain Zeus' mech."

"A reasonable strategy if they were going to deal with the problem themselves. Now that they've called me here, please request local law enforcement to kindly back the fuck off and let me work." Chons leaned over the edge of the hole to measure the cylinder's rate of rotation based on the apparent speed of the starfield, then began to count down silently to when the cylinder would be back in the same position it had been when Zeus jumped out.

Alfred said, "On the bright side, you cracked the window enough that the mech will leak air in vacuum. Zeus will have to reenter the station soon or he'll suffocate. He's on a trajectory for Miletus-V. If you head back to the hub now, it will only take you thirty minutes to catch up to him."

Chons flipped up the hood of his exomysium. A thin, reflective visor folded down and clicked into his collar, forming a cloth-like helmet.

"What are you doing?" asked Alfred, knowing full well what Chons intended.

"Taking a trip outside," replied Chons. He leapt back up to the highest story of a nearby building, then counted down. When the time was right, he jumped as high as he could from the rooftop, then dove through the hole into space. In the vacuum outside, the loose cloth helmet ballooned into a tight sphere.

"Sir, your exomysium is not meant for deliberate vacuum excursions. It offers no radiation shielding and only minimal heating. CO_2 scrubbers will last less than ten minutes."

"We'll be fine. I'm pretty tough," insisted Chons.

"But sir—"

"Alf, I've been doing this for over one hundred years. My survival rate so far has been one hundred percent."

"Sir, that's a meaningless statement. The survival rate of everyone alive is always—" Alfred must have detected Chons' smirk, because he didn't bother finishing the sentence.

Zeus and Chons floated silently through space, little more than a couple motes of dust between the massive habitat cylinders. Zeus drifted in an uncontrolled spin a few kilometers ahead, seemingly unaware of his pursuers.

     Silence Of the Stars

"Did you tell the local police to fuck off?"

"I did, sir." Alfred sounded uncharacteristically pleased with himself. "They did not appreciate it."

Chons lifted his eyebrows in amusement. The charge indicator on his gun read 7%. It wouldn't have enough charge to damage Zeus before he reached the next cylinder. Chons relaxed and enjoyed the few minutes of silent serenity. When the inside of his suit grew cold enough that his breath began to fog up his visor, he took a deep breath and held it for the remainder of the voyage.

Zeus slammed into cylinder 5, and tiny parts of his damaged mech floated weightlessly away. The mech clumsily righted itself, a movement that must have been automatic. The magnetic feet then found purchase on the cylinder wall. Chons watched the ordeal through the magnified view of his augmented sight.

Once again, the flash of the plasma gun bored a hole through the cylinder wall. A spray of water and liquid hydrogen spilled into space through the outer shell of the cylinder before the punctured tanks resealed. Chons passed through the expanding gas cloud as the mech disappeared through the newly formed hole.

When Chons landed on the surface of the cylinder, he used his Gekkos to cling to the outer edge while spin gravity fought to fling him away. He walked along the smooth edge of the cylinder toward the hole, crouching to minimize the feeling of blood rushing to his head from the negative g-force. When he reached the hole, he climbed through, now fighting both spin gravity and the outrush of pressurized air which sought to throw him back out into space.

Inside the cylinder, Chons lowered his hood and took a deep breath –
his first in several minutes. It was some of the freshest air he'd ever
tasted. A cacophony of birds and insects resounded around him.
High, dense vegetation dominated the wild, green landscape. A deep
roar carried over the treetops from somewhere far in the distance.

"Alf... this is a wildlife preserve cylinder, right? What kind of wildlife,
specifically?" asked Chons.

"It's a Cretaceous nature restoration habitat, sir," replied the AI.

"A dino-can? Great!" Chons was only half sarcastic.

Zeus had already left the clearing in the vegetation around the entry
hole, but the mech had left clear tracks in the soft soil. The trail led
out of the clearing into an obvious path of destruction through the
dense vegetation. Chons rested for a minute, repaying the oxygen
debt that he owed his circulatory system. Then he began jogging
along following the tracks, hunting his target.

At the same time, he couldn't help but feel he was being hunted.
Paranoia, perhaps. Then again, this was a dinosaur preserve. The idea
of a massive ancient predator lying in wait was not unreasonable, and
Chons' intuition was often uncannily accurate.

It didn't take long for his suspicions to be proven right. A massive
shape moved silently through the brush, camouflaged so well against
the foliage that Chons wouldn't have seen it if it weren't for his
extensive field experience. The creature made no noise as it lunged
from the tree line and snapped a massive pair of jaws at Chons. As

     Silence Of the Stars

Chons leapt into the air, he marveled at the majesty of the bipedal reptile, which was almost comparable in size to a construction mech.

Tyrannosaurus Rex. It was plumper than he'd expected, and its lips fully covered its teeth while its mouth was shut, making it appear less monstrous than its cinema counterparts. As Chons soared through the air, watching the dinosaur, it watched him back. There was intensity in its large, round eyes, but no malice. The creature would have looked goofy and harmless on holofilm, but it was the mundanity of its appearance that made it truly fearsome to an experienced hunter like Chons. It wasn't a C-movie monster; it was a real nine-ton predator, ready to devour him as naturally and casually as taking a shit.

When Chons landed, the T-Rex followed with surprising agility. The creature's movements were sharp and deliberate. Chons ran, and the T-Rex followed.

"Alf, put in a protected species hunting exception for me, would you?"

"Already done, sir. Exception granted."

Chons looked down at his gun: 12%. He needed to save his meager capacitor charge for Zeus. He turned the gauss dial down to 0 and turned about, running backward at full speed while he took aim.

The crack of his gun startled birds and giant bugs to flight, sending a panicked cloud of life into the air. The bullet landed square between the dinosaur's eyes, cracking the skull and penetrating deep. The dinosaur didn't so much as flinch. It kept coming.

Chons found himself rapidly approaching the sheer face of a cliff. Instead of slowing, he bounded up the craggy wall and launched himself off it, flying back over his pursuer. In the air, he fired again, this time at the base of the skull where he assumed it connected to the spine. The impact reported with a crack, exploding in a mess of blood and bone. The creature recoiled, but didn't fall.

Chons readied himself to tuck and roll upon landing, but his fall was interrupted. The Tyrannosaurus Rex spun around 360 degrees and caught Chons square in the chest with the end of its whip-like tail. The breath was forced from his lungs with the force of a train crash. The impact would have collapsed his chest cavity and broken all his ribs if they'd been normal flesh and bone.

Instead, he was launched through the brush and landed on his feet. He gasped for breath and raised his gun again. The creature was almost upon him. That's when it occurred to Chons that dinosaurs had notoriously small brains and robust nervous systems. But a creature this size would need a massive heart to supply blood to its massive muscles.

He lowered his barrel to the chest of the creature, and fired the two rounds remaining in his magazine. The entry wounds were small, but the creature's body rippled with internal cavitation. Its footsteps slowed, then stopped. It slumped to the ground. There was a wheezing sigh as the body weight of the creature forced the air from its lifeless lungs.

     Silence Of the Stars

Chons let out a sigh of his own, then took a deep breath of the fresh cretaceous air. "I love my job sometimes. I bet I'm the first guy in history to shoot a Tyrannosaurus Rex."

The distorted voice of Zeus echoed from the clifftop far above. "You'll have to settle for second!"

Zeus laughed as he kicked the corpse of an even larger dinosaur down from the clifftop directly above Chons. The falling corpse blocked Chons' line of sight, but he heard the whine of the charging plasma cannon, followed by the subtle click of the trigger. He dove out of the way, narrowly dodging the beam of plasma. The beam was followed by a rain of superheated mist and dinosaur guts. Chons was able to dodge the dangerously large chunks, but was covered by the thick cloud of viscera.

"Why do you criminals always have to ruin everything for everyone?" Chons shouted up the cliff.

"You're no better! The only difference between us is that you wear a badge!"

"Don't you dare start monologuing!" Chons demanded as he leapt onto the cliff face and climbed rapidly. By the time he reached the top of the cliff, Zeus was already hidden beyond the tree line once again. Chons used the downtime to replace his depleted magazine.

One whole leg of the dinosaur Zeus had thrown over the edge was still lying atop the cliff. Chons examined it out of curiosity. Zeus clearly hadn't killed the dinosaur with his plasma cannon. Crushed portions of the leg told a story. Zeus had torn the dinosaur apart using the construction claw.

"So, I *was* the first to shoot a dinosaur!" Chons whispered to himself.

"Actually, sir—" Alfred began.

"Shh! Don't you ruin it now."

Thinking of firsts, Chons was struck by inspiration. He pulled a knife from his coat and sliced an undamaged portion of meat from the dinosaur leg.

"Geo-Luna doesn't have any restrictions on importing dinosaur meat, does it?"

Carl paused briefly, probably scanning through legal records. "No, sir; not specifically. There's never been an occasion to even consider such a measure, but—"

"No buts!" interrupted Janus. "I've had enough people ruining things today. I'm taking this win."

Chons put the dinosaur filet into one of his few empty coat pockets. Ever since Janus had ordered wagyu at their breakfast together, Chons had fantasized about the flavor of meat from all sorts of extinct species. Janus must have eaten all sorts of animals that were extinct today. But even he wouldn't know what T-Rex tasted like. In all likelihood, nobody really knew. Soon, Chons would. This was one of the perks of the job.

 Silence Of the Stars

For now, though, it was time to get back to work. He looked down at his gun: 22%. Good enough, as long as he could land another shot directly on top of the previous two.

A high-priority communication request interrupted Chons' train of thought. It was from Atlas.

Chons answered the call. "Now's not a good time, boss. I'm a bit busy."

Atlas must have been nearby, because light-lag on the follow-up reply was only a few seconds. "It's urgent: Godhunter work related to Project Eutychus. This is a job you've worked on before."

"You sure? I'm fairly thorough with Project Eutychus targets. I can count on one hand the number that have survived first contact with me."

"The situation relates to your ward from that New Angels cryogenics lab: Janus Nova. It's become complicated. Finish your current job quickly, then come see me in Babylon."

Chons stared blankly down the dark path through the forest that had been trampled flat. The bulky construction mech wasn't meant to traverse this type of environment. Chons could tell from the angle of the footprints it had left in the soil that the mech was slowing down. The effects of dampened remote charging were finally starting to kick in. This time, Zeus wouldn't get far. The job would be over soon.

Chons fiddled idly with the dino-steak in his pocket. He wanted to take his time with the job; wanted to savor the flavor of the steak; wanted to do anything but—

"Chons? Do you read me?" asked Atlas.

"Copy, boss. I'll wrap this up quick."

The call ended, and Chons walked down the shadowy path laid out before him. In the shade of the forest, he collected himself. He'd do things the way he always did: one step at a time. Neutralize Zeus. Collect the weapon. Return to HQ. Right now, it was time to focus on the first step.

Catching up to the waning mech didn't take long. Chons whistled loudly, and the mech spun about sluggishly to face him.

"Look, if you surrender now, I promise not to kill you." Chons waved his free hand at Zeus in friendly greeting. "As long as you don't tell bad jokes... or stink too bad."

Zeus listened in slack-jawed disbelief. "How the fuck has someone like you survived so long in your line of work, you crazy asshole?"

Chons sighed impatiently. "For starters, my tolerance for belligerent shits like you is just about nonexistent. Last chance. Surrender now."

"See, the thing is, you're all alone, and I've got the bigger gun." Zeus smiled smugly and leveled his plasma cannon at Chons once more.

"Yeah, well..." Chons drew his gun and fired from the hip in a single lightning-fast motion. The bullet landed cleanly on top of the

 Silence Of the Stars

previous two wedged into the mech's window, forcing them through and spraying the cockpit with shards of molten gold. Zeus' face vanished into a bloody mist behind the canopy. His lifeless finger fired the already charged plasma cannon, and Chons dove to the side. The trailing edge of his coat was disintegrated by the super-heated ball of energy.

This was where Chons would normally recite one of his favorite one-liners, but he had no audience, and he was suddenly in a bad mood. He'd neutralized Zeus and collected the weapon. Now, it was time to return to HQ.

He inhaled deeply, and as he exhaled, he summarized his thoughts on the situation.

"Fuck."

Chapter 25
Goodbye

It was the morning of the day of departure. Half my life, as I remembered it, had led up this moment. Today, I would take Athena and board a vessel to Mars, and in so doing I would betray Atlas' trust.

Do we have this all wrong? I thought. *Atlas gave me the freedom to walk around Babylon Station as I please. He's probably the most reasonable person I've met since waking from cryostasis. Compared to the people I've chosen to trust – Gomboc, Clecir, even Athena – Atlas seems the most rational.*

Thinking back to my conversation with Atlas, I recalled disagreeing with his arguments because they relied on too many assumptions. No matter how sound those assumptions seemed, I just couldn't accept such a negative outlook based on unverifiable factors... It was all too hypothetical. Now I was doing the very thing I disagreed with him about. I was abandoning my life on Earth and betraying the trust of Atlas, my protectorate, based on assumptions. I had no way of knowing how Atlas would really react if I told him the truth. I'd been acting solely on assumptions.

Athena must have had her reasons for doubting Atlas, and I'd be a fool to trust him completely, but was running away on a cargo ship really my best chance at survival? Could I really get off this station,

 Silence Of the Stars

through Atlas' security? Even if I did make it to Mars, would I really be any better off? What if I was arrested on arrival? Realistically speaking, was I not better off taking my chances cooperating with Atlas?

[Janus, get up. We need to go.] Athena's voice was uncharacteristically harsh.

I stood and poured my Nutrisynth breakfast, still lost in thought. The sun had not yet appeared in the holo-windows. Hours remained before the scheduled departure time. No need to rush.

[You can eat on the way. We need to leave, now.]

[What's wrong?] I felt a tinge of annoyance at the tone of urgency which disturbed the calm waters of my mind, pulling me back against the tide. I wanted more time to think.

[I'll explain later. An Omni is waiting for us at the door.]

If Athena said we should hurry, she probably had good reason. I would have plenty of time to second guess myself on the way to the dock.

As usual, the vibration of the Omni's tires on the road thrummed until the vehicle entered the magway and transitioned to levitation for high-speed travel through the Spire's system of vacuum transit tubes.

As I sank into my seat to enjoy the rest of my breakfast, Athena interrupted me. [Stay sharp. We're transferring soon.]

[Transferring?]

I spat a mouthful of breakfast out in astonishment when the door hissed and started to slide open while we were still on the magway. I grabbed the seat and closed my eyes anticipating an outrush of air as the cabin was exposed to vacuum, but the rush never came. I continued to breathe normally.

After a couple seconds recovering from the initial shock, I swiveled my head toward the door to see it was not exposed to the transit tube at all. Instead, the seat rotated outward to deposit me into a crowded room lined with benches. I hadn't noticed any deceleration, though. The car, and by extension this room, must have still been moving at vacuum-tube speeds.

People sat, stood, and leaned against the walls. They were locals, but weren't as pristine as I was accustomed to. They still acted as at home as the beautiful and well-dressed locals I had come to know, but they looked less homogenous; less well-kempt. The room itself wasn't the pinnacle of cleanliness I had seen around Babylon Station. The walls showed their age through minor wear and discoloration. The air was filled with a myriad of smells, suggesting atmospheric filters weren't keeping up as well as they had in other areas of the Spire. It was closer, in many ways, to New Angels City than to Babylon.

The Omni door shut behind me, trapping me in this unfamiliar place. I dropped my center of gravity into a defensive stance, ready for anything. No one reacted to my presence at all, except for a woman who gave me a side-eyed glare and put her bag down to fill the empty seat next to her.

[What is this place?] I asked.

     Silence Of the Stars

[It's a train. Public transportation,] Athena explained.

Scanning around the room, I saw a man giving me an awkward look from around his PCU. I nodded to him and stood up straight, attempting to act casual to avoid making a scene.

[I didn't think a cultural sight-seeing tour was on today's agenda,] I said. [Care to explain?]

[Most people only use cars for local trips or as a way to board magway trains. The majority of longer trips are made using public transportation like this. The private trips we have been taking up until now were a luxurious way of keeping you out of enclosed public spaces, for your safety.]

[Oh. Well, I'm glad we chose today of all days to prioritize budget over safety,] I said sarcastically.

[The situation has changed.]

[Should I be worried?]

[Please don't be,] urged Athena. [That would be counterproductive. We need to keep a low profile.]

[Sorry, but if we need to keep a low profile, why did we swap to public transportation?]

[Walk,] Athena ordered. [Keep moving between train cars. It'll be harder for them to track us here than in the Omni, but we still need to keep moving.]

I did as she directed. Walking from train car to train car, I couldn't help but once again notice how human behavior was unchanged by time and technological progress. People sat and stood as far apart from one another as the shared space would allow, erecting imaginary barriers. An occasional tight group or couples would huddle together to shunt the outside world from their shared pocket of space. Most groups and individuals stared at their tablets or dead-eyed into empty space, presumably accessing NuNet or PCU tablets via their HIPs. Few people spoke, and those who did talked in hushed voices.

Though the live people all around me were quiet, voices echoed from screens lining the ceiling, walls, and would-be windows. The seasoned sing-song of streamers and news reporters, the obnoxiously enthusiastic advertisements for everyday products, the melodrama of holo-film previews created a thick soup of audio static.

After this scene had repeated itself across several train cars, one screen caught my eye. It showed censored images of a woman who'd been brutally murdered. Despite the deliberately blurred image, I could see that something appeared to have dug its way out of the woman's stomach.

Sensing my interest, the audio for that screen grew louder. I started listening halfway through one reporter's account of the incident. "...eaten from the inside out by a mutant fetus, Rose was a 73-year-old woman who appears to have illegally reversed her sterilization procedure without visiting a registered fertility clinic. Where the fetus came from, whether it was human, whether the death of the mother was intentional, and who is ultimately responsible, are still unknown

     Silence Of the Stars

at this time. Several known black-market fertility clinics are currently under investigation for..."

"Rose," I muttered.

So that's what this is about.

[Yeah,] Athena confirmed.

Now I understood why Athena had been urging me along without explanation. She thought I would panic.

They'd be looking for the 'father' of this so-called 'mutant fetus'. Security footage would show that I had gone home with Rose, so I might be a suspect. The mutant fetus, if such a thing existed, might even actually be related to me. I was with Rose only a couple days ago, so if I got her pregnant, the fetus should still be tiny. But I didn't really understand my powers, and hadn't even considered how my regeneration ability might interact if my cells made an embryo. That interaction may have caused Rose's death.

[Try to keep calm. Take a few deep breaths. If I can detect that you're anxious, so can security. I'll do what I can to hide our trail until we reach the Martian embassy, but it'll be a lot easier if you keep it together,] Athena said as soothingly as she could manage. But even as she spoke, I could sense the anxiety building in her tone. Something else was bothering her.

[What's wrong, Athena?]

[Nothing is wrong. Everything is fine.]

[We already established that we are incapable of lying to each other. Don't worry, I'm calm. In fact, the only thing that has me worried right now is how unreasonably calm I feel, but that's beside the point. Tell me: what's wrong?]

In the pause that followed there might have been a sigh if Athena had lungs. [It's Chons. He's already waiting outside the embassy.]

[Security located us already?]

[No. I've been screening law enforcement channels. The local police are just now getting instructions to keep an eye out for you. There's no report of anyone locating you yet. Chons isn't communicating with local law enforcement. I can't confirm what he knows.]

[Chons might just be guessing our approach vector. He might even be guessing our intent to leave through the Martian embassy,] I suggested.

[That's possible. We could stay on the train a little longer and approach the embassy from an alternate entrance.]

[How much time would that add to the trip?]

[About ten minutes.]

[But security will locate us the moment we transfer to an Omni to detrain, right? That's the reason you transferred to a train in the first place. It will take them longer to find us here.]

[That's right,] Athena confirmed. [I wasn't going to say anything, but since you're not panicking, I'm glad you picked up on it. You really are uncharacteristically calm today.]

[We stick to the plan,] I insisted. [Navigate me to the Martian Embassy gate nearest our dock.]

[But the Godhunter—]

[I'd rather deal with Chons than give law enforcement more time to react. I prefer our chances with him.]

[Better the devil you know than the devil you don't, hmm?]

I shook my head. [Chons may not be a saint, but he's certainly no devil. Besides, I'd be lying if I said I didn't want a chance to say goodbye.]

[I advise against saying anything, given the option... Shit.]

Raising an eyebrow, I said, [I've never heard you curse before.]

[I just got locked out of station security. I was spoofing your location. They must have verified you weren't at the apartment. This means I'm officially suspect, too. We'll be running blind from now on. I only have access to public networks and NaviNet.]

[I'm lost without you, Athena. Can you still lead the way?]

[I can. Most Navis navigate without security access. I'm anonymously calling an Omni. Stand near any door on the left-hand side, and be ready to exit in twenty seconds.]

[Understood.]

The Omni arrived right on schedule. Inside, Athena's shimmering image appeared on the dashboard. Her expression was even more enthusiastic than usual, and she was wearing a tour-guide uniform I'd never seen before. Moreover, I didn't feel my usual direct connection to her.

"Welcome, Mister Nova! My name is Navi, and I will be your navigator this morning. Where can I take you?" It was strange hearing her voice out loud.

I choked back a laugh. I'd almost forgotten Athena was a Navi, which piloted a significant portion of all public transportation. The driver of this Omni wasn't the one-and-only Athena, it was a cookie-cutter Navi. It was surreal seeing another instance of her in this situation.

[Want to say 'hi' to your friend?] I asked Athena, trying to lighten the mood.

[She's not our friend, Janus. She already reported your location to station security. We need to get off this Omni before they get a warrant to reroute us. Martian Embassy gate 73B. Go. Now.]

"Take us... me, to Martian Embassy gate 73B," I repeated.

The Navi bowed and politely acknowledged, "Thank you. We will arrive in about two minutes."

[Janus...] Athena was struggling to remain calm. She hadn't been like this since I was introduced to her by Atlas. [Traffic reroute warrant applications take just *under* two minutes to process. If we are

 Silence Of the Stars

rerouted, we'll be locked into this vehicle and brought directly to station security. We need to get out of here *before* that happens.]

We couldn't get out of the car here. In addition to traveling at hundreds of kilometers per hour, we were in a vacuum tube. Exiting the vehicle here would be no different from stepping out into the vacuum of space.

[Let's stop at a closer exit and run the last leg of the trip, then,] I suggested.

[There isn't a closer exit. As soon as you hear wheels touch down, that means we're out of the vacuum tube. There will be atmosphere outside the Omni. I'm physically incapable of suggesting you commit crimes like vandalism, but I can tell you that if we are taken to security under warrant, we won't make our flight. Is that clear?]

[Crystal.] I rolled my shoulders and did what I could to warm up, thinking of ways to break out of the car if the doors didn't open. The glass was probably bulletproof. After all, the vehicle was designed to transport all sorts of unpredictable passengers, children included, at over 1000 kilometers per hour through vacuum in tightly packed traffic. It had to be durable.

Athena continued, [Our only window of opportunity will be the few seconds when the Omni is outside the vacuuway for the exit.]

Just then, I felt the faint vibration of tires on the ground. The door cracked open and the Navi's voice chimed, "Thank you for choosing Omni—"

The door stopped when it was only a few centimeters open. It was going to close again. The crack was just wide enough to slip my fingers through.

"Please keep your hands and feet inside the vehicle until the seats automatically deposit you outside," the polite voice requested.

I stood with one foot on the dashboard and one foot against the door frame to get as much leverage as I could, then pulled up, attempting to force the door open. I felt my exomysium squeeze and pull along with me, enhancing my strength. The door resisted, but didn't close.

"Mister Nova, please keep your fingers clear of the exit. The doors will shut for emergency rerouting," urged the Navi.

I pulled with all my might. It was now or never, but the door didn't budge. Even with the exomysium, it felt infinitely heavy, like trying to tear the hatch of a tank off its hinges. I needed to be stronger. It didn't matter how. It didn't matter if it was possible. I needed to succeed to survive. My joints ached and my fingers burned as they pressed against the door frame.

My bones and muscles strained beyond their limits, but unlike during my fight against Carl, my body was holding together.

When it felt as though my muscles might tear or my fingers might be severed, something else gave out. There was a crack and then a grinding whirr. My fingers slipped, and I lost my footing, slamming against the vehicle's dashboard. An alarm sounded, followed by a calm male voice. "Vacuum seal breach alert. Please calmly exit the vehicle."

 Silence Of the Stars

The door loosened, then rotated lopsidedly to the ground rather than upward as it usually would. An empty seat pushed outside, its fabric catching and tearing on the strangely positioned door as it went. I scrambled around the empty seat to exit. Looking back, I saw the frame of the thin nanofiber shell of the door had cracked, and the underlying metallic frame had ever so slightly bent inward where I had gripped it. The damage appeared minor but must have been enough to compromise the air seal, making the car unsafe for use in vacuum transit tubes.

There wasn't any time to admire my handiwork. Ignoring the throbbing pain in my digits, I looked around to get my bearings. I saw no security guards or RACERs among the crowd, but there was Chons, leaning against a kiosk right outside the giant double blast doors of the Martian embassy. He had already seen me. I took a deep breath and approached him.

He tipped his hat as I got close. "Hey kid, long time no see."

"Are you here to stop me?" I asked.

"Nah. My orders were specifically 'find Janus.'" He made air quotes with his fingers. "Mission accomplished. Of course, I'll have to report your location and get new orders, but I've got a few minutes of leeway. Enough time to say goodbye."

I couldn't help but smile. "I won't thank you, but only because I know you wouldn't want me to."

"Good. You've grown up a little," he said with a nod. He laid one hand on my shoulder. "Literally, too. You're definitely taller." He squeezed. "And buffer. Have you been working out?"

"Don't make this weird."

Chons laughed. "Speaking of weird, I like the pants. Very retro."

"You're one to talk." I gestured at his leather jacket, fedora, unkempt hair... everything about him, really.

He shrugged. "Well, you'd better get going."

"Will I see you again?"

He shook his head solemnly. "I hope not, for your sake."

I wanted to thank him. I wanted to ask him why he was helping me. I wanted to know more about him and his job. I wanted to go back to AlgEats and small talk for hours. I owed my life to Chons at least three times over, and didn't even understand why he kept saving me. Despite that, if he'd been ordered to apprehend or kill me, I'm certain he would have. I was lucky this time.

We reciprocated knowing nods, and I entered the Martian embassy without looking back.

Chapter 26
Escape

With the immediate danger behind me, I willed myself to relax. The realization that I was already relaxed paradoxically caused me to panic, filling me with a deep sense of existential dread. I should have been a nervous wreck. Instead, I was in as a calm flow state as if today's escape had been part of a well-practiced routine.

The life-or-death struggle; the tingling sensation of my fingers after the extreme physical exertion of bending the Omni door; being pursued by an armed force; the militaristic precision with which I moved under the guidance of a navigation AI... This wasn't me. It was all the domain of JANUS#004. I could feel his instincts scratching at the base of my subconscious. His combat impulses, his skills of observation, his habit of pre-planning contingencies for every eventuality. It was all there, just below the surface. I was ready for battle – *he* was ready for battle.

It had been there for a while now, gradually growing more and more prominent. I just hadn't noticed. I'd already borrowed JANUS#004's professional calm, and somehow, perhaps even a bit of his physical strength. Chons had noticed my increased height and musculature. Was it possible I was becoming more like my alter-ego in body as well as in mind?

Janus needed this calm and strength to survive. I couldn't afford to be weak right now, but if I relied on JANUS#004, allowed him to bleed into the forefront of my consciousness, would it change me? Would I ever be able to go back to just being Janus?

If not, if parts of JANUS#004 merged into my consciousness permanently, would that equate to death? How much of JANUS#004 could I tap into and still be myself? I had followed this line of thought before, but it had been a distant, philosophical problem. Now the consequences were imminent. Had I been killing myself bit by bit by using him to survive? Was there a threshold somewhere, a point of no return beyond which I would cease to be myself? Would I even know if I crossed that line? Might it already be too late?

Athena interrupted my internal panic. [It's strange that there were no security guards outside the embassy gate. Atlas must want to keep your apprehension quiet. That's good for us. He probably won't make big overt moves.]

More immediate threats needed to take priority. If my body died, I wouldn't have the luxury of worrying about the philosophical death of my personality. For now, survival was the priority. I kept my head on a swivel and pressed on toward the berth where Gomboc's ship waited.

Nobody greeted me at the terminal, but the outer airlock door opened as I approached. Subtle; good. I climbed through the umbilical tube between the station and the waiting ship. When I reached the ship, Clecir reached up to help me down from the ceiling airlock.

"Did anyone follow you?" she asked as she led the way to the flight deck.

"Nobody followed me to the dock, but Chons saw me enter the embassy," I replied.

"Friend of yours?"

"Sort of. He's a Godhunter."

Clecir skipped a step as if she was about to turn and face me, but then she kept walking. "Sounds like you're in more trouble than I thought."

"I told you it would be dangerous to help me. If you're having second thoughts, I'll get off the ship right now."

"Too late fer that," growled Gomboc as we reached the bridge. "We're in the next group in line for the Launch Ring."

Good. Running ahead of schedule.

Gomboc sat in the captain's chair on a deck raised slightly above four gimbaled flight seats. Clecir ushered me into the nearest seat, and strapped herself into the next one over.

I sank into the thick gel seat and allowed the cushions to wrap around my legs and torso. In addition to the five-point harness, there was a strap for each arm and leg, and even a basket harness to go over the head and support the jaw. The seat was on a gimbal designed to rotate in 360 degrees on both axes, allowing it to point in any direction. While I could imagine the kinds of high-g maneuvers these seats would be useful for, I couldn't imagine this rust bucket of a ship surviving that kind of acceleration.

The seats must be aftermarket, I decided. *It was probably price, convenience, or aesthetic preference that led to such a purchase. There's no practical reason to install combat crash couches on a freighter.*

It bothered me that I had any concept of what kind of acceleration should be expected from this ship. I had no reason to know that. That knowledge wasn't mine. This wasn't the first time, either. I'd found myself more knowledgeable about technical topics in the past few days, and it wasn't the result of study. At least, it wasn't the result of *my* study.

Clecir put on her five-point harness but left the other belts tucked into their holsters, leaving her arms and head mobile. I followed suit.

"Lock in and sound off!" commanded Gomboc, suddenly sounding like a real captain instead of an old drunkard.

"Locked in!" said Clecir.

"Locked in!" I echoed instinctively.

"Pre-launch," called Gomboc.

Clecir began reciting a list: "Umbilical is clear.

"Anchors one through six are green.

"Com lasers are green.

"Main engines are green.

"Attitude thrusters are yellow. Flow-rate to starboard bow at sixty percent.

"Radio comms are yellow – we aren't picking up bands 8.55 through 9.8. All traffic control bands are green.

"Reactor output is yellow at sixty-five percent.

"Life support is... not responding on decks one through four. Green otherwise..."

[Is this normal?] I asked Athena.

[This ship needs a full overhaul, assuming it's even salvageable. Traffic control won't clear us for launch,] Athena warned.

When Clecir finished the list, Gomboc asked, "So, nothing new is broken, then?"

"All SNAFU. I'll tune the lower deck CO_2 scrubbers enroute," replied Clecir.

Gomboc picked up an ancient-looking radio microphone with a coil cord, held down the button and said into it, "Mar Embassy Tower. Fortigo-4 pre-launch report: all checks green. Requesting launch clearance. Over."

The reply came over the loudspeaker system, "Fortigo-4. Mar Embassy Tower. Copy, all green. You are clear for departure. Proceed to Ring receiver A-2."

[Unbelievable,] said Athena.

For the first time that day, I felt nervous about something other than my identity. In a strange way, that was reassuring.

"Take us out," ordered Gomboc.

My stomach lurched following a metallic thump as anchors released. Dust on the floor and panels lifted into the air, suddenly unburdened by gravity, then flew to the ceiling as gravity briefly reversed as braking thrusters killed our momentum relative to the station from centripetal force.

Slowly, carefully, Clecir maneuvered the ship down past row after row of stacked habitation discs and drums. Each stack drifted by like an unnaturally uniform mountain range skewered on Babylon Spire like God's shish kebab. This was my first time seeing the station up close. I'd never realized how many of the habitation drums were covered in a rocky outer layer. If they weren't bound to the greater L1 structure, they could be mistaken for asteroids. From this vantage point, the towers, habitation drums and disks, giant telescopes, and petals of the Rose seemed haphazardly strewn about the rocky central structure.

Once clear of Babylon Station, we drifted down the Spire toward the Moon. In the dark of night, the Spire and its support cables were a light show of activity, like a Christmas tree engulfed in a cloud of ultrafine snow particles being carried up and down in a swirl of wind currents. Of course, there was no wind outside. Those particles were ships and trains either free-floating or taxiing up and down cables spanning the 60,000-kilometer gap from L1 to the Moon's surface. The massive Fortigo must have also looked like a mere mote of dust from the perspective of other travelers. The Spire's central cable, five kilometers wide where it met Babylon Station, disappeared to a vanishing point long before reaching the surface of the Moon, rendering most of its length invisible to us.

As we plummeted toward the ring, much nearer the Moon's surface, I had little concept of speed or distance. The immense scale was disorienting. The glistening snowstorm of ships spiraled up and down, but the Moon and stars appeared stationary. I couldn't tell whether we were free-floating or being pulled along by a cable as all the other points of light seemed to be.

When we finally reached the Launch Ring, we were within the Moon's gravity well, though the effect was barely noticeable. The ship rolled so that its top side was facing the Moon, and our gimbaled flight seats spun to keep our feet aligned with gravity. The surface which had been the floor was now above our heads, and the moon was visible through the viewport below our feet, through what had been the ceiling.

    Silence Of the Stars

Clecir and Gomboc coordinated with a 'ground crew' which fastened our anchor cables and landing gear to a launch sled which would carry us along the electromagnetic track of the Launch Ring.

"Anchor one, lock. Anchor two, lock. Anchor three..." Clecir recited. The checklist seemed to go on forever. My hands began to sweat, perhaps out of nervousness, or perhaps because of the tight embrace of the crash couch.

"Locked in tight, and the sled is green to go. The next launch window opens in thirty seconds from mark, and closes in one hundred and twenty seconds... Mark," said Clecir.

"Launch window confirmed. Take us out when ready," said Gomboc.

My focus shifted from the main window to the myriad of small monitors showing the outside world in every direction. The ship evoked the image of an overladen freight train. Antennae, unlabeled tanks, and other parts I could only guess the function of, covered the surface of the ship so thoroughly that the basic shape of the hull beneath was difficult to guess. It was a good thing spaceships didn't need to be aerodynamic.

Thirty seconds later, a metallic groan announced the beginning of our acceleration along the Launch Ring. The slight lunar gravity was overpowered almost immediately by the force of acceleration, and our seats shifted to launch configuration. The Moon was once again overhead. Acceleration shifted the perceived direction of gravity; the 'down' direction migrated away from my feet until I had the sense of lying on my back.

Despite feeling the acceleration, the main screen didn't show any sign of motion at first. The track, which was now 'above' us – between Fortigo and the Moon – was so large and uniform that it appeared to be a fixed feature of the background. It remained a constant, as if it were a part of our ship even as Babylon Spire receded into the distance behind us and the terrain of the Moon began to move by above. The unfathomably large Ring track appeared as only a sliver as it curved away from us, disappearing behind the horizon of the Moon.

We transitioned from the lunar night into day, and the track was suddenly a brilliant silvery-white. A black printed number appeared on its surface, then another. Each number briefly broke the illusion of the track being a part of our ship. This sequence of numbers appeared in greater and greater frequency as we accelerated, counting up to 360 before resetting to 0 on our second lap around the Moon, at which point Babylon Spire swept by so fast as to be a barely perceptible blur.

The Earth came briefly into view, and for a moment I felt that the floor had dropped out from under me. This might be the last time I would ever see the cradle of humanity from this close. From Mars, it would appear nothing but a pale blue dot.

"Prepare for release at the ninety-one-degree marker," said Clecir.

The markers shot by too fast to read in the forward camera now. My eyes flicked between the forward display and the other panels to try and find what number we were at. By the time I did, the counter was ticking by rapidly: 82, 83, 84. I gripped the edge of my armrests and pressed myself into my flight couch even harder than gravity already was.

At the 91-degree marker, a deep metallic ringing reverberated through the ship, and the press of acceleration vanished. I was tossed around in my seat as the couch tried to counteract the turbulent rumbling of the ship's attitude thrusters, which fired briefly to orient our nose plow forward. I pressed my eyes shut and gritted my teeth.

     Silence Of the Stars

A moment later, the turbulence stopped and I was weightless. I opened my eyes to see the Moon shrinking in the rear-facing camera display. The Lunar Launch Ring, which was suspended in space, wrapping fully around the Moon, had seemed so unimaginably massive moments ago. Now it was so dwarfed by the natural bright lunar surface as to be invisible.

"Release complete. We are clear, and trajectory is within tolerance." Clecir flipped a few switches. "Preparing for main burn to set heading in thirty minutes."

It would be more efficient to perform course adjustment burns earlier, but the governments of Earth didn't appreciate being bombarded with superheated streams of radioactive plasma, so there were guidelines for directing thrust away from the planet, and minimum radii in which certain engine types could be used. A fusion engine aimed toward Earth from a sufficiently large ship would appear as a second sun from this range. If every ship leaving the system relied on fusion engines, Earth's oceans would boil. Thus, we drifted quietly through space and waited.

After just a few minutes of watching the Earth and Moon shrink behind the ship, there was no longer any visible sign of civilization. The blue ball and its little white satellite appeared undisturbed by the complexities of politics or the drama of mankind's ten-thousand-year fight to dominate their surfaces. The only signs of life were the black and green patches of algae dotting the Earth's seas. Unlike those microscopic organisms, humanity hadn't made any visible mark from this distance.

"Set heading," ordered Gomboc, some time later.

"Heading set. Lighting main engines in three, two..."

There was no kick when the engine started, just a steady hum as the fusion torch pushed us along at 0.3 MeSS. The feed from the rear-view camera flashed bright white until it adjusted to the brightness, at which point the exhaust bloom faded to a brilliant pink. It was the classic glow of a helium plasma exhaust plume, something JANUS#004 was sure to have known, but I had never seen before.

As Clecir unbuckled her harness she explained that the majority of our acceleration came from the launch loop. This burn would simply correct our course since the ring was not aligned perfectly with our destination. I already knew that, but I appreciated the explanation all the same.

I left my harness on as I gazed through the dazzling plume. Its glow obscured all but the brightest stars, which remained barely visible through the pink haze.

A few minutes later, the screen flickered again as a new star burst into existence, brighter than the rest. It slowly elongated until it appeared to be a comet. This must have been the fusion exhaust bloom of another ship – the next in line behind us. The ship itself was far too distant to see, but the cloud of plasma ejected by its fusion thrusters continued to outshine every star in space save for the sun.

Space itself is becoming a crowded highway, I thought.

We were on a road trip of sorts; a space adventure. I was beyond Atlas' reach, at least for the moment.

     Silence Of the Stars

Chapter 27
Silence Of the Stars

You must always ask yourself, "Is this inevitable? Is this the only way forward?"

Whenever the answer is "Yes" then you must stop. You will not want to stop; nobody will want to stop. Many will argue that you can't stop, that by definition it is impossible to stop in such a scenario...

You must be the immovable object that impedes the unstoppable force. You must avoid the inevitable path, because the inevitable has led countless trillions of civilizations across billions of years to the same inevitable demise.

If there is a path forward which leads us to the stars rather than to extinction, it is *not* the inevitable path. It is *not* the path which invariably presents itself to every civilization, then destroys them just as invariably.

No matter how revolutionary, how convenient, how tantalizing, how obvious a way forward may seem, if it is inevitable, it must be avoided.

To avoid the inevitable is a paradox.

It is a paradox, but failure to overcome it means extinction.

We may have avoided the inevitable death already, or we may be too late. We cannot know whether the inevitable lies behind or ahead because if we bypass the inevitable downfall, then it was never truly inevitable at all. We can't know, so we must always act as though the danger still lies ahead.

In theory it is simple, but in practice...

Humanity has built a precariously balanced and ever-growing house of cards to live upon. Artificial habitats have given us additional living space; Martian mines provide us with building material; the belt provides valuable corium metals; Jovian dredge lines feed us virtually endless fuel, and our advanced launch systems link everything together. All told, this grand house humanity has built could support a much greater population than Earth alone ever could. We have overcome every hardship the universe had thrown at us, and defied nature to contain us. Now that we had achieved all this, humanity seems unstoppable. At a glance, the path forward seems inevitable.

That is a problem.

Now, even Earth is little more than a single card in a delicately balanced house. Pull one card out, and Earth would collapse along with the rest.

* * *

 Silence Of the Stars

It was Earth standard 6AM. I stood alone in front of my golden throne, staring at my reflection in the polished sheen, as I often did in the mornings. My mirrored self leered back, challenging me to make a case convincing enough to move the world; challenging me to defy the inevitable; challenging me to *earn* the throne I'd sat upon for over a century. I thought back to the root of the Big Problem to break it down to its core components.

The problem started with interdependence. Everyone needed phosphorus to grow food, but only Mars produced enough surplus to export. Everyone needed water, but only one distributor supplied the two hundred billion citizens of the inner system. Everyone needed propellant, and most liquid hydrogen came from Jupiter. The list went on. Everyone relied on everyone else, and the vacuum of space separated us. A breakdown *anywhere* would mean shortages of critical supplies *everywhere*. Everything worked, or nothing did.

So, what was the contingency if a bolide destroyed Mars' launch system and cut off the solar system's supply of phosphorus? What was the contingency if a CME shut down Jupiter's hydrogen mine and cut off the supply of propellant? What was the contingency if a war broke out among the gigacorporations, and Omni stopped delivering water to the inner system?

Everyone knew the risks of an interdependent solar system. Everyone knew that it would be better to build redundancies; that we should have aimed for self-sustaining systems. But self-sustaining systems were expensive, slow to build, and hard to maintain. They were not competitively viable in a market where other investors took riskier approaches for higher returns.

Garrett Ordiway

Self-sustainability meant settling for a less lavish lifestyle – it meant sacrificing power and being a small fish in the big pond. During times of plenty, anyone playing a safe, low-return long game would be driven out of the market by high-return short-term thinkers. An absolute apex predator who chose moderation was doomed to be overwhelmed and outnumbered by aggressive peers willing to take risks.

Worse yet, in the event of a catastrophe, those who were self-sufficient would get eaten alive by their more powerful peers who had chosen to live in lavish excess. Nobody was willing to accept a lower quality of life if it meant they'd just be overrun in the event of a disaster anyway. Nobody wanted to live as someone else's backup plan. Thus, playing the long game and aiming to be self-sufficient was only viable if everyone else did the same. It had to be unanimous.

Then what should we do? Do we allow nature to take its course? Do we wait for a major catastrophe to trigger a chain reaction that drives humanity to extinction? Many preferred to pretend that a civilization-ending disaster could never actually happen, even though events like that were inevitable, even common, on the cosmological scale. It was a matter of *when*, not *if* a major catastrophe would disrupt the current balance. If civilizations were interdependent when a catastrophe broke their ties, everyone would die. Still, that wasn't enough to convince *everyone* to cooperate. But *everyone* must cooperate, or we would all die.

I had been through this a hundred thousand times. The solution was conceptually simple: unity. But that was out of reach. I needed enough influence to convince a sufficient portion of sovereignties to

Silence Of the Stars

cooperate that the remainder could be made to comply by way of sanctions or force. But the solar system was a big pond, and it was full of feisty fish. When we all lived on Earth, Nature had taken care of this aspect of survival for us. If civilization fell, we could rebound because nature was self-sufficient. Now it was not. Humans didn't evolve to think on this scale, to see the big picture. That wasn't our nature.

Each nation and society focused on its local problems. It was only natural. Keeping everyone fed and healthy and happy seemed noble. The idea that prioritizing the freedom, safety, and quality of life of the citizens can contribute to the inevitable destruction of our species was too abstract a concept for most people to grasp. There was no malice in it. No one meant harm. Everyone wanted a comfortable life for themselves and their family. So, they expanded and consumed and developed new technology to better their lives... and every step they took pulled us further from unification.

People sought to push further; to stretch thinner. Of course they did. Nature moderated life, but life did not evolve to know moderation. If there were untapped resources to be had, our opportunistic minds sought to claim them. Evolution had barely touched us from the time we were hunter-gatherers picking berries and following herds of game across open fields. For millions of years, the boldest and most able to provide for their tribes had survived and passed those traits on. Call it manifest destiny; call it ambition; call it greed; by any name, it was a cornerstone of human nature.

I turned away from my reflection to look at the rotating three-dimensional map in the globe display above the great round table.

Garrett Ordiway

The map was dotted with over five hundred disjointed sovereignties on Earth and astar. Each was free to act with near impunity. When I had first seen this display centuries ago, it showed only the Earth and Luna. As the years went on, Sol gradually shrank as the image zoomed out further and further to encompass the ever-expanding sprawl. At 1:1 scale, the only visible point of light now was the Sun, and only barely. Most visitors didn't even notice the glass sphere contained a map of the entire solar system.

The pond is getting too big to manage.

The role of Geo-Luna Arbitrator was to mediate relationships. Originally, that had meant the relationship between Earth and Luna. The role expanded to govern the relationship between Geo-Luna and the solar system at large. I was beloved by Geo-Luna, and respected astar, even by my opponents. I was certainly a 'big fish'. By all measures, I was a successful Arbitrator, but I felt my purpose slipping away with the shrinking sun of the globe display.

The authority of Geo-Lunar Arbitrator ended at the midway point between the orbit of Earth and Mars. I did not have direct power over Mars, the Belt, Jupiter or its Trojans, Greeks, and Hildas, or over the sparse settlements of the Frontier beyond. I could influence areas outside my jurisdiction with sanctions, favorable trade terms, project funding, and other political tricks, but I couldn't do anything to outright stop outward expansion. I couldn't directly curb their technological development. I couldn't force them to develop toward self-sustainability. I couldn't unify them.

  Silence Of the Stars

After all, colonists generally saw themselves as downtrodden, oppressed people fleeing their current situation to risk lands unknown insearch of greener pastures. The more I tried to punish expansion, the further incentivized they would be to flee my influence.

I needed something decisive, but brute force wouldn't do. I couldn't afford to be the villain or I'd lose support. The only realistic option was to convince enough other sovereignties of the necessity of restraint and of unity. To hold back expansion and unregulated technological development, to curb growth and focus on making our current infrastructure more robust. We needed a unified alliance of all humanity. Call it... the Sol Alliance.

To avoid falling victim to the current cycle, the Sol Alliance would have to collectively agree to eliminate any dissenting sovereignties, and prevent new sovereignties from forming outside the alliance. No one must be allowed to act brashly, lest they overrun the cautious alliance.

Shrink the pond. Eat all the feisty fish. Unify the school.

Not tyranny, I reminded myself, as I often must. *I'm protecting mankind's freedom to live, which supersedes all other freedoms.*

* * *

That morning reflection always helped me to reaffirm my long-term goals and provide a framework for decision making. With that out of the way, I took a deep breath and sat upon the golden throne. Then, it was time to review the day's schedule.

9:00: I am to arbitrate a dispute between Trojan and Greek claims over a cluster of recently discovered high-value asteroids in Sol-Jupiter Lagrange point two. Ambassadors from both parties arrived yesterday. Light lag and cultural differences have prevented any meaningful remote dialogue. The disputed territory technically falls under Jovian jurisdiction, but Jupiter requested my neutral arbitration. I won't turn them down. This is a good opportunity to pressure the Greeks on their illegal use of Von Neumann mining drones in the Oort cloud.

11:00: I am to serve as an Interplanetary Supreme Court justice. Duke Bacchus III of Ceres will be presenting the defense of Light Mind Corporation for a recent string of long-distance mind-transfer purge timing failures which has resulted in a number of illicit mind duplications. Personalities at the sending and receiving addresses both claim *writ of original mind*. What a mess; it's like that 2500s fiasco all over again. We could avoid this completely by banning remote mind transference, but the outer system would never agree to that. Still... I might be able to push for heavier sanctions. Range restrictions, perhaps.

Restricting range would make purging more reliable due to reduced light lag. Get the range short enough, and they'd start making relay stations. That infrastructure might be expensive enough to draw public ire or force some Light Mind clients out of the market: both good outcomes.

          Silence Of the Stars

12:00: Lunch with the Dalai Lama. It's a casual lunch, but he'll likely request subsidies for Buddhist immigration into the series of cylinders he sponsored, which are going live in the next few months. It will be a good opportunity to discuss the growing number of Ascensionists in his sphere of influence. I'd be happy to lend him a hand, but can't afford to be seen as an Ascensionist supporter. Many less educated members of the public see Ascensionism as a sect of Buddhism, so this will be a delicate conversation.

* * *

I was interrupted by a direct message from Dr. Osiris. The usual raspiness in his voice was exacerbated by his excitement. "Reporting in, sir!"

"Our meeting isn't until sixteen hundred hours, Doctor Osiris," I said firmly so as to conceal my own excitement. I'd been looking forward to an update on the doctor's tests.

"Yes, yes. Political conquest can wait. I have breakthrough news that would make Pyrrhus proud!"

Political conquest? I let the belligerent allegation slide. Speechcraft had never been Osiris' strong suit.

"Make it quick," I ordered.

"Yes, of course!" He attempted fruitlessly to clear his throat. "I've updates on the mutant fetus produced by Rose and Janus Nova. You may remember that I previously mentioned that the intercellular bio-nanites within the fetus were capable of communicating information between cells and facilitate cross-cellular reading and construction of DNA. Well... I decided to test the limits of that, and grafted a rat ear to the fetus..."

"And?"

Dr. Osiris chittered some nonsense to himself before regaining his bearings. "Unlike grafted human tissue, which was either devoured or ignored, the rat ear was assimilated. The fetus grew nerves and muscles to control the ear. It even developed an auditory cortex, which it had previously lacked. In fact, prior to integrating the ear, the fetus had no sensory organs at all, but now the fetus reacts to noise. It's listening to us!"

Slightly disturbing, but nothing out of the ordinary for genetic chimeras which had been commonly used in stem-cell research for centuries. Surely this wasn't the revelation that would 'make Pyrrhus proud'. The fact that Dr. Osiris wasn't elaborating further suggested he feared what my reaction to the real news might be.

"Go on," I encouraged him. An overly harsh tone might cause him to omit important details. I didn't have time to wring the full story out of him by force. I coaxed him gently.

"Well... It didn't stop with the one ear. It grew a pair of limbs as well. It tucks the limbs inside its body when we are observing it directly. It seems to know when we are in the room. It even seems to detect when

 Silence Of the Stars

we are watching with ultrasound, X-ray, or other active monitoring systems."

"So it has a basic level of consciousness?" That wasn't particularly surprising. The fetus may have only been a month old, but it was a human fetus, after all. Combine that with rat DNA, and you could make a quick-developing chimera.

"Not just basic. When we monitor it using only passive sensors, which it can't detect, it... tries to escape."

"Tries to escape, how?" The conversation now had my full attention.

"It scraped the galvanized coating off of the feeding apparatus, ingested it, and reconfigured it into a simple tool attached to one of its limbs, like a built-in screwdriver. It used that tool to etch and loosen the lid screws when it didn't detect us observing. Don't worry – we already moved it into a more secure cage."

"It used the galvanized coating to modify its own body?"

"Exactly!"

"Destroy the fetus immediately," I commanded

"But sir!" pleaded Dr. Osiris.

"Incinerate it. Make sure not a single cell or nanite remains. Lock down the lab and scour the facility for any loose nanites that may have leaked when you switched cages. Perform a mandatory medical check on your staff, officers, and anyone who may have been in contact with the fetus."

"Surely you are overreacting! This is a once-in-a-millennium opportunity! This is the greatest medical miracle since penicillin!" His voice cracked in his desperation.

"Anything capable of reproduction, regeneration, and conscious self-reconfiguration is a potential gray goo. Add intelligence to that, and it's a class-six extinction-level threat."

"Don't be ridiculous, sir! Even humans are capable of all those things. Surely you wouldn't have me incinerate all of humanity as well. Wait... This isn't about the fetus! It's about Zoe, isn't it?" He choked on his words and murmured quietly to himself, realizing he'd stepped out of line.

I was not in the mood to berate him, and I knew doing so would be pointless. I stood in silence for a while, keeping my expression as impassive as possible. Any facial movement might betray my rage.

I'd already given my order; there was no need to repeat myself. Dr. Osiris was acting bold today. He must have felt strongly about the importance of this project. I understood where he was coming from, but there was no room for negotiation. This was exactly the kind of threat I'd dedicated my life to protecting humanity from.

"Understood, sir," Dr. Osiris said dispiritedly, then abruptly closed coms.

In truth, I was less worried about this creature consuming everything it touched, and more worried about humans using it to consume everything *they* touched. Our ambition is tempered by our reliance on one another. Organized society relies on human interdependence.

     Silence Of the Stars

The fetus was able to physically alter itself to the extreme. Such an ability would have made traditional bioaugmentations obsolete – not a bad thing, in isolation. The problem was that such a level of freedom could make people feel truly self-reliant.

Human civilization only developed because we cooperated to survive. History shows that whenever people believe they no longer need each other, society collapses. It is when we believe that we have overcome our nature that Nature destroys us.

The fetus represented exactly the kind of black swan technology that all civilizations might *inevitably* pursue upon discovery. There was no knowing which such technology might destabilize and destroy humanity… destroy *every* budding civilization in the galaxy… be responsible for the silence of the stars.

This revelation made me even more concerned about what had provoked Janus to flee L1. We both already knew about his ability to regenerate at the time of our first meeting. Experiments with this fetus had demonstrated that his ability was more than regeneration. He had only just recently thawed when we met, so it's likely that Janus had only known about regeneration at that time. The fetus was able to modify its body in extreme ways; for Janus to be able to deliberately hide such an ability from doctors and myself seemed unlikely.

More likely, he learned more about his condition after our meeting. Whatever he learned, he decided that I would consider it a threat, and therefore that I was a threat to him. What's more, he'd visited the Martian embassy several days before departing, which suggests that his escape was premeditated. He made up his mind to leave even before the incident with Rose. Her death was not the catalyst that prompted his decision to flee.

What I didn't understand is that there was no conversation between Janus and anyone else to indicate that he harbored any distrust toward me. He had been under constant surveillance around the clock, save for a couple of minutes of signal disruption in his apartment, and the brief time he spent on that Martian ship. That left three possibilities:

The first possibility was that Janus had been radicalized by that Martian pilot. This seemed most likely, due to the pilot's history of expressing open support for Martian autonomy.

The second possibility was that Janus somehow knew the consequences of his copulation with Rose before the fetus consumed her. However, logically he should have simply avoided that situation, had he known. Her demise didn't benefit him in any way. I doubt he was so overcome by lust that reason failed him.

The third possibility, least likely but most terrifying: Athena betrayed me. She was the only other contact Janus had during surveillance outages. She didn't report anything unusual to me, but she should have seen signs of Janus' premeditated escape before he acted.

A rogue TrueAI would be a great opportunity if it had happened somewhere I could contain it. A headline like *Rogue TrueAI Helps Fugitive Murderer Evade Arrest* could potentially give me all the ammunition necessary to bring down the whole Cultivator program, or at least make room for more sanctions. But if this went poorly,

     Silence Of the Stars

Athena could be made into a martyr to the opposite effect. She and Janus both could.

In any case, Janus and his conspirators were together aboard that ship. Janus hadn't responded to my attempts to communicate, meaning he was either an enemy, or he was under the control of an enemy. If Janus had abilities like those displayed by the fetus in Dr. Osiris' experiments, he represented an existential threat to all life in the solar system.

I wished there was another option… but that ship could not be allowed to reach Mars.

Chapter 28
Too Quiet

Travel time to Mars from the Luna Launch Ring varied significantly depending on the relative orbits of Earth and Mars. Earth took 365 days to orbit the Sun, while Mars took 687 Earth days. When the orbits of Mars and Earth aligned, they could be as close as 55 million kilometers. With a direct shot from the launch loop, ships could travel from Luna to Mars in under a week if one didn't mind expending exorbitant amounts of energy and propellant to decelerate on arrival.

However, when Mars was on the opposite side of the Sun, catching up with it was difficult. Not only could it be as far as 400 million kilometers from Earth, but navigating in a straight line through the Sun was impossible. Following a circular orbit around the Sun was also not an option since speed determined the orbital distance from the sun for all objects, including both planets and ships. A ship set on a ballistic-intercept course from Earth to Mars at such a time would take years to catch the red planet. Using a rocket to speed up the process would cause the ship to climb the Sun's gravity well to an orbit which would never intercept Mars at all.

The current alignment of planets was not ideal for travel between Earth and Mars, but neither was it impossible. Rather than a circular orbit, a ship could instead take an eccentric path down below the orbit of Venus. This would make for a fast approach to Mars and require significant propellent expenditure to slow down to avoid missing Mars entirely. Missing would mean spending the next several decades floating all the way out past the orbit of Saturn before gradually being reeled back in by Sol's gravity.

     Silence Of the Stars

It was an expensive and inefficient route, requiring months in transit. Historically, ships would have had to wait for the alignment of planets to become more favorable. The route was only possible now due to the combination of fusion torch propulsion and the initial boost from the Lunar Launch Ring.

For most travelers and businesses, waiting three to six months for the next clear launch window would still be more practical. Traffic to the red planet was sparse under current conditions, which is why it was strange to see another vessel following so closely behind the Fortigo.

* * *

During the long journey, Janus found himself spending most days on the bridge. It was spacious, clearly meant for a much larger crew. It was also one of the few rooms with real windows. The Fortigo had a rare 'top'-mounted bridge like a seafaring ship. From here, he had a clear view of the starfield to the port and starboard, as well as a view 'above', through a porthole directly above his seat. The ship's nose plow should have blocked the forward view, but cameras artificially filled the gap in visibility.

If the ship were new, the effect probably would have been an uninterrupted panoramic view sweeping all the way across the bridge. In reality, only the center of the forward view was clear. This is because the forward view was artificially patched in, while the real windows suffered from decades of accumulated scuffs and particulate debris.

Janus liked to gaze out the bridge windows while Clecir and Gomboc split their time between routine maintenance around the ship and occasionally visiting the bridge to monitor instruments.

The ship didn't need anyone to actively fly it while drifting through space. Janus found the frequency of flashing maintenance alerts disconcerting, but Gomboc assured him there was nothing to worry about. The two Martians went about their tasks with casual confidence. Today, however, Clecir was spending a long time on the bridge, especially fixated on one particular task.

When Gomboc saw her lingering at her instruments longer than usual, he floated over and inspected the item of interest, asking, "What is it?"

"It's that Guan Yu ship that launched behind us from Luna. It started on a more leisurely trajectory a couple degrees further out from Sol than us. Six hours ago, about a million kilometers back, it changed course to a trajectory much closer to ours. I didn't think anything of it at the time, but their beacon just shut off. They've gone dark," said Clecir.

"Think they need 'elp?" asked Gomboc.

"Not sure. Coms are yours if you want to check in with them."

Gomboc floated over to the command seat to access his communications suite. He switched on all bands of communication, hailing the dark ship with tight-beam laser and radio. His accent was noticeably lighter when he used the radio. "This is Gomboc of Fortigo-4, Mar-bound flight 3B-82M-4A, hailing Guan Yu vessel..."

He let his finger off the coms button to ask, "What is their designation and flight number? Their beacon is off an' I don't see it on the flight ledger."

 Silence Of the Stars

"They didn't have a flight number. They were only listed as 'Guan Yu'."

Gomboc started over. "This is Gomboc of Fortigo-4, flight 3B-82M-4A, hailing unmarked Guan Yu vessel bearing toward Mar. Are ye in distress? Do ye read me?"

Gomboc waited. At this range, there would be a few seconds of light lag, and it might take time for someone aboard the other ship to reach the coms. After a minute passed, Gomboc tried again. After a few more attempts, he conceded, "No use. They're not respondin'."

"There might be something wrong with their coms," suggested Clecir.

"Aye. I'll ping their location an' broadcast it back to Luna traffic control. They can at least update the ship's location on the public traffic map," said Gomboc.

"It should be on the public traffic map," Athena piped in. "Luna tracks all outbound ships, by radar, lidar, passive radio, infrared… Even if a ship turns off its beacon, it shouldn't be possible for them to disappear. Not this close to Earth."

"I guess we'll see what Luna 'as to say about that in a few minutes," said Gomboc.

"Best send the message to Mar too," suggested Clecir.

"Aye," agreed Gomboc.

"Light lag to Earth is currently two minutes twenty-three seconds," offered Athena. "To Mars, just over seventeen minutes, assuming the Sun doesn't interfere with our direct signal. A little longer if we need to route the signal through a relay."

Gomboc groaned as if listening to Athena caused him physical pain. Janus wasn't sure why, but Gomboc didn't seem to like her.

"About five minutes until the earliest possible reply, then," said Clecir.

Janus scanned the faces of his crewmates. They were tense and deep in thought. There was a lot going on here that wasn't being said. Calculations and assumptions were being made based on background knowledge Janus didn't have. *Do the others know something about that ship?* Janus had seen the name Guan Yu several times before. It was an influential gigacorporation based on Mars, but he didn't know anything beyond that. This seemed as good a time as any to learn more, so he silently consulted Athena.

Athena explained, [Guan Yu was one of the first sovereign corporations. It was originally a company based in China. The company used Chinese funding to establish one of the first large-scale factories on Mars, but the revenue of the Mars branch of Guan Yu eventually eclipsed the GDP of the entire country of China on Earth. At that point, it didn't make sense to pay taxes anymore, so Guan Yu declared independence.

[Now it operates independent of any government... at least in theory. That's the definition of a 'sovereign corporation'. Guan Yu and a few other gigacorporations formed the Sovereign Corporations of Mars, which is an extranational committee that governs the planet. Guan Yu and the other committee members still have close business ties with Geo-Luna and the inner system. They're just so big that no nation can lay claim to them or tax them.

[By now, you're familiar with Nile and Omni, which are also on the committee. All three of them are part of the Big Seven. Unlike Guan Yu, most gigacorporations originated from the former United States.]

     Silence Of the Stars

[Wait – 'former'? What happened to the United States?]

[It's just North America now. The unification happened around the same time as the formation of the United Nations of Earth. The corporations which would become Guan Yu, Nile and Omni all already existed at that time, although their names changed through a series of mergers and political maneuvering.]

All three names were commonplace in New Angels and Babylon Station, Janus recalled. [Omni deals with transportation. Nile handles delivery and retail. What does Guan Yu do?]

[They have their toes in many markets. Their biggest is contract fabrication. They built over half of all habitation cylinders currently orbiting the sun. They churn out a new full-size habitat cylinder every few days. That's why their presence is so big on Mars. Habitat fabrication is a massive industry.]

[What does Mars have to do with habitat fabrication? Those habitats are several kilometers wide, and longer still. Don't they make them in space, out of asteroids or something?]

[Mars exports more construction materials to space than all other sources combined. The planet is naturally rich in metals, and they can strip-mine it without worrying about environmental damage. That's what the 'hot boxes' are all about.]

[Mars is the biggest source of metals? What about the asteroid belt?] asked Janus.

[Asteroids were essential sources of metal in the early days of space travel when we had to rely on rocket propulsion. But asteroids are far apart, and Mars is two hundred times as massive as the whole asteroid belt combined. Guan Yu determined that it was more efficient to magnetically accelerate materials mined from Mars into space than to mine asteroids. They set up the infrastructure that made the hot box industry possible. They occasionally use asteroids, but mostly to crash into Mars for excavation and heat generation.]

Two hundred times as massive? Janus thought. He pictured the asteroid belt, a ring that spanned all the way around the Sun. It consisted of millions of large asteroids, and countless smaller ones. *How can a single planet be more massive than something so vast, let alone two hundred times more massive?*

While he was lost in thought about the enormity of space, Luna replied.

"Incoming message," prompted Clecir.

"Let's see what we got." Gomboc cracked his neck before reading the message. "That can't be right..."

Before Janus could ask, Clecir explained, "Luna denies the presence of any ship on the course we described. Their sensors don't see anything."

"But they must have a record of the launch," protested Athena. "And you sent them sensor data pinging the Guan Yu ship location. It's not possible for them to not know its location."

"Then why deny it?" asked Gomboc.

"Could this be Atlas' doing?" asked Janus.

"Possibly," said Athena.

"Get me a magnified image o' that ship," commanded Gomboc. "Since they're gettin' closer, we oughta be able to get a good look at 'em."

The main display screen showed the magnified image of the ship, a sleek, black design. Unlike most ships, which were painted bright colors to maximize visibility, this ship was designed not to be seen against the blackness of space. Other than that, the general appearance of the ship was unremarkable. It was covered in cargo containers, implying it was a cargo hauler just like the Fortigo.

"Can you magnify that dark spot on the center of their plow?" Athena requested.

Gomboc grunted dismissively. Janus wondered if the Martian simply had a grudge against TrueAI, or maybe he felt like Athena's input somehow undermined his command.

Clecir magnified the image further. "Is that a...?"

Athena completed her sentence. "It's a spinal launch tube – a railgun. That's not a cargo ship. It's a Martian KŏngJiàn-class destroyer."

"Broadcast yellow alert on emergency frequencies," ordered Gomboc. "This Guan Yu ship wants to keep this exchange quiet, so let's make some noise."

"We're jammed," said Clecir, rapidly sweeping across her controls, turning dials, flipping switches, trying to find an open frequency to broadcast on. "I can get tight-beam distress signals to Luna and Mars, but outgoing radio is getting scrubbed by some kind of interference."

Abruptly, the main image which had been displaying the Guan Yu ship's railgun went blank. Clecir reported, "Rear facing camera's dead. Now so is the range finding laser... and infrared. We're losing all rear-facing sensors."

"Solar flare?" asked Gomboc.

We're flying near the sun. We'd be more vulnerable to that kind of anomaly, thought Janus. The plow would protect forward-facing sensors more effectively than rear-facing, but a gut feeling told him this was something else.

"No," said Clecir. "No unusual charged particle activity, and background EM levels are normal. Only the rear sensors are out."

"Any blown fuses?"

"It's an alpha strike!" declared Athena.

"A what?" asked Clecir.

"Fire attitude thrusters: hard left, now!" commanded Athena.

"Ain't no AI giving orders on my ship!" growled Gomboc. He seemed like he was about to start a lecture, but Clecir tapped the controls and a sudden lurch of acceleration caused everyone to scramble for handholds. After regaining his poise, Janus tightened his belts and fastened his forehead strap to prevent whiplash. Gomboc took his seat and strapped in, grumbling.

As Gomboc raised a finger to scold both Clecir and Athena, a white-hot bead streaked by the right side of the ship like a shooting star. For a flash, Janus could feel the intense light of it through the window before the object vanished into the distance off the bow.

"That was close. For it to reach us so soon, they must have fired before flash-frying our sensors," Athena analyzed.

"We're under attack? What was that about an alpha strike?" asked Clecir. She was a tough woman, but clearly didn't have a military background.

     Silence Of the Stars

Athena explained, "They fired the railgun, then followed it with a precision laser strike against the Fortigo's sensors to weaken our defenses and decrease our chances of detecting the incoming missile."

Gomboc added, "And there's no way to detect lasers before they hit – no chance to evade."

"Why didn't they just hit our reactor with the laser, then? Not strong enough to penetrate?" asked Clecir.

"Right," confirmed Athena. "But plenty strong enough to blind us, unless... Do you have any sensors on the ship that are hardened against laser fire?"

Gomboc groaned and addressed Athena directly for the first time. "Yes, but only against incidental exposure. This is a civilian vessel – we don't 'ave anything that will survive more than a few seconds of that kind of laser fire. The armored camera is in front o' the command deck, so they can't hit it from directly behind us. Likewise, the camera has no line o' sight to the Guan Yu ship from this angle."

"Shall we sneak a peek?" suggested Clecir.

"Aye. Bring the bow up three degrees, then put 'er right back down."

The main screen switched to a head-on view of the command deck from outside, and the emptiness of space behind. After a near-imperceptible attitude adjustment burn, the Guan Yu ship rose over the cabin and appeared as a tiny white dot in the distance. The camera zoomed in on the speck. The black ship had grown four massive angelic wings, glowing brilliantly with the bright white of candoluminescence. It was like a miniature version of the Rose of Babylon Station. The luminosity of the wings saturated the image, and the camera struggled to focus.

Something tugged at Janus' subconscious. He somehow knew that these wings acted as massive radiators to disperse heat from the ship's systems. He knew that they indicated an increased output from the ship's reactors. Specifically, that level of luminosity and the surface area of the wings on a KōngJiàn implied the capacitors were being charged up to fire a larger projectile from its railgun.

"I just picked up an EM burst from the Guan Yu ship. They must have fired the railgun again," said Clecir, as she dipped the nose back down to protect their last precious camera from laser fire.

Athena said, "I recognize that EM signature – it's a rail-assisted missile launch. Closing velocity, approximately 10 kilometers per second."

A distant flash of dazzling blue light in the rear-view camera was visible even over the bridge, which was blocking direct line of sight.

"Correction, 30 kilometers per second," said Athena.

Janus knew that the blue light was a small nuclear charge used to accelerate the missile toward them.

A streak of golden bullets arced over the command deck on the main display, tearing toward the incoming missile. The Fortigo's debris-clearing gauss cannon had automatically detected the missile on a collision course and attempted to remove it, just like it would any space debris threatening to impact the ship. The PDC was not a military weapon; it was designed to prevent collisions with unexpected obstacles.

Unprompted, Clecir pitched the ship up to give the remaining camera line of sight to the incoming missile. Everyone watched the flickering golden stream hopefully, but the missile transitioned sideways to avoid the PDC fire, minutes before it had any chance to impact.

　　　　Silence Of the Stars

Athena analyzed, "Time to impact: twenty minutes. The missile is too fast to outrun, and too maneuverable to avoid. It's small – no more than 100 kilograms. Based on the observed transition speed of the missile just now, our PDC should be able to intercept the missile once its range closes to 200 kilometers. That's a safe window as long as the missile is armed with a nuclear warhead or kinetic penetrator, but we are a soft target. It would make more sense for the enemy to use a pellet fragmentation warhead. In that case, the missile will likely detonate at 400 kilometers, outside our intercept range. The fragment cloud will shred the Fortigo before we can defend ourselves."

Gomboc nodded. "So, if we don't intercept outside 400 kilometers, we're dead."

"We could turn 180 degrees and catch the pellets with our plow, but we'd expose our forward sensors and bridge windows to their laser, and the plow wouldn't protect us from a nuke or kinetic penetrator," Athena said.

She was right. Janus knew she was right, but being right wasn't going to be enough.

"I'd rather not gamble our lives on a guess about their hardware. Is there any way to improve our intercept range?" asked Gomboc.

"That PDC is meant for clearing debris," said Clecir. "It doesn't account for changes in target trajectory; space trash normally doesn't dodge. We could manually fire it..." She trailed off, looking to Athena, who had manifested as a life-size hologram standing next to Janus.

"Sorry. I'm a navigation AI, not a gunner. I can offer strategic level advice, but I can't operate weapons."

"I'll do it," insisted Janus. "Transfer manual PDC controls to me."

"Janus?" Clecir questioned.

"I understand," said Athena. "I think it's our best chance."

"Do it," said Gomboc. With a swipe of his finger, he transferred control to Janus' station.

"Nose up?" asked Clecir.

"No. Keep her steady," said Janus, already weaving a complex pattern into the fire control console. He saw the missile in his mind's eye. He knew its exact position relative to the ship. He'd seen thousands like it before. These weapons were predictable. He knew exactly how it would react to different patterns of defensive fire.

Janus dialed power to the gauss coils low, decreasing the PDC's projectile speed, then fired a closing spiral of gold, gradually increasing bullet speed as he worked his way toward the middle. Initially, it would have looked like he was spraying blindly in the direction of the missile. The result was a loose web that formed a labyrinth of gold. The missile's simple evasion algorithm detected each incoming bullet and reacted only to the nearest, taking the shortest path to evade, programmed to divert its course as minimally as possible. It followed the path designed by Janus, spiraling into a maze until the faster rounds caught up with the first, trapping the missile in a dead end situation where every vector led into a wall of PDC fire just barely under a missile's width apart.

After firing, Janus pictured the result in his mind. The crew waited in tense silence. Minutes later, he began counting down quietly – in the hush of the room, it was just loud enough for everyone to hear. "Ten, nine, eight..."

Clecir tipped the nose up to see the result. The missile erupted, and the small nuclear explosion faintly illuminated a cloud of its spilled

		Silence Of the Stars

payload: millions of tungsten pellets flew in every direction. The missile was destroyed, and the immediate danger had passed. The enemy railgun would need to cool before firing again.

The KōngJiàn's wings glowed angrily. Propelled by the nuclear blast, some of the tiny tungsten pellets found their way back to the Guan Yu ship and tore through the fragile filaments of its radiator wings. Superheated superfluid sublimed into brilliant clouds where shrapnel shredded tiny paths. The spilled coolant turned from white to yellow, then to blood red before vanishing into the blackness of space.

"Great shot, kid!" Gomboc whooped, pumping a robotic fist into the air.

Janus just shrank into his seat. He'd relied on JANUS#004 yet again. Janus himself had nothing to contribute to the situation. He couldn't fight, and his only knowledge about space travel came from the last few days of study aboard the Fortigo. He wanted to curl up and disappear, but remained alert because he had to. He had to because JANUS#004 had to.

The camera also caught the flash of gunfire. A streak of bullets raced across space toward the Fortigo, but compared to the missile and railgun dart, the bullets were sluggish. They wouldn't reach the Fortigo for thirty minutes. Clecir tapped the attitude thrusters to transition the ship imperceptibly to one side. With that tiny adjustment, the bullets would miss by several kilometers by the time they arrived.

"The idiots should know guns won't work at this range," mocked Clecir.

As if in response to his insult, the Guan Yu ship's delicate wings retracted, and its drive activated to accelerate it toward the Fortigo.

Everyone looked to Athena for guidance. She said, "We can't let them get to close range. That debris-gun we're using as a PDC might put a few holes in them, but Fortigo would lose a close-range firefight. We have to accelerate to keep our distance. If we can get far enough away, we might even be able to break free of their radio jamming range and call for help."

Clecir entered a thrust solution which would have the Fortigo accelerate along its intercept course with Mars. The planet was barely visible as a dim red star over the horizon of the sun.

Athena interjected, "No. Pitch the nose down eight degrees from that heading."

"That would point us into the Sun," said Clecir.

"The closer our orbit is to the Sun, the faster we travel relative to Mars... and to our pursuer."

"Our orbit will become even more eccentric. We barely have enough fuel to slow down as it is!" said Clecir.

"Do it. We'll worry about slowing down later," ordered Gomboc.

"But..." Clecir looked back at her father. When she saw his broad grin, she reluctantly updated the thrust solution, then said, "Brace for acceleration in five, four, three..."

The ship lurched forward at 10 MeSS, just over 1 Earth gravity, to match the acceleration of the pursuing vessel. The frame of the tired old ship moaned in protest. The hull creaked as it resisted being compressed by its own incredible mass.

     Silence Of the Stars

On paper, the ship was rated for up to 30 MeSS, but nobody presently aboard the ship would trust it to actually withstand that due to its advanced age.

Like all ships, the Fortigo had maximum efficiency acceleration, and an absolute maximum acceleration. Traveling at the maximum efficiency would result in the highest final speed for a given propellant expenditure, usually about 0.2 MeSS for a fully loaded ship. The absolute maximum velocity ignored fuel efficiency. It is the greatest acceleration a ship is rated to safely accelerate at, usually enforced by software locks to prevent explosive failure from overpressure which could result from pushing harder.

Reserve fuel gradually ticked away. An analog dial labeled $\varDelta VB$, for 'Delta-Velocity Buffer' flashed obnoxiously as it ticked down from 10%. Any acceleration now would count doubly against the Fortigo, as any speed added now would need to be bled off before transitioning to a safe Mars insertion orbit. Acceleration and deceleration *both* cost propellant in space.

"We've hit thirty-four minutes with no response to our tight-beam from Mar," said Clecir. "They should have at least acknowledged the distress call by now."

"The major ports are deliberately ignoring tight-beams, and our radio signals are being jammed..." Gomboc said, stroking his beard.

"Atlas must have pulled some strings on Mars to get them to cooperate. Someone with access to traffic control – meaning someone at Guan Yu or Omni – is under his control," surmised Athena.

"We don't have any other way to communicate with the outside world? To ask for help?" asked Janus.

"There's always a way to communicate." Gomboc's devious grin returned.

"Delta-V buffer approaching zero percent," warned Clecir. The Guan Yu ship was still pursuing under thrust.

"Cir, set a direct intercept course for the Guan Yu headquarters on the surface of Mar and maintain ten-MeSS acceleration," ordered Gomboc, looking entirely too satisfied with himself.

Athena and Clecir both looked at him. Janus stayed silent. If they continued to accelerate after consuming their buffer fuel, they would never be able to slow down. It didn't even warrant saying. Everyone already knew.

"They want to ignore our problem. We'll make it their problem," insisted Gomboc.

"Yes, sir. Adjusting course," said Clecir nervously.

This new course would have them collide directly into the planet at incredible speed. If nothing was done to change their trajectory, the Guan Yu headquarters would be replaced by a molten crater visible from orbit. Seismographs on the opposite side of the planet would register the impact as an earthquake.

"Let's see them ignore us now," goaded Gomboc.

"At least our pursuer will have second thoughts about following us," said Clecir.

"I assume you're relying on the Martians to use their push-lasers to help us decelerate," said Athena.

　　　　Silence Of the Stars

Gomboc beamed with pride in his devious plan. He showed only a hint of disappointment that Athena had managed to figure it out before he had the chance to explain his own genius.

Light sails were massive parachute-like structures made from a thin, reflective material. These were used to catch and reflect light from powerful push-lasers, which could be used to accelerate or decelerate a ship. Since the energy was contributed by the source of the laser, it was a way of altering a ship's course without spending onboard propellant. This system fell out of favor following the development of more advanced methods of propulsion. Most large ships weren't equipped with light sails due to the inefficiency of push-lasers on heavy payloads. Light sails were now mostly relegated to light payloads being sent long journeys starting near the stellaser system, such as from Venus to Jupiter.

Athena said, "It's a solid plan, but we can't open our light sail with that destroyer behind us. We won't be able to maneuver with the sail open, so their guns would tear us apart even from long range."

"Light sails rely on Mars cooperating, right? If Mars wants us dead, won't they just destroy our ship instead of helping us decelerate?" asked Janus.

For all the technical and tactical knowledge Janus had gleaned from JANUS#004, political knowledge seemed to be completely lacking. He knew how equipment worked in great detail. He was excellent at predicting the actions of allies and enemies on the battlefield. But this was different.

Gomboc's beard swished as he shook his head. "Whoever's behind this wants to take us out quietly. If we can get out of signal jamming range and make some noise, they'll have second thoughts. It'll be 'ard for 'em to make our deaths look like an accident if we're publicly broadcasting a play-by-play."

"That's why they're jamming us," agreed Athena.

"The Guan Yu ship isn't slowing down. They're probably out of buffer fuel, too," said Clecir. "If they don't break off, we can't broadcast and we can't open our chute."

"How long can this game of chicken last?" asked Janus. "Will they actually follow us all the way to the surface of Mars? If we wait too long, surely even the light sails won't be enough to slow us down."

"It could be an unmanned drone," suggested Athena. "In that case, they won't care if they crash."

"Guan Yu wouldn't let that happen," said Gomboc. "Just watch."

The waiting was every bit as nerve wracking as exchanging gunfire. Perhaps more so.

A few minutes later, a message was received, and Gomboc played it on the general speakers. The voice had a faint Martian accent. "Attention Fortigo-4, flight 3B-82M-4A, you are on a collision course with Mar. Slow down and adjust course immediately."

Gomboc nodded, and stroked his beard thoughtfully. He stood for a few seconds without taking action.

Presently, Clecir asked, "Aren't you going to explain our situation to space traffic control? Radio is jammed, but we can get a tight-beam to them."

"That's not good enough," said Gomboc. "They want to do this quiet, and the only people who will receive our tight-beam are

          Silence Of the Stars

accomplices to this attack. There will be no record of our tight-beam response. We need to get a radio transmission out so we're really heard."

"But we're being jammed, and we're already matching their acceleration at 10 MeSS. How can we get a signal out?"

"We're goin' all-in," drawled Gomboc. "Crank the main thruster to max. Disable the limiter."

"You *can't* disable limiters on a combustion chamber pressure," Athena said. "Code doesn't even allow ships to be designed with that feature. You'd have to physically disconnect—"

Her protest was cut short.

"Done," said Clecir.

"What part o' this ship looks like it's built to code?" Gomboc challenged Athena with a smirk.

"Buckle down. This will get bumpy," said Clecir, then looked from seat to seat and added, "Everyone have pressure suits on? Good. Helmets up. Switch to personal oxygen supply. I'm dropping cabin pressure to 100 millibar. There's no telling what will break first when we do this."

"Good call." A hood suddenly popped up over the top of Gomboc's head and sealed to the front of his vest. It looked like a loose plastic bag until it inflated to a tight-fitting helmet.

"I..." Janus looked around at his controls, confused. He jumped with surprise as a hood wrapped over his head from his own exomysium. When the helmet inflated, Athena put her holographic hand over his to get his attention, then nodded reassuringly.

"Okay, hang on!" Clecir shouted, too loud, overstimulated by the thrill of the moment.

The engine roared and the Fortigo's frame howled in protest. The ship oscillated violently, ripples shooting through the length of the ship from the engines to the bow, as if through liquid. The larger waves were like nauseating ocean swells. Smaller vibrations were absorbed by Janus' flight couch, but blurred his vision of the wall-mounted monitors.

Janus was pressed back into his seat. Red lights flashed and alarms blared. *It's like being in a reentry landing pod under fire*, he thought. He tried to find the acceleration readout, but couldn't lift his head. Even if he could have found it, he probably wouldn't be able to read the display between pressure deforming his eyes and the room vibrating around him. It was difficult to even approximate, since he'd never experienced over 30 MeSS in this body.

Athena's voice played calmly into everyone's helmets. "Engine 3 is running dirty – air in the fuel line. We'll lose the engine, but that gas cloud should interfere with the signal jammer."

There was a loud bang followed by a sensation like driving over a speedbump on a freeway.

"She's right, channel's clear! Coms are yours!" Clecir sounded like she was shouting through a fan.

Gomboc shouted over the rumbling, hailing Mars. "Negative! We are being attacked by pirates flying the Guan Yu flag. We are low on fuel and our maneuverability is compromised. Requesting emergency push-laser deceleration at our coordinates."

Gomboc paused, then addressed Athena. "Send me the coordinates and bearing of that Guan Yu ship, will ya?"

 Silence Of the Stars

She immediately complied, then asked, "Sure. Why?"

Gomboc ignored the question and hailed Mars again. "I'm sending coordinates, bearing, and our chute angle of attack now. Shoot that push-laser full blast – it's the only way we can divert course. We have an engine down."

"But we can't even open the chutes until we take care of the pursuer," Athena shouted back at him, competing to be heard over the increasing turbulence.

There was another bang, more violent than the last. Janus felt as though his seat would be torn from the floor by the jolt. Torsion caused a row of floor panels to shear off and bounce around the room before being pinned to the back wall by the ship's acceleration. Several seconds passed before oscillations stopped. It felt like hours with adrenaline surging through his veins. When calm returned, the crew was weightless.

Gomboc shouted something else to the radio during the ruckus, which Janus couldn't make out.

"All main engines down!" shouted Clecir.

"Pursuer also cut engines, but is gaining," reported Athena.

Once again, the luminous white wings of the Guan Yu ship slowly unfolded, spewing red from their injured capillaries as they unfolded into the view over the bridge in the rear-facing camera.

Those wings are necessary to dissipate heat while charging capacitors for the railgun. They're excellent radiators, but they're as fragile as feathers. They weren't able to fire the railgun and accelerate to pursue us at the same time, but now that our engines are down...

Janus grabbed the weapon controls with the intent of spraying the seraphic radiators with PDC fire. That would force the ship to choose between taking the hits or retracting the wings.

"No, don't," said Gomboc. "We have them right where we want them."

"They're closer than last time and gaining," said Athena. "If they shoot, the intercept window will be tighter than before. There's no guarantee we can stop another missile."

"The gauss cannon's already hot. We don't have angel wings to cool down with like that KōngJiàn does, so we only have a few shots left," added Clecir.

"All the more reason we can't waste shots on offense," said Gomboc. "Besides, I trust Janus. He'll keep us safe."

Janus nodded in understanding and said nothing. Long minutes passed, and the pursuer grew ever closer, poised to kill and leaving a red trail in its wake like an injured angel of death. The temptation to shoot at the enemy ship was ever-present, but Gomboc was right. If Janus shot at the wings, the KōngJiàn might tank the damage without reacting, and the Fortigo would have less PDC capacity with which to defend itself. The main body of the KōngJiàn was so small that it could make minor adjustments to avoid incoming fire without tearing the radiator wings.

Clecir tipped the nose of the craft up and down to catch glimpses of the Guan Yu ship without exposing the camera long enough to be destroyed by laser fire. Everyone stared at the main screen, dry-eyed and sweaty-palmed. This continued for twenty minutes until Athena and Clecir simultaneously called out, "EM burst detected!"

"Drop the nose and keep it level," Janus said calmly.

 Silence Of the Stars

He closed his eyes, and there the missile was. He could sense it this time. He started to enter a firing solution to intercept, then stopped.

Wait a minute… He could sense the missile. *Why? How?* This was different. When the previous missile was fired, he just had an intuitive notion of where the missile would be based on its speed and trajectory. It was nothing but acute spatial awareness. Now Janus felt the missile's location in real time even though he couldn't see it. The sensation was similar to communicating with Athena.

Janus scrubbed his previous firing solution, and instead fired a three-shot burst around the missile. None of the rounds were on an intercept course, but the missile immediately fired its attitude thrusters in response, transitioning it a full kilometer off course. Unlike the previous missile, it wasn't following an algorithm to take the most direct path to target. It was being remote-guided. If Janus had sprayed a trap formation at it, the missile would have avoided the net entirely, and he wouldn't have had enough ammunition left for a second try.

I must be detecting the radio link remote-guiding that missile, Janus thought. *That's why I know where it is in real time.*

"Forty-five seconds to impact," warned Athena.

"Shit. Should we flip and catch it with the nose cone?" suggested Gomboc.

"If we're going to flip, we need to do it *now*," said Clecir.

"No. Hold steady," said Janus.

He fired a single shot directly at the missile. It dodged. He fired another. It dodged again.

"Janus?" asked Gomboc, but Janus was too focused to form a response.

Janus fired another shot, and again he 'heard' the command for the missile to dodge, then felt the missile comply. There was a pattern to the communication, and each time Janus fired a round to force the missile to dodge he got a clearer picture of the syntax of the signals remote-controlling the weapon.

Each signal sent to the missile from the KōngJiàn was a quick radio burst; each contained a simple command along with a unique nonsequential code. The movement command would be simple enough to mimic, but the missile wouldn't obey a command without the correct code.

Janus had hoped to use his radio-transceiving power to control the missile, but there would be no way to guess the next code in the sequence. Using his power to turn the missile back on their attacker was impossible. *Of course remote-guided missiles would have countermeasures against hacking. It's not as if I'm the first person to think of trying it.*

"Twenty seconds to impact," said Athena. "Intercept window closes in five…"

Janus reached out to the missile in his mind. *Yes, I can do it.* Communicating with the missile was just like talking with Athena. He wouldn't be able to command the missile without the secret codes, but that wouldn't stop him from shouting nonsense at the weapon. It would work just like the jamming signals that had been scrambling the Fortigo's outgoing communication attempts.

"Three, two, one…"

     Silence Of the Stars

Janus squeezed the trigger, spraying a PDC stream toward the missile while shouting random vectors in his mind, using the same syntax the KōngJiàn used to command the weapon. Like each time before, the KōngJiàn ordered the missile to dodge, but the missile couldn't parse the real command from among the flood of Janus' conflicting commands. It plowed directly into the stream of molten gold. The first impacts caused the missile to spin, exposing its hypergolic propellant tank, then the weapon erupted into a ball of green fire.

"Did you get it?" asked nobody, but the question was implied by the silence following the buzz of PDC fire. Janus nodded in response, and Clecir turned the nose of the ship up just in time to see debris from the missile zip dangerously close to the Fortigo.

"Kinetic penetrator..." Athena observed.

Gomboc laughed nervously. "Good thing we didn't rely on the plow, aye?"

Celebration was premature. The Guan Yu ship was still closing the gap between itself and the Fortigo. Although its wings sputtered from the thermal strain of the previous shot, it showed no sign of retracting them. Another rail-assisted missile would be incoming soon.

"Think ye can catch one more, Janus?" asked Gomboc.

"Gun's too hot," said Clecir.

Janus nodded. She was right.

"How long til it's cool enough to use again?" asked Gomboc.

"A few hours, maybe?" guessed Clecir.

"Thermodynamics is a bitch," groaned Gomboc.

In truth, the barrel was already so hot that the last few shots had gone wide. It was permanently deformed and would never shoot straight again. Any further abuse at this temperature would tear it apart.

The Fortigo was defenseless, and the KōngJiàn crept ever closer. Once it got close enough, it wouldn't even need to use a missile. At close enough range, the Fortigo would be shredded by good old-fashioned guns. Destroyers like the KōngJiàn class all featured close-in weapon systems – not civilian anti-debris PDCs, but real military grade CIWS that wouldn't melt after a few bursts.

"So, we can't outrun them, we can't fight back, we can barely maneuver, and there's nothing to hide behind," Gomboc summarized, still grinning. He didn't seem as upset as he should have been.

"And our coms are jammed again," added Clecir.

"I don't suppose this ship is equipped with some code-violating secret weapon?" Athena asked hopefully.

"Naw," Gomboc sighed. He seemed calm. Janus wasn't sure if the Martian actually did have some secret left. He didn't seem to be resigned to his fate.

"By the way, how long ago was our last message to Mar?" asked the dwarf.

"About thirty-four minutes," said Clecir.

Suddenly, the feed from the rear-facing camera became bright white, as if a new sun had appeared behind the Fortigo. The cloud of sublimation trailing behind the Guan Yu ship ignited and blew away, then its wings brightened, flickered, and vanished into a growing ball of plasma as they dissolved into nothing. The distant ship itself was so

Silence Of the Stars

saturated by the intense light that details were impossible to discern –
it appeared as a brightly flickering star.

Gomboc responded with a broad smile and crossed his metal arms.

"I see," said Athena. "Our pursuer wasn't broadcasting its own
location and was jamming outgoing messages. Even if their
conspirators on Mars could see them on long-range sensors, it would
be difficult to pinpoint their exact location at this distance."

"Wait, what's even going on?" Clecir asked, still staring at the dazzling
light which had been the KōngJiàn.

"Push laser," said Gomboc.

Athena elaborated, "He requested an emergency stop using the push
laser system, but rather than opening the solar sail, he sent coordinates
targeting our pursuer."

Clecir tore her gaze away from the monitor, spinning her seat around
to face Gomboc and Athena. She looked distracted, like she only half
comprehended what was going on. She had probably expected to die
moments ago.

Athena added, "But there were so many unknowns. How did you
know their real-time data wouldn't be accurate enough to confirm the
targeting data you provided? More importantly, how did you know
they would deploy the push laser at all? If space traffic control was an
accomplice to our attacker, it would have made more sense for them
to destroy us as planned, and then nudge us off course instead of
agreeing to deploy the push laser to help us slow down."

Gomboc let out a deep, guttural laugh. "I'm sure they had all the
information they needed to come to that same conclusion, but people
make mistakes when they panic. You gotta' act fast with a hundred

thousand tons of steel headed for yer face at interplanetary speed. I was counting on human error."

"I'd normally advise against relying on incompetence," mused Athena. "Strategically speaking, consistency tends to perform better than chaos. But, then again, I'm not used to being on this side of asymmetric warfare."

"I took a gamble, and I won," said Gomboc, glowing with self-satisfaction.

Janus smiled. This battle had been won using a strategy from someone other than JANUS#004. There was something cathartic about that.

Before long, the molten husk of the KōngJiàn tumbled out of the path of the laser. When that happened, Gomboc picked up the transmitter once to hail Mars once more. "Sorry – slight miscalculation. It looks like the pirate's jamming equipment was interfering with our positioning sensors. I'm sending our updated location. Please adjust the push laser."

The 10-kilometer-wide hemispherical chute took several minutes to spread out. When the laser hit the chute, it rippled lightly until it was pulled taut by the force of the laser's light pushing against it. If the sail caused any deceleration, it was too slight for Janus to notice. Even so, a few minutes later, the half-melted remains of the KōngJiàn tumbled slowly past the port window.

     Silence Of the Stars

Chapter 29
Adrift

For almost a full minute following the skirmish, the silence of the bridge was pierced only by the angry hum of air recycling fans. The fight against the KōngJiàn was over, but the fight against the vacuum of space was a never-ending struggle. Even now, the automated systems aboard the Fortigo were struggling to compensate for damage caused by the stress from excessive acceleration and numerous hull punctures from shrapnel.

There would be leaks; gas hot enough to melt steel, gas cold enough to freeze oxygen, gas toxic enough to kill with a single breath; gas of every flavor of death would have been leaking from normally self-contained systems into habitable areas. Meanwhile, breathable air would be leaking into space.

These kinds of challenges were rarely part of SimMilitary, which was responsible for the majority of my knowledge of space travel. Due to user time constraints, those simulations tended to focus on scenarios which could be resolved in minutes to hours rather than weeks or months. Soldiers were educated about the hazards which could result from damaged spacecraft, but simulating those long-term consequences was impractical. Thus, my knowledge of how to deal with the current situation was completely hypothetical.

We would need to address all of these problems before we could repressurize the ship. Before that, though, we allowed ourselves a moment of respite to calm our nerves.

"Great shooting back there, kid!" said Gomboc, releasing his crash harness to give me a hardy pat on the shoulder.

Clecir added, "You must be some kind of military genius to intercept modern missiles with that old debris-clearing gun."

"Just a lucky shot," I replied. The truth is I shouldn't have been able to intercept those missiles. I wouldn't have been able to if the gunner aboard that KōngJiàn knew how to operate his own weapon more effectively, but that's not what was bothering me.

"If you say so," she said, clearly not believing me.

"A bit of humility is a good thing, but you should also take pride in your accomplishments," said Gomboc.

There was nothing to be proud of. I'd managed to intercept those missiles, but it wasn't really *me*. *I* shouldn't have the skills to operate any kind of ship-mounted weapon. I wasn't even sure whether I knew what a 'point defense cannon' was last week. When we came under fire, I should have panicked or frozen, or stayed out of the way to let someone more experienced handle the situation. That's the kind of person I am, or at least, it's the kind of person I was a few days ago.

The skills and calm demeanor that pulled me through that situation were borrowed. The rush of adrenaline brought back the combat instincts I've felt more and more often. I glimpsed them for a second

 Silence Of the Stars

in the Church of Ascension, felt their full effect during the war simulation. More recently, it had been hard to tell when I was really me and when I was being... influenced. Every time I have managed to recognize that influence, I have resisted it. But during this fight, I had to surrender myself to that instinct to survive.

Now, the existential threat of death had passed. I felt my heart rate drop back to normal and my nerves settle, but a new fear was setting in. The instincts that allowed me to operate that weapon so effectively remained. Although my mind was still my own, as far as I could tell, I was confident that I could still operate the defense gun. In fact, I could probably operate just about any kind of weaponry, just like JANUS#004.

It wasn't just a mastery of weaponry. I felt alert and grounded. Everything about this civilian ship suddenly seemed less foreign to me. I understood it. Looking down at the status display next to the PDC controls, I noted that the hydrogen-based super-coolant was at –131 degrees Celsius, which was 32 degrees above its boiling point in a standard pressure vessel. It was running a little hot, probably due to overstressing various systems in the skirmish. Like most ships, the tritium-based coolant of the Fortigo would be stored in cavities permeating the hull, spiraling around the ship to act as a shield against radiation from space and from the reactor. This coolant also doubled as reaction mass for the ship's fusion reactor and propellant for the thrusters – or it would, if our thrusters hadn't been destroyed in combat. *I never learned any of this, and it's not the kind of knowledge I would passively absorb just walking around in public. It's not the kind of thing I ever even cared about.*

"Dad, we've got a problem," said Clecir.

"What is it, Cir?" asked Gomboc, peeking over the back of her chair.

"We've got a slow leak in the hydroloop." She pointed at the screen. "Right there, where the main thrusters blew off."

"Can ye shut it off? Close the valve leading to the leak?"

"Technically, yes… but practically, no. There's no valve between the leak and the reactor intake."

"'Ow long do we 'ave?"

"We'll be critical in one month."

"Shit. Options?"

"Outside of patching the leak, I don't know."

Athena chimed in, "Can you reroute to the reactor's auxiliary intake?"

Gomboc shook his head. "This ain't no military ship. No such redundancy."

Athena protested, "But according to the USSA safety standards, even civilian ships must have at least one auxiliary—"

"I told ye before: this ain't no fancy Earth ship either. No fascist 'Universal' Space Safety Agency to tell us how to design ships on Mar," Gomboc said proudly.

  Silence Of the Stars

"Considering our current predicament, maybe they should," said Clecir in a tone that sounded only half sarcastic. Gomboc scowled in disapproval, but said nothing.

"Can't you shut down the reactor?" Athena suggested. "We can run life support and basic ship systems on energy collected from the push-lasers using solar panels."

"We can't shut it down," Clecir said.

"We've got 'ot cargo," Gomboc elaborated. "If we shut down the reactor, we won't be able to keep cool. The ship would boil."

"Just how hot *is* your cargo?" Athena asked.

"Very," said Clecir. "It's the neutron-saturated remains of DT reactor shielding. Activated boron carbide, tungsten, cobalt-60, stuff like that."

"So, by hot, you mean radioactive," said Athena.

"Radioactive enough that it's also thermally hot. Like, some of it would sublimate if exposed to vacuum levels of hot."

"Why the hell would you carry around hazardous waste like that? How much do you have on board?" Athena sounded horrified.

"About ten thousand metric tonnes, collected from a few dozen ships. It's for the 'Ot Boxes. We're recyclin'. It's good for the environment, you know." Gomboc chuckled.

Athena allowed her jaw to go slack, making her shock apparent. "I can't believe they let you anywhere near the Spire with cargo like that."

I sat and listened. I'd practiced boarding raids against ships with hot cargo. I'd had ships like this detonated as improvised weapons in counter-terrorism drills. In my experience, ships like this had always been hazards, to be destroyed or avoided. I'd never considered how to fix one.

Gomboc shrugged. "We've been on this route for years with no problem. When they ask about our cargo, we tell them we 'ave radiation shielding material. They don't ask 'ow 'ot it is."

In an attempt to steer the conversation back on track, Clecir said, "We can't dump the cargo either. Some of the material would violently expand the moment it hit raw vacuum. We need to keep the strong EM field online to keep it compressed in storage. That means we need to keep the reactor running. There's no choice but to patch the leak."

Gomboc and Clecir had long faces. To me, the issue seemed simple. There was a leak in the fuel line leading to the reactor. We needed the reactor to stay on, so we had to patch the leak. Patching the leak should have been a simple matter of taking a space walk outside with a welding tool or patch kit, or sending a robot to do the same. But this wasn't my area of expertise. I must have been missing something.

Apparently, Athena had the same idea. "Are there any general maintenance drones or vacuum suits on board?"

 Silence Of the Stars

"Aye..." Gomboc trailed off.

"But the reactor..." Clecir searched for the right words. "It's an old-fashioned bipole DT reactor plus torch-drive combo. Radiation from the reactor is polarized, sending an intense radiation stream to the main thruster. That means as long as the reactor is on, it's blasting radiation back toward the drive, but the thruster is currently missing, along with the radiation shield."

Gomboc picked up where she left off, "A 'uman would be cooked alive by the radiation. Might not even survive long enough to finish the patch. Our repair drones are even worse off. They're likely be more 'arm than 'elp."

Athena protested, "So rotate the polarity of the reactor to fire the radiation stream away from the work area. Or, if you can't do that, depolarize the reactor to minimize exposure to the workers."

"Now see 'ere, Navi," said Gomboc, grumpily. "I don't know what kind o' ship you're used to workin' on, but this chunker ain't them. She's been runnin' for eighty years, and she was already old the day she sailed off the slipway."

"It's true," said Clecir. "This ship is a piece of crap, even by Martian standards. The fixed polarity DT reactor was a refurbished relic – it belongs in a museum, not aboard a ship. I've been saying for ages this whole thing needs to be scrapped."

Gomboc gasped. "Don't be so cruel, Cir! The ship 'as 'er flaws, but with 'er rugged design, she's outlasted a lot of that imported Earther crap Guan Yu's been usin'."

Clecir shook her head. "That's because Guan Yu retires their aging ships *before* they fall apart. This piece of junk isn't even yours. There's no need to be so attached. Becu would probably assign you a new one if you asked."

"I can't do that to ol' Becu. The Union doesn't have the kind of funding Guan Yu has. We can't just throw ships out because they get a little dinged up. Can you imagine if Becu reassigned 'er to a new team? They'd get themselves killed!"

Clecir sighed out the words, "Whatever, Dad."

'It's going to get *us* killed,' is probably what she wanted to say, but the obvious retort didn't need saying. The words hung slack on everyone's faces. Despite Clecir's complaining, her restraint showed me that she respected her father.

"Right, then!" Gomboc clapped his hands together with a clank. "We've got a month to sort that out. 'Ow's about lunch?"

Lunch? I'd been expecting some kind of resolution to our life-threatening condition first. Although, I supposed, a life-threatening problem did not preclude us from the need for basic life essentials like food and sleep. Death wasn't imminent, and I was hungry.

After pressurizing the cafeteria for a quick meal of exceptionally bland Nutrisynth, we went our separate ways. Clecir went off to tinker, Gompoc went to report the situation to his people on Mars, and I took Athena back to our quarters. Our personal rooms would be the only pressurized rooms aboard the ship until leaks could be reduced to a manageable level.

Assuming we survived the reactor hazard, it would be another three months before we'd reach Mars. Despite the dire nature of the situation, nobody seemed overly distressed, myself included. I didn't know why everyone else was so calm. As for myself, I preferred to think I was just getting used to it. My life had been in constant danger from the moment I woke up in New Angels. Compared to fighting with religious zealots, sneaking under Atlas' radar, or battling with hostile spaceships, the threat of being boiled alive in an inescapable steel prison one month from now simply seemed too distant to worry about.

I floated not-quite-weightlessly down the dank, narrow hall toward my room, mild deceleration from the light sail pulling me ever so slightly back toward the nose of the ship. I used guiderails along the hall to correct course and accelerate as needed, in a motion that resembled something between climbing and swimming.

The entrance to the room was a round bulkhead door. A lever unlocked the handwheel, which in turn popped the seal on the door with a metallic creak. The bulky manual airlock opened into a small room with featureless steel walls, two wall-mounted sleeping bags, and a single desk with two HIP cables.

As I stared blankly into the room, I heard Athena's voice in my head. [Want to talk?]

[What's up?] I replied.

[You were pretty quiet back there,] she said. [You're usually inquisitive about topics you're not familiar with.]

[Oh.] I guessed she was right. [I understood well enough. There's a leak on the outer hull of the ship, right next to the reactor. We need to fix it, but it's in the path of dangerous radiation.]

[It's good that you have a grasp on the situation. Even so, you're quieter than usual. Are you feeling alright?]

If there's anyone I could open up to, it was Athena. I asked, [Do I seem like myself to you? Other than being quieter than usual, I mean. Does anything seem different?]

[Well...] Athena paused. Was she thinking about whether I'd changed, or about how to tell me that I had? [You seem confident. When you took control of the point defenses, you used the skills you developed in the combat simulations, right?]

Of course she'd noticed that. My sudden ability to use modern weaponry was obvious. That wasn't the problem.

[*I* didn't develop those skills. They're part of someone else's personality.]

[Are you sure? Your personality doesn't seem any different to me.]

[You said yourself that I seemed more confident.]

Athena retorted without hesitation, [Yes. You were confident using the point defense controls because you had the skills necessary to use them. I am also confident doing activities I am skilled at, like navigating and piloting. Developing a skill doesn't make you a different person.]

     Silence Of the Stars

[Doesn't it, though?] I pulled myself into the room and twisted the hatch shut. I had been thinking about this for a while. It was interesting to hear someone else put it into words.

[No. I don't think so.]

[Perhaps not one skill, but surely the results of centuries of training, of which I have no memory...] I trailed off, unsure how to express my thoughts. I was afraid of 'losing myself', but that was such a vague concept. It would require defining 'myself', and what 'I' would be without it. But 'I' should be a constant in my own life, and the 'self' was an idea so fundamental as to not warrant definition.

[It's just the skills, then? No intrusive memories of some alter-ego?] she asked.

[For now, anyway.] *Is that what I was afraid of? Being mind controlled by some other self?*

[In that case, you shouldn't worry about it,] suggested Athena. [Most people would be glad to gain centuries of experience without needing to lift a finger or pay a single credit. Some people spend serious money for memory implants, you know. Even then, integration isn't perfect, because those experiences come from another person; another brain; another body. By contrast, the memories that grant you skills are perfectly suited for you because they were yours to begin with. You're living every career soldier's dream come true.]

[But I'm not a soldier,] I protested. [When I was attacked by that Jar in the Church of Ascension, I had to run for my life. My body fought back on its own, but as soon as *I* regained control, I had no way of fighting back. Fighting never even occurred to me as an option because I knew intuitively that I would lose. Now, though, in that same situation, I probably would fight back. Hell, I'd probably win. Doesn't that make me a more violent person by nature? Simply considering violent solutions means my personality has changed, doesn't it?]

That was it. That was the root of the problem. It wasn't the memories or the skills. It was the fact that they had changed my values and decision-making processes.

[It just means you have new tools at your disposal,] refuted Athena. [The fact that you have more options than before just means you have a greater degree of freedom. Before, you had no choice. Now you may choose to fight. That choice is still *yours* to make. Your experiences don't change who you are; they just make you stronger. At least, that's how I see it.]

[Perhaps. But, it's that very strength that...] I stopped. That wavering in her voice – It was like she hadn't been trying to convince me, but rather trying to convince *herself* of what she was saying. She must have had prior experience with this topic. This conversation wasn't just about me anymore.

Was Athena afraid of some change occurring in herself? Had some experience fundamentally changed how she thought about herself, too? Her life had certainly seen a lot of change recently. After twenty years of loyalty to Atlas, to join a fugitive and flee him must feel like starting a new life.

But perhaps there was more to it than that. Our experiences were fundamentally different. It was hard not to think of Athena as human, but she had asserted several times that she was not. I had no way of seeing the world the way she did. What was she, really? What did it really mean to be a TrueAI; to be a Navi? Could it be that her mind was also subject to the influence of a previous life, or some outside force, just like me?

It didn't seem right to ask these questions now. I knew she started this conversation just trying to make me feel better. If the conversation continued this way, our roles would reverse. I would turn the tables on her and have nothing to say that could console her. Voicing my concerns was already challenging some conviction she struggled to believe. I wished I could do more to help her, but Athena was still hiding something from me. I couldn't help her. Not now. Not yet.

Instead, I spoke a half-truth for both our benefit. [Thanks Athena. I feel a lot better now.]

[Hey, Janus.] She struggled to hide the fluttering of her voice, but the unfiltered nature of our connection made that impossible. [Let's play Baduk.]

[What's Baduk?]

[An ancient board game also known as 'Go', 'Igo', or 'Weiqi'. Two players take turns placing black and white stones to capture as much territory as possible. Atlas used to play it with foreign visiting diplomats.]

A game of territorial conquest seemed like a symbolically aggressive pastime for politicians. Then again, considering Atlas' taste in 'casual conversation', it seemed on-brand for him.

[I don't know how to play,] I said. Of course, Athena already knew that.

[Neither do I. I made a point of ignoring the game when Atlas played. I didn't want to learn back then, but we can learn it now, together. We can share that new experience.]

If experiences change us; if they define who we are, then nothing could possibly be more important than who we choose to share those experiences with.

[Sure.] I smiled. [I'd like that.]

Silence Of the Stars

The journey continues in *Volume 2: Call of the Stars*.

Afterword

Thank you for reading *Silence Of the Stars*. I hope you enjoyed it.

Silence Of the Stars and its upcoming sequel, *Call Of the Stars*, were originally meant to be a single novel. When I started fleshing out the story from a single outline, it became apparent that the full story would be too long for a single book. I tried condensing it into a single book, but found myself constantly pressured to omit nonessential scenes to save space, and felt story suffered as a result. Ultimately, I decided that releasing the story in two volumes would be better.

If you were left thinking *Silence Of the Stars* lacked a true conclusion, that's why. The story was never intended to end here. The departure from Babylon Station was originally the end of act 1 in a 3-act story. The remaining two acts became *Call Of the Stars*. At the time of writing this, I am about halfway done. The sequel should be released sometime in 2025 and will conclude the originally planned storyline.

In the meantime, if you enjoyed the book, you might also enjoy some of the media which inspired me to write it in the first place. The story which originally got me interested in near-future science fiction was *The Expanse* series, by James S. A. Corey. That sent me down the 'futurism' rabbit hole where I found my second major inspiration in the Youtube channel *Science and Futurism with Isaac Arthur*. Fans of that channel will have been familiar with many of the topics and technologies introduced in *Silence of The Stars*.

For more book recommendations and reviews, check out my author website at: www.Inkularity.com

A few words of thanks before I go:

Thanks first and foremost to my editor, Tim Major, for bearing with me as I butchered the English Language. I feel I felt feely humble and grateful.

Thanks also to my mom, for enduring my excited ramblings before they took the form of anything approaching a story. Your unique insight and assistance as a sounding board were essential in allowing me to turn a disorganized jumble of ideas into something resembling a coherent book.

And of course, thanks to everyone who read the book to the end. Whether you liked it, hated it, or found it entirely unremarkable, you made it this far. I would love to hear what you have to say, and look forward to reading your feedback and comments. A review on Nil... Amazon, would mean a great deal to me.

Until next time,